CROSSCURRENTS / MODERN FICTION

HARRY T. MOORE, *General Editor*
MATTHEW J. BRUCCOLI, *Textual Editor*

PREFACE BY

HARRY T. MOORE

A NOTE ON THE TEXT BY

MATTHEW J. BRUCCOLI

D. H. LAWRENCE
AND
M. L. SKINNER

The
Boy in the Bush

❧ ❧
❧

SOUTHERN ILLINOIS UNIVERSITY PRESS
CARBONDALE AND EDWARDSVILLE

FEFFER & SIMONS, INC.
LONDON AND AMSTERDAM

CONTENTS

PREFACE

By Harry T. Moore

AMERICAN readers are now offered a book which has long been out of print in the United States and difficult to obtain there: D. H. Lawrence's *The Boy in the Bush*. Lawrence's publishers in England, William Heinemann, Ltd., are also bringing out a new edition, all of which makes the reissuing of this novel something of a literary event. Perhaps the true worth of the book will at last be recognized, for its Lawrencean qualities, for its cinematic force, and for its exciting adventures.

The Boy in the Bush (1924) has undeservedly been the most neglected among Lawrence's novels. Commentators have usually either ignored the book or passed it over lightly because Lawrence shares the title page with a collaborator, M. L. Skinner. But now that so many readers appreciate so much of Lawrence's work, the reappearance of this novel which contains a good deal of his own writing is timely and important. The passages which are so uniquely Lawrence's often show him at his finest.

Before considering the literary merits of this novel, it is necessary to investigate the background and origins of the collaboration. Readers who are not interested in such matters may turn to page xxi, where the discussion of the novel itself begins.

M. L. (Mollie) Skinner was not the first woman to work (or try to) on a novel with Lawrence. His widow Frieda said in her memoir *"Not I, But the Wind . . ."* (1934) that as Lawrence scratched away at the final draft of his third novel, *Sons and Lovers,* in Italy in 1912, "I lived and suffered with that book, and wrote bits of it when he would ask me: 'What do you think my mother would have felt like then?' I had to go deeply into the character of Miriam and all the others." Such procedure was not really unusual with Lawrence, for he always wanted to be sure of the woman's point of view. As I have shown elsewhere, providing examples, at a somewhat earlier time in the progress of *Sons and Lovers* Lawrence even asked Jessie Chambers, the Miriam of the story, to write and even correct several passages of that novel, and he adapted these, revising and using them in his own manner.

There are other examples of his interest in having women associates in his literary and even in his artistic production. His second novel, *The Trespasser*, was rewritten from a manuscript by his friend Helen Corke. And Mable Dodge Luhan recalled, in her *Lorenzo in Taos* (1932), that when Lawrence first arrived in New Mexico ten years earlier, he suggested that she tell him about her personal experiences and that the two of them could make a novel out of them. Mrs. Luhan in her memoir included an outline of part of the proposed novel, as Lawrence saw it; and a six-page fragment exists (in his handwriting). But Frieda ("I did not want this") broke up the proposed collaboration.

The following year, in London, Lawrence heard his friend Catherine Carswell mention some aspects of a novel she wanted to write. He almost immediately gave her a synopsis and implied that he was to be her collaborator. She found herself unable to begin the story and, because Lawrence soon left England, nothing more was done about it. Fortunately, in her later biography of him, *The Savage Pilgrimage* (1932), she included his synopsis, which indicated that he would have dealt with the story as the semimystical adventures of members of the Clan Maclure, on a Scottish island and elsewhere. As Lawrence outlined the novel, he seemed at his imaginative best, this time drawing upon Celtic mythology, and those who enjoy his writings may regret that he never fleshed out this story, the idea of which leads toward his later novel, *The Plumed Serpent,* and such tales as "Sun" and "The Woman Who Rode Away."

Any account of Lawrence's proposed or realized collaborations with women would be incomplete unless it mentioned that, in New Mexico in 1925, he worked with his wife and the Honorable Dorothy Brett in painting a picture of his ranch with the surrounding mountains and distant valleys. As Mervyn Levy notes in *Paintings of D. H. Lawrence* (1964), "The horses, their riders, and other figures and animals were painted by Lawrence; the white chickens by Frieda; and the landscape by Brett"; all three of them signed the picture.

We needn't feel surprised, then, to find Lawrence sharing a title page with a woman. He met Maria Louisa Skinner in Western Australia in 1922. She had been born there in 1876, but grew up in Great Britain after her family moved away. Her father was an army officer, her mother a descendant of pioneer settlers of Australia. Mollie Skinner as a girl nearly went blind and had to spend several months in a darkened room. By the time her family had returned to Western Australia in 1900, she considered herself a writer, and soon she began contributing articles and fiction to various regional newspapers.

She served as a nurse, mostly in Burma and India, during the First World War, and while she was still a member of the Voluntary Aid Detachment she brought out *Letters of a V. A. D.* (1918) under the pseudonym of R. E. Leake (a family name). When the middle-aged spinster met Lawrence, she and another woman friend were operating a combined guest-house and nursing-home in Darlington, where the Lawrences stayed as guests, not patients. When Mollie Skinner showed Lawrence the original draft of the story—which concerned a girl and a convict and another man—he found it promising though amateurish. He told her to write out of her experience.

Meanwhile he was drawing Australia into his own consciousness. With his sense of what, in his essay, "The Novel," he called "quickness," he could almost immediately discover "the spirit of place." Once when Lawrence met Rebecca West in Florence, she was somewhat surprised and doubtless amused to find him writing about the town very soon after he had arrived there. (But Rebecca West was one of the first to appreciate the brilliant vitality of his work, which apparently was sometimes published in rough draft and at other times extensively rewritten.) Lawrence's impressions of people and places remained with him. One magnificent example of his writing power, his superb introduction (now in *Phoenix II,* 1968) to Maurice Magnus's *Memoirs of the Foreign Legion,* was sent off to an agent, apparently soon after he completed it, a year after the events it dealt with. There are other examples of Lawrence's ability to retain impressions, and to do so in abundant detail.

In 1922, after landing at Fremantle, in Western Australia, he and Frieda stayed a few days in nearby Perth, and about 7 May they moved inland. As he said in a letter from Darlington on 15 May, "We are here about sixteen miles out of Perth —bush all around—marvellous air, marvellous sun and sky— strange, vast empty country—hoary unending 'bush' with a pre-primeval ghost in it." As so often, he didn't want to settle, and on 18 May he and Frieda sailed to the opposite end of the continent, stopping briefly at Sydney and then moving to a bungalow on the east coast, where in about six weeks he wrote *Kangaroo*, published in 1923. This is another of Lawrence's unduly neglected works. A book more like *Sartor Resartus* or *Also Sprach Zarathustra* than a traditional novel, *Kangaroo* is set along that part of the coast where the Lawrences lived, near Sydney, and in the city itself. But Lawrence hadn't forgotten Western Australia, and in one of the many autobiographical passages in *Kangaroo* he writes of a man's first encounter with the bush at night; when walking in it he feels an "icy sensation of terror." Lawrence would always remember the bush.

After Australia, he went to New Mexico, which he continued to revisit across the next three years. In 1923 he stayed for a while in Los Angeles and from there traveled down the western coast of Mexico. Before he left on this trip, he received from Mollie Skinner the manuscript of the novel he had suggested that she should write, which she called "The House of Ellis." He wrote to her on 2 September, telling her that her book lacked harmony and unity. She had "no constructive power," and the manuscript wouldn't attract a publisher although it had considerable merit. But: "If you like I will take it and re-cast it, and make a book of it. In which case we should have to appear as collaborators, or assume a pseudonym. If you give me a free hand, I'll see if I can't make a complete book out of it." On 1 November he wrote to her from Guadalajara, Mexico, to say that he had been working on the novel as he traveled. "The only thing was to write it all out again, following your MS almost exactly, giving it a unity, a rhythm, and a little more psychic development than you have done. . . . The end will have to be different, a good deal different." And he became more specific about his own approach to the book:

> Your hero Jack [based on Mollie Skinner's brother Jack] is not quite so absolutely blameless an angel, according to me. You left the character psychologically at a standstill all the way: same boy at the beginning and at the end. I have tried, taking your inner cue, to make a rather daring development, psychologically. You may disapprove.

"I did," Mollie Skinner recalled. "I wept." But she liked Lawrence's new title, *The Boy in the Bush*. He told her, "There have been so many houses in print." Apparently neither she nor Lawrence knew that an earlier novel about Australia, published in London in 1869 and reissued in 1885 (the year of Lawrence's birth), was called *The Boy in the Bush*.

Lawrence's statement to the effect that he had rewritten Mollie Skinner's book completely, although keeping her story as substructure, was repeated in the preface he wrote for her novel *Black Swans*. Mollie Skinner had revised this after finishing "The House of Ellis," and it came out in the year after *The Boy in the Bush* appeared. But the London publishers (Jonathan Cape) didn't use Lawrence's preface — possibly because it was based only upon his memory of the first version of *Black Swans*. When the rewritten book came out Lawrence told Middleton Murry, "It irritates me, by its foolish facility. She herself knows life isn't like that — conceited slipshod nonsense — so why does she write it!" In the *Black Swans* preface, which finally went into print in *Phoenix II*, Lawrence dealt at far greater length with *The Boy in the Bush* than with *Black Swans*. He gave a lively picture of M. L. Skinner in her native setting:

> There was Miss Skinner, in the house on the hills at the edge of the bush, in Western Australia, darting about rather vaguely in her white nurse's dress, with the nurse's white band over her head, looking after her convalescents who, mercifully, didn't need much looking after. Miss Skinner darting about on the brink of all the balances, and her partner, a wise, strong woman, sitting plumb at the centre of equilibrium.
>
> Oh, and the ponderous manuscript, tangled, and simply crepitating with type-writer's mistakes, which I read in despair in that house in Western Australia. Such possibilities: And such impossibilities!
>
> But the possibilities touched with magic. Always hovering over the borderline where probability merges into magic: then tumbling, like a bird gone too far out to sea, flopping and splashing into the wrong element, to drown soggily.

It was after reading the early draft of *Black Swans* that Lawrence suggested that Mollie Skinner write more directly out of what she really knew. "The House of Ellis" was the first product of her new effort, followed by the revision of *Black Swans* and several more books, published either in Australia or England, before her death in 1955. She left among her papers a novel, "Eve in the Land of Nod," which, a friend of hers has pointed out, contains "notes in Lawrence's handwriting on just about every page. Years later Mollie re-wrote it, using Lawrence's suggestions, but although the book was apparently given to an agent, it was never published." Another book of hers which has not yet appeared in print is her autobiography, entitled "The Fifth Sparrow."

The question remains, How much of *The Boy in the Bush* is M. L. Skinner's and how much is D. H. Lawrence's?

I have already quoted Lawrence as saying that he had rewritten the whole book, following Mollie Skinner's pattern, but adding that the ending would have to be changed. In the *Black Swans* preface he said, "I am not good at suggesting and criticizing. I did the only thing I knew well how to do: that is, I wrote the whole book over again, from start to finish, putting in and leaving out, yet keeping the main subject of Miss Skinner's work." She was, however, not to be blamed for anything "shocking"; and he took full responsibility for the last chapters.

The original Skinner manuscript, "The House of Ellis," seems to be lost. If it were available, we could tell exactly how much Lawrence really contributed. As John Middleton Murray wrote, if that manuscript had survived "it would be a priceless document." But we do have some bits of evidence that throw some light on the circumstances of collaboration. One typewritten manuscript is in Columbia University Library's Special Collections, with what is recognizably Lawrence's hand making occasional alterations. Another hand which has also marked some changes can hardly have been Mollie Skinner's since she apparently saw only one copy of the typescript which was given to the printer. The Columbia alterations were probably taken from her comments on her extra typescript.

Mollie Skinner herself said, in 1950, in an article in the Australian magazine *Meanjin*, that from the time when she cabled permission for Lawrence to rewrite the story she didn't see anything further until the book itself appeared. But her memory was certainly in error, for Lawrence wrote to her from London on 13 January 1924 to say that he was sending one of the typescripts to her in a few days and that she should return it at once (it was the time of slow mail before transoceanic air service); and on 4 April he wrote from Taos to say that her letter about the manuscript had been sent there: "I have written to [Martin] Secker to make the alterations you wish, if it is not too late. Also, I tell them they may leave out both chapters at the end, if they wish. But here, if the book is set up, the publishers will not agree unless they wish to of their own account."

Another letter of 4 April, to Lawrence's English publisher (first printed in the *Letters from D. H. Lawrence to Martin Secker,* 1970), says that he had had a request from Mollie Skinner "asking for a few alterations in *Boy in the Bush.* I copy these out and send them to you. If there is time, please make these little changes to please her." It is evident that Mollie Skinner had merely written a letter to Lawrence with a list of suggestions. The typescript she apparently mailed to Curtis Brown, Lawrence's London agent, with a similar list, making changes between the lines, and the other handwriting on the document at Columbia University may be that of Curtis Brown or one of his associates.

On 3 April, the day before Lawrence's letter sending M. L. Skinner's suggestions to Martin Secker in London, Secker wrote to him (see *Letters from a Publisher: Martin Secker to D. H. Lawrence and Others, 1911–1929,* published in 1970), saying that two sets of printed proof-copy had been mailed to Taos, and that Lawrence's agent Curtis Brown had given Secker "a second typescript which contained some small alterations and suggestions, presumably from Mrs. [sic] Skinner. These have been transferred to the marked set, and you will also find among its pages some of the suggestions, which you may like to adopt. When you have corrected this will you transfer the alterations from the second set, which will do for [Thomas] Seltzer [the American publisher] to set up from." It is possible that the typescript came from Curtis Brown before the original manuscript went to the printer, and that the emendations were made before the typed version had gone to him.

The references to the "marked set" in Secker's letter certainly refer to the proof sheets, though he also apparently sent the typescript to Lawrence, who must have added his changes earlier; and if it were not someone in Brown's office who incorporated Mollie Skinner's suggestions, it may have been Secker or one of *his* associates. In any case, it is an interesting puzzle.

Secker wrote to Lawrence again on 25 April, said that he found Mollie Skinner's suggestions "quite unimportant," and that he felt strongly about those Lawrencean last chapters, which "should not be scrapped."

The typescript which went to the English printer is probably the one at Columbia University, since it bears evidence of being the copy sent to him; and it was probably the English compositor, since Seltzer, to judge from Secker's 3 April letter, apparently had the book set up from the British proof sheets. That the Columbia typescript had gone to a printer is suggested by a marking on page 143, "gal 30," indicating that another of the galley proofs begins at that point. Galley 30 came out, in the printing, as page 99: Jack is with his Ellis cousins on a kangaroo hunt, and the cries of the men and boys ("Coo-ee!") coming through the bush seem to Jack like a manifestation of God. One of the sentences in the typescript read: "The long deep 'coo,' rising again more imperious than the 'ee!' thrilling and holding aloft." Here there is an emendation, not in Lawrence's hand, which makes the sentence into two sentences reading: "The deep long 'coo' mastering the silence, the high summons of the long 'eee.' The 'coo' rising more imperious, and then the 'eee!' thrilling and holding aloft."

That looks as if it might be Lawrence correcting Lawrence, but it is in an exceedingly neat script-writing. Lawrence's own hand, identifiable and easy enough to read, appears throughout, as on page 269 of the typescript (page 182 in print). At the point where the text read, "The fear that the great liquid fire of the cold moon would dissolve him, dissolve him right away, in some transcendent, pure, white-shining acid"—Lawrence changed this to: "The fear that the broad liquid fire of the cold moon would capture him, capture him and destroy him, like some white tiger that slowly and coldly tastes and devours its prey." In the printed version, the word *tiger* becomes *demon,* an alteration Lawrence probably made on the final proofsheets.

Perhaps the most interesting document relating to *The Boy in the Bush* which has survived is the copy of it which M. L. Skinner marked up for Edward Garnett when she was in London during the summer of 1924. She brought her manuscript of *Black Swans,* which Secker, who didn't meet her, thought was "quite hopeless." When Edward Garnett met her at a London party, he told her—as she recollected—"with a roar" that her work was "damn damn bad," but added, "with an angelic smile," that it was also "so damn good, he couldn't bear it." At his suggestion she made the red-chalk marginal indications as to which parts of *The Boy in the Bush* (in the copy now at the University of Texas' Humanities Research Center) she recalled as hers, and which ones Lawrence had apparently added.

On page 66, for example, when Jack is learning to tame the difficult horse, Stampede, Lawrence wrote: "He wanted just to hold it hard with his legs until it soothed down a little, and he and it could come to an understanding. But he must never relax the hold of his hard legs, or he was dead." The Australian novelist Katherine Susannah Prichard, an admirer of Lawrence's writing in general, wrote that "no Australian with any knowledge of horses would ask us to believe that the newly arrived young Englishman 'conquered' an unbroken stallion like Stampede, which neither Australian nor native stockmen could ride." But the passages in question partly reflect Lawrence's own experiences in New Mexico, where he had become a horseback rider; and M. L. Skinner, who knew Western Australia so well, had perhaps originally written some of the sentences about Jack's experiences with the horse and his conquest of the animal (pages 65–67). In the copy which she marked up for Garnett, she merely chalked off a few of Lawrence's additions, such as the one just quoted. On page 67, for example, she indicated that the last part of the longest paragraph was a Lawrence correction or addition, beginning "But Jack had the pride . . ." One of the sentences here tells us that Jack "was not going to yield his manliness before the colonial way of life: the brutishness, the commonness."

Another passage Mollie Skinner attributed to Lawrence begins six lines from the bottom of page 70 and continues to the end of the passage at the conclusion of section v on page 71. This underscores Jack's need of the Ellis family, which he wanted to be a part of, yet without "the slow and lonely process of babies coming." In his reflections, "He didn't want his own children. He wanted this family: always this family. And yet there was something gruesome to him about the empty bedrooms and the uncanny privacies even of this family. He didn't want to think of their privacies." These complications are Lawrencean enough.

At the top of page 174, Mollie Skinner noted "All DHL" and, at the beginning of the following page, it was again "all." Page 174 is chiefly a projection of Jack's private religion, greatly similar to Lawrence's own, as we can piece it together from various bits:

> Now, in [Jack's] pain and battered fever, he was fighting for his Lord again.
>
> "Lord, I don't love Easu [as Easau is called], and I'll kill him if you want me to. But if you don't want me to. I won't. I won't. I won't bother any more."
>
> This pledge and this submission, [comma as in text] soothed him strangely. He felt he was coming back to his own Lord. It was a pledge, and he would keep it. He gave no pledge to love Easu. Only not to kill him, if the Lord didn't want it; and to kill him, if the Lord did.

Jack Grant was, like Lawrence himself, somewhat ahead of his time in communicating with a Lord of his own devising, thereby anticipating so many people brought up in a later age who cannot reconcile themselves to churchgoing, but who are not always atheists. This kind of "worship" would be alien to M. L. Skinner, whose writings in general show an orthodox approach to Christianity.

She wrote vertically in the margin of page 176, "A good deal changed." The first two paragraphs on page 201, discussing Jack's "passion" for and "cherishing" of Monica contain the note, "Changed a bit." On page 298, M. L. Skinner said, "Very little change, can't piece it out," but on the following page she indicated at line 18 that the passage about "the Lords of Death" is Lawrence's, as well as the long paragraph a few lines after, in which Jack in his flow of consciousness says, "I can't bear to think of Monica messy with Easu." On page 341 Mollie Skinner wrote, "To end DHL," which meant not only to the conclusion of the chapter on page 354 (it had begun on page 329), but also the two chapters which follow, completing the book—the chapters which Lawrence, at once irritated and indifferent, told Secker he could remove if he so wished.

Mollie Skinner's marginal comments were written when she apparently could still remember the manuscript she had sent to Lawrence barely a year before and apparently could show how much of the book was hers. Yet the writing throughout is

distinctly Lawrencean. Mollie Skinner's style, as in her un-
published autobiography ("The Fifth Sparrow"), is quite different from that of Lawrence, as Mrs. Rose Anne Lee showed
in a dissertation written at the University of Texas. She found
that M. L. Skinner's prose "is marked by numerous allusions
to Biblical references and hymns [that much is fairly Lawrencean — H.T.M.] and a fondness for effusive phrases. Her
preference for metaphor rather than more direct statement is
found continually in such phrases as 'The Hand on the
Shoulder' for Chance and references to herself as the 'fifth
sparrow.' In contrast to the slangy, direct and forceful style
of Lawrence, Miss Skinner's prose seems to gush and to be
overly 'sweet.' "

Mrs. Lee, who has worked out some statistics on the basis
of her examination of the Texas copy of the book and the Columbia typescript, believes that "the majority of the credit
must go to Miss Skinner . . . The total of almost 238 pages
out of 369 pages of the novel clearly gives her the ascendancy.
This indicates, to me at least, that Lawrence's claim to have
rewritten the entire novel cannot be verified!"

One of the reviewers of the published novel said that "two-
thirds of the book are very good, the life in the bush, the Ellis
family, the raw pioneering atmosphere of Australia — all this
is strong, vivid and often beautiful." Katherine Susannah
Prichard, who thinks that Mollie Skinner's "share in the book
should have more recognition," points out that the two-thirds
of it mentioned in the quotation from the reviewer were
"chiefly Mollie Skinner's." But she says further:

> Anyone who knows the style of both writers under-
> stands how much Miss Skinner's material owes to Law-
> rence's twist and turn of a sentence, to his subtle adjec-
> tives, to streaks of verbal magic, to paragraphs which
> flow with the rhythm of an elusive thought. Miss Skinner
> herself is the first to acknowledge this.
>
> But Lawrence knew nothing of those pioneering days
> in Australia. They were too far from his experience to
> have been given in such intimate detail by him. Despite
> the fact that the chapters about early Fremantle were re-
> ferred to [apparently by reviewers] as "pure Lawrence,"
> I guessed when I first read the book that those chapters,
> Mr. George, the Ellis family, the incidents and anecdotes
> of bush life, belonged to Miss Skinner.

None of this really confutes Lawrence's statements on the subject, to the effect that the final version is his prose. The writing throughout is distinctly Lawrencean, and the book should rank as a Lawrence novel, though Mollie Skinner's extremely important contribution should be noted. The Australian frontier of the 1880s was familiar to her, and many of the people in the book, as well as most of the incidents, were originally hers. But so far it seems that only Mrs. Pritchard and Mrs. Lee have dealt with this problem. If Lawrence's part in putting the book together has generally been passed over, so has M. L. Skinner's. The American "uniform edition" of 1930, made from the plates which A. and C. Boni used (taken over from Thomas Seltzer's 1924 American edition) doesn't even list M. L. Skinner on the title page, although Seltzer had done so. But the Bonis, in the year of Lawrence's death, simply cut off the title-page existence of M. L. Skinner.

They were not alone in such actions. Mollie Skinner recollected, in "The Fifth Sparrow," that when *The Boy in the Bush* came out in 1924, the reviewer [Humbert Wolfe?] for the *Weekly Westminster* wondered whether there was "any sich [sic] person as M. L. Skinner," and subsequently wrote of the "suppositious Skinner." Another reviewer ventured, "It may be a gentleman or it may be a lady." The *Times Literary Supplement* spoke of a "Mr. Skinner." Yet its anonymous review was for the most part favorable, and its conclusion was friendly enough: "We have written throughout as if the novel were all Mr. Lawrence's work. Whatever Mr. Skinner's share in it may be, the best and the worst of it are the best and the worst of Mr. Lawrence. And the best is Mr. Lawrence's very best."

On the other hand, L. P. Hartley spoke ill of the book in the *Spectator,* and several critics in the United States also treated the book badly, among them Joseph Wood Krutch in the *Nation* and Matthew Josephson in the *Saturday Review of Literature*. Lloyd Morris in the *New York Times Book Review* gave the novel a friendly welcome, and A. D. Douglas, in the "Literary Review" of the *New York Evening Post* could say that the book "glitters with all light and all color and all freshness and beauty. Its humor has nothing in common with the rather awful humor of Mr. Lawrence's literary essays. A boy in Mr. Lawrence's bush is worth two in any other writer's hand." In the *New York World,* J. W. C. found that *"The Boy in the Bush* is one of the most entertaining books Lawrence has written, and is, none the less, profound and searching and truthful." Edwin Muir, in the *Nation and Athenaeum* (London), said that Lawrence "can be intense or magnificent, but he has neither wit nor humor. The jocularity is as painful as Herman Melville's, and *The Boy in the Bush* is very bad and very good in much the same way as *Moby-Dick*"—which is very high praise, by today's standards. John Franklin in the *New Statesman* wrote, "Admirable is the impression he [Lawrence] conveys of looseness, freedom, irresponsibility, with a wonderful harmony between the emotional setting and the details."

Whatever may be said of these reviews—and there were others—we must admit that literary editors and their reviewers didn't ignore this novel as most of those who have subsequently written books about Lawrence have ignored it. The first of them, Herbert J. Seligmann's *D. H. Lawrence: An American Interpretation* (1924), still an excellent critique, came out too soon for the author to note *The Boy in the Bush*. The first volume about Lawrence to appear after his death, Stephen Potter's *D. H. Lawrence: A First Study* (1930), neglected *The Boy in the Bush,* though John Middleton Murry's *Son of Woman* (1931) didn't—but more of Murry later. William York Tindall's iconoclastic *D. H. Lawrence and Susan His Cow* (1939) made several references to the novel under discussion, mostly in support of a special theme. *D. H. Lawrence and Human Existence* (1951), by "Father William Tiverton" (Father Martin Jarrett-Kerr), one of the most penetrating studies of Lawrence, passed by *The Boy in the Bush,* apparently because it was "not Lawrence's designing altogether." F. R. Leavis, in *D. H. Lawrence: Novelist* (1955), completely ignored *The Boy in the Bush,* and Graham Hough in *The Dark Sun: A First Study* (1956) granted it a paragraph; it was one of praise, saying that although Lawrence rewrote someone else's story, he did so with "dash and conviction," turning out "an admirable novel of action—the career of a young settler in West Australia in the early part of the century" [it is actually the last part of the nineteenth century]. Eliseo Vivas's *D. H. Lawrence: The Failure and the Triumph of Art* (1960), a shrewdly aesthetic study, apparently didn't consider *The Boy in the Bush* either a triumph or a failure. Eugene Goodheart's *The Utopian Vision of D. H. Lawrence* (1963) failed to mention Jack Grant's important vision of a Utopia. Nor did Julian Moynahan's otherwise excellent book, *The Deed of Life: The Novels and Tales of D. H. Lawrence* (1963), even mention *The Boy in the Bush,* that significant part of Lawrence's Utopian vision, of his sense of the deed of life. But E. W. Tedlock's valuable *D. H. Lawrence: Artist and Rebel* (1963) devotes three pages to *The Boy in the Bush,* describing and analyzing it. The first of the later critics to examine the book seriously, Professor Tedlock finds in it "a psychological and cultural borderline having certain geographical analogies, and of borderline beings who are potentially capable of crossing over from death into a new way of life." As he says further,

> The demarcations are between civilization and nature; between man's incomprehensible behavior and nature's unambiguous and strengthening habits; between the weakness or lack of commitment and the fight to avoid decadence by making new communities, and the pride and strength of the vitalistic soldier in the face of both inward and physical death. In Lawrence's imagination the Australian frontier had become the borderline situation of contemporary culture.

That is a fine approach to the story.

Ronald P. Draper, who knows Australia from his own experience, dealt in his *D. H. Lawrence* (1964) more fully with *Kangaroo* than with the other Australian novel in which Lawrence was involved. George H. Ford, in *Double Measure: A Study of the Novels and Stories of D. H. Lawrence* (1965), takes up *The Boy in the Bush,* but discusses it mostly as a projection of Lawrence's "aloneness," attributable to a temporary estrangement from Frieda at the time he was writing the book. Keith Sagar's comprehensive volume, *The Art of D. H. Lawrence* (1966), mentions the appearance of Lawrence's dark gods in *The Boy in the Bush* and discusses Jack's communion with God, though the treatment is synoptic rather than evaluative.

Several other critical studies which fail to mention or discuss *The Boy in the Bush,* or which merely notice it in passing, are not included in this brief summary. Among the more recent books of Lawrence criticism I'll mention only *Conflict in the Novels of D. H. Lawrence* (1969), by an author whose only name, as given in the book, is Yudhishtar; he makes the point that Lawrence was a worshiper of life and then scolds virtually every critic who has written on Lawrence for not accepting this as enough, for going on to apply "artistic" standards to the holy man, who in *The Boy in the Bush* would have given this Yudhishtar even more ammunition for his argument —but this book dealing with "conflict" in Lawrence's novels doesn't give any suggestion that its author had ever heard of that novel, which is charged with all kinds of conflict.

John Middleton Murry, whose strange relationship with Lawrence was at once friendly and inimical, sometimes saw Lawrence the writer precisely as he should be seen. His statement, in *Son of Woman*, about *The Boy in the Bush* is partly outlandish, although he begins well:

> *The Boy in the Bush* is a strangely beautiful book. It is so largely because Lawrence did not have to invent it. He could clothe his collaborator's story in an added glory of flesh and blood, and pour out the riches of his imagination upon the given theme.

The "given theme" is of course the one embodied in the title. In *Kangaroo*, written a year before Lawrence began to revise M. L. Skinner's manuscript, he shows how emotionally involved he was with the Western Australian atmosphere of the later book. He speaks of his own experience in the guise of his character Richard Lovat Somers:

> And then one night at the time of the full moon he walked alone into the bush. A huge electric moon, huge, and the tree-trunks like naked pale aborigines among the dark-soaked foliage, in the moonlight. And not a sign of life—not a vestige.
>
> Yet something. Something big and aware and hidden! He had walked on, had walked a mile or so into the bush, and had just come to a clump of tall, nude, dead trees, shining almost phosphorescent with the moon, when the terror of the bush overcame him. He looked so long at the vivid moon, without thinking. And now, there was something among the trees, and his hair began to stir with terror, on his head. There was a presence. He looked at the weird, white, dead trees, and into the hollow distances of the bush. Nothing! Nothing at all. He turned to go home. And immediately the hair on his scalp stirred and went icy cold with terror. What of? He knew quite well it was nothing. He knew quite well. But with his spine cold like ice, and the roots of his hair seeming to freeze,

he walked on home, walked firmly and without haste. For
he told himself he refused to be afraid, though he ad-
mitted the icy sensation of terror. But then to experience
terror is not the same thing as to admit fear into the conscious soul. Therefore he refused to be afraid.

But the horrid thing in the bush! He schemed as to
what it would be. It must be the spirit of the place. Something fully evoked to-night, perhaps provoked, by that
unnatural West-Australian moon. Provoked by the moon,
the roused spirit of the bush. He felt it was watching, and
waiting. Following with certainty, just behind his back.
It might have reached a long black arm and gripped him.
But no, it wanted to wait. It was not tired of watching
its victim. An alien people—a victim. It was biding its
time with a terrible ageless watchfulness, waiting for a
far-off end, watching the myriad intruding white men.

The Boy in the Bush is at one level an adventure story,
with various excursions into romance. But it is also a tale
which delineates the changes that time makes in communities
and their members, especially in such individuals as Jack
Grant. Jack is seventeen when he arrives at Fremantle in
1882. Expelled from his English school, he is resentful and
somewhat antisocial. But Australia offers him a *vita nuova,*
and his experiences become a form of *rites de passage.* By the
end of the book he is, in his early manhood, still vigorously
independent, but responsive to his environment, having in
every way developed psychologically, as Lawrence had fore-
told in his letter to Mollie Skinner on 1 November 1923, noted
earlier. Jack has had experiences with several women and has
married one of them, his tawny-eyed cousin Monica; but in his
youthful vision of himself as a patriarch-to-be, this marriage
hasn't stopped him from responding to other women.

Lawrence said, in the preface to *Black Swans:*

Miss Skinner had quite another conclusion [to *The Boy
in the Bush*]. In her "House of Ellis" . . . Monica went
to the bad and disappeared, among the tears of the family. Jack set off to find her: got lost: and "came to" with
Mary gazing lovingly at him. In that instant, he knew he
loved Mary far, far more than Monica. In fact, his love
for Monica was a dead bluebottle. Mary and Jack lived
happily ever after, virtue rewarded, *finale!*

Now I have my own ideas of morality. A young man who is supposed to love a young girl through years, with passion, and whose love goes pop when she gets in a mess, bores me. He has no real integrity: and that, to my mind, is immorality.

At the same time, this Jack always had a second "feeling" for Mary. Australia is a land which believes not at all in externally imposed authority. There is no limit to love. The popular method would be for a hero, having got his Monica, and not having got his Mary, for whom he had a latent feeling all the time, suddenly realizes that he no longer "loved" Monica, but only Mary: then an "affair," Monica left in the lurch, sympathy streaming towards the virtuous, long-neglected Mary.

Public, popular morality seems to me a pig's business. If a man has ever cared for a woman enough to marry her, he always cares for her. And divorce is all bunk. Forgetting, as Miss Skinner's Jack forgot Monica, is all bunk. Once you care, and the connection is made, you keep the connection, if you are half a man.

But the further question, as to whether this one connection is final and exclusive, is up to us to settle. Largely a question of discipline. And since Australia is the most undisciplined country I have met, discipline won't settle the question there. Fall back on evasions and sentimentalism.

Discipline is a very good thing. Evasions and sentimentalism very bad.

These statements will give the potential reader an idea of some of the problems of *The Boy in the Bush* which lie beneath the vital adventure story. And this reader may be amused to learn how Lawrence worked out these problems in his final chapter, "The Rider on the Red Horse."

The Jack Grant who arrives in Fremantle looks innocent as a lamb, but this appearance is deceptive. At the dock he meets the frontier lawyer, Mr. George, who will introduce him to his relatives, and he soon goes inland to stay with them. The boy is in the bush, the adventures begin. Mollie Skinner's contribution lies under Lawrence's prose like the original material on a palimpsest. Mr. George suggests Jaggers in *Great Expectations,* but he comes to life in his own way, although he is, like Jaggers, something of a background figure.

The Ellis family is superbly projected, obviously taken from life, life as Mollie Skinner knew it there; but we must remember Lawrence's skill at depicting families in his early short stories, in *Sons and Lovers,* and in the novella of his last phase, *The Virgin and the Gipsy.* Like them, *The Boy in the Bush* breathes with life. But it is not only the Ellis family that is delineated, for as Jack wanders through Western Australia with Tom Ellis, he meets many frontier characters who have a Dickens-like vitality. They are various types, some amusingly eccentric. Far from being a book devoted exclusively to Jack's inner development, *The Boy in the Bush* is also a brilliant surface story of the people who inhabit the wilderness, the white settlers rather than the black aborigines; Lawrence knew nothing of the latter, and Mollie Skinner perhaps knew them only in a peripheral way. Nevertheless, the book presents interesting and entertaining types. One remembers Lawrence's knack at capturing out-of-the-way figures; in *The Rainbow,* for example, the man and woman Ursula and Skrebensky talk with on the canal-barge, or, in *Women in Love,* the couple Ursula and Birkin encounter at the Nottingham marketplace. *The Boy in the Bush* is full of such characters, their oddity intensified by their lonely existence so far from the madding crowd.

The reader will himself be able to follow the story as it goes from point to point, imbued with that psychological development which Lawrence thought was so essential to the character of Jack. Eventually, after many vicissitudes, he finds at least one thing he has sought, and this results in a change of his fortunes. Some readers may find this a bit incredible, just too pat, but it is simply one of the ingredients of the surface adventure-story. In such a tale we must learn to accept the fabulous. And there is much more.

Earlier, Jack had engaged in a life-or-death battle with an enemy he hated in a strange way, as if he loved him in spite of the hate—which was never really a loathing. The relationship reaches its climax in a violent scene of the kind Lawrence could bring off so effectively; and afterward Jack wanders about feverishly. He lies abed half-delirious—this is his Descent into Avernus. He nearly yields to the Lord of Death, of whom he has had visions; but his cousin and friend Tom Ellis, "in a gloomy, reproachful tone," says, "Y' aren't desertin' us, are y' . . . Are y' desertin' us, mate?"

It was the Australian, lost but unbroken on the edge of the wilderness, looking through the wilderness, looking with grim mouth into the void, and calling to his mate not to leave him. Man for man, they were up against the great dilemma of white men, on the edge of the white man's world, looking into the vaster, alien world of the undawned era, and unable to enter, unable to leave their own.

Jack smiles faintly at Tom: "In some subtle way, both men know the mysterious responsibilities of living." Jack comes slowly back to life: "The boy Jack never rose from that fever. It was a man who got up again. A man with all boyishness cut away from him, all the childishness gone, and a certain unbending recklessness in its place."

It was his eyes that had changed most. From being the warm, emotional dark-blue eyes of a boy, they had become impenetrable, and had a certain fixity. There was a touch of death in them, a little of the fixity and changelessness of death. And with this, a peculiar power. As if he had lost his softness in the otherworld of death, and brought back instead some of the relentless power that belongs there. And the inevitable touch of mockery.

He has several desires, one of them for masterhood. This is "not mastery. He didn't want to master anything. But to be the dark lord of his own folk: that was a desire in his heart." And he goes forth more than ever an adventurer, seeking the fortune that inevitably comes to him. He knows that he can never conform. His relatives "all love me exceedingly the moment they think I am in line with them," but let him do anything beyond the social shibboleths "and they would like to destroy me off the face of the earth, like a rattlesnake." If he would admit himself a sinner, grovel in repentance, and "submit to their judgment, I could do all the wicked things I like, and they would love me better. . . . I must take great care to ask them for nothing, to take nothing from them." These complications, and the varied episodes of the narrative make this a fine story, worthy of the author who has at last attained the stature he deserves.

Altogether, *The Boy in the Bush* gives a great deal: the change in a man, his experiences in love, a fight to the death, and ultimate good fortune. And Lawrence adds, among other ingredients, Jack Grant's Utopian vision.

This Old Testament, patriarchal vision has been prepared for earlier. Jack's sense of the Bible and its meaning and its poetry appear in the opening section of the story, when he is standing on the wharf at Fremantle, just after landing:

> The only prize Jack had ever won at school was for Scripture. The Bible language exerted a certain fascination over him, and in the background of his consciousness the Bible images always hovered. When he was moved, it was Scripture that came to his aid. So now he stood, silent with the shyness of youth, thinking over and over: "There shall be a new heaven and a new earth."

Again, in chapter X ("Shadows Before"), Jack's consciousness is filled with Biblical ideas:

> Jack knew the Bible pretty well, as a well-brought-up nephew of his aunts. He had no objection to the Bible. On the contrary, it supplied his imagination with a chief stock of images, his ear with the greatest solemn pleasure of words, and his soul with a queer heterogeneous ethic. He never really connected the Bible with Christianity proper, the Christianity of aunts and clergymen. He had no use for Christianity proper: just dismissed it. But the Bible was perhaps the foundation of his consciousness. Do what seems good to you in the sight of the Lord. This was the moral he always drew from Bible lore. And since the Lord, for him, was always the Lord Almighty, Almighty God, Maker of Heaven and Earth, Jesus being only a side issue; since the Lord was always Jehovah the great and dark, for him, one might do as David did, in the sight of the Lord, or as Jacob, or as Abraham or Moses or Joshua or Isaiah, in the sight of the Lord. The sight of the Lord was a vast strange scope of vision, in the semi-dark.

A few pages earlier, in the "New Year's Eve" chapter, Jack had thought he would like to build a brick house in Australia and always be near Monica, Tom, and their brother Lennie: "He hoped he would never, in all his life, say good-bye to them."

Then, after all his adventures but one, in chapter XXV, the next to the last, Jack has his vision of the future, with the ideal community Lawrence so often projected; but, like Lawrence, Jack realizes that he can't create such a community "with the people that are on earth today." The vision is too splendid to become a reality, so Jack will go his own way until he finally becomes "a lord of death."

Lawrence had even thought of sending him to death at the end of the novel. We learn this from the Hon. Dorothy Brett, the only "disciple" who followed Lawrence to New Mexico, where he had hoped to establish a colony. Miss Brett recalls that, when she and Lawrence were discussing *The Boy in the Bush,* she said Jack should have died in the story. Lawrence said he had first written it that way, but Frieda had made him change it. Frieda is reported as looking up from her embroidery, to boom, "Yes, I made him change it. I couldn't stand the superiority of the man, always the same self-importance. 'Let him become ordinary,' I said. 'Always this superiority and death.'" When Miss Brett said that the ending had spoiled the book, Lawrence sighed, "Yes, he should have died."

Since the story is not in any way a tragic one, many readers who enjoy this book will be glad that Jack, who is abundantly alive, will continue to live. They may also be amused because Lawrence in the final chapter, "The Rider on the Red Horse," provides Jack with another woman.

And although the story is more than just another airing of Lawrencean doctrine, though here he gives us much more of it than usual, a point which has too often been overlooked by those who undertake critiques of Lawrence.

What will strike the reader above all is the sense of life this book gives—something Lawrence usually projected, the vibrancy of his own artistic vision. M. L. Skinner's contribution was a notable one, but it is Lawrence who breathed life into her people and the setting. Yet there is a great deal more to this novel. It is an engrossing story of a certain place at a certain time, and Lawrence's magic touches all of it to life.

Southern Illinois University
March 17, 1971

(*Postcript:* For valuable assistance in helping me with background material for this Preface, I should like to thank Messrs. Kenneth Lohf and Bernard Crystal of the Columbia

University Library's Special Collections Department; Professor Matthew J. Bruccoli, University of South Carolina; Mr. David Koch, Rare Books Librarian of Southern Illinois University Library; Mrs. Rose Anne Lee; and Professor Warren Roberts, Director, Humanities Center, University of Texas. — H.T.M.)

THE BOY IN THE BUSH

CHAP : 1. JACK ARRIVES IN AUSTRALIA

i

HE stepped ashore, looking like a lamb. Far be it from me to say he was the lamb he looked. Else why should he have been sent out of England? But a good-looking boy he was, with dark blue eyes and the complexion of a girl, and a bearing just a little too lamb-like to be convincing.

He stepped ashore in the newest of new colonies, glancing quickly around, but preserving his lamb-like quietness. Down came his elegant kit, and was dumped on the wharf : a kit that included a brand-new pigskin saddle and bridle, nailed up in a box straight from a smart shop in London. He kept his eye on that also, the tail of his well-bred eye.

Behind him was the wool ship that had brought him from England. This nondescript port was Fremantle, in West Australia; might have been anywhere or nowhere. In his pocket he had a letter of introduction to a well-known colonial lawyer, in which, as he was aware, was folded also a draft on a West Australian bank. In his purse he had a five pound note. In his head were a few irritating memories. In his heart he felt a certain excited flutter at being in a real new land, where a man could be *really* free. Though what he meant by " free " he never stopped to define. He left everything suitably vague.

Meanwhile, he waited for events to develop, as if it were none of his business.

This was forty years ago, when it was still a long, long way to Australia, and the land was still full of the lure of promise. There were gold and pearl findings, bush and bush-ranging, the back of beyond and everything desirable. Much misery, too, ignored by all except the miserable.

And Jack was not quite eighteen, so he ignored a great deal. He didn't pay much attention even to his surroundings, yet from the end of the wharf he saw pure sky above, the pure, unknown, unsullied sea to westward; the ruffled, tumbled sand glistened like fine silver, the air was the air of a new world, unbreathed by man.

The only prize Jack had ever won at school was for

1

Scripture. The Bible language exerted a certain fascination over him, and in the background of his consciousness the Bible images always hovered. When he was moved, it was Scripture that came to his aid. So now he stood, silent with the shyness of youth, thinking over and over : " There shall be a new heaven and a new earth."

Not far off among the sand near the harbour mouth lay the township, a place of strong, ugly, oblong houses of white stone with unshuttered bottle-glass windows and a low white-washed wall going round, like a sort of compound ; then there was a huge stone prison with a high white-washed wall. Nearer the harbour, a few new tall warehouse buildings, and sheds, long sheds, and a little wooden railway station. Further out again, windmills for milling flour, the mill-sails turning in the transparent breeze from the sea. Right in the middle of the township was a stolid new Victorian Church with a turret : and this was the one thing he knew he disliked in the view.

On the wharf everything was busy. The old wool steamer lay important in dock, people were crowding on deck and crowding the wharf in a very informal manner, porters were running with baggage, a chain was clanking, and little groups of emigrants stood forlorn, looking for their wooden chests, swinging their odd bundles done up in coloured kerchiefs. The uttermost ends of the earth ! All so lost and yet so familiar. So familiar, and so lost. The people like provincial people at home. The railway running through the sand hills. And the feeling of remote unreality.

This was his mother's country. She had been born and raised here, and she had told him about it, many a time, like a fable. And this was what it was like ! How could she feel she actually *belonged* to it ? Nobody could belong to it.

Himself, he belonged to Bedford, England. And Bedford College. But his mind turned away from this in repugnance. Suddenly he turned desirously to the unreality of this remote place.

Jack was waiting for Mr George, the lawyer to whom his letter of introduction was addressed. Mr George had shaken hands with him on deck ; a stout and breezy gentleman, who had been carried away again on the gusts of his own breeze, among the steamer crowd, and had forgotten his young charge. Jack patiently waited. Adult and responsible people with stout waistcoats had a habit, he knew, of being needed elsewhere.

Mr George! And all his mother's humorous stories about him! This notable character of the Western lonely colony, this rumbustical old gentleman who had a " terrific memory " who was " full of quotations " and who " never forgot a face "—Jack waited the more calmly, sure of being recognised again by him—was to be seen in the distance with his thumbs hooked in his waistcoat armholes, passively surveying the scene with a quiet, shrewd eye, before hailing another acquaintance and delivering another sally. He had a " tongue like a razor " and frightened the women to death. Seeing him there on the wharf, elderly, stout and decidedly old-fashioned, Jack had a little difficulty in reconciling him with the hearty colonial hero of his mother's stories.

How he had missed a seat on the bench, for example. He was to become a judge. But while acting on probation, or whatever it is called, a man came up before him charged with wife-beating, and serious maltreatment of his better half. A verdict of " not guilty " was returned. " Two years' hard labour," said Mr George, who didn't like the looks of the fellow. There was a protest. " Verdict stands! " said Mr George. " Two years' hard labour. Give it him for *not* beating her and breaking her head. He should have done. He should have done. 'Twas fairly proved! "

So Mr George had remained a lawyer, instead of becoming a judge. A stout, shabby, provincial-looking old man with baggy trousers that seemed as if they were slipping down. Jack had still to get used to that sort of trousers. One of his mother's heroes!

But the whole scene was still outside the boy's vague, almost trance-like state. The commotion of unloading went on—people stood in groups, the lumpers were already at work with the winches, bringing bales and boxes from the hold. The Jewish gentleman standing just there had a red nose. He swung his cane uneasily. He must be well-off, to judge by his links and watch-chain. But then why did his trousers hang so low and baggy, and why was his waistcoat of yellow cloth—that cloth cost a guinea a yard, Jack knew it from his horsey acquaintances—so dirty and frayed?

Western Australia in the year 1882. Jack had read all about it in the official report on the steamer. The colony had three years before celebrated its fiftieth anniversary. Many people still remembered the fiasco of the first attempt at the Swan River Settlement. Captain Stirling brought the first boatload of prospective settlers. The Government promised not to defile the land with convicts. But the promise was broken. The convicts had come : and that stone prison-building must have been the convict station. He knew from his mother's stories. But he also knew that the convicts were now gone again. The " Establishment " had been closed down already for ten years or more.

A land must have its ups and downs. And the first thing the old world had to ship to the new world was its sins, and the first shipments were of sinners. That was what his mother said. Jack felt a certain sympathy. He felt a sympathy with the empty " Establishment " and the departed convicts. He himself was mysteriously a " sinner." He felt he was born such : just as he was born with his deceptive handsome look of innocence. He was a sinner, a Cain. Not that he was aware of having committed anything that seemed to himself particularly sinful. No, he was not aware of having " sinned." He was not aware that he ever would " sin."

But that wasn't the point. Curiously enough, that wasn't the point. The men who commit sins and who know they commit sins usually get on quite well with the world. Jack knew he would never get on well with the world. He was a sinner. He knew that as far as the world went, he was a sinner, born condemned. Perhaps it had come to him from his mother's careless, rich, uncanny Australian blood. Perhaps it was a recoil from his father's military-gentleman nature. His father was an officer in Her Majesty's Army. An officer in Her Majesty's Army. For some reason there was always a touch of the fantastic and ridiculous, to Jack, in being an officer in Her Majesty's Army. Quite a high and responsible officer usually stationed in command in one or other of Her Britannic Majesty's Colonies.

Why did Jack find his father slightly fantastic? Why

was that gentleman in uniform who appeared occasionally, very resplendent and somehow very " good," why was he always unreal and fantastic to the little boy left at home in England ? Why was he even more fantastic when he wore a black coat and genteel grey trousers ? He was handsome and pleasant, and indisputably " good." Then why, oh why, should he have appeared fantastic to his own little boy, who was so much like him in appearance ?

" The spitten image ! " one of his nurses had said. And Jack never forgave it. He thought it meant a spat-upon image, or an image in spit. This he resented and repudiated absolutely, though it remained vague.

" Oh, you little sinner ! " said the same nurse, half caressingly. And this the boy had accepted as his natural appellation. He was a little sinner. As he grew older, he was a young sinner. Now, as he approached manhood, he was a sinner without modification.

Not, we repeat, that he was ever able to understand wherein his sinfulness lay. He knew his father was a " good man "—" The colonel, your father, is such a *good man*, so you must be a *good little boy* and grow up like him "—" There is no better example of an English gentleman than your father, the general. All you have to do is to grow up like him."

Jack knew from the start that he wouldn't. And therein lay the sin, presumably. Or the root of the sin.

He did not dislike his father. The general was kind and simple and amiable. How could anyone dislike him ? But to the boy he was always just a little fantastic, like the policeman in a Punch and Judy show.

Jack loved his mother with a love that could not but be intermittent, for sometimes she stayed in England and " lived " with him, and more often she left him and went off with his father to Jamaica or some such place—or to India or Khartoum, names that were in his blood—leaving the boy in the charge of a paternal aunt. He didn't think much of the aunt.

But he liked the warm, flushed, rather muddled delight of his mother. She was a handsome, ripe Australian woman with warm colouring and soft flesh, absolutely kindly in a humorous, off-hand fashion, warm with a jolly sensuousness, and good in a wicked sort of way. She sat in the sun and laughed and refused to quarrel, refused also to weep. When she had to leave her little boy a spasm would contract her face and make her look ugly, so the child was glad if she went quickly. But she was in love with her husband, who was still more in love with her, so off she went laughing sensuously across seven seas, quarrelling with nobody, pitching her camp in true colonial fashion wherever she found herself, yet always with a touch of sensuous luxury, Persian rugs and silk cushions and dresses of rich material. She was the despair of the true English wives, for you couldn't disapprove of her, she was the dearest thing imaginable, and yet she introduced a pleasant, semi-luxurious sense of—of what? Why, almost of sin. Not positive sin. She was really the dearest thing imaginable. But the feeling that there was no fence between sin and virtue. As if sin were, so to speak, the unreclaimed bush, and goodness were only the claims that the settlers had managed to fence in. And there was so much more bush than settlement. And the one was as good as the other, save that they served different ends. And that you always had the wild and endless bush all round your little claim. And coming and going was always through the wild and innocent, but non-moral bush. Which non-moral bush had a devil in it. Oh, yes! But a wild and comprehensible devil, like bush-rangers who did brutal and lawless things. Whereas the tame devil of the settlements, drunkenness and greediness and foolish pride, he was more scaring.

" My dear, there's tame innocence and wild innocence, and tame devils and wild devils, and tame morality and wild morality. Let's camp in the bush and be good."

That was her attitude, always. " Let's camp in the bush and be good." She was an Australian from a wild Australian homestead. And she was like a wild sweet animal. Always the sense of space and lack of restrictions, and it didn't matter *what* you did, so long as you were good inside yourself.

Her husband was in love with her, completely. To him it mattered very much what you did. So perhaps her easy indifference to English rail-fences satisfied in him the iconoclast that lies at the bottom of all men.

She was not well-bred. There was a certain " cottage " geniality about her. But also a sense of great, unfenced spaces, that put the ordinary ladylikeness rather at a loss. A real colonial, from the newest, wildest, remotest colony.

She loved her little boy. But also she loved her husband, and she loved the army life. She preferred, really, to be with her husband. And you can't trail a child about. And she lived in all the world, and she couldn't bear to be poked in a village in England. Not for long. And she was used to having men about her. Mostly men. Jolly men.

So her heart smarted for her little boy. But she had to leave him. And he loved her, but did not dream of depending on her. He knew it as a tiny child. He would never have to depend on anybody. His father would pay money for him. But his father was rather jealous of him. Jealous even of his beauty as a tiny child, in spite of the fact that the child was the " spitten " image of the father : dark blue eyes, curly hair, peach-bloom skin. Only the child had the easy way of accommodating himself to life and circumstances, like his mother, and a certain readiness to laugh, even when he was by himself. The easy laugh that made his nurse say " You little sinner !"

He knew he was a little sinner. It rather amused him.

Jack's mind jolted awake as he made a grab at his hat, nearly knocking it off, realizing that he was being introduced to two men : or that two men were being introduced to him. They shook hands very casually, giggling at the same time to one another in a suppressed manner. Jack blushed furiously, embarrassed, not knowing what they were laughing at.

Just beside him, the Jewish gentleman was effusively greeting another Jewish gentleman. In fact, they were kissing : which made Jack curl with disgust. But he couldn't move away, because there were bales behind him, people on two sides, and a big dog was dancing and barking in front of him, at something which it saw away below through a crack in the wharf timbers. The dog seemed to be a mixture of wolf and grey-hound. Queer specimen ! Later, he knew it was called a kangaroo dog.

" Mr A. Bell and Mr Swallow. Mr Jack Grant from England." This was Mr George introducing him to the two men, and going on without any change, with a queer puffing of the lips : " Prh ! Bah ! Wolf and Hider ! Wolf and Hider ! "

This left Jack completely mystified. And why were Mr Bell and Mr Swallow laughing so convulsedly? Was it the dog?

" You remember his father, Bell, out here in '59—Captain Grant. Married Surgeon-Captain Reid's youngest daughter, from Woolamooloo Station."

The gentleman said : " Pleased to make your acquaintance," which was a phrase that embarrassed Jack because he didn't know what to answer. Should one say, " Thank you ! "—or " The pleasure is mine ! "—or " So am I to make yours ! " He mumbled : " How do you do ! "

However, it didn't matter, for the two men kept the laugh between themselves, while Mr George took on a colonial *distrait* look, then blew out his cheeks and ejaculated : " Mercy and truth have met together : righteousness and peace have kissed each other." This was said in a matter-of-fact way. Jack knew it was a quotation from the Psalms, but not what it was aimed at. The two men were laughing more openly at the joke.

Was the joke against himself? Was it his own righteousness that was funny? He blushed furiously once more.

ii

But Mr George ignored the boy's evident embarrassment, and strolled off with one of the gentlemen—whether Bell or Swallow Jack did not know—towards the train.

The remaining gentleman—either Bell or Swallow—clapped the uncomfortable youth comfortably on the shoulder.

" New chum, eh? Not in the know? I'll tell you." They set off after the other two.

" By gad, 's a funny thing ! You've got to laugh if old George is about, though he never moves a muscle. Dry as a ship's biscuit. D'y'see the Jews kissing? They've been at law for two years, those two blossoms. One's name is Wolf and the other's Hider, and Mr George is Wolf's attorney. Never able to do anything, because you couldn't get Hider into the open. See the joke? Hider ! Sneak Hider ! Hider under the rafters ! Hider hidden ! And the Wolf couldn't unearth him. Though George showed up Wolf for what he is : a mean, grasping, contentious mongrel of a man. Now they meet to kiss. See them? The suit ended in a mush. But that dog there hunting a rat right under their feet—wasn't that beautiful? Old George couldn't miss it—' Mercy and truth have met together,' ha! ha! However he finds his text for everything beats me—— "

Jack laughed, and walked in a daze beside his new acquaintance. He felt he had fallen overhead into Australia, instead of arriving naturally.

The wood-eating little engine was gasping in front of a little train of open carriages. Jack remarked on her tender piled high with chunks of wood.

" Yes, we stoke 'er with timber. We carry all we can. And if we're going a long way, to York, when she's burned up all she can carry she stops in the bush and we all get down, passengers and all, to chop a new supply. See the axe there? She carries half a dozen on a long trip."

The three men, all wearing old-fashioned whiskers, pulled out tobacco pouches the moment they were seated, and started their pipes. They were all stout, and their clothes were slack, and they behaved with such absolute unconcern that it made Jack self-conscious.

He sat rather stiffly, remembering the things his mother had told him. Her father, Surgeon-Captain Reid, had arrived at the Swan river on a man-of-war, on his very first voyage. He had landed with Captain Fremantle from H.M.S. " Challenger," when that officer took formal possession of the country in the name of His Majesty King George IV. He had seen the first transport, the " Parmelia," prevented by heavy gales from landing her goods and passengers on the mainland, disembark all on Garden Island, where the men of the " Challenger " were busy clearing ground and erecting temporary houses. That was in midwinter, June, 1827; and Jack's grandfather. Now it was mid-winter, June, 1882; and mere Jack.

Midwinter! A pure blue sky and a warm, crystal air. The brush outside green, rather dull green, the sandy country dry. It was like English June, English midsummer. Why call it midwinter? Except for a certain dull look of the bushes.

They were passing the convict station. The " Establishment " had not lasted long; from about 1850 to 1870. Not like New South Wales, which had a purely convict origin. Western Australia was more respectable.

He remembered his mother always praised the convicts, said they had been a blessing to the colony. Western Australia had been too big and barren a mouthful for the first pioneers to chew, even though they were gentlemen of pluck and education, and bit off their claims bravely. Came the rush that followed occupation, a rush of estimable and highly respectable British workmen. But even these were unprepared for the hardships that awaited them in Western Australia. The country was too much for them.

It needed the convicts to make a real impression : the convicts with their law, and discipline, and all their governmental outfit, and their forced labour. Soldiers, doctors, lawyers, spiritual pastors and earthly masters . . . and the convicts condemned to obey. This was the beginning of the colony.

Thought speaks ! Mr Swallow, identified as the gentleman with the long, lean, ruddy face and large nose and vague brown eye, leaned forward and jerked his pipe stem towards the open window.

" See that beautiful road running through the sand, sir ? That road extends to Perth and over the Causeway and away up country, branching in all directions, like the arteries of the human body. Built by the sappers and miners with *convict labour*, sir. Yes, with *convict* labour. Also the bridge over which we are crossing."

Jack looked out at the road, but was much more enchanted by the full, soft river of heavenly blue water, on whose surface he looked eagerly for the black swans. He didn't see any.

" Oh, yes ! Oh, yes ! You'll find 'em wild in their native state a little way up," said Mr Swallow.

Beyond the river were sheets of sand again, white sand stretching around on every side.

" It must have been here that the Carpenter wept," Jack said in his unexpected young voice that was still slightly hoarse, as he poked his face out of the window.

The three gentlemen were silent in passive consternation, till Mr George swelled his cheeks and continued :

" Like anything to see such quantities of sand." Then he snorted and blew his nose.

Mr Bell at once recognised the Westralian joke, which had been handed on to Jack by his mother.

" Hit it, my son ! " he cried, clapping his hands on his knees. " In the first five minutes. Useless ! Useless ! A gentleman of discernment, that's what you are. Just the sort we want in this colony—a gentleman of discernment. A gentleman without it planted us here, fifty years ago, in the blank, blank sand. What's the consequence ? Clogged, cloyed, cramped, sand-smothered, that's what we are."

" Not a bit of it," said Mr Swallow.

" Sorrow, Sin, and Sand," repeated Mr Bell.

Jack was puzzled and amused by their free-and-easy, confidential way, which was still a little ceremonious. Slightly ceremonious, and in their shirt-sleeves, so to speak. The same with their curious, cockney pronunciation, their accurate grammar, and their slight pomposity. They never said " you," merely " y' "—" That's what y'are." And their drawling, almost sneering manner was very odd, contrasting with the shirt-sleeves familiarity, the shabby clothes and the pleasant way they had of nodding at you when they talked to you.

" Yes, yes, Mr Grant," continued Mr Bell, while Jack wished he wouldn't Mister him—" A gentleman without discernment induced certain politicians in the British Cabinet to invest in these vast areas. This same gentleman got himself created King of Groperland, and came out here with a small number of fool followers. These fool followers, for every three quid's worth of goods they brought with them, were given forty acres of land apiece——"

" Of sand," said Mr George.

" ——and a million acres of fine promises," continued Mr Bell unmoved. " Therefore the fool followers, mostly younger sons of good family, anxious to own property—— "

" In parties of five females to one male—Prrrh !" snorted Mr George.

" ——came. They were informed that the soil was well adapted to the cultivation of tobacco ! Of cotton ! Of sugar ! Of flax ! And that cattle could be raised to supply His Majesty's ships with salt beef—and horses could be reared to supply the army in India—— "

" With Kangaroos and Wallabies."

" ——the cavalry, that is.   So they came and were landed in the sand—— "

" And told to stick their head in it, so they shouldn't see death staring at 'em."

" ——along with the goods they had brought."

" A harp ! " cried Mr George. " My mother brought a harp and a Paisley shawl and got five hundred acres for 'em—estimated value of harp being twenty guineas. She'd better have gone straight to heaven with it."

" Yes, sir ! " continued Mr Bell, unheeding.

" No, sir ! " broke in Mr George. " Do you wish me unborn."

Mr Bell paused to smile, then continued :

" Mr Grant, sir, these gentle ladies and gentlemen were dumped in the sand along with their goods. Well, there were a few cattle and sheep and horses. But what else ? Harps. Paisley shawls. Ornamental glass cases of wax fruit, for the mantelpiece ; family Bibles and a family coach, sir. For that family coach, sir, the bringer got a thousand acres of land. And it ended its days where they landed it, on the beach, for there wasn't an inch of road to drive it over, nor anywhere to drive it to. They took off its wheels and there it lay. I myself have sat in it."

" Ridden in his coach," smiled Mr George.

" My mother," continued Mr Bell, " was a clergyman's daughter. I myself was born in a bush humpy, and my mother died shortly after—— "

" Of chagrin ! Of chagrin ! " muttered Mr George.

" We will draw a veil over the sufferings of those years—— "

" Oh, but we made good ! We made good ! " put in Mr Swallow comfortably. " What are you grousing about ? We made good. There you sit, Bell, made of money, and grousing, anybody would think you wanted a loan of two bob."

" By the waters of Babylon there we sat down—— " said Mr George.

" Did we ! No, we didn't. We rowed up the Swan River. That's what my father did. A sturdy British yeoman, Mr Grant."

" Where did he get the boat from ? " asked Mr Bell.

" An old ship. I was a baby, sir, in a tartan frock.

Remember it to this day, sitting in my mother's lap. My father got that boat off a whaler. It had been stove in, and wasn't fit for the sea. But he made it fit for the river, and they rowed up the Swan—my father and a couple of ' indented ' servants, as we called them. We landed in the Upper Swan valley. I remember that camp fire, sir, as well as I remember anything."

" Better than most things," put in Mr George.

" We cleared off the scrub, we lifted the stones into heaps, we planted corn and wheat—— "

" The babe in the tartan frock steering the plough."

" Yes, sir, later on. Our flocks prospered, our land bore fruit, our family flourished—— "

" On milk and honey—— "

" Oh, cry off, Swallow! " ejaculated Mr Bell. " Your father fought flood and drought for forty odd years. The floods of '62 broke his heart, and the floods in '72 ruined *you*. And this is '82, so don't talk too loud."

" Ruined! When was I ever ruined? " cried Mr Swallow. " Sheep one-hundred-and-ten per cent; for some herds, as you know, gentlemen, throw twins and triplets. Cattle ninety per cent., horses fifty; and a ready market for 'em all."

" Pests," Mr Bell was saying, "one million per cent. Rust destroys fourteen thousand acres of wheat crop, just as the country is getting on its feet. Dingoes breed 135 per cent., and kill sheep to match. Cattle run wild and are no more seen. Horses cost the eyes out of your head before you can catch 'em, break 'em, train 'em, and ship 'em to the Indian market."

" Moth and rust! Moth and rust! " murmured Mr George absently.

iii

Jack, with the uncomfortable philosophy of youth, sat still and let the verbal waters rage. Until he was startled by a question from Mr George.

" Well, sir, what were you sent out for? "

This was a colonial little joke at the " Establishment " identity's expense. But, unfortunately, it hit Jack too. He had been sent out, really, because he was too tiresome to keep at home. Too fond of " low " company. Too often a frequenter of the stables. Too indifferent to the higher claims of society. They feared a waster in the bud. So they shipped the bud to the antipodes, to let it blossom there upside down.

But Jack was not going to give himself away.

" To go on the land, sir," he replied. Which was true. But what had his father said in the letter? He flushed and looked angry, his dark blue eyes going very dark. " I was expelled from school," he added calmly. " And I was sent down from the Agricultural College. That's why I have come out a year before my time. But I was coming—to go on the land—anyway—— "

He ended in a stammer. He rather hated adults; he definitely hated them in tribunal.

Mr George held up his hand deprecatingly.

" Say nothing! Say nothing! Your father made no mention of anything. Tell us when you know us, if y'like. But you aren't called on to indict yourself. That was a silly joke of mine. Forget it. You came to go on the land, as your father informs me. I knew your father, long before you were born. But I knew your mother better."

" So did I," said Mr Swallow. " And grieved the day that ever a military gentleman carried her away from Western Australia. She was one of our home-grown flowers, was Katie Reid, and I never saw a Rose of England that could touch her."

Jack now flushed deeper than ever.

" Though," said Mr George slyly, " if you've got a prank up y'r sleeve, that you can tell us about—come on with it, my son. We've none of us forgotten being shipped to England for a schooling."

" Oh, well! " said Jack. He always said " Oh, well! " when he didn't know what to say. " You mean at the Agricultural College. Oh, well!—Well I was the youngest there, stable-boy and harness-cleaner, and all that. Oh, well! You see there'd been a chivoo the night before. The lads had a grudge against the council, because they gave us bread and cheese, and no butter, for supper, and cocoa with no milk. And we weren't just little nippers. We were—Oh, well! Most of the chaps were men, really— eighteen—nineteen—twenty. As much as twenty-three. I was the youngest. I didn't care. But the chaps were different. There were many who had failed at the big entrance exams. for the Indian Civil, or the Naval or Military, and they were big, hungry chaps, you can bet—— "

" I should say so," nodded Mr George approvingly.

" Well, there was a chivoo. They held me on their shoulders and I smashed the principal's windows."

You could see by Jack's face how he had enjoyed breaking those windows.

" What with? " asked Mr George.

" With a wooden gym club."

" Wanton destruction of property. Prrrh ! "

" The boss was frightened. But he raised Old Harry and said he'd go up to town and report us to the council. So he ordered the trap right away, to catch the nine o'clock train. And I had to take the trap round to the front door—— "

Here Jack paused. He didn't want to go further.

" And so—— " said Mr George.

" And so, when I stepped away from the horse's head, the principal jerked the reins in the nasty way he had and the horse bolted."

" Couldn't the fellow pull her up? Man in a position like that ought to know how to drive a horse."

Jack watched their faces closely. On his own face was that subtle look of innocence, which veiled a look of life-and-death defiance.

" The reins weren't buckled into the bit, sir. No man could drive that horse," he said quietly.

A look of amusement tinged with misgiving spread over Mr George's face. But he was a true colonial. He had to hear the end of a story against powers-that-be.

" And how did it end? " he asked.

" I'm sorry," said Jack, " he broke his leg in the accident."

The three Australians burst into a laugh. Chiefly because when Jack said " I'm sorry," he really meant it. He was really sorry for the hurt man. But for the hurt Principal he wasn't sorry. As soon as the Principal was on the ground with a broken leg, Jack saw only the hurt man, and none of the office. And his heart was troubled for the hurt man.

But if the mischief was to do again he would probably do it. He couldn't repent. And yet his feelings were genuinely touched. Which made him comical.

" You're a corker ! " said Mr George, shaking his head with new misgiving.

" So you were sent down," said Mr Bell. " And y'r father though he'd better ship you straight out here, eh ? Best thing for you, I'll be bound. I'll bet you never learned a ha'porth at that place."

" Oh, well. I think I learned a lot."

" When to sow and when to reap and a Latin motto attached ! "

" No, sir, not that. I learned to vet."

" Vet. ? "

" Well, sir, you see, the head groom was a gentleman veterinary surgeon and he had a weakness, as he called it. So when he was strong he taught me to vet, and when he had his attacks I'd go out with the cart and collect him at a pub and bring him home under the straw, in return for kindness shown."

" A nice sort of school ! Prrrh ! Bah ! " snorted Mr George.

" Oh, that wasn't on the curriculum, sir. My mother says there'll be rascals in heaven, if you look for them."

" And you keep on looking, eh ? Well—I wouldn't, if I were you. Especially in this country, I wouldn't. I wouldn't go vetting any more for any drunken groom in the world, if I were you. Nor breaking windows, nor leaving reins unbuckled either. And I'll tell you for why. It becomes a habit. You get a habit of going with rascals, and then you're done. Because in this country you'll find plenty of scamps, and plenty of wasters. And the sight of them is enough—nasty, low-down lot. This is a great big country, where an honest man can go his own way into the back of beyond, if he likes. But the minute he begins to go crooked, or slack, the country breaks him. It breaks him, and he's neither fit for god nor man any more. You beware of this country, my boy, and don't try to play larks with it. It's all right playing a prank on an old fool of a fossil out there in England. They need a few pranks played on them, they do. But out here—no ! Keep all your strength and all your wits to fight the bush. It's a great big country. And it needs men, *men*, not wasters. It's a great big country, and it wants men. You can go your way and do what you want : take up land, go on a sheep station, lumber, or try the gold fields. But whatever you do, live up to your fate like a man. And keep square with yourself. Never mind other people. But keep square with *yourself*."

Jack, staring out of the window, saw miles of dull dark-green scrub spreading away on every side to a bright sky-line. He could hear his mother's voice :

" Earn a good opinion of yourself and never mind the world's opinion. You know when there's the right glow inside you. That's the spirit of God inside you."

But this " right glow " business puzzled him a little. He was inclined to believe he felt it while he was smashing the Principal's window-glass, and while he was " vetting " with the drunken groom. Yet the words fascinated him : " The right glow inside you—the spirit of God inside you."

He sat motionless on his seat, while the Australians kept on talking about the colony. " Have y'patience? Perseverance? Have ye that? She wants y' and y' offspring. And the bones y'll leave behind y'. All of y' interests, y' hopes, y' life, and the same of y' sons and son's sons. An' she doesn't care if y' go nor stay, neither. Makes no difference to her. She's waiting, drowsy, no hurry. Wants millions of yer. But she's waited endless ages and can wait endless more. Only she must have *men*—understand? If they're lazy derelicts and ne'er-do-wells, she'll eat 'em up. But she's waiting for real men—British to the bone—— "

" The lad's no more than a boy, yet, George. Dry up a bit with your *men—British to the bone*."

" Don't toll at *me*, Bell. I've been here since '31, so let me speak. Came in old sailing-ship, ' Rockingham '— wrecked on coast—left nothing but her name, township of Rockingham. Nice place to fish. Was sent back to London to school, '41, in another sailing-vessel and wasn't wrecked this time. ' Shepherd,' laden colonial produce. The first steam vessel didn't come till '45—the ' Driver.' Wonderful advancement—wonderful advancement in the colony, too, when I came back. Came back a notary. Couple of churches, Mill Street Jetty, Grammar School opened,

Causeway built, lot of exploration done. Eyre had legged it from Adelaide—all in my time, all in my time—— "

iv

Jack felt it might go on for ever. He was becoming stupefied. Mercifully, the train jerked to a standstill beside a wooden platform, that was separated from a sandy space by a picket fence. A porter put his hand to his mouth and yelled " Perth," just for the look of the thing—because where else could it be ? They all burst out of the train. The town stood up in the sand : wooden houses with wooden platforms blown over with sand.

And Mr George was still at it. " Yes, Bell, wait for the salty sand to mature. Wait for a few of *us* to die—and decay ! Mature—manure, that's what's wanted. Dead men in the sand, dead men's bones in the gravel. That's what'll mature this country. The people you bury in it. Only good fertilizer. Dead men are like seed in the ground. When a few more like you and me, Bell, are worked in——"

CHAP : II. THE TWIN LAMBS

i

JACK was tired and a little land-sick, after the long voyage. He felt dazed and rather unhappy, and saw as through a glass, darkly. For he could not yet get used to the fixed land under his feet, after the long weeks on the steamer. And these people went on as if they were wound up, curiously oblivious of him and his feelings. A dream world, with a dark glass between his eyes and it. An uneasy dream.

He waited on the platform. Mr George had again disappeared somewhere. The train was backing already away.

It was evening, and the setting sun from the west, where the great empty sea spread unseen, cast a radiance in the etherealised air, melting the brick shops and the wooden houses and the sandy places in a sort of amethyst glow. And again Jack saw the magic clarity of this new world, as through a glass, darkly. He felt the cool snap of night in the air, coming strange and crude out of the jewel sky. And it seemed to him he was looking through the wrong end of a field-glass, at a far, far country.

Where was Mr George? Had he gone off to read the letter again, or to enquire about the draft on the bank? Everyone had left the station, the wagonette cabs had driven away. What was to be done? Ought he to have mentioned an hotel? He'd better say something. He'd better say——

But here was Mr George, with a serious face, coming straight up to say something.

" That vet," he said, " did he think you had a natural gift for veterinary work ? "

" He said so, sir. My mother's father was a naval surgeon—if that has anything to do with it."

" Nothing at all. I knew the old gentleman—and another silly old cuckoo he was, too. But he's dead, so we'll make the best of him. No, it was your character I wanted to get at. Your father wants you to go on a farm or a station for twelve months, and sends a pound a week for your board. Suppose you know——? "

" Yes—I hope it's enough."

" Oh, it's enough, if you're all right yourself—I was thinking of Ellis's place. I've got the twins here now. They're kinsmen of yours, the Ellises—and of mine, too. We're all related, in clans and cliques and gangs, out here in this colony. Your mother belongs to the Ellis clan. Well, now. Ellis's place is a fine home farm, and not too far. Only he's got a family of fine young lambs, my step-sister's children into the bargain. And y'see, if y're a wolf in sheep's clothing—for you *look* mild enough—why, I oughtn't to be sending you among them. Young lasses and boys bred and reared out there in the bush, why—— Come now, son—y'father protected you by silence—but you're not in court, and you needn't heed me. Tell me straight out what you were expelled from your Bedford school for."

Jack was silent for a moment, rather pale about the nose.

" I was nabbed," he said, in a colourless voice, " at a fight with fists for a purse of sovereigns, laid either side. Plenty of others were there. But they got away, and the police nabbed me for the school colours on my cap. My father was just back from Ceylon, and he stood by me. But the Head said for the sake of example and for the name of the school I'd better be chucked out. They were talking about the school in the newspapers. The Head said he was sorry to expel me."

Mr George blew his nose into a large yellow red-spotted handkerchief, and looked for a few moments into the distance.

" Seems to me you let yourself be made a bit of a cat's paw of," he said dubiously.

" I suppose it's because I don't care," said Jack.

" But you ought to care. Why don't y' ? "

There was no answer.

" You'll have to care some day or other," the old man continued.

" Do you know, sir, which hotel I shall go to ? " asked Jack.

" You'll go to no hotel. You'll come home with me. But, mind y'. I've got my two young nieces, Ellis' twins, couple of girls, Ellis' daughters, where I'm going to send you. They're at my house. And there's my other niece,

Mary, who I'm very fond of. She's not an Ellis, she's a Rath, and an orphan, lives with her Aunt Matilda, my sister. They don't live with me. None of 'em live with me. I live alone, except for a good plain cook, since my wife died. But I tell you, they're visiting me. And I shall look to you to behave yourself, now; both here and at Wandoo, which is Ellis' station. I'll take you there in the morning. But y'see now where I'm taking you : among a pack of innocent sheep that's probably never seen a goat to say Boh! to—or Baa! if you like—makes no difference. We don't raise goats in Western Australia, as I'm aware of. But I'm telling you, if you're a wolf in sheep's clothing—— No, you needn't say anything. You probably don't know what you are, anyhow. So come on. I'll tell somebody to bring your bags—looks a rare jorum to me—and we'll walk."

ii

They walked off the timber platform into the sand, and Jack had his first experience of " sand-groping." The sand was thick and fine and soft, so he was glad to reach the oyster-shell path running up Wellington Street, in front of the shops. They passed along the street of brick cottages and two-storied houses, to Barrack Street, where Jack looked with some surprise on the pretentious buildings that stood up in the dusk : the handsome square red brick tower of the Town Hall, and on the sandy hill to the left, the fine white edifice of the Roman Catholic Church, which building was already older than Jack himself. Beyond the Town Hall was the Church of England. " See it ! " said Mr George. " That's where your father and mother were married. Slap-dash, military wedding, more muslin and red jackets than would stock a shop."

Mr George spoke to everybody he met, ladies and gentlemen alike. The ladies seemed a bit old-fashioned, the gentlemen all wore nether garments at least four sizes too large for them. Jack was much piqued by this pioneering habit. And they all seemed very friendly and easy-going, like men in a pub at home.

" What did the Bedford Headmaster say he was sorry to lose you for? Smart at your books, were you? "

" I was good at Scripture and Shakespeare, but not at the other things. I expect he was sorry to lose me from the football eleven. I was the cock there."

Mr George blew his nose loudly, gasped, prrrhed, and said, " You'd better say *rooster*, my son, here in Australia; especially in polite society. We're a trifle more particular than they are in England, I suppose. Well, and what else have you got to crow about ? "

If Jack had been the sulky sort, he would now have begun to get sulky. As it was, he was tired of being continually pulled up. But he fell back on his own peculiar callous indifference.

" I was captain of the first football eleven," he said in his indifferent voice. " And not bad in front of the sticks. And I took the long distance running cup a year under age. I tell you because you ask me."

Then Mr George astonished Jack again by turning and planting himself in front of him like Balaam's ass, in the middle of the path, standing with feet apart in his big elephant trousers, snorting behind a walrus moustache, glaring and extending a large and powerful hand. He shook hands vigorously, saying, " You'll do, my son. You'll do for me."

Then he resumed his walk.

iii

" Yes, sir, you'll do for me," resumed the old man. " For I can see vou're a gentleman."

Jack was rather taken aback. He had come to Australia to be a Man, a wild, bushy man among men. His father was a gentleman.

" I think I'd rather be a man than a gentleman," he said.

Mr George stood still, feet apart, as if he had been shot. " What's the difference ? " he cried in a falsetto, sarcastic tone. " What's the difference ? Can't be a man unless you *are* a gentleman. Take that from me. You might say I'm not a gentleman. Sense of the ridiculous runs away with me, for one thing. But, in order to be the best man I could, I've tried to be all the gentleman I could. No hanky-pankying about it. You're a gentleman born. I'm not, not *altogether*. Don't you go trying to upset what you are. But whether you're a bush-whacker or a lumper you can be a gentleman. A gentleman's a man who never laughs to wound, who's honest with himself, and his own judge in the sight of the Almighty. That's the Government House down there among the trees, river just beyond. That's my house, there, see. I'm going to hand you over to the girls once we get there. So I shan't see you again, not to talk to. I want to tell you, then, that I put my confidence in you, and you're going to play up like a gentleman. And I want you to know, as between gentlemen, not merely between an old man and a boy, but as between gentlemen, if you ever need any help, or a word of advice, come to me. Come to me, and I'll do my best."

He once more shook hands, this time in a conclusive manner.

Jack had looked to left and right as they walked, half listening to the endless old man. He saw sandy blocks of land beside the road, and scattered, ugly buildings, most of them new. He made out the turrets and gables of the Government House, in the dusk among trees, and he imagined the wide clear river below those trees.

Turning down an unmade road, they approached a two-storied brick house with narrow verandahs, whose wooden supports rested nakedly on the sand below. There was no garden, fence, or anything : just an oyster-shell path across the sand, a pipe-clayed doorstep, a brass knocker, a narrow wooden verandah, a few flower-pots.

Mr George opened the door and showed the boy into the narrow wooden hall. There was a delicious smell of cooking. Jack climbed the thin, flimsy stairs, and was shown into his bedroom. A four-poster bed with a crochet quilt and frilled pillows, a mahogany chest of drawers with swivel looking-glass, a washstand with china set complete. England all over again. Even his bag was there, and his brushes were set out for him.

He had landed !

iv

As he made his toilet he heard a certain fluttering outside his door. He waited for it to subside, and when all seemed still, opened to go downstairs. There stood two girls, giggling and blushing, waiting arm in arm to pounce on him.

" Oh, isn't he *beau!* " exclaimed one of the girls, in a sort of aside. And the other broke into a high laugh.

Jack remained dumbfounded, reddening to the roots of his hair. But his dark-blue eyes lingered for a moment on the two girlish faces. They were evidently the twins. They had the same thin, soft, slightly-tanned, warm-looking faces, a little wild, and the same marked features. But the brows of one were level, and her fair hair, darkish fair, was all crisp, curly round her temples, and she looked up at you from under her level brows with queer yellow-grey eyes, shy, wild, and yet with a queer effrontery, like a wild-cat under a bush. The other had blue eyes and a bigger nose, and it was she who said, " Oh, isn't he *beau!*"

The one with the yellow eyes stuck out her slim hand awkwardly, gazing at him and saying :

" I suppose you're cousin Jack, Beau."

He shook hands first with one then with the other, and could not find a word to say. The one with the yellow eyes was evidently the leader of the two.

" Tea is ready," she said, " if you're coming down."

She spoke this over her shoulder. There was the same colour in her tawny eyes as in her crisp, tawny hair, but her brows were darker. She had a forehead, Jack decided, like the plaster-cast of Minerva. And she had the queerest way of looking at you under her brows, and over her shoulder. Funny pair of lambs, these.

The two girls went downstairs arm in arm, at a run. This is quite a feat, but evidently they were used to it.

Jack looked on life, social life inside a house, as something to be borne in silence. These two girls were certainly a desperate addition. He heard them burst into the parlour, the other one repeating :

" He's coming. Here comes Beau."

" I thought his name was Jack. *Bow*, is it ! " exclaimed a voice.

He entered the parlour with his elbows at his sides, his starched collar feeling very stiff. He was aware of the usual hideous room, rather barer than at home : plush cushions on a horse-hair sofa, and a green carpet : a large stout woman, with reddish hair, in a silk frock, and gold chains, and Mr George introducing her as Mrs Watson, otherwise Aunt Matilda. She put diamond-ringed hands on Jack's shoulders and looked into his face, which he thought a repellant procedure.

"So like your father, dear boy; how's your dear mother?"

And in spite of his inward fury of resistance, she kissed him. For she was but a woman of forty-two.

"Quite well, thank you," said Jack, though considering he had been at sea for six weeks, he knew as little about his mother's health as did Aunt Matilda herself.

"Did y' blow y' candle out?" asked Mr George.

"No, he didn't," answered the tawny girl. "*I'll* go and do it."

And she flashed away upstairs like a panther.

"I suppose the twins introduced themselves," said Mr George.

"No, they didn't," said the other one.

"Only christened you Bow. You'll be somebody or other's beau before very long, I'll warrant. This is Grace, Grace Ellis, you know, where you're going to live. And her sister who's gone upstairs to blow your candle out, is Monica. Can't be too careful of fire in these dry places. Most folks say they can't tell 'em apart, but I call it nonsense."

"Ancien, beau, bon, cher, adjectives which precede," said the one called Monica, jerking herself into the room, after blowing out the candle.

"There's your father," said Mr George. And Aunt Matilda fluttered into the hall, while the twins betrayed no interest at all. The tawny one stared at Jack and kept slinking about like a lean young panther, to get a different view of him. For all the world as if she was going to pounce on him, like a cat on a bird. He, permanently flushed, kept his self-possession in a boyish and rather handsome, if stiff, manner.

Mr Ellis was stout, clean-shaven, red-faced, and shabby and baggy and good-natured in appearance.

"This is the young gentleman—Mr Grant—called in Westralia Bow, so named by Miss Monica Ellis."

"By Miss Grace, if you please," snapped Monica.

"Tea's ready. Tea's ready."

They trooped into the dining room where a large table was spread. Aunt Matilda seated herself behind the tea-kettle, Mr George sat at the other end, before the pile of plates and the carvers, and the others took their places where they would. Jack modestly sat on Aunt Matilda's left hand, so the tawny Monica at once pounced on the chair opposite.

Entered the Good Plain Cook with a dish covered with a pewter cover, and followed by a small, dark, ugly, quiet girl carrying the vegetable dishes.

" That's my niece, Mary, Jack. Lives with Aunt Matilda here, who won't spare her or I'd have her to live here with me. Now you know everybody. What's for tea? "

He was dangerously clashing the knife on the steel. Then lifting the cover, he disclosed a young pig roasted in all its glory of gravy. Mary meanwhile had nodded her head at Jack and looked at him with her big, queer, very black eyes. You might have thought she had native blood. She sat down to serve the vegetables.

" Grace, there's a fly in the milk," said Aunt Matilda, who was already pouring large cups of tea. Grace seized the milk jug and jerked from the room.

" Do you take milk and sugar, as your dear father used to, John? " asked Aunt Matilda of the youth on her left.

" Call him Bow. Bow's his name out here—John's too stiff and Jack's too common! " exclaimed Mr George, elbows deep in carving.

" Bow'll do for me," put in Mr Ellis, who said little.

" Mary, is there any mustard? " said Aunt Matilda.

Jack rose vaguely to go and get it, but Aunt Matilda seized him by the arm and pushed him back.

" Sit still. She knows where it is."

" Monica, come and carry the cups, there's a good girl."

" Now which end of the pig do you like, Jack? " asked Mr George.

" Matilda, will this do for you? " He held up a piece on the fork. Mary arrived with a ponderous gyrating cruet-stand, which she made place for in the middle of the table.

" What about bread? " said Aunt Matilda. " I'm sure John eats bread with his meat. Fetch some bread, Grace, for your cousin John."

" Everybody did it," thought Jack in despair, as he tried to eat amid the bustle. " No servants, nothing ever still. On the go all the time."

" Girls going to the concert to-night ? " asked Mr George.

" If anybody will go with us," replied Monica, with a tawny look at Jack.

" There's Bow," said Mr George, " Bow'll like to go."

Under the she-lion peering of Monica, Jack was incapable of answer.

" Let the poor boy rest," said Aunt Matilda. " Just landed after a six thousand mile voyage, and you rush him out next minute to a concert. Let him stop at home quietly with me, and have a quiet chat about the dear ones he's left behind. Aren't *you* going to the concert with the girls, Jacob ? "

This was addressed to Mr Ellis, who took a gulp of tea and shook his head mutely.

" I'd rather go to the concert, I think," said Jack, under the queer yellow glower of Monica's eyes, and the full black gaze of Mary's.

" Good for you, my boy," said Mr George. " Bow by name and Bow by nature. And well set up, with three strings to his Bow already."

Monica once more peered tawnily, and Mary glanced a black, furtive glance. Aunt Matilda looked down on him, and Grace, at his side, peered up.

For the first time since childhood, Jack found himself in a really female setting. Instinctively he had avoided women : but particularly he avoided girls. With girls and women he felt exposed to some sort of danger—as if something were going to seize him by the neck, from behind, when he wasn't looking. He relied on men for safety. But curiously enough, these two elderly men gave him no shelter whatever. They seemed to throw him a victim to these frightful " lambs." In England, there was an *esprit de corps* among men. Man for man was a tower of strength against the females. Here in this place men deserted one another as soon as the women put in an appearance. They left the field entirely to the females.

In the first half-hour Jack realised he was thrown a victim to these tawny and black young cats. And there was nothing to do but bear up.

" Have you got an evening suit? " asked Grace, who was always the one to ponder things out.

" Yes—a sort of a one," said Jack.

" Oh, good! Oh, put it on! Do put it on."

" Leave the lad alone," said Mr George. " Let him go as he is."

" No," said Aunt Matilda. " He has his father's handsome presence. Let him make the best of himself. I think I'll go to the concert after all."

After dinner there was a bustle. Monica flew up to light his candle for him, and stood there peering behind the flame when he came upstairs.

" You haven't much time," she said, as if she were going to spear him.

" All right," he answered, in his hoarse young voice. And he stood in torment till she left his room.

He was just tying his tie when there came a flutter and a tapping. Aunt Matilda's voice was saying : " Nearly time. Are you almost ready? "

" Half a minute! " he crowed hoarsely, like an unhappy young cock.

But the door stealthily opened, and Aunt Matilda peeped in.

"Oh, tying his tie! " she said, satisfactorily, when she perceived that he was dressed as far as discretion demanded. And she entered in full blow. Behind her hovered Grace—then Monica—and in the doorway, Mary. It seemed to Jack that Aunt Matilda was the most objectionable of the lot, Monica the brazenest, Grace the most ill-mannered, and Mary the most repulsive, with her dark face. He struggled in discomfort with his tie.

" Let Mary do it," said Aunt Matilda.

" No, no," he barked. " I can do it."

" Come on, Mary. Come and tie John's tie."

Mary came quietly forward.

" Let me do it for you, Bow," she said in her quiet, insinuating voice, looking at him with her inky eyes and standing in front of him till his knees felt weak and his throat strangled. He was purple in the face, struggling with his tie in the presence of the lambs.

" He'll never get it done," said Monica, from behind the yellow glare.

" Let me do it," said Mary, and lifting her hands decisively she took the two ends of the tie from him.

He held his breath and lifted his eyes to the ceiling and felt as if the front of his body were being roasted. Mary, the devil-puss, seemed endless ages fastening the tie. Then she twitched it at his throat and it was done, just as he was on the point of suffocation.

" Are those your best braces? " said Grace. " They're awfully pretty with rose-buds." And she fingered the band.

" I suppose you put on evening dress for the last dinner on board," said Aunt Matilda. " Nothing makes me cry like *Auld Lang Syne*, that last night, before you land next day. But it's fifteen years since I went over to England."

" I don't suppose we shall any of us ever go," said Grace longingly.

" Unless you marry Bow," said Monica abruptly.

" I can't marry him unless he asks me," said Grace.

" He'll ask nobody for a good many years to come," said Aunt Matilda with satisfaction.

" Hasn't he got lovely eyelashes," said Grace impersonally.

" He'd almost do for a girl," said Monica.

" Not if you look at his ears," said Mary, with odd decision. He felt that Mary was bent on saving his manhood.

He breathed as if the air around him were red-hot. He would have to get out, or die. He plunged into his coat, pulling down his shirt-cuffs with a jerk.

" What funny green cuff-links," said Grace. " Are they pot? "

" Malachite," said Jack.

" What's malachite? "

There was no answer. He put a white silk muffler round his neck to protect his collar.

" Oh, look at his initials in lavender silk ! "

At last he was in his overcoat, and in the street with the bevy.

" Leave your overcoat open, so it shows your shirt-front as you walk," said Grace, forcibly unbuttoning the said coat. " I think that looks so lovely. Doesn't he look lovely, Monica? Everybody will be asking who he is."

" Tell them he's the son of General Grant," said Aunt Matilda, with complete satisfaction, as she sailed at his side.

Life is principally a matter of endurance. This was the sum of Jack's philosophy. He put it into practice this evening.

It was a benefit concert in the Town Hall, with the Episcopalian Choir singing " Angels Ever Bright and Fair," and a violinist from Germany playing violin solos, and a lady vocalist from Melbourne singing " home " solos, while local stars variously coruscated. Aunt Matilda filled up the end of the seat—like a massive book-end; and the others like slender volumes of romance were squeezed in between her and another stout book-end. Jack had the heaving warmth of Aunt Matilda on his right, the electric wriggle of Monica on his left, and he continued to breathe red-hot air.

The concert was a ludicrous continuation of shameful and ridiculous noise, to him. Each item seemed inordinately long and he hoped for the next, which, when it came, seemed worse than the last. The people who performed seemed to him in a ghastly humiliating position. One stout mother-of-thousands leaned forward and simply gurgled about riding over the brow of a hill and seeing a fair city beyond, and a young knight in silver armour riding toward her with shining face, to greet her on the spot as his lady fair and lady dear. Jack looked at her in pained amazement. And yet when the songstress from Melbourne, in a rich contralto, began to moan in a Scotch accent :

" And it's o-o-oh ! that I'm longing for my ain folk,
Though the-e-ey be but lowly, puir and plain folk—
I am far across the sea
But my heart will ever bee-ee
At home in dear old Scotland with my ain folk."

Jack suddenly wanted to howl. He had never been to Scotland and his father, General Grant, with his mother, was at present in Malta. And he hadn't got any " ain folk," and he didn't want any. Yet it was all he could do to keep the tears from showing in his eyes, as his heart fairly broke in him. And Aunt Matilda crowded him a little more suffocatingly on the right, and Monica wriggled more hatefully than ever on the left, and that beastly Mary leaned forward to glance appreciatively at him, with her low-down black eyes. And he felt as if the front of his body was scorched. And a smouldering desire for revenge awoke deep down in him.

People were always trying to " do things " to you. Why couldn't they leave you alone? Dirty cads, to sing " My Ain Folk," and then stare in your face to see how it got you.

But life was a matter of endurance, with possible revenge later on.

When at last he got home and could go to bed, he felt he had gained a brief respite. There was no lock to the door —so he put the arm-chair against it, for a barricade.

And he felt he had been once more sold. He had thought he was coming to a wild and woolly world. But all the way out he had been forced to play the gentlemanly son of his father. And here it was hell on earth, with these women let loose all over you, and these ghastly concerts, and these hideous meals, and these awful, flimsy, choky houses. Far better the Agricultural College. Far better England.

He was sick with homesickness as he flung himself into bed. And it seemed to him he was always homesick for some place which he had never known and perhaps never would know. He was always homesick for somewhere else. He always hated where he was, silently but deeply.

Different people. The place would be all right, but for the people.

He hated women. He hated the kind of nausea he felt after they had crowded on him. The yellow cat-eyes of that deadly Monica! The inky eyes of that low-down Mary! The big nose of that Grace : she was the most tolerable. And the indecency of the red-haired Aunt Matilda, with her gold chains.

He flung his trousers in one direction, and the loathsome starched shirt in another, and his underwear in another. When he was quite clear of all his clothing he clenched his fists and reached them up, and stretched hard, hard as if to stretch himself clear of it all. Then he did a few thoughtless exercises, to shake off the world. He wanted the muscles of his body to move, to shake off the contact of the world.   As a dog coming out of the water shakes himself, so Jack stood there slowly, intensely going through his exercises, slowly sloughing the contact of the world from his young, resistant white body.   And his hair fell loose into curl, and the alert defiance came into his eyes as he threw apart his arms and opened his young chest. Anything, anything to forget the world and to throw the contact of people off his limbs and his chest.   Keen and savage as a Greek gymnast he struck the air with his arms, with his legs.

Till at last he felt he had broken through the mesh.   His blood was running free, he had shattered the film that other people put over him, as if snails had crawled over him. His skin was free and alive.   He glowered at the door, and made the barricade more safe.

Then he dived into his night-shirt, and felt the world was his own again.   At least in his own immediate vicinity. Which was all he cared about for the moment.

CHAP. III. DRIVING TO WANDOO

i

JACK started before dawn next morning, for Wandoo. Mr George had business which took him south, so he decided to carry the boy along on the coach. Mr Ellis also was returning home in the coach, but the twins, those lambs, were staying behind. In the chilly dark, Jack climbed the front of the buggy to sit on the seat beside the driver. He was huddled in his overcoat, the happiest boy alive. For now at last he was " getting away," as he always wanted to " get away." From what, he didn't stop to consider, and still less did he realise *towards* what. Because however far you may get away from one thing, by so much do you draw near to another.

And this is the Fata Morgana of Liberty, of Freedom. She may lead you very definitely away from to-day's prison. But she also very definitely leads you towards some other prison. Liberty is a changing of prisons, to people who seek *only* liberty.

Away went the buggy at a spanking trot, the driver pointing out the phosphoric glow of the river, as they descended to the Causeway. Stars still shone overhead, but the sky was beginning to open inland. The buggy ran softly over the damp sand, the two horses were full of life. There was an aroma of damp sand, and a fresh breeze from the river as they crossed.

Jack didn't want to talk. But the driver couldn't miss the opportunity.

" I drives this coach backards and forrards to Albany week in week out, years without end, amen, and a good two hundred miles o' land to cover, taking six days clear with two 'osses, and them in relays fifteen or twenty miles, sometimes over, as on the outland reach past Wagin."

" Ever get held up ? "

" No, sir, can't say as I do. Who'd there be to hold me up in Western Australia ? And if there was, the mounted police'd soon settle 'em. There's nobody to hold me up but my old woman, and she drives the coach for me up Middle Swan way."

" Can she drive ? "

" You back your life she can. Bred and born to it.
Drive, an' swear at the 'osses like a trooper, when she's a
mind. Swear ! I'd never ha' thought it of 'er, when I rode
behind 'er as a groom."

" How ? "

" Oh, she took me in, she did, pretty. But, after all,
what's a lady but a woman ! Though far be it from me to
say : ' What's a woman but a lady ' ! If I'd gone down
on my hands an' knees to her in them days I should have
expected her to kick me. And what does she do ? Rode
out of the park gates and stopped. So she did. Turns
to me. ' Grey,' she says, ' here's money. You go to
London and buy yourself clothes like what a grocer would
buy. Avoid looking like a butler or a groom. And when
you've got an outfit, dress and make yourself look like a
grocer,' she said, though I never had any connections with
grocery in my life, ' and go to the office in Victoria Street
and take two passages to Australia.' That was what she
said. Just Australia. When the man in the office asked me
where to in Australia, I didn't know what to say. ' Oh,
we'll go in at the first gate,' I said. And so it was Fremantle. ' Yes,' she said, ' we're going to elope.' ' Nice
thing for me,' thinks I. But I says, ' All right, miss.' She
was a pearl beyond price, was Miss Ethel. So she seemed
to me then. Now she's a termagant as ever was : in double
'arness, collar-proud."

The coachman flicked the horses. Jack looked at him
in amazement. He was a man with a whitish-looking beard,
in the dim light.

" And did she have any children ? "

" She's got five."

" And does she regret it ? "

" At times, I suppose. But as I say to her, if anybody
was took in, it was me. *I* always thought her a perfect
lady. So when she lets fly at me : ' Call yourself a man ? '
I just say to her : ' Call yourself a lady ? ' And she comes
round all right."

Jack's consciousness began to go dim. He was aware of
a strange dim booming almost like guns in the distance, and
the driver's voice saying, " Frogs, sir. Way back in the
days before ever a British ship came here, they say the

Dutchmen came and was frightened off by the croaking of the bull frogs. Couldn't make it out a-nohow "! The horses' hoofs were echoing on the boarded Causeway, and from the little islands alongside came the amazing croaking, barking, booing and booming of the frogs.

ii

When Jack looked round again it was day. And the driver's beard was black. He was a man with a thin red face and black beard and queer grey eyes that had a mocking sort of secret in them.

" I thought your beard was white," said Jack.

" Ay, with rime. With frost. Not with anything else."

" I didn't expect hoar-frost here."

" Well—it's not so *very* common.   Not like the Old Country."

Jack realised they always spoke patronisingly of the Old Country, poor old place, as if it couldn't help being what it was.

The man's grey eyes with the amused secret glanced quickly at Jack.

" Not quite awake yet ? " he said.

" Oh, yes," said Jack.

" Coming out to settle, I hope," said the driver. " We can do with a few spruce young lads. I've got five daughters to contend with. Why, there's six A.1. families in Perth, maybe you've heard, and six in the country, and possibly six round Fremantle, and nary one of 'em but's got seven daughters. Seven daughters . . ."

Jack did not hear. He seemed to be saying, in reply to some question, " I'm Jack Hector Grant."

" Contrary " the servants had called him, and " naughty little boy," his aunts. Insubordinate, untrustworthy. Such things they said of him. His soul pricked from all the things, but he guessed they were not far wrong.

What did his mother think of him ? And his father ? He didn't know them very well. They only came home sometimes, and then they seemed to him reasonable and delightful people. The Wandering Grants, Lady Bewley had called them.

Was he a liar ? When they called him a liar, was it true ?

It was. And yet he never really *felt* a liar. " Don't ask, and you'll get no lies told you." It was a phrase from his nurse, and he always wanted to use it to his hateful Aunts. " Say you're sorry! Say you're sorry! " Wasn't that *forcing* him to tell lies, when he *wasn't* sorry. His aunts always seemed to him despicable liars. He himself was just an ordinary liar. He lied because he *didn't* want them to know what he'd done, even when he'd done right.

So they threatened him with that loathsome " police-man." Or they dropped him over the garden fence into the field beyond. There he sat in a sort of Crusoe solitary con-finement. A vast row of back fences, and a vast, vast field. Himself squatting immovable, and an Aunt coming to demand sharply through the fence : " Say you're sorry. Say you want to be a good little boy. Say it, or you won't come in to dinner. You'll stay there all night."

He wasn't sorry, he didn't want to be a good little boy, therefore he wouldn't " say it "; so he got a piece of bread and butter pushed through the fence. And then he faced the emptiness of the field and set off, to find himself some-how in the kitchen-garden of the manor-house. A servant had seen him, and brought him before her ladyship, who was herself walking in the garden.

" Who are you, little boy? "

" I'm Jack Hector Grant "—a pause—" Who are you? "

" I'm Lady Bewley."

They eyed one another.

" And where were you wandering to, in my garden? "

" I wasn't wand'rin'. I was walkin'."

" Were you? Come then, and walk with me, will you? "

She took his hand and led him along a path. He didn't quite know if he was a prisoner. But her hand was gentle, and she seemed a quiet, sad lady. She stepped with him through wide-open window-doors. He looked uneasily round the drawing-room, then at the quiet lady.

" Where was *you* born? " he asked her.

" Why, you funny boy, I was born in this house."

" My mother wasn't. She was born in Australia. And my father was born in India. And I can't remember where I was born."

A servant had brought in the tea-tray. The child was

sitting on a foot-stool. The lady seemed not to be listening. There was a dark cake.

" My mother said I wasn't never to ask for cake, but if somebody was to offer me some I needn't say No fank you."

" Yes, you shall have some cake," said the lady. " So you are one of the wandering Grants, and you don't know where you were born ? "

" But I think I was born in my mother's bed."

" I suppose you were. And how old are you ? "

" I'm four. How old are you ? "

" A great deal older than that. But tell me, what *were* you doing in my garden ? "

" I don't know. Well, I comed by mistake."

" How was that ? "

" 'Cause I wouldn't say I was sorry I told a lie. Well, I wasn't sorry. But I wasn't wandrin' in your garden. I was only walkin'. I was walkin' out of the meadow where they put me—— "

" ——And as I says, she may have been born in a 'all, but she'll die in a wooden shack—— "

" Who ? Who will ? "

" I was tellin' you about my old woman. Look ! There's a joey runnin' there along the track."

Jack looked and saw a funny little animal half leaping, half running along.

" We call them baby 'roos joeys, you understand, and they make the cutest little pets you ever did imagine."

They were still in sandy country, on a good road not far from the river, and Jack saw the little chap jump to cover. The tall gum trees with their brownish pale smooth stems and loose strips of bark stood tall and straight and still, scattered like a thin forest that spread unending, rising from a low, heath-like undergrowth. It seemed open, and yet weird, enclosing you in its vast emptiness. This bush, that he had heard so much of ! The sun had climbed out of the mist, and was becoming gold and powerful in a limpid sky. The leaves of the gum trees hung like heavy narrow blades, inert and colourless, in a weight of silence. Save when they came to a more open place, and a flock of green parrots flew shrieking " Twenty-eight ! Twenty-eight ! " At least that was what the driver said they cried. The lower air was still somewhat chilly from the mist. A

number of black-and-white handsome birds, that they call
magpies, flew alongside in the bush, keeping pace for a
time with the buggy. And once a wallaby ran alongside
for a while on the path, a bigger 'roo than the joey, and
very funny, leaping persistently alongside with his little
hands dangling.

It *was* a new country, after all. It *was* different. A small
exultance grew inside the youth. After all, he *had* got
away, into a country that men had not yet clutched into
their grip. Where you could do as you liked, without being
stifled by people. He still had a secret intention of doing
as he liked, though what it was he would do when he could
do as he liked, he did not know. Nothing very definite. And
yet something stirred in his bowels as he saw the endless
bush, and the noisy green parrots and the queer, tame
kangaroos : and no man.

"It's dingy country down here," the coachman was saying : "Not good for much. No good for nothing except
cemetery, though Mr George says he believes in it. And
there's nothing you *can* do with it, seeing as how many
gents what come in the first place has gone away for ever,
lock, stock and barrel, leaving nothing but their ' claims '
on the land itself, so nobody else can touch it." Here he
shook the reins on the horses' backs. "But I hopes you
settles, and makes good, and marries and has children, like
me and my old woman, sir. She've put five daughters into
the total, born in a shack, though their mother was born
in Pontesbeach Hall——"

But Jack's mind drifted away from the driver. He was
in that third state, not uncommon to youth, which seems
to intervene between reality and dream. The bush, the
coach, the wallabies, the coach-driver were not very real to
him. Neither was his own self and his own past very real
to him. There seemed to him to be another mute core to
himself. Apart from the known Jack Grant, and apart
from the world as he had known it. Even apart from this
Australia which was so unknown to him.

As a matter of fact, he had not yet come-to in Australia.
He had not yet extricated himself from England and the
ship. Half of himself was left behind, and the other half
was gone ahead. So there he sat, mute and stupid.

He only knew he wanted something, and he resented

something. He resented having been so much found fault with. They had hated him because he preferred to make friends among " good-for-nothings." But as he saw it, " good-for-nothings " were the only ones that had any daring. Not altogether tamed. He loathed the thought of harness. He hated tameness, hated it, hated it. The thought of it made his innocent face take on a really devilish look. And because of his hatred of harness, he hated answering the questions that people put to him. Neither did he *ask* many, for his own part. But now one popped out.

" There *are* policemen here, are there ? "

" Yes, sir, a good force of mounted police, a smart body of men. And they're needed. Western Australia is full of old prisoners, black fellers, and white ones too. The whites, born here, is called ' gropers,' if you take me, sir. Sand-gropers. And they all need protection one from the other. And there's half-pay officers, civil and military, and clergy, scattered through the bush—— "

" Need protecting from one another, and yet he says there's nobody to hold up the coach," thought Jack to himself, cynically.

The bush had alternated with patches of wild scrub. But now came clearings : a little wooden house, and an orchard of trees planted in rows, with a grazing field beyond. Then more flat meadows, and ploughed spaces, and a humpy or a shack here and there : children playing around, and hens : then a regular homestead, with verandah on either side, and creepers climbing up, and fences about.

" The soil is red ! " said Jack.

" Clay ! That's clay ! No more sand, except in patches, all the way to Albany. This is Guildford where the roses grow."

They clattered across a narrow wooden bridge with a white railing, and up to a wooden inn where the horses were to be changed. Jack got down in the road, and saw Mr George and Mr Ellis both sleepily emerge and pass without a word into the place marked BAR.

" I think I'll walk on a bit," said Jack, " if you'll pick me up."

But at that moment a fleecy white head peering out of the back of the coach cried :

" Oh, Mr Gwey! Mr Gwey! They've frowed away a perfeckly good cat."

The driver went over with Jack to where the chubby arm was pointing, and saw the body of a cat stretched by the trodden grass. It was quite dead. They stood looking at it, Grey explaining that it was a good skin and it certainly was a pity to waste it, and he hoped someone would find it who would tan it before it went too far, for as for him, he could not take it along in the coach, the passengers might object before they reached Albany, though the weather was cooling up a bit.

Jack laughed and went back to the coach to throw off his overcoat. He loved the crazy inconsequence of everything. He stepped along the road feeling his legs thrilling with new life. The thrill and exultance of new life. And yet somewhere in his breast and throat tears were heaving. Why? Why? He didn't know. Only he wanted to cry till he died. And at the same time, he felt such a strength and a new power of life in his legs as he strode the Australian way, that he threw back his head in a sort of exultance.

Let the exultance conquer. Let the tears go to blazes.

When the coach came alongside, there was the old danger-look in his eyes, a defiance, and something of the cat-look of a young lion. He did not mount, but walked on up the hill. They were climbing the steep Darling Ranges, and soon he had a wonderful view. There was the wonderful clean new country spread out below him, so big, so soft, so ancient in its virginity. And far beyond, the gleam of that strange empty sea. He saw the grey-green bush ribboned with blue rivers, winding to an unknown sea. And in his heart he was *determining* to get what he wanted. Even though he did not know what it was he wanted. In his heart he clinched his determination to get it. To get it out of this ancient country's virginity.

He waited at the top of the hill. The horses came clop-clopping up. Morning was warm and full of sun. They had rolled up the flaps of the wagonette, and there was the beaming face of Mr George, and the purple face of Mr Ellis, and the back of the head of the floss-haired child.

Jack looked back again, when he had climbed to his seat and the horses were breathing, to where the foot of the grey-bush hills rested in a valley ribboned with rivers and patched with cultivation, all frail and delicate in a dim ethereal light.

" A land of promise ! A land of promise," said Mr George. " When I was young I bid £1080 for 2,700 acres of it. But Hammersley bid twenty pounds more, and got it. Take up land, Jack Grant, take up land. Buy, beg, borrow or steal land, but get it, sir, get it."

" He'll have to go farther back to find it," said Mr Ellis from his blue face. " He'll get none of what he sees there."

" Oh, if he means to stay, he can jump it. The law is always bendin' and breakin', bendin' and breakin'.' "

" Well, if he's going to live with me, Mr George, don't put him on to land-snatching," said Mr Ellis. And the two men fell to a discussion of Land Acts, Grants, Holdings, Claims, and Jack soon ceased to listen. He thought the land looked lovely. But he had no desire to own any of it. He never felt the possibility of " owning " land. There the land was, for eternity. How could he own it ? Anyhow, it made no appeal to him along those lines.

But Mr Ellis loved " timber " and broke the spell by pointing and saying :

" See them trees, Jack, my boy ? Jarrah ! Hills run one into the other way to the Blackwood River. Hundreds of miles of beautiful Jarrah timber. The trees like this barren ironstone formation. It's well they do, for nothing else does."

" There's one o' the mud-brick buildings the convicts lived in, while they were building the road," said the driver, not to be done out of his say. " One of the convicts broke and got away. Mostly when they went off they was driven in by the bush. But this one never. They say he's wandering yet. I say, dead."

Mr George was explaining the landscape.

" Down there, Darlington. Governor Darling went down and never came back. Went home the quick way. Boya, native word for rock. Mahogany Creek just above there. They'll see us coming. Kids watch from the rise, run back and holloa. Pa catches rooster, black girl blows fire, ma mixes paste, yardman peels spuds—dinner when we get there."

" And, sir, Sam has a good brew, none better. Also, sir, though it looks lonesome, he's mostly got company."

" How's that ? "

" Well, sir, everyone comes for miles round to hear his missus play the harmonium. Got it out from England, and if it doesn't break your heart to hear it ! The voice of the past ! You'd love to hear it, Mr Grant, being new from home."

" I'm sure I should," said Jack, thinking of the concert.

The dinner at Mahogany Creek was as Mr George had said. Afterwards, on again through the bush.

Towards the end of the afternoon the coach pulled up at a little by-road, where stood a basket-work shay, and a tall young fellow in very old clothes lounging with loose legs.

" 'Ere y'are ! " said Grey, and walking the horses to the side of the road, he scrambled down to pull water from a well.

" Here we are ! " said Mr Ellis from the back of the coach, where the tall youth was just receiving the floss-haired baby between his big red hands. Fat Mr Ellis got down. The youth began pulling out Jack's bags and boxes, and Jack hurried round to help him.

" This is Tom," said Mr Ellis.

" Pleased to meet you," said Tom, holding out a big hand and clasping Jack's hand hard for a moment. Then they went on piling the luggage on the wicker shay.

" That's the lot ! " called Mr Ellis.

" Good-bye, Jack ! " said Mr George, leaning his grey head out of the coach. " Be good and you'll be happy."

Over which speech Jack puzzled mutely. But the floss-haired baby girl was embracing his trouser legs.

" I never knew you were an Ellis," he said to her.

" Ay, she's another of 'em," said Mr Ellis.

The coach was going. Jack went over awkwardly and offered the driver a two-shilling piece.

" Put it back in y'r pocket, lad, y'll want it more than I shall," said Grey unceremoniously. " The best o' luck to you, an' I mean it."

They all packed into the shay, Jack sitting with his back to the horses, the little girl tied in beside him, his smaller luggage bundled where it could be stowed; and in absolute silence they drove through the silence of the standing, motionless gum-trees. Jack had never felt such silence.

At last they pulled up. Tom jumped down and drew a slip-rail, and they passed a log fence, inside which there were many sheep, though it was still bush. Tom got in again and they drove through bush with occasional sheep. Then Tom got down again—Jack could not see for what purpose. The youth fetched an axe out of the cart and started chopping. A tree was across the road : he was chopping at the broken part. There came a sweet scent.

" Raspberry jam ! " said Mr Ellis. " That's *acacia acuminata*, a beautiful wood, good for fences, posts, pipes, walking-sticks. And they're burning it off by the million acres."

Tom pulled the trunk aside, and drove on again till he came to another gate. Then they saw ahead a great clearing in the bush, and in the midst of the clearing a " gingerbread " house, made of wood slabs, with a shingle roof running low all round to the verandahs. A woman in dark homespun cloth with an apron and sunbonnet, and a young bearded man in moleskins and blue shirt, came out with a cheery shout.

" You get along inside and have some tea," said the young bearded man. " I'll change the horses."

The woman lifted down the baby, after having untied her.

There was a door in the front of the house, a window on each side. But they all went round under the eaves to the mud-brick kitchen behind, and had tea. The woman hardly spoke, but she smiled and passed the tea and nursed Ellie. When the young bearded man came in he smiled and said :

" I've got the mail out of the shay, Mr Ellis."

" That's all right," said Mr Ellis.

After which no one spoke again.

When they set off once more there was a splendid pair of greys on either side the pole.

" Bill and Lil," said Mr Ellis. " My own breed. Angus lends us his for the twenty miles to the cross roads. We've just changed them and got our own. There's another twenty miles yet."

It now began to rain, and gradually grew dark and cold. The bush was dree, the dreest thing Jack had ever known. Rugs and mackintoshes were fetched out, the baby was fastened snug in a corner out of the wet, and the horses kept up a steady pace. And then, as Nature went to roost, Mr Ellis woke up and pulled out his pipe, to begin a conversation.

" How's Ma ? "

" Great ! "

" How's Gran ? "

" Same."

" All well ? "

" Yes."

" He's come twenty miles," thought Jack, " and he only asks now ! "

" See the doctor in town, Dad ? " asked Tom.

" I did."

" What'd he say ? "

" Oh, heart's wrong all right, just what Rackett said. But might live to be older than he is. So I might too, lad."

" So you will an' all, Dad."

And then Mr Ellis, as if desperate to change the conversation, pulling hard at his pipe :

" Jersey cow calved ? "

" Yes."

" Bull again ? "

" No, heifer. Beauty."

They both smiled silently. Then Tom's tongue suddenly was loose.

" Little beauty she is. And the Berkshire has farrowed nine little prize-winners. Cowslip came on with 'er butter since she come on to the barley. I cot them twins Og an' Magog peltin' the dogs with eggs, an' them so scarce, so I wopped 'em both. That black spaniel bitch I had to kill her for she worried one o' the last batch o' sucking pigs, though I don't know how she come to do such a thing. I've finished fallowin' in the bottom meadow, an' I'm glad you're back to tell us what to get on wif."

" How's clearing in th' Long Mile Paddock ? "

" Only bin down there once. Sam's doin' all right."

" Hear anything of the Gum Tree Gully clearing gang ?"

" Message from Spencer, an' y' t'go down some time— as soon's y' can."

" Well, I want the land reclaimed this year, an' I want it gone on with. Never know what'll happen, Tom. I'd

like for you to go down there, Tom. You c'n take th'
young feller behind here with you, soon's the girls come
home."

"What's he like?"

"Seems a likely enough young chap. Old George put
in a good word for'm."

"Bit of a toff."

"Never you mind, s' long's his head's not toffy."

"Know anything?"

"Shouldn't say so."

"Some fool?"

"Don't know. You find out for y'self."

Silence.

Jack heard it all. But if he hadn't heard it, he could
easily have imagined it.

"Yes, you find out," he thought to himself, going dazed
with fatigue and indifference as he huddled under the
blanket, hearing the horses' hoofs clop-clop! and the rain
splash on his shoulders. Sometimes the horses pulled slow
and hard in the dark, sometimes they bowled along. He
could see nothing. Sometimes there was a snort and jangle
of harness, and the wheels resounding hollow. "Bridging
something" thought Jack. And he wondered how they
found their way in the utter dark, for there were no lamps.
The trees dripped heavily.

And then, at the end of all things, Tom jumped down
and opened a gate. Hope! But on and on and on. Stop!
—hope!—another gate. On and on. Same again. And so
interminably.

Till at last some intuition seemed to communicate to
Jack the presence of home. The rain had stopped, the
moon was out. Ghostly and weird the bush, with white
trunks spreading like skeletons. There opened a clearing,
and a dog barked. A horse neighed near at hand. There
were no trees, a herd of animals was moving in the dusk.
And then a dark house loomed ahead, unlighted. The shay
drove on, and round to the back. A door opened, a woman's
figure stood in the candle-light and firelight.

"All right, Ma!" called Tom.

"All right, dear," called Mr Ellis.

"All right!" shrilled a little voice . . .

Well, here they were in the kitchen. Mrs Ellis was a

brown-haired woman with a tired look in her eyes. She looked a long time at Jack, holding his hand in her one hand and feeling his wet coat with the other.

" You're wet. But you can go to bed when you've had your supper. I hope you'll be all right. Tom'll look after you."

She was hoping that he would only bring good with him. She was all mother : and mother of her own children first. She felt kindly towards him. But he was another woman's son.

When they had eaten, Tom led the newcomer away out of the house, across a little yard, threw open a door in the dark, and lit a candle stuck in the neck of a bottle. Jack looked round at the mud floor, the windowless window, the unlined wooden walls, the calico ceiling, and he was glad. He was to share this cubby hole, as they called it, with the other Ellis boys. His truckle bed was fresh and clean. He was content. It wasn't stuffy, it was rough and remote.

When he opened his portmanteau to get out his night-shirt he asked Tom where he was to put his clothes. For there was no cupboard or chest of drawers or any-thing.

" On your back or under your bed," said Tom. " Or I might find y' an old packing case, if y're decent. But say, ol' bloke, lemme give y' a hint. Don't y' get sidey or nosey up here, puttin' on jam an' suchlike, f'r if y' do y'll shame me in front of strangers, an' I won't stand it."

" Jam did you say ? "

" Yes, jam, macaroni, cockadoodle. We're plain people out here-aways, not mantle ornaments nor dickey-toffs, an' we want no flash sparks round, see ? "

" *I'm* no flash spark," said Jack. " Not enough for 'em at home. It's too much fist and too little toff, that's the matter with me."

" C'n y' use y'r fists ? "

" Like to try me ? "

Jack shaped up to him.

" Oh, for the love o' Mike," laughed Tom, " stow the haw-haw gab ! You'll do me though, I think."

" I'll try to oblige," said Jack, rolling into bed.

" Here ! " said Tom sharply, " out y' get an' say y'

prayers. What sortta example for them kids of ours, gettin' into bed an' forgettin' y'r prayers? "

Jack eyed the youth.

" You say yours? " he asked.

" Should say I do. Gran is on ter me right cruel if I don't see to it, *whoever* sleeps in this cubby. They has ter say their prayers, see? "

" All right! " said Jack laconically.

And he obediently got up, kneeled on the mud floor, and gabbled through his quota. Somewhere in his heart he was touched by the simple honesty of the boy. And somewhere else he was writhing with slow, contemptuous repugnance at the vulgar tyranny.

But he called again to his aid that natural indifference of his, grounded on contempt. And also a natural boyish tolerance, because he saw that Tom had a naive, if rather vulgar, good-will.

He gabbled through his prayers wearily, but scrupulously, to the last Amen. Then rolled again into bed to sleep till morning, and forget, forget, forget! He depended on his power of absolute forgetting.

CHAP : IV. WANDOO

i

Two things struggled in Jack's mind when he awoke in the morning. The first was the brave idea that he had left everything behind, that he had done with his boyhood and was going to enter into his own. The second was a noise of somebody quoting Latin and clicking wooden dumb-bells.

Jack opened his eyes. There were four beds in the cubby hole. Between two beds stood a thin boy of about thirteen, swinging dumb-bells, and facing two small urchins who were faithfully imitating him, except that they did not repeat the Latin tags. They were all dressed in short breeches loosely held up by braces, and under-vests.

Veni, up went their arms smartly—*vidi*, down came the clubs to horizontal—*vici*, the clubs were down by their sides.

Jack smiled to himself and dozed again. It was scarcely dawn. He was dimly aware of the rain pattering on the shingle roof.

" Ain't ye gettin' up this morning? "

It was Tom standing contemplating him. The children had run out barefoot and bare-armed in the rain.

" Is it morning? " asked Jack stretching.

" Not half. We've fed th' 'osses. Come on."

" Where do I wash? "

" At the pump. Look slippy and get your clothes on. Our men live over at Red's, we have to look sharp in the morning."

Jack looked slippy, and went out to wash in the tin dish by the pump. The rain was abating, but it seemed a damp performance.

By the time he was really awake, the day had come clear. It was a fine morning, the air fresh with the smell of flowering shrubs : silver wattle, spirea, daphne and syringa which Ellis grew in his garden. Already the sun was coming warm.

The house was a low stone building with a few trees

round it. But all the life went on here at the back, here where the pump was, and the various yards and wooden out-buildings. There was a vista of open clearing, and a few huge gum-trees. The sky was already blue, a certain mist lay below the great isolated trees.

In the yard a score of motherless lambs were penned, bleating, their silly faces looking up at Jack confidently, expecting the milk bottle. He walked with his hands in the pockets of his old English tweeds, feeling over-dressed and a bit out of place. Cows were tethered to posts or standing loose about the fenced yard, and the half-caste Tim, and Lennie, the dumb-bell boy, and a girl, were silently milking. The heavy, pure silence of the Australian morning.

Jack stood at a little distance. A cat whisked across the yard and ran up a queer-looking pine-tree, a dissipated old cow moved about at random.

" Hey, you ! " shouted Tom impatiently, " Take hoult of that cart 'oss nosin' his way inter th' chaff-house, and bring him here. An' see to that grey's ropes : she's chewin' 'em free. Look slippy, make yourself useful."

There was a tone of amiability and intimacy mixed with this bossy shouting. Jack ran to the cart 'oss. He couldn't help liking Tom and the rest. They were so queer and naive, and they seemed oddly forlorn, like waifs lost in this new country. Jack had always had a leaning towards waifs and lost people. They were the only people whose bossing he didn't mind.

The children at their various tasks were singing in shrill, clear voices, with a sort of street-arab abandon. Lennie, the boy, would break the shrilling of the twin urchins with a sudden musical yell, from the side of the cow he was milking. And they seemed to sing anything, songs, poetry, nonsense, anything that came into their heads, like birds singing variously and at random.

" The blue, the fresh, the ever free
I am where I would ever be
With the blue above, and the blue below—— "

Then a yell from Lennie by the cows :

" And wherever thus in childhood s'our "

The twins :

> " I never was on the dull tame shore
> But I loved the great sea more and more "

Again a sudden and commanding yell from Lennie :

> " I never loved a dear gazelle
> To glad me with its soft black eye,
> But, when it came to know me well
> And love me—— "

Here the twins, as if hypnotised, howled out :

> " It was sure to die."

They kept up this ragged yelling in the new soft morning, like lost wild things. Jack laughed to himself. But they were quite serious. The elders were dumb-silent. Only the youngsters made all this noise. Was it a sort of protest against the great silence of the country? Was it their young, lost effort in the noiseless antipodes, whose noiselessness seems like a doom at last? They yelled away like wild little lost things, with an uncanny abandon. It pleased Jack.

ii

They had all gone silent again, and collected under the peppermint tree at the back door, where Ma ladled out tea into mugs for everybody. Ma was Mrs Ellis. She still had the tired, distant look in her eyes, and a tired bearing, and she seemed to take no notice of anybody, either when she was in the kitchen or when she came out with pie to the group squatting under the tree. When anyone said : " Some more tea, Ma ! " she silently ladled out the brew. Jack was not a very intent observer. But he was struck by Mrs Ellis' silence and her " drawn " look.

Tom came and hitched himself up against the trunk of the tree. Lennie was sitting opposite on a log, holding his tin mug and eyeing the stranger in silence. On another log sat the two urchins, sturdy, wild little brats, barefooted, bare-legged, bare-armed, as Jack had first seen

them, their dress still consisting of a little pair of pants
and a cotton undervest, and a pair of braces. The last
seemed by far the most important garment. Lennie was
clothed, or unclothed, the same, while Tom had added a
pair of boots. The bare arms out of the cotton vests were
brown and smooth, and they gave the boys and the youth
a curiously naked look. A girl of about twelve, in a dark-
blue spotted pinafore and a rag of red hair-ribbon, sat on
a little stump near the twins. She was silent like her
mother—but not yet " drawn."

" What d'e think of Og an' Magog? " said Tom, pointing with his mug at the twins. " Called for giants cos
they're so small."

Jack did not know what to think. He tried to smile
benevolently.

" An' that's Katie," continued Tom, indicating the girl,
who at once looked foolish. " She's younger'n Lennie, but
she's pretty near his size. He's another little 'un. Little
an' cheeky, that's what he is. Too much cheek for his age
—which is fourteen. You'll have to keep him in his place,
I tell you straight."

" Ef ye *ken!* " murmured Len with a sour face.

Then, chirping up with a real street-arab pertness, he
seemed to ignore Jack as he asked brightly of Tom :

" An' who's My Lord Duke of Early Risin,' if I might be
told? For before Gosh he sports a tidy raiment."

" Now, Len, none o' yer lingo ! " warned Tom.

" Who is he, anyway, as you should go tellin' him to
keep me in my place ? "

" No offence intended, I'm sure," said Jack pleasantly.

" *Taken* though ! " said Lennie, with such a black look
that Jack's colour rose in spite of himself.

" You keep a civil tongue in your head, or I'll punch it
for you," he said. He and Lennie stared each other in the
eye.

Lennie had a beautiful little face, with an odd pathos
like some lovely girl, and grey eyes that could change to
black. Jack felt a certain pang of love for him, and in the
same instant remembered that she-lioness cub of a Monica.
Perhaps she too had the same odd, lovely pathos, like a
young animal that runs alert and alone in the wood. Why
did these children seem so motherless and fatherless, so

much on their own? It was very much how Jack felt himself. Yet he was not pathetic.

Lennie suddenly smiled whimsically, and Jack knew he was let into the boy's heart. Queer! Up till now they had all kept a door shut against him. Now Len had opened the door. Jack saw the winsomeness and pathos of the boy vividly, and loved him, too. But it was still remote. And still mixed up in it was the long stare of that Monica.

"That's right, you tell 'im," said Tom. "What I say here, goes—no back chat, an' no tales told. That's what's the motto on this station."

> "Obey an' please my Lord Tom Noddy,
> So God shall love and angels aid ye—— "

said Lennie, standing tip-toe on his log and balancing his bare feet, and repeating his rhyme with an abstract impudence, as if the fiends of air could hear him.

"Aw, shut up, you!" said Tom. "You've got ter get them 'osses down to Red's. Take Jack an' show him."

"I'll show him," said Len, munching a large piece of pie as he set off.

"Ken ye ride, Jack?"

Jack didn't answer, because his riding didn't amount to much.

iii

Len unhitched four heavy horses, led them into the yard, and put the ropes into Jack's hands. The child marched so confidently under the noses of the great creatures, as they planted their shaggy feet. And he was such a midget, and with his brown bare arms and bare legs and feet, and his vivid face, he looked so " tender." Jack's heart moved with tenderness.

"Don't you ever wear boots?" he asked.

"Not if I k'n help it. Them kids now, they won't neither, 'n I don't blame 'em. Last boots Ma sent for was found all over the manure heap, so the old man said he'd buy no more boots an' a good job too. The only thing as scares me is double-gees : spikes all roads and Satan's face on three sides. Ever see double-gees?"

Len was leading three ponderous horses. He started peering on the road, the horses marching just behind his quick little figure. Then he found a burr with three queer sides and a sort of face on each side, with sticking-out hair.

He was a funny kid, with his scraps of Latin and tags of poetry. Jack wondered that he wasn't self-conscious and ashamed to quote poetry. But he wasn't. He chirped them off, the bits of verse, as if they were a natural form of expression.

They had led the horses to another stable. Len again gave the ropes to Jack, disappeared, and returned leading a saddled stock-horse. Holding the reins of the saddle-horse, the boy scrambled up the neck of one of the big draft horses like a monkey.

" Which are you goin' to ride ? " he asked Jack from the height. " I'm taking three an' leading Lucy. You take the other three."

So he received the three halter ropes.

" I think I'll walk," said Jack.

" Please y'self. You k'n open the gates easy walkin', and comin' back I'll do it, 'n you k'n ride Lucy an' I'll ride behind pinion so's I can slip down easy."

Yes, Lennie was a joy. On the return journey, when Jack was in the saddle riding Lucy, Len flew up behind him and stood on the horse's crupper, his hands on Jack's shoulders, crying : " Let 'er go ! " At the first gate he slid down like a drop of water, then up again, this time sitting back to back with Jack, facing the horse's tail, and whistling briskly.

Suddenly he stopped whistling, and said :

" Y've seen everybody but Gran an' Doc. Rackett, haven' you ? He teaches me—a rum sortta dock he is, too, never there when he's wanted. But he's a real doctor all right : signs death certificates an' no questions asked. Y' c'd do a murder, 'n if you was on the right side of him, y'd never be hung. He'd say the corpse died of natural causes."

" I didn't know a corpse died," said Jack laughing.

" Didn't yer ? Well, yer know now ! Gran's as good as a corpse, an' she don't want ter die. She put on Granfer's grave : ' Left desolate, but not without hope.' So they all thought she'd get married again. But she never. Did y' go to one of them English schools ? "

" Yes."

" Ever wear a bell-topper? "

" Once or twice."

" Gosh! May I never go to school, God help me. I should die of shame and disgrace. Arrayed like a little black pea in a pod, learnin' to be useless. Look at Rackett. School, an' Cambridge, an' comes inter money. Wastes it. Wastes his life. Now he's teachin' me, an' th' only useful thing he ever did."

After a pause, Jack ventured.

" Who is Doctor Rackett? "

" A waster. Down and out waster. He's got a sin. I don't know what it is, but it's wastin' his soul away."

iv

It was no use Jack's trying to thread it all together. It was a bewilderment, so he let it remain so. It seemed to him, that right at the very core of all of them was the same bewildered vagueness : Mr Ellis, Mrs Ellis, Tom, the men—they all had that empty bewildered vagueness at the middle of them. Perhaps Lennie was most on the spot. The others just could attend to their jobs, no more.

Jack still had no acquaintance with anyone but Tom and Len. He never got an answer from Og and Magog. They just grinned and wriggled. Then there was Katie. Then Harry, a fat, blue-eyed small boy. And then that floss-haired Ellie who had come from Perth. And smaller than her, the baby. All very confusing.

The second morning, when they were at the proper breakfast, Dad suddenly said :

" Ma! D'ye know where the new narcissus bulbs are gone? I was waiting to plant 'em till I got back."

" I've not seen them since ye put them in the shed at the end of the verandah, dear."

" Well, they're gone."

Dead silence.

" Is 'em like onions? " asked Og, pricking up intelligently.

" Yes. They are! Have you seen them? " asked Dad sternly.

" I see baby eatin' 'em, Dad," replied Og calmly.

" What! My bulbs as I got out from England! Why, what the dickens, Ma, d'you let that mischievous monkey loose for? My precious narcissus bulbs, the first I've ever had. An', besides, Ma! I'm not sure but what they're poison."

The parents looked at one another, then at the gay baby. There is a general consternation. Ma gets the long, evil, blue bottle of castor oil and forcibly administers a spoonful to the screaming baby. Dad hurries away, unable to look on the torture of the baby—the last of his name. He goes to hunt for the bulbs in the verandah shed. Tom says, " By gosh! " and sits stupefied. Katie jumps up and smacks Og for telling tales, and Magog flies at Katie for touching Og. Jack, as a visitor, unused to family life, is a little puzzled.

Lennie meanwhile calmly continues to eat his large mutton chop. The floss-haired Ellie toddles off talking to herself. She comes back just as intent, wriggles on her chair on her stomach, manages to mount, and puts her two fists on the table, clutching various nibbled, onion-like roots.

" Vem's vem, ain't they, Dad? She never ate 'em. She got 'em out vis mornin', and was suckin' 'em, so I took 'em from her an' hid 'em for you."

" Should Dad have said narcissi or narcissuses? " asked Len from over his coffee mug, in the hollow voice of one who speaks out of his cups.

Nobody answered. The baby was shining with castor oil. Jack sat in a kind of stupefaction. Everybody ate mutton chops in noisy silence, oppressively, and chewed huge door-steps of bread.

Then there entered a melancholy, well-dressed young fellow who looked like a daguerreotype of a melancholy young gentleman. He sauntered in in silence, and pulling out his chair, sat down at table without a word. Katie ran to bring his breakfast, which was on a plate on the hearth, keeping warm. Then she sat down again. The meal was even more oppressive. Everybody was eating quickly, to get away.

And then Gran opened the door leading from the parlour, and stood there like the portrait of an old, old lady, stood there immovable, just looking on, like some ghost. Jack's blood ran cold. The boys, pushing back their empty plates, went quietly out to the verandah, to the air. Jack followed, clutching his cap, that he had held all the time on his knee.

Len was pulling off his shirt. The boys had to wear shirts at meal times.

This was the wild new country ! Jack's sense of bewilderment deepened. Also he felt a sort of passionate love for the family—as a savage must feel for his tribe. He felt he would never leave the family. He must always be near them, always in close physical contact with them. And yet he was just a trifle horrified by it all.

CHAP : V.   THE LAMBS COME HOME

i

A MONTH later Tom and Lennie went off with the greys, Bill and Lil, to fetch the girls. It had been wet, so Jack had spent most of his day in the sheds mending corn sacks. He was dressed now in thick cotton trousers, coloured shirt, and grey woollen socks, and copper-toed boots. When he went ploughing, by Tom's advice, he wore " lasting " socks—none.

His tweed coat hung on a nail on the wall of the cubby, his good trousers and vest were under the mattress of his bed. The only useful garment he had brought had been the old riding breeches of the Agricultural College days.

On the back of his Tom-clipped hair was an ant-heap of an old felt hat, and so he sat, hour after hour, sewing the sacks with a big needle. He was certainly not unhappy. He had a sort of passion for the family. The family was almost his vice. He felt he *must* be there with the family, and then nothing else mattered.   Dad and Ma were the silent, unobtrusive pillars of the house.   Tom was the important young person. Lennie was the soul of the place. Og and Magog were the mischievous life. Then there was Harry, whom Jack didn't like, and the little girls, to be looked after. Dr. Rackett hovered round like an uneasy ghost, and Gran was there in her room. Now the girls were coming home.

Jack felt he had sunk into the family, merged his individuality and he would never get out. His own father and mother, England, or the future, meant nothing to him. He loved this family.   He loved Tom, and Lennie, and he wanted always to be with all of them. This was how it had taken him : as a real passion.

He loved, too, the ugly stone house, especially the south side, the shady side, which was the back where the peppermint tree stood. If you entered the front door—which nobody did—you were in a tiny passage from which opened the parlour on one side, and the dying room on the other. Tom called it the dying room because it had never been used for any other purpose, by the family. Old Mr Ellis had been carried down there to die. So had his brother Willie. As Tom explained : " The staircase is too narrow to handle a coffin."

Through the passage you dropped a step into the living room. On the right from this you stepped up a step into the kitchen, and on the left, up a step into Gran's room. Gran's room had once been the whole house : the rest had been added on. It is often so in Australia.

From the sitting room you went straight on to the back verandah, and there were the four trees, and a fenced-in garden, and the yards. The garden had gay flowers, because Mr Ellis loved them, and a round, stone-walled well. Alongside was the yard, marked off by the four trees into a square : a mulberry one side the kitchen door, a pepper the other, a photosphorum with a seat under it a little way off, and across, a Norfolk pine and half a fir tree.

Tom would talk to Jack about the family : a terrible tangle, they both thought. Why there was Gran, endless years old ! Dad was fifty, and he and Uncle Easu (dead) were her twins and her only sons. However, she had seven daughters and, it seemed to Jack, hundreds of grand-children, most of them grown up with more children of their own.

" I could never remember all their names," he declared.

" I don't try," said Tom. " Neither does Gran. And I don't believe she cares a tuppenny for 'em—for any of 'em, except Dad and us."

Gran was a delicate old lady, with a lace cap, and white curly hair, and an ivory face. She made a great impression on Jack, as if she were the presiding deity of the family. Over her head as she sat by the sitting-room fire an old clock tick-tocked. That impressed Jack, too. There was something weird in her age, her pallor, her white hair and white cap, her remoteness. She was very important in the house, but mostly invisible.

Lennie, Katie, Og and Magog, Harry, Ellie with the floss-hair, and the baby : these counted as " the children." Tom, who had had another mother, not Ma, was different. And now the other twins, Monica and Grace, were coming. These were the lambs. Jack, as he sat mending the sacks, passion-ately in love with the family and happy doing any sort of work there, thought of himself as a wolf in sheep's clothing, and laughed.

He wondered why he didn't like Harry. Harry was six, rather fat and handsome, and strong as a baby bull. But he was always tormenting baby. Or was it baby tormenting Harry?

Harry had got a picture book, and was finding out letters. Baby crawled over and fell on the book. Harry snatched it away. Baby began to scream. Ma interfered.

" Let baby have it, dear."

" She'll tear it, Ma."

" Let her, dear. I'll get you another."

" When? "

" Some day, Harry. When I go to Perth."

" Ya! Some day! Will ye get it Monday? "

" Oh, Harry, do be quiet, do . . ."

Then Baby and Harry tore the book between them in their shrieking struggles, while Harry battered the cover on the baby's head. And a hot, dangerous, bullying look would come into his eyes, the look of a bully. Jack knew that look already. He would know it better before he had done with Australia.

And yet Baby adored Harry. He was her one god.

Jack always marvelled over that baby. To him it was a little monster. It had not lived twelve months, yet God alone knew the things it knew. The ecstasy with which it smacked its red lips and showed its toothless gums over sweet, sloppy food. The diabolic screams if it was thwarted. The way it spat out " lumps " from the porridge. How on earth, at that age, had it come to have such a mortal hatred for lumps in porridge? The way its nose had to be held when it was given castor oil! And, again, though it protested so violently against lumps in porridge, how it loved such abominations as plaster, earth, or the scrapings of the pig's bucket.

When you found it cramming dirt into its mouth, and scolded it, it would hold up its hands wistfully to have them cleaned. And it didn't mind a bit, then, if you swabbed its mouth out with a lump of rag.

It was a girl. It loved having a new clean frock on. Would sit gurgling and patting its stomach, in a new smart frock, so pleased with itself. Astounding!

It loved bulls and stallions and great pigs, running between their legs. And yet it yelled in unholy terror if fowls or dogs came near. Went into convulsions over the friendly old dog, or a quiet hen pecking near its feet.

It was always trying to scuttle into the stable, where the horses stood. And it had an imbecile desire to put its hand in the fire. And it adored that blue-eyed bully of a Harry, and didn't care a straw for the mother that slaved for it. Harry, who treated it with scorn and hate, pinching it, cuffing it, shoving it out of its favourite positions—off the grass patch, off the hearth-rug, off the sofa-end. But it knew exactly the moment to retaliate, to claw his cap from his head and clutch his fair curls, or to sweep his bread and jam on to the floor, into the dust, if possible. . . .

To Jack it was all just incredible.

ii

But it was part of the family, and so he loved it.

He dearly loved the cheeky Len.

" What d'y'want ter say ' feece ' for? Why can't yer say ' fyce ' like any other bloke? And why d'y'wash y' fyce before y'wash y'hands? "

" I like the water clean for my face."

" What about your dirty hands, smarmin' them over it? "

" You use a flannel or a sponge."

" If y've got one! Y'don't find 'em growin' in th' bush. Why can't y'learn offa me now, an' be proper. Ye'll be such an awful sukey when y'goes out campin', y'll shame y'self. Y'should wash y'hands first. Frow away th' water if y'not short, but y' will be. Then when y've got y'hands all soapy, sop y' fyce up an' down, not round an' round like a cat does. Then pop y' nut under th' pump an' wring it dry. Don't never waste y' huckaback on it. Y'll want that f' somefin' else."

" What else shall I want my towel for? "

" Wroppin' up things in, meat an' damper, an't'lay down for y'meal, against th' ants, or to put over it against th' insex."

Then from Tom :

" Hey, nipper knowall, dry up! I've taught you the

way you should behave, haven't I ? Well, I can teach Jack
Grant, without any help from you. Skedaddle ! "

" Hope y' can ! Sorry for y', havin' to try," said Len
as he skedaddled.

Tom was the head of the clan, and the others gave him
leal obedience and a genuine, if impudent homage.

" What a funny kid ! " said Jack. " He's different from
the rest of you, and his lingo's rotten."

" He's not dif ! " said Tom. " 'Xactly same. Same's
all of us—same's all the nips round here. He went t' same
school as Monica an' Grace an' me, to Aunt's school in th'
settlement, till Dr. Rackett came. If he's any different,
he got it from *him* : he's English."

Jack noticed they always spoke of Dr. Rackett as if he
were a species of rattlesnake that they kept tame about the
place.

" But Ma got Dad to get the Doc, cos she can't bear to
part with Len even for a day—to give 'm lessons at home. I
suppose he's her eldest son—Dock needn't, he's well-to-do.
But he likes it, when he's here. When he's not, Lennie
slopes off and reads what he pleases. But it makes no
difference to Len, he's real clever. And "—Tom added
grinning—" he wouldn't speak like you do neither, not for
all the tin in a cow's bucket."

To Jack, fresh from an English public school, Len was
amazing. If he hurt himself sharply, he sat and cried for
a minute or two. Tears came straight out, as if smitten
from a rock. If he read a piece of sorrowful poetry, he
just sat and cried, wiping his eyes on his arm without heed-
ing anybody. He was greedy, and when he wanted to, he
ate enormously, in front of grown up people. And yet you
never minded. He talked poetry, or raggy bits of Latin,
with great sententiousness and in the most awful accent,
and without a qualm. Everything he did was right in his
own eyes. Perfectly right in his own eyes.

His mother was fascinated by him.

Three things he did well : he rode, bare-back, standing
up, lying down, anyhow. He rode like a circus rider. Also
he boasted—heavens high. And thirdly, he could laugh.
There was something so sudden, so blithe, so impish, so daring, and so wistful in his lit-up face when he laughed, that
your heart melted in you like a drop of water.

Jack loved him passionately : as one of the family.

And yet even to Lennie, Tom was the hero. Tom, the slow Tom, the rather stupid Tom. To Lennie Tom's very stupidity was manly. Tom was so dependable, so manly, such a capable director. He never gave trouble to anyone, he was so complacent and self-reliant. Lennie was the love-child, the elf. But Tom was the good, ordinary Man, and therefore the hero.

Jack also loved Tom. But he did not accept his manliness so absolutely. And it hurt him a little, that the strange, sensitive Len should put himself so absolutely in obedience and second place to the good plain fellow. But it was so. Tom was the chief. Even to Jack.

iii

When Tom was away Jack felt as if the pivot of all activity was missing. Mr Ellis was not the real pivot. It was the plain, red-faced Tom.

Tom had talked a good deal, in snatches, to Jack. It was the family that bothered him, as usual. He always talked the family.

" My grandfather came out here in the early days. He was a merchant and lost all his money in some East India business. He married Gran in Melbourne, then they came out here. They had a bit of a struggle, but they made good. Then Granpa died without leaving a will : which complicated things for Gran. Dad and Easu was twins, but Dad was the oldest. But Dad had wandered : he was gone for years, and no one knows what he did all the time.

" But Gran liked him best, and he was the eldest son, so she had this place all fixed up for him when he came back. She'd a deal of trouble getting the Reds out. All the A'nts were on their side—on the Red's side. We always call Uncle Easu's family the Reds. And Aunt Emmie says she's sure Uncle Easu was born first, and not Dad. And that Gran took a fancy to Dad from the first, so she said he was the eldest. Anyhow, it's neither here nor there. I hope to goodness I never get twins. It runs in the family, and of all the awful things ! Though the Easu's have got no twins. Seven sons and no girls, and no twins. Uncle Easu's dead, so young Red runs their place.

" Uncle Easu was a nasty scrub, anyway. He married the servant girl, and a servant girl no better than she should be, they say.

" He didn't make no will, either. Making no wills runs in the family, as well as twins. Dad won't. His Dad wouldn't, and he won't neither."

Which meant, Jack knew, that by the law of the colony, the property would come to Tom.

" Oh, Gran's crafty all right! She never got herself talked about, turning the Reds out! She saved up a stocking—Gran always has a stocking. And she saved up an' bought 'em out. She persuaded them that the land beyond this was better'n this. She worked in with 'em while Dad was away, like the fingers on your hand : and bought that old barn of a place over yonder for 'em, and bounced 'em into it. Gran's crafty, when it's anyone she cares about. Now it's Len.

" Anyhow, there it was when Dad came back, ' Wandoo ' all ready for him. He brought me wrapped in a blanket. Old Tim, our half-caste man, was his servant, and there was my old nurse. That's all there is we know about me. I know no more, neither who I am nor where I sprung from. And Dad never lets on.

" He came back with a bit of money, and Gran made him marry Ma to mind me. She said I was such a squalling little grub, and she wanted me brought up decent. So Ma did it. But Gran never quite fancied me.

" It's a funny thing, seeing how I come, that I should be so steady and ordinary, and Len should be so clever and unsteady. You'd ha' thought I should be Len and him me.

" Who was my mother? That's what I want to know. Who was she? And Dad won't never say.

" Anyhow, she wasn't black, so what does it matter, anyhow?

" But it *does* matter ! " Tom brought his fist down with a smack in the palm of his other hand. " Nobody is ordinary to their mother, and I'm ordinary to everybody, and I wish I wasn't."

Funny of Tom. Everybody depended on him so, he was the hero of the establishment, because he *was* so steady and ordinary and dependable. And now even he was wishing himself different. You never knew how folks would take themselves.

iv

As for the Reds, Jack had been over to their place once or twice. They were a rough crowd of men and youths, father and mother both dead. A bachelor establishment. When there was any extra work to be done, the Wandoos went over there to help. And the Reds came over to Wandoo the same. In fact they came more often to Wandoo than the Ellises went to them.

Jack felt the Reds didn't like him. So he didn't care for them. Red Ellis, the eldest son, was about thirty years old, a tall, sinewy, red-faced man with reddish hair and reddish beard, and staring blue eyes. One morning when Tom and Mr Ellis were out mustering and tallying, Jack was sent over to the Red house. This was during Jack's first fortnight at Wandoo.

Red the eldest met him in the yard.

" Where's y'oss ? "

" I haven't one. Mr Ellis said you'd lend me one."

" Can y' ride ? "

" More or less."

" What d'ye want wearin' that Hyde Park costume out here for ? "

" I've nothing else to ride in," said Jack, who was in his old riding breeches.

" Can't y' ride in trousers ? "

" Cant' keep 'em over my knees, yet."

" Better learn then, smart n' lively. Keep them down, n' y'socks up. Come on then, blast ye, an' I'll see about a horse."

They went to the stockyard, an immense place. But it was an empty desert now, save for a couple of black boys holding a wild-looking bay. Red called out to them :

" Caught Stampede, have y' ? Well, let 'im go again afore y' break y' necks. Y'r not to ride him, d'y hear. What's in the stables, Ned ? "

" Your mare, master. Waiting for you."

" What y' got besides, ye grinning jackasses. Find something for Mr Grant here, an' look slippy."

"Oh, master, no horse in, no knowin' stranger come."

Red turned to Jack. Easu was a coarse, swivel-eyed, loose-jointed tall fellow.

"Y' hear that. Th' only thing left in this yard is Stampede. Ye k'n take him or leave him, if y'r frightened of him. I'm goin' tallyin' sheep, an' goin' now. If ye stop around idlin' all day, y'needn't tell Uncle 'twas my fault."

Jack hesitated. From a colonial point of view he couldn't ride well, and he knew it. Yet he hated Easu's insulting way. Easu went grinning to the stable to fetch his mare, pleased with himself. He didn't want the young Jackeroo planted on *him*, to teach any blankey thing to.

Jack went slowly over to the quivering Stampede, and asked the blacks if they had ever ridden him. One answered :

"Me only fella ride 'em some time master not to-morrow. Me an' Ned catch him in mob longa time. Try break him —no good. He come back paddock one day. Ned wantta break him. No good. Master tell 'im let 'im go now."

Red Easu came walking out of the stable, chewing a stalk.

"Put the saddle on him," said Jack to the blacks. "I'll try."

The boys grinned and scuffled round. They rather liked the job. By being very quick and light, Jack got into the saddle, and gripped. The boys stood back, the horse stood up, and then whirled around on his hind legs, and round and down. Then up and away like a squib round the yard. The boys scattered, so did Easu, but Jack, because it was natural for his legs to grip and stick, stuck on. His bones rattled, his hat flew off, his heart beat high. But unless the horse came down backwards on top of him, he could stay on. And he was not really afraid. He thought : " If he doesn't go down backwards on top of me, I shall be all right." And to the boys he called : " Open the gate." Meanwhile, he tried to quiet the horse. " Steady now, steady ! " he said, in a low, intimate voice. " Steady, boy ! " And all the time he held on with his thighs and knees, like iron.

He did not believe in the innate viciousness of the horse. He never believed in the innate viciousness of anything, except a man. And he did not want to fight the horse for simple mastery. He wanted just to hold it hard with his legs until it soothed down a little, and he and it could come to an understanding. But he must never relax the hold of his hard legs, or he was dead.

Stampede was not ready for the gate. He sprang fiercely at it as if it had been guarded by fire. Once in the open, he ran, and bucked, and bucked, and ran, and kicked, and bucked, and ran. Jack stuck on with the lower half of his body like a vice, feeling as if his head would be jerked off his shoulders. It was becoming hard work. But he knew, unless he stuck on, he was a dead man.

Then he was aware that Stampede was bolting, and Easu was coming along on a grey mare.

Now they reached the far gate, and a miracle happened. Stampede stood still while Red came up and opened the gate. Jack was conscious of a body of live muscle and palpitating fire between his legs, of a furious head tossing hair like hot wire, and bits of white foam. Also he was aware of the trembling in his own thighs, and the sensual exertion of gripping that hot wild body in the power of his own legs. Gripping the hot horse in a grip of sensual mastery that made him tremble with a curious quivering. Yet he dared not relax.

" Go! " said Red. And away they went. Stampede bolted like the wind, and Jack held on with his knees and by balance. He was thrilled, really; frightened externally, but internally keyed up. And never for a moment did he relax his mind's attention, nor the attention of his own tossed body. The worst was the corkscrew buck, when he nearly went over the brute's head. And the moments of vindictive hate, when he would kill the beast and be killed a thousand times rather than be beaten. Up he went, off the saddle, and down he came again, with a shattering jerk, down on the front of the saddle. The balance he kept was a mystery even to himself, his body was so flung about by the volcano of furious life beneath him. He felt himself shaken to pieces, his bones rattled all out of socket. But they got there, out to the sheep paddock where a group of Reds and black boys stood staring in silence.

Jack jumped off, though his knees were weak and his hands trembling. The horse stood dark with sweat. Quickly he unbuckled the saddle and bridle and pulled them off, and gave the horse a clap on its wet neck. Away it went, wild again, and free.

Jack glanced at the Reds, and then at Easu. Red Easu met his eyes, and the two stared at one another. It was the defiance of the hostile colonial, brutal and retrogressive, against the old mastery of the old country. Jack was barely conscious. Yet he was not afraid, inside himself, of the swivel-eyed brute of a fellow. He knew that Easu was not a better man than himself, though he was bigger, older, and on his own ground. But Jack had the pride of his own, old, well-bred country behind him, and he would never go back on his breeding. He was not going to yield his manliness before the colonial way of life : the brutishness, the commonness. Inwardly he would not give in to it. But the best of it, the colonial honesty and simplicity, that he loved.

There are two sides to colonials, as to everything. One side he loved. The other he refused and defied.

These decisions are not mental, but they are critical in the soul of a boy of eighteen. And the destiny of nations hangs on such silent, almost unconscious, decisions.

Esau—they called him Easu, but the name was Esau—turned to a black, and bellowed :

" Give master your horse, and carry that bally saddle home."

Then silently they all turned to the sheep-tallying.

v

Jack was still sewing sacks. It was afternoon. He listened for the sound of the shay, though he did not expect it until nightfall at least.

His ear, training to the Australian alertness, began to detect unusual sounds. Or perhaps it was not his ear. The old bushman seems to have developed a further faculty, a psychic faculty of " sensing " some unusual disturbance in the atmosphere, and reading it. Jack was a very new Australian. Yet he had become aware of this faculty in Tom, and he wanted it for himself. He wanted to be able to hear the inaudible, like a sort of clair-audience.

All he could hear was the audible : and all he could see was the visible. The children were playing in the yard :

he could see them in the dust. Mrs Ellis was still at the wash-tub : he saw the steam. Katie was upstairs : he had seen her catching a hornet in the window. The men were out ploughing, the horses were away. The pigs were walking round grunting, the cows and poultry were all in the paddock. Gran never made a sound, unless she suddenly appeared on the scene like the Lord in Judgment. And Dr. Rackett was always quiet : often uncannily so.

It was still rainy season, but a warm, mellow, sleepy afternoon, with no real sound at all. He got up and stood on the threshold to stretch himself. And there, coming by the grain-shed, he saw a little cortege in which the first individual he distinguished was Red Easu.

" Go in," shouted Red, " and tell A'nt as Herbert's had an accident, and we're bringin' him in."

Sure enough, they were carrying a man on a gate.

Mrs Ellis clicked :

" Tt-tt-tt-tt-tt ! They run to us when they're in trouble." But she went at once to the linen closet, and on into the living room.

Gran was sitting in a corner by a little fire.

" Who's hurt ? " she inquired testily. " Not one of the family, I hope and pray."

" Jack says it's Red Herbert," replied Mrs Ellis.

" Put him in the cubby with the boys, then."

But Mrs Ellis thought of her beloved boys, and hesitated.

" Do you think it's much, Jack ? " she asked.

" They're carrying him on a gate," said Jack. " It looks bad."

" Dear o'me ! " snapped Gran, in her brittle fashion. " Why couldn't you say so. Well, then, if you don't want to put him in the cubby, there's a bed in my room. Put him there. But I should have thought he could have had Tom's bed, and Tom could have slept here on the sofa."

" Poor Tom," thought Jack.

" Don't "—Gran banged her stick on the floor—" stand there like a pair of sawneys ! Get to work ! Get to work ! "

Jack was staring at the ground and twirling his hat. Gran hobbled forward. He noticed to his surprise that she had a wooden leg. And she stamped it at him :

" Go and fetch that rascal of a doctor," she cried, in a startling loud voice.

Jack went. Dr. Rackett was not in his room, for Jack halloed and knocked at every door. He peeped into the rooms, whose doors were slightly opened. This must be the girls' room—two beds, neat white quilts, blue bow at the window. When would they be home? Here was the family bed, with two cots in the room as well. He came to a shut door. This must be it. He knocked and halloed again. No sound. Jack felt as if he were bound to come upon a Bluebeard's chamber. He hated looking in these bedrooms.

He knocked again, and opened the door. A queer smell, like chemicals. A dark room, with the blind down : a few books, a feeling of dark dreariness. But no doctor. " So that's that ! " thought Jack.

In spite of himself his boots clattered going down, and made him nervous. Why did the inside of the house, where he never went, seem so secret, and rather horrible? He peeped into the dismal little drawing room. Not there, of course ! Opposite was the dying room, the door wide open. Nobody ever was there.

Rackett was not in the house, that was certain. Jack slunk out, went to the paddock, caught Lucy, the saddle-horse, saddled her and cantered aimlessly round, within hearing of the homestead. The afternoon was passing. Not a soul was in sight. The gum-trees hung their sharp leaves like obvious ghosts, with the hateful motionlessness of gum-trees. And though flowers were out, they were queer, scentless, unspeaking sort of flowers, even the red ones that were ragged like fire. Nothing spoke. The distances were clear and mellow and beautiful, but soulless, and nobody alive in the world. The silent, lonely gruesomeness of Australia gave Jack the blues.

It surely was milking time. Jack returned quietly to the yard. Still nobody alive in the world. As if everyone had died. Yes, there was the half-caste Tim in the distance, bringing up the slow, unwilling cows, slowly, like slow dreams.

And there was Dad coming out of the back door, in his shirt sleeves : bluer and puffier than ever, with his usual serene expression, and his look of boss, which came from his waistcoat and watchchain. Dad always wore his waistcoat and watchchain, and seemed almost over-dressed in it.

Came Og and Magog running with quick little steps, and Len slinking round the doorpost, and Harry marching alone, and Katie dragging her feet, and baby crawling. Jack was glad to see them. They had all been indoors to look at the accident. And it had been a dull, dead, empty afternoon, with all the life emptied out of it. Even now the family, the beloved family, seemed a trifle gruesome to Jack.

He helped to milk : a job he was not good at. Dad even took a stool and milked also. As usual, Dad did nothing but supervise. It was a good thing to have a real large family, that made supervising worth while. So Tom said, " It's a good thing to have nine children, you can clear some work with 'em, if you're their dad." That's why Jack was by no means one too many. Dad supervised him too.

They got the milking done somehow. Jack changed his boots, washed himself, and put on his coat. He nearly trod on the baby as he walked across to the kitchen in the dying light. He lifted her and carried her in.

Usually " tea "—which meant mutton chops and eggs and steaks as well—was ready when they came in from milking. To-day Mr Ellis was putting eucalyptus sticks under the kettle, making the eternally familiar scent of the kitchen, and Mrs Ellis was setting the table there. Usually they lived in the living room from breakfast on. But to-day tea was to be in the kitchen, with a silence and a cloud in the air like a funeral. But there was plenty of noise coming from Gran's room.

Jack had to have baby beside him for the meal. And she put sticky hands in his hair and leaned over and chewed and sputtered crumbs, wet crumbs, in his ear. Then she tried to wriggle down, but the evening was chill and her hands and feet were cold and Mrs Ellis said to keep her up. Jack felt he couldn't stand it any longer, when suddenly she fell asleep, the most unexpected thing in the world, and Mrs Ellis carried off her and Harry to bed.

Ah, the family ! the family ! Jack still loved it. It seemed to fill the whole of life for him. He did not want to be alone, save at moments. And yet, on an afternoon like to-day, he somehow realised that even the family wouldn't last for ever. What then ? What then ?

He couldn't bear the thought of getting married to *one*

woman and coming home to a house with only himself and this one woman in it. Then the slow and lonely process of babies coming. The thought of such a future was dreadful to him. He didn't want it. He didn't want his own children. He wanted this family : always this family. And yet there was something gruesome to him about the empty bedrooms and the uncanny privacies even of this family. He didn't want to think of their privacies.

vi

Three of the Reds trooped out through the sitting-room, lean, red-faced, hairy, heavy-footed, uncouth figures, for their tea. The Wandoo Ellises were aristocratic in comparison. They asked Jack to go and help hold Herbert down, because he was fractious. " He's that fractious ! "

Jack didn't in the least want to have to handle any of the Reds, but he had to go. He found himself taking the two steps down into the dark living room, and the two steps up into Gran's room beyond.

Why need the family be so quiet in the kitchen, when there was such a hubbub in here ? Alan Ellis was holding one leg of the injured party, and Ross Ellis the other, and they both addressed the recumbent figure as if it were an injured horse with a *Whoa there! Steady on, now! Steady, boy, steady!* Whilst Easu, bending terribly over the prostrate figure, clutched both its arms in a vice, and cursed Jack for not coming sooner to take one arm.

Herbert had hurt his head, and turned fractious. Jack took the one arm. Easu was on the other side of the bed, his reddish fair beard glowing. There was a queer power in Easu, which fascinated Jack a little. Beyond, Gran was sitting up in bed, among many white pillows, like Red Riding Hood's grandmother. A bright fire of wood logs was burning in the open hearth, and four or five tallow candles smoked duskily. But a screen was put between Gran's four-poster and Herbert's bed, a screen made of a wooden clothes-horse covered with sheets. Jack, however, from his position by Herbert's pillow, could see beyond the screen to Gran's section.

His attention was drawn by the patient. Herbert's movements were sudden and convulsive, and always in a sudden jerking towards the right side of the bed. Easu had given Jack the left arm to hold, and as soon as Herbert became violent, Jack couldn't hold him. The left arm, lean and hard as iron, broke free, and Easu jumped up and cursed Jack.

Here was a pretty scene! With Gran mumbling to herself on the other side the hideous sheeted screen!

There was nothing for it but to use cool intelligence—a thing the Reds did not possess. Jack had lost his hold again, and Easu, like a reddish, glistening demon, was gripping the sick man's two arms and arching over him. Jack called up his old veterinary experience and proceeded to detach himself.

He noticed first that Herbert was far less fierce when they didn't resist him. Second, that he stopped groaning when his eyes fell away from the men around him. Third, that all the convulsive jerky movements, which had thrown him out of the bed several times, were towards the right side of the bed. Every time he had fallen out on the right side of the bed.

Then why not bind him to the left?

The left arm had again escaped his grasp, and Easu's exasperated fury was only held in check by Gran's presence. Jack went out of the room and found Katie.

" Hunt me out an old sheet," he said.

" What for? " she asked, but went off to do his bidding. When she came back she said :

" Mother says they don't want to bandage Herbert, do they ? "

" I'm going to try and bind him. I shan't hurt him," he replied.

" Oh, Jack, don't let them send for me to sit with him —I hate sickness."

" You give us a hand then with this sheet."

Between them they prepared strong bands. Jack noosed one with sailor's knots round Katie's hands, and fastened it to the table leg.

" Pull ! " he ordered. " Pull as hard as you can." And as she pulled : " Does it hurt now? "

" Not a bit," she said.

Jack went back to the sick room. Herbert was quiet, the three brothers were sulky and silent. They wanted above all things to get out, to get away. You could see that. Easu glanced at Jack's hand. There was something tense and alert about Easu, like a great, wiry bird with enormous power in its lean, red neck and its lean limbs.

" I thought we'd best bind him so as not to hurt him," said Jack. " I know how to do it, I think."

The brothers said not a word, but let him go ahead. And Jack bound the left arm and the left leg, and put a band round the body of the patient. They looked on, rather distantly interested. Easu released the convulsive left arm of his brother. Jack took the sick man's hand soothingly, held it soothingly, then slipped his hand up the hairy fore-arm and got the band attached just above the elbow. Then he fastened the ends to the bed-head. He felt quite certain he was doing right. While he was busy Mrs Ellis came in. She watched in silence, too. When it was done Jack looked at her.

" I believe it'll do," she said with a nod of approval. And then, to the cowed, hulking brothers, " You might as well go and get your tea."

They bumped into one another trying to get through the door. Jack noticed they were in their stocking feet. They stooped outside the door to pick up their boots.

" Good idea! " he thought. And he took off his own boots. It made him feel more on the job.

Mrs Ellis went round the white bed-sheet screen to sit with Gran. Jack went blowing out the reeking candles on the sick man's side of the same screen. Then he sat on a hard chair facing the staring, grimacing patient. He felt sorry for him, but repelled by him. Yet as Herbert tossed his wiry, hairy free arm and jerked his hairy, sharp-featured face, Jack wanted to help him.

He remembered the vet's advice : " Get the creatures' confidence, lad, and you can do anything with 'em. Horse or man, cat or canary, get the creature's confidence, and if anything can be done, you can do it."

Jack wanted now to proceed to get the creature's con-fidence. He knew it was a matter of will : of holding the other creature's will with his own will. But gently, and in a kindly spirit.

He held Herbert's hard fingers softly in his own hand, and said softly : " Keep quiet, old man, keep quiet. I'm

here. I'll take care of you. You rest. You go to sleep.
I won't leave you. I'll take care of you."

Herbert lay still as if listening. His muscles relaxed.
He seemed dreadfully tired—Jack could feel it. He was
dreadfully, dreadfully tired. Perhaps the womanless,
brutal life of the Reds had made him so tired. He seemed
to go to sleep. Then he jerked awake, and the convulsive
struggling began again, with the frightful rolling of the
eyes.

But the steady bonds that held him seemed to comfort
him, and Jack quietly took the clutching fingers again.
And the sick man's eyes, in their rolling, rested on the
quiet, abstract face of the youth, with strange watching.
Jack did not move. And again Herbert's tension seemed to
relax. He seemed in an agony of desire to sleep, but the
agony of desire was so great, that the very fear of it jerked
the sick man into horrible wakefulness.

Jack was saying silently, with his will : " Don't worry !
Don't worry, old man ! Don't worry ! You go to sleep.
I'll look after you."

And as he sat in dead silence, saying these things, he
felt as if the fluid of his life ran out of his fingers into the
fingers of the hurt man. He was left weak and limp. And
Herbert began to go to sleep, really to sleep.

Jack sat in a daze, with the virtue gone out of him. And
Herbert's fingers were soft and childlike again in their
relaxation.

The boy started a little, feeling someone pat him on the
shoulder. It was Mrs. Ellis, patting him in commendation,
because the patient was sunk deep in sleep. Then she went
out.

Following her with his eyes, Jack saw another figure in
the doorway. It was Red Easu, like a wolf out of the
shadow, looking in. And Jack quietly let slip the heavy,
sleeping fingers of the sick man. But he did not move his
posture.

Then he was aware that Easu had gone again.

vii

It was late, and the noise of rain outside, and weird
wind blowing. Mrs. Ellis had been in and whispered that

Dr. Rackett was not home yet—that he had probably waited somewhere for the shay. And that she had told the Reds to keep away.

There was dead silence save for the weather outside, and a noise of the fire. The candles were all blown out.

He was startled by hearing Gran's voice :

" Out of the mouths of babes and sucklings. . . ."

" She's reading," thought Jack, though there was no light to read by. And he wondered why the old lady wasn't asleep.

" I knew y'r mother's father, Jack Grant," came the thin, petulant voice. " He cut off my leg. Devil of a fella wouldn't let me die when I wanted to. Cut it off without a murmur, and no chloroform."

The thin voice was so devilishly awake, in the darkness of the night, like a voice out of the past piercing the inert present.

" What did he care ! What did he care ! Not a bit," Gran went on. " And y're another. You take after him. You're such another. You're a throw-back, to your mother's father. I was wondering what I was going to do with those great galoots in my room all night. I'm glad it's you."

Jack thought : " Lord, have I got to sit here all night ! "

" You've got the night before you," said Gran's demonishly wakeful voice, uncanny in its thin alertness, in the deep night. " So come round here to the fireside an' make y'self comfortable."

Jack rose obediently and went round the screen. After all, an arm-chair would be welcome.

" Well, say something," said Gran.

The boy peered at her in the dusk, in a kind of fear.

" Then light me a candle, for the land's sake," she said pettishly.

He took a tin candle-stick with a tallow candle, blew the fire and made a yellow light. She looked like a carved ivory Chinese figure, almost grotesque, among her pillows.

" Yes, y'r like y'r grandfather : a stocky, stubborn man as didn't say much, but dare do anything. And never had a son. Hard as nails the man was."

" More family ! " thought Jack wearily, disapproving of Gran's language thoroughly.

" Had two daughters though, and disowned the eldest.
Your mother was the youngest. The eldest got herself into
trouble and he turned her out. Regular obstinate fool,
and no bowels of compassion. That's how men are when
y' let 'em. You're the same."

Jack was so sleepy, so sleepy, and the words of the old
woman seemed like something pricking him.

" I'd have stood by her—but I was her age, and what
could I do ? I'd have married her father if I could, for he
was a widower. But he married another woman for his
second, and I went by ship to Melbourne, and then I took
poor old Ellis."

What on earth made her say these things, he didn't know,
for he was dead sleepy, and if he'd been wide awake he
wouldn't have wanted her to unload this sort of stuff on
him. But she went on, like the old demon she was :

" Men are fools, and women make 'em what they are.
I followed your Aunt Lizzie up, years after. She married
a man in the mounted police, and he sent the boy off. The
boy was a bit weak-minded, and the man wouldn't have
him. So the lad disappeared into the bush. They say he
was canny enough about business and farming, but a bit
off about people. Anyway he was Mary's half-brother :
you met Mary in Perth. Her scamp of a father was father
of that illegitimate boy. But she's an orphan now, poor
child : like that illegitimate half-brother of hers."

Jack looked up pathetically. He *didn't* want to hear.
And Gran suddenly laughed at him, with the sudden daring,
winsome laugh, like Lennie.

" Y're a bundle of conventions, like y'r grandfather,"
she said tenderly. " But y've got a kinder heart. I suppose that's from y'r English father. Folks are tough in
Australia : tough as whit-leather. Y'll be tempted to sin,
but y' won't be tempted to condemn. And never you
mind. Trust yourself, Jack Grant. *Earn a good opinion
of yourself*, and never mind other folks. You've only got
to live once. You know when you're spirit glows—trust
that. That's *you!* That's the spirit of God in you. Trust
in that, and you'll never grow old. If you knuckle under,
you'll grow old."

She paused for a time.

" Though I don't know that I've much room to talk,"

she ruminated on. " There was my son, Esau, he never knuckled under, and though he's dead, I've not much good to say of him. But then he never had a kind heart : never. Never a woman loved Esau, though some feared him. I was not among 'em. Not I. I feared no man, not even your grandfather : except a little. But look at Dad here now. He's got a kind heart : as kind a heart as ever beat. And he's gone old. And he's got heart disease. And he knuckled under. Ay, he knuckled under to me, he did, poor lad. And he'll go off sudden, when his heart gives way. That's how it is with kind-hearted men. They knuckle under, and they die young. Like Dad here. He'll never make old bones. Poor lad ! "

She mused again in silence.

" There's nothing to win in life, when all's said and done, but a good opinion of yourself. I've watched and I know. God is y'rself. Or put it the other way if you like : y'rself is God. So win a good opinion of yourself, and watch the glow inside you."

Queer, thought Jack, that this should be an old woman's philosophy. Yourself is God ! Partly he believed it, partly he didn't. He didn't know what he believed. Watch the glow inside you. That he understood.

He liked Gran. She was so alone in life, amid all her children. He himself was a lone wolf too : among the lambs of the family. And perhaps Red Easu was a lone wolf.

" But what was I telling you ? " Gran resumed. " About your illegitimate cousin. I followed him up too. He went back beyond Atherton, and took up land. He's got a tidy place now, and he's never married. He's wrong in his head about people, but all right about the farm. I'm hoping that place'll come to Mary one day, for the child's got nothing. She's a good child—a good child. Her mother was a niece of mine."

She seemed to be going to sleep. But, like Herbert, she roused again.

" Y'd better marry Mary. Make up your mind to it," she said.

And instantly he rebelled against the thought. Never.

" Perhaps I'd ought to have said : ' The best in yourself is God,' " she mused. " Perhaps that's more it. The best in yourself is God. But then who's going to say what *is*

the best in yourself. A kind man knuckles under, and
thinks it's the best in himself. And a hard man holds out,
and thinks that's the best in himself. And it's *not* good
for a kind man to knuckle under, and it's *not* good for a
hard-hearted man to hold out. What's to be done, dreary-
me, what's to be done. And no matter what we say, people
will be as they are. You can but watch the glow."

She really did doze off. And Jack stole away to the other
side of the screen to escape her, leaving the candle burning.

viii

He sat down thankfully on the hard chair by Herbert's
side, glad to get away from women. Glad to be with men,
if it was only Herbert. Glad to doze and feel alone : to
feel alone.

He awoke with a jerk and a cramped neck, and there
was Tom peeping in. Tom ? They must be back. Jack's
chair creaked as he made a movement to get up. But Tom
only waved his hand and disappeared. Mean of Tom.

They must be back. The twins must be back. The
family was replenished. He stared with sleepy eyes, and
a heavy, sleepy, sleepy head.

And the next thing he heard was a soft, alert voice
saying :

" Hello, Bow ! "

Queer how it echoed in his dark consciousness as he slept,
this soft, " Hello, Bow ! "

There they were, both laughing, fresh with the wind and
rain. Grace standing just behind Monica, Monica's hair
all tight crisp with rain, blond at the temples, darker on
the head, and her fresh face laughing, and her yellow eyes
looking with that long, meaningful look that had no meaning, peering into his sleepy eyes. He felt something stir
inside him.

" Hello, Bow ! " she said again, putting her fingers on
his sleeve. " We've got back." And still in his sleep-
stupor he stared without answering a word.

" You aren't awake ! " she whispered, putting her cold
hand suddenly on his face, and laughing as he started back.
A new look came into his eyes as he stared startled at her,
and she bent her head, turning aside.

" Poo ! Smells of stinking candles in here ! " whispered Grace.

Someone else was there. It was Red Easu in the doorway, saying in a hoarse voice :

" Want me to take a spell with Herbert ? "

Monica glanced back at him with a strange look. He loomed weird and tall, with his rather long, red neck and glistening beard and quick blue eyes. A certain sense of power came with him.

" Hello, girls, got back ! " he added to the twins, who watched him without speaking.

" Who's there ? " said Gran's voice from the other side of the screen. " Is it the girls back ? Has Mary come with you ? "

As if in answer to the summons, Mary appeared in the doorway, wearing a white apron. She glanced first at Jack, with her black eyes, and then at Gran. Monica was watching her with a sideways lynx look, and Grace was looking at everybody with big blue eyes, while Easu looked down from his uncouth, ostrich height.

" Hello, Gran ! " said Mary, going to the other side of the screen to kiss the old lady. The twins followed suit.

" Want me to take a spell in here ? " said Easu, jerking his thumb at the sleeping Herbert. Easu wore black trousers hitched up high with braces over a dark-grey flannel shirt, and leather leggings, but no boots. His shirt-sleeves were rolled up from his sinewy brown arms. His reddish fair hair was thick and rather long. He spoke in a deep gruff voice, that he made as quiet as possible, and he seemed to show a gruff sort of submissiveness to Jack at the moment.

" No, Easu," replied Gran. " I can't do with you. Jack Grant will manage."

The sick man was sleeping through it all like the dead.

" I can take a turn," said Mary's soft, low, insidious voice.

" No, not you either, Mary. You go to sleep after that drive. Go, all of you, go to bed. I can't do with you all in here. Has Dr. Rackett come ? "

" No," said Easu.

" Then go away, all of you. I can't do with you," said Gran.

Mary came round the screen and shook hands with Jack,

looking him full in the eyes with her black eyes, so that he was uncomfortable. She made him more uncomfortable than Monica did. Monica had slunk also round the screen, and was standing with one foot trailing, watching. She watched just as closely when Mary shook hands with the embarrassed Easu.

They all retreated silently to the door. Grace went first. And with her big, dark-blue eyes she glanced back inquisitively at Jack. Mary went next—she too turning in the door to give him a look and an intimate, furtive-seeming smile. Then came Monica, and like a wolf she lingered in the door looking back with a long, meaningful, meaningless sidelong look before she took her departure. Then on her heels went Easu, and he did not look back. He seemed to loom over the girls.

" Blow the light out," said Gran.

He went round to blow out the candle. Gran lay there like an old angel. Queer old soul—framed by pillow frills.

" Yourself is God ! "

Jack thought of that with a certain exultance.

He went over and made up the fire. Then he sat in the arm-chair. Herbert was moving. He went over to soothe him. The sick man moaned steadily for some time, for a long time, then went still again. Jack slept in the hard chair.

He woke up cramped and cold, and went round to the arm-chair by the fire. Gran was sleeping like an inert bit of ivory. He softly attended to the fire and sat down in the arm-chair.

He was riding a horse a long, long way, on a journey that would never end. He couldn't stop the horse till it stopped of itself. And it would never stop. A voice said : What has he done?   And a voice answered : Conquered the world. But the horse did not stop. And he woke and saw shadows on the wall, and slept again. Things had all turned to dough—his hands were heavy with dough. He woke and looked at his hands to see if it were so. How loudly and fiercely the clock ticked.

Not dough, but boxing-gloves. He was fighting inside a ring, fighting with somebody who was and who wasn't Easu. He could beat Easu—he couldn't beat Easu. Easu had knocked him down : he was lying writhing with pain and couldn't rise, while they were counting him out. In three more seconds he would be counted out! Horror!

He woke, it was midnight and Herbert was writhing.

" Did I sleep a minute, Herbert? " he whispered.

" My head! My head! It jerks so! "

" Does it, old man. Never mind."

And the next thought was : " There must have been gun-powder in that piece of wood, in the fire."

ix

It was half-past one, and Mary unexpectedly appeared with tray and lighted candle, and cocoa-milk for Jack and arrowroot for Herbert. She fed Herbert with a spoon, and he swallowed, but made no sign that he understood.

" How did he get the accident? " Jack whispered.

" His horse threw him against a tree."

" Wish Rackett would come," whispered Jack.

Mary shook her head and they were silent.

" How old are you, Mary? " Jack asked.

" Nineteen."

" I'm eighteen at the end of this month."

" I know—but I'm much older than you."

Jack looked at her queer dark muzzle. She seemed to have a queer, humble complacency of her own.

" She "—Jack nodded his head towards Gran—" says that knuckling under makes you old."

Mary laughed suddenly.

" Then I'm a thousand," she said.

" What do you knuckle under for? " he asked.

She looked up at him slowly, and again something quick and hot stirred in him, from her dark, queer, humble, yet assured face.

" It's my way," she said, with an odd smile.

" Funny way to have," he replied, and suddenly he was embarrassed. And he thought of Monica's dare-devil way. He felt embarrassed.

" I must have my own way," said Mary, with another odd, beseeching, and yet darkly confident smile.

" Yourself is God," thought Jack. But he said nothing, because he felt uncomfortable.

And Mary went away with the tray and the light, and he was glad when she was gone.

x

The worst part of the night. Nothing happened—and that was perhaps the worst part of it. Fortified by the powers of darkness, the slightest sounds took on momentous importance, but nothing happened. He expected something—but nothing came.

Gran asleep there, in all the fixed motionlessness of her years, a queer white clot. And young Herbert asleep or unconscious, sending wild vibrations from his brain.

The thought of Monica seemed to flutter subjectively in Jack's soul, the thought of Mary objectively. That is, Monica was somehow inside him, in his blood, like a sister. And Mary was outside him, like a black-boy. Both of them engaging his soul. And yet he was alone, all alone in the universe. These two only beset him. Or did he beset them?

The oppossums made a furious bombilation as they ran up and down, back and forth between the roof and ceiling, like an army moving. And suddenly, shatteringly, a nut would come down on the old shingle roof from the Moreton Bay fig outside, with a crash like a gun, while the branches dangled and clanked against the timber walls. An immense uncanny strider! And him alone in the lonely, uncanny, timeless core of the night.

Slowly the night went by. And weird things awoke in the boy's soul, things he could never quite put to sleep again. He felt as if this night he had entered into a dense impenetrable thicket. As if he would never get out. He knew he would never get out.

He awoke again with a start. Was it the first light? Herbert was stirring. Jack went quickly to him.

Herbert opened dazed eyes, and mutely looked at Jack. A look of intelligence came, and as quickly passed. He groaned, and the torment came over him once more. Whatever was the matter with him? He writhed and struggled, groaning—then relapsed into a cold, inert silence. It was as if he were dying. As if he, or something in him, had decided to die.

Jack was terribly startled. In terror, he mixed a little

brandy and milk, and tried to pour spoonfuls down the unresisting throat. He quickly fetched a hot stone from the fire, wrapped it in a piece of blanket, and put it in the bed.

Then he sat down and took the young man's hand softly in his own and whispered intensely : " Come back, Herbert ! Come back ! Come back ! "

With all his will he summoned the inert spirit. He was terribly afraid the other would die. He sat and watched with a fixed, intent will. And Herbert relaxed again, the life came round his eyes again.

" Oh, God ! " thought Jack. " I shall die. I shall die myself. What sort of a life have I got to live before I die ? Oh, God, what sort of a life have I got between me and when I die ? "

And it all seemed a mystery to him. The God he called on was a dark, almost fearful mystery. The life he had to live was a kind of doom. The choice he had was no choice. " Yourself is God." It wasn't true. There was a terrible God somewhere else. And nothing else than this.

Because, inside himself, he was alone, without father or mother or place or people. Just a separate living thing. And he could not choose his doom of living nor his dying. Somewhere outside himself was a terrible God who decreed.

He was afraid of the thicket of life, in which he found himself like a solitary, strange animal. He would have to find his way through : all the way to death. But what sort of way ? What sort of life ? What sort of life between him and death ?

He didn't know. He only knew that something must be. That he was in a strange bush, and by himself. And that he must find his way through.

CHAP : VI.   IN THE YARD

i

Ah, good to be out in the open air again! Beyond all telling good! Those indoor rooms were like coffins. To be dead, and to writhe unreleased in the coffin, that was what those indoor rooms were like.

" God, when I die, let me pass right away," prayed Jack. " Lord, I promise to live my life right out, so that when I die I pass over and don't lie wriggling in the coffin! "

Mary had come as soon as it was light, and found Herbert asleep and Jack staring at him in a stupor.

" You go to sleep now, Bow," said Mary softly, laying her hand on his arm.

He looked at her in a kind of horror, as if she were part of the dark interior. He didn't want to go to sleep. He wanted to wake. He stood in the yard and stared around stupefied at the early morning. Then he went and hauled Lennie and the twins out of their bunks. Tom was already up. Then he went, stripped to the waist, to the pump.

" Pump over my nut, Lennie," he shouted, holding his head at the pump spout. Oh, 'twas so good to shout at somebody. He must shout.

And Lennie pumped away like a little imp.

When Jack looked out of the towel at the day, he saw the sky fresh with yellow light, and some red still on the horizon above the grey gum-trees. It all seemed crisp and snappy. It was life.

" Ain't yer goin' ter do any of yer monkey trickin' this morning? " shouted Lennie at him.

Jack shook his head, and rubbed his white young shoulders with the towel. Lennie, standing by the wash-tin in his little under-vest and loose little breeches, was watching closely.

" Can you answer me a riddle, Lennie? " asked Jack.

" I'll try," said Len briskly, and Og and Magog jumped up in gay expectation.

" What *is* God, anyhow? " asked Jack.

" Y'd better let my father hear y'," replied Lennie, with a dangerous nod of the head.

" No, but I mean it. Suppose Herbert had died. I want to know what God is."

Jack still had the inner darkness of that room in his eyes.

" I'll tell y'," said Len briskly. " God is a Higher Law than the Constitution."

Jack thought about it. A higher law than the law of the land. Maybe! The answer left him cold.

" And what is self ? " he asked.

" Crickey! Stop up another night! It'ud make ye sawney. But I'll tell y' what self is.

> " ' Self is a wilderness of sweets. And selves
> They eat, they drink, and in communion sweet
> Quaff immortality and joy.' "

Len was pleased with this. But Jack heard only words.

" Ask *me* one, Jack! Ask *me* one! " pleaded Og.

" All right. What's success, Og? " asked Jack, smiling.

" Success! Success! Why, success—— "

" Success is t'grow a big bingy like a bloke from town, 'n a watch-chain acrost it with a gold dial in y' fob, and ter be allowed ter spout as much gab as y've got bref left over from y' indigest," cut in Lennie, with delight.

" That was *my* riddle," yelled Og, rushing at him.

" Ask me one! Ask me one, Jack! Ask me one," yelled Magog.

" What's failure? " asked Jack, laughing.

" T' be down on y' uppers an' hev no visible means of supporting y'r pants up whilst y' slog t' th' nearest pub t'cadge a beer spot," crowed Lennie in delight, while he fenced off Og.

Both twins made an assault and battery upon him.

" D'ye know y'r own answers? " yelled Len at Jack.

" No."

The brazenness of the admission flabbergasted the twins. They stalked off. Len drew up a three-legged stool, and sat down to milk, explaining impatiently that success comes to those that work and don't drink.

" But "—he reverted to his original thought—" ye've gotta work, not go wastin' y'r time as you generally do of a morning—boundin' about makin' a kangaroo of y'self; tippin' y'elbows and holdin' back y' nut as if y' had a woppin' fine drink in both hands, and gone screwed with joy afore you drained it; lyin' flat on y' hands an' toes, an' heavin' up an' down, up an' down, like a race-horse iguana frightened by a cat; an' stalkin' an' stoopin' as if y'wanted ter catch a bird round a corner; or roundin' up on imaginary things, makin' out t'hit 'em slap-bang-whizz on the mitts they ain't got; whippin' round an' bobbin' like a cornered billy-goat; skippin' up an' down like sis wif a rope, an' makin' a general high falutin' ass of y'self."

" I see you and the twins with clubs," said Jack.

" Oh, that ! That's more for music an' one—two—three —four," said Len.

" You see I'm in training," said Jack.

" What for ?   Want ter teach the old sows to start dancin' on th' corn-bin floor ? "

" No, I want to keep in training, for if I ever have a big fight."

" Who with ? "

" Oh, I don't know. But I love a round with the fists. I'll teach you."

" All right. But why don't y' chuck farmin' an' go in f' prize fightin' ? "

" I wish I could. But my father said no. An' perhaps he's right. But the best thing I know is to fight a fair round. I'll teach you, Len."

" Huh ! What's the sense ! If y' want exercise, y' c'n rub that horse down a bit cleaner than y' are doin'."

" Stop y' sauce, nipper, or I'll be after y' with a strap !" called Tom. " Come on, Jack. Tea ! Timothy's bangin' the billy-can. And just you land that nipper a clout."

" Let him 'it me ! Garn, let him ! " cried Len, scooting up with his milk-stool and pail and looking like David skirmishing before Goliath. He wasn't laughing. There was a demonish little street-arab hostility in his face.

" Don't you like me, Len ? " Jack asked, a bit soft this morning. Len's face at once suffused with a delightful roguishness.

" Aw, yes—if y'like. I'll be dressin' up in Katie's skirts n' spoonin' y' one of these bright nights."

He whipped away with his milk-pail, like a young lizard.

ñ

" Look at Bow, he looks like an owl," said Grace at breakfast.

" What d'y call 'im Bow for? " asked Len.

" Like a girl, with his eyes double size," said Monica.

" You'd better go to sleep, Jack," said Mrs Ellis.

" Take a nap, lad," said Mr Ellis. " There's nothin' for y' to do this morning."

Jack was going stupefied again as the sun grew warm. He didn't hear half that was said. But the girls were very attentive to him. Mary was not there : she was sitting with Herbert. But Monica and Grace waited on him as if he had been their lord. It was a new experience for him : Monica jumping up and whipping away his cup with her slim hand, to bring it back filled, and Grace insisting on opening a special jar of jam for him. Drowsy as he was, their attention made his blood stir. It was so new to him.

Mary came in from the sitting-room : they were still in the kitchen.

" Herbert is awake," she said. " He wants to be untied. Bow, do you think he ought to? "

Jack rose in silence and went through to Gran's room. Herbert lay quite still, but he was himself. Only shattered and wordless. He looked at Jack and murmured :

" Can't y'untie me? "

Jack went at once to unfasten the linen bands. The twins, Monica and Grace, stood watching from the doorway. Mary was at his side to help.

" Don't let 'em come in," said Herbert, looking into Jack's face.

Jack nodded and went to the door.

" He wants to be left alone," he said.

" Mustn't we come, Bow? " said Monica, making queer yellow eyes at him.

" Best not," he said. " Don't let anybody come. He wants absolute quiet."

" All right." She looked at him with a heavy look of obedience, as if making him an offering. They were not going to question his authority. She drew Grace away : both the girls humble. Jack slowly and unconsciously flushed. Then he went back to the bed.

"I want something," murmured Herbert wanly. "Send that other away."

"Go away, Mary. He wants a man to attend to him," said Jack.

Mary looked a long, dark look at Jack. Then she, too, submitted.

"All right," she said, turning darkly away.

And it came into his mind, with utter absurdity, that he ought to kiss her for this submission. And he hated the thought.

Herbert was a boy of nineteen, uncouth, and savagely shy. Jack had to do the menial offices for him.

The sick man went to sleep again almost immediately, and Jack returned to the kitchen. He heard voices from outside.

Ma and Grace were washing up at the slab. Dad was sitting under the photosphorum tree, with Effie on one knee, cutting up tobacco in the palm of his hand. Tom was leaning against the tree, the children sat about. Lennie skipped up and offered a seat on a stump.

"Sit yourself down, Bow," he said, using the nickname. "I'd be a knot instead of a bow if I had to nurse Red Herbert."

Monica came slinking up from the shade, and stood with her skirt touching Jack's arm. Mary was carrying away the dishes.

"I've been telling Tom," said Mr Ellis, "that he can take the clearing gang over to his A'nt Greenlow's for the shearing, an' then get back an' clear for all he's worth, till Christmas. Y'might as well go along with him, Jack. We can get along all right here without y', now th' girls are back. Till Christmas that is. We s'll want y' back for the harvest."

There was a dead silence. Jack didn't want to go.

"Then y' can go back to the clearing and burn off. I need that land reclaimed, over against the little chaps grows up and wants to be farmers. Besides "—and he looked round at Ma—" we're a bit overstocked in the house just now, an' we'll be glad of the cubby for Herbert, if he's on the mend."

Dad resumed cutting up his tobacco in the palm of his hand.

" Jack can't leave Herbert, Uncle," said Mary quietly,
" he won't let anybody else do for him."

" Eh ? " said Mr Ellis, looking up.

" Herbert won't let me do for him," said Mary. " He'll
only let Bow."

Mr Ellis dropped his head in silence.

" In that case," he said slowly, " in that case, we must
wait a bit. Where's that darned Rackett put himself ? This
is his job."

There was still silence.

" Somebody had best go an' look for him," said Tom.

" Ay," said Mr Ellis.

There was more silence. Monica, standing close to Jack,
seemed to be fiercely sheltering him from this eviction.
And Mary, at a distance, was like Moses' sister watching
over events. It made Jack feel queer and thrilled, the
girls all concentrating on him. It was as if it put power in
his chest, and made a man of him.

Someone was riding up. It was Red Easu. He slung
himself off his horse, and stalked slowly up.

" Herbert dead ? " he asked humorously.

" Doing nicely," said Dad, very brief.

" I'll go an' have a look at 'm," said Easu, sitting on
the step and pulling off his boots.

" Don't wake him if he's asleep. Don't frighten him,
whatever you do," said Jack, anxious for his charge.

Easu looked at Jack with an insolent stare : a curious
stare.

" Frighten him ? " he said. " What with ? "

" Jack's been up with him all night," put in Monica,
fiercely.

" He nearly died in the night," said Jack.

There was a dead silence. Easu stared, poised like some
menacing bird. Then he went indoors in his stocking feet.

" Did he nearly die, Jack ? " asked Tom.

Jack nodded. His soul was feeling bleached.

" If Doctor Rackett isn't coming—see if you can trail
him up, Tom. And, Len, can you go on Lucy and fetch
Doctor Mallett ? "

" Course I can," said Len, jumping up.

" You go and get a nap in the cubby, son," said Mr Ellis.

They were now all in motion. Jack followed vaguely into

the kitchen. Lennie was the centre of excitement for the moment.

" Well, Ma, I has no socks fitta wear. If y'll fix me some, I'll go." For he was determined to go to York in decent raiment, as he said.

" Find me a decent shirt, Ma; *decent!* None o' your creases down th' front for me. 'N a starch collar, real starch."

And so on. He was late. Lennie was always late.

" Ma, weer's my tie—th' blue one wif gold horse-shoes? Grace—there's an angel—me boots. Clean 'em up a bit, go on. Monica! Oh, Monica; there y'are! Fix this collar on for me, proper, do! Y're a bloke at it, so y'are, an' I'm no good. . . . Gitt outta th' way, you nips—how k'n I get dressed with you buzzin' round me feet? Ma! Ma! Come an' brush me 'air with that dinkey nice-smellin' stuff. . . . There, Ma, don't your Lennie look a dream now? Ooha, Ma, don't kiss me, Ma, I 'ate it."

" Lennie, love, don't drop your aitches."

" I never, Ma. I said I 'ate it. Y' kissed me, did y' or *didn't* y'? Well, I 'ate it."

He was gone on Lucy, like a little demon. Jack, sitting stupid on a chair, felt part of his soul go with him.

" Come on, Bow! " said Monica, taking him by the arm. " Come and go to sleep. Mary will wake you if Herbert wants you."

And she led him off to the door of the cubby, while he submitted and Easu stood in his stocking feet on the verandah watching.

" He saved Herbert's life," said Monica, looking up at Easu with a kind of defiance, when she came back.

" Who asked him? " said Easu.

iii

Tom and Jack were to leave the next day. The girls brought out a lot of stores from the cupboard, and blankets and billies and a lantern. They packed the sacks standing there.

" Get y' swag f'y'selves," said Dad. " The men have everything for themselves. Take an axe an' a gun apiece."

" Gun! Gee! K'n I go, Dad? "

" Shut up, Len. Destroy all the dingoes y' can. I'll give
y' sixpence a head, an' the Government gives another.
Haven't y' a saddle, Jack Grant, somewhere in a box.
Because I'd be short of one off the place, if you took one
from here."

" It must be somewhere," said Jack.

" Get it unpacked. An' you can have Lucy to put it
across. It's forty mile from here to virgin forest : real
forest. If you get strayed, ever, all you have to do is to
drop th' reins on Lucy's neck 'n she'll bring y' in."

The saddle came out of the dusty box. All were there in
a circle to look on. Jack expected deep admiration. But
he was hurt to feel Monica laughing derisively. Everybody
was laughing, but he minded Monica most. She could jeer
cruelly.

" Jolly good saddle," said Jack.

" Mighty little of it," said Len.

" What's wrong with it, Tom ? " said Jack.

" Slithery. No knee-pads, saddle-bags, strap-holder,
scooped seat, or any sortta comfort. It's a whale, on the
wrong side."

Lennie closely examined the London ticket. The unpacking continued in silence, under Tom's majestic eye. Whip,
yellow horse-rug, bridle, leathers, a heavy bar bit with
double rings and curb, saddle cloths, reins, extra special
blue-and-gold girths wrapped in tissue paper, nickel cross
rowell jockey spurs, and glittering steel stirrup-irons. Cord
breeches, assam silk coat, white water-proof linen stocks,
leather gaiters, and a pair of leather gauntlets completed
the amazing disclosure. It was all a mighty gift from one
of the unforgiven aunts.

Half way through the unpacking Tom gave a groan and
walked away; but walked back. Og and Magog stole the
saddle, slung it across a bar, and slid off and on rapturously.
Monica was laughing at him disagreeably : strange and
brutal, as if she hated him : rather like Easu. And Lennie
was tittering with joy.

" Oh, Og ! Here ! Y're missin' it. Leave that hog's
back saddle, No. 1 Grade—picked material—hand forged—
tree mounted, guaranteed—a topper off; see this princess
palfrey bridle for you, rosettes ornamented, periwinkle an'
all. An', oh, look you ! a canary belly-band f'r Dada

t'strap round th' heifer's neck when she gets first prize at the Royal York show. Look at that crush-bone cage to put round Stampede's mouth when the niggers catches him again. Oh, Lor', oh, my—— "

" Shut up ! " said Tom abruptly, catching the boy by the back of his pants and tossing him out of the barn. " Now, roll up y'r bluey "—meaning the new rug, which was yellow. " Fix them stirrup leathers, take the bridle off that bit an' we'll find you something decent to put the reins on. An' kick th' rest t'gether. What a gear. Glad it's you, not me, as has got to ride that leather, me boy. But ride on't y'll have to, for there's nought else. Now, Monica, close down that mirth of yours. You're not asked for it."

" Let brotherly love continue," said Monica spitefully. " Wonder if it will, even unto camp."

She went, leaving Jack feeling suddenly tired.

CHAP : VII.   OUT BACK AND SOME LETTERS

i

JACK was absolutely happy, in camp with Tom. Perhaps the most completely happy time in his life. He had escaped the strange, new complications that life was weaving round him. Yet he had not left the beloved family. He was with Tom : who, after all, was the one that mattered most. Tom was the growing trunk of the tree.

All real living hurts as well as fulfils. Happiness comes when we have lived and have a respite for sheer forgetting. Happiness, in the vulgar sense, is just a holiday experience. The life-long happiness lies in being used by life; hurt by life, driven and goaded by life, replenished and overjoyed with life, fighting for life's sake. That is real happiness. In the undergoing, a large part of it is pain. But the end is like Jack's camping expedition, a time of real happiness.

Perhaps death, after a life of real courage, is like a happy camping expedition in the unknown, before a new start.

It was spring in Western Australia, and a wonder of delicate blueness, of frail, unearthly beauty. The earth was full of weird flowers, star-shaped, needle-pointed, fringed, scarlet, white, blue, a whole world of strange flowers. Like being in a new Paradise from which man had not been cast out.

The trees in the dawn, so ghostly still. The scent of blossoming eucalyptus trees : the scent of burning eucalyptus leaves and sticks in the camp fire. Trailing blossoms wet with dew; the scrub after the rain; the bitter-sweet fragrance of fresh-cut timber.

And the sounds !   Magpies calling, parrots chattering, strange birds flitting in the renewed stillness. Then kangaroos calling to one another out of the frail, paradisal distance. And the birr ! of crickets in the heat of the day. And the sound of axes, the voices of men, the crash of falling timber. The strange slobbering talk of the blacks ! The mysterious night coming round the camp fire.

Red gum everywhere !   Fringed leaves dappling, the glowing new sun coming through, the large, feathery,

93

honey-sweet blossoms flowering in clumps, the hard, rough-marked, red-bronze trunks rising like pillars of burnt copper, or lying sadly felled, giving up the ghost.   Everywhere scattered the red gum, making leaves and herbage under-neath seem bestrewed with blood.

And it was spring : the short, swift, fierce, flower-strange spring of Western Australia, in the month of August.

Then evening came, and the small aromatic fire was burning amid the felled trees. Tom stood, hands on hips. giving directions, while the blackened billy-can hung sus-pended from a cross-bar over the fire. The water bubbling, a handful of tea is thrown in. It sinks. It rises. " Bring it off ! " yells Tom. Jack balances the cross-stick, hold-ing the wobbling can, until it rests safely on the ground. Then snatching the handle holds the can aloft. Tea is made.

The clearing gang had a hut with one side for the horses, the other for the men's sleeping place. Inside were stakes driven into the ground, bearing cross-bars with sacks fastened across, for beds. On the partition-poles hung the wardrobes, and in a couple of boxes lay the treasures, in shape of watches, knives, razors, looking-glasses, etc., safe from the stray thief. But the men were always tormenting one another, hiding away a razor, or a strop, or a beloved watch.

Just in front of this shelter the camp oven had been built, for baking damper and roasting meat, and to one side was the well, a very important necessity, built by contract, timbered, and provided with winch, rope and bucket.

All around, the bush was dense like a forest, much denser than usual. The slim-girthed trees grew in silent array, all alike and all asleep, with undergrowth of scrub and fern and flowers, banksia short and sturdy with its cone-shaped, red-yellow flowers like fairy lamps, and here and there a perfect wattle, or mimosa tree, with its pale gold flowers like little balls of sun-dust, and here and there sandal-wood trees. Jack never forgot the beauty of the first bushes and trees of mimosa, in a damp place in the wild bush. Occasionally there was still an immense karri tree, or a jarrah slightly smaller, though this was not the region for these giants.

And far away, unending, upslope and downslope and
rock-face, one far unending dimness of these changeless
trees, going on and on without variation, open enough to
let one see ahead and all around, yet dense enough to form
a monotony and a sense of helplessness in the mind, a sense
of timelessness. Strongly the gang impressed on Jack that
he must not go even for five minutes' walk out of sight of
the clearing. The weird silent timelessness of the bush
impressed him as nothing else ever did, in its motionless
aloofness. " What would my father mean, out here ? " he
said to himself. And it seemed as if his father and his
father's world and his father's gods withered and went to
dust at the thought of this bush. And when he saw one
of the men on a red sorrel horse galloping like a phantom
away through the dim, red-trunked, silent trees, followed
by another man on a black horse; and when he heard their
far, far-off yelling Coo-ee ! or a shot as they fired at a dingo
or a kangaroo, he felt as if the old world had given him up
from the womb, and put him into a new weird grey-blue
paradise, where man has to begin all over again. That
was his feeling : that the human way of life was all to be
begun over again.

The home that he and Tom made for themselves seemed
to be a matter of forked sticks. If you wanted an upright
of any sort, drive a forked stick into the ground, or dig it
in, fork-end up. If you wanted a cross bar, lay a stick or
a pole across two forks. Down the sides of your house you
wove brushwood. For the roof you plaited the long,
stringy strips of gum-bark. With a couple of axes and a
jack-knife they built a house fit for a savage king. Then
they went out and made a kitchen, with pegs hammered
into the bole of a tree, for the frying-pans, the sawn surface of a large stump for a table, and logs to lie back against.

North of the clearing lay the nucleus of a settlement, with
pub, sawmill, store, one or two homes, and a farm or two
out-lying. And as they cleared the land, the teamsters
carried the best of the timber on jinkers, or dragged it with
chains hitched to bullock or horse teams, to the mill. But
milling was expensive, and most of the wood was hand-
split. Jack learned to cut palings and poles, and then to
split slabs that would serve to build slab houses, or sheds.
In the spare time they would have little hunts of wallabies

or bandicoots or bungarras, or boody-rats; or they would snare opossums or stalk dingoes.

But because he was really away in the wild, Jack felt he must write letters home. So it is. The letters from home hardly interested him at all. The thin sheets with their interminable writing were almost repulsive to him. He would stow them in the barn and leave them for days without reading them : he was " busy." And sometimes the mice nibbled them, and in that way read them for him. He was a little ashamed of this indifference. But he noticed other men were the same. When they got these endless thin sheets from home, covered with ink of words, they stowed them away in a kind of nausea, without reading more than a few lines. And the people at home had such a pitying admonishing tone : like the young naval lieutenant who made friends with the black aborigines by promptly shaving them. And then letters were not profitable. A stamp home cost sixpence, and a letter took about two months on the way. It was always four months before you got an answer. And after you'd written to your mother about something really important—like money—and waited impatiently several months for the answer, when it came it never mentioned the money and made a mountain of a cold in your head which you couldn't remember having had. What was the good of people at home writing : " We are having true November weather, very cold, with fog and sleet," when you were grilling under a fierce sun and the rush of the intense antipodal summer. What was the good of it all? All dull as ditchwater, and no use to anybody. He had promised his mother he would write once a week. And his mother was his mother, he wanted to keep his promise. Which he did for a month. But in camp, he didn't even know what day it was, hardly what month : though the mail did come once a fortnight, via the sawmill. He took out his mother's letter. " You said in your letter from Colombo that you were sneezing. Do take care in Australia in the rainy season. Ask not to be sent out in the rain. I recollect the climate, always sunny and bright between showers. That is what we miss so much now we are back in England, the sunny skies. Of course, I do not want you to be a mollycoddle, but I know the climate of Western Australia, it is very trying, particularly so in the

rainy season.   I do hope and pray you are on a good
station with a good woman who will see you are not out
getting drenched in those cold downpours—— "

Jack groaned aloud, astonished that his mother had got
so far from her own early days. How in the name of heaven
had he come to mention sneezing? Never again. He would
not even say he was camping.

" Dear Mother,
                    " I am quite well and like farming out
here all right. Old Mrs Ellis knew your father. She says
he cut off her leg. I hope Father has got rid of his Liver,
you said he was taking variolettes for it. I hope they have
done him good. Mr Ellis says a cockles pill and a ten-mile
walk will cure anything. He says it would cure a pig's
liver. But when old Tim, the half-caste, tried to swallow
the pill it came out of the gap where his front tooth used
to be, so Mrs Ellis gave him a teaspoonful of sulphur, which
he said would make him blow up. But it didn't. I think
I was more likely to blow up because she gave me a big
teaspoon of paraffin which they call kerosene out here. She
is a fine doctor, far better than the medical man who lodges
here, whose name is Rackett.

" I hope you are quite well. Give my love to all my
aunts and sister and father. I hope they are all quite
well—— "

Jack hurried this letter in confusion into its envelope, and
spent sixpence on it, knowing perfectly well it was all
nonsense.

ii

There was a pause in the clearing work, after the early
hot spell, and word from Lennie that there was to be a
kangaroo hunt, and they were to come down. An old man
kangaroo, a king of boomers, had been seen around, hoof-
marks, and paw-pad trails near the pool.

They met at dawn, by the well : Easu with two kangaroo
hounds, like greyhounds, on leash ; Lennie peacocking on an
enormous hairy-heeled roadster ; a " superior " young
Queenslander who had been sent west because his father

found him unmanageable and who wasn't a bad sort, though his nickname was Pink-eye Percy; Lennie's " Cornseed " friend, Joe Low; Alec Rice, the young fellow who was courting Grace; Ross Ellis, and Herbert, who was well again, then Tom on a grey stallion; and Jack, in riding breeches and gaiters and clean shirt, astride the famous Lucy.

Easu was born in the saddle, he rode easy on his big roan. He waved his hat excitedly at the group, and led off into the scrub, through the slender, white-barked trees of the open bush. The others rode fast in ragged order, among the thin, open trees. Jack let Lucy pick her way, sometimes ahead, sometimes in sight of the others. They rode in silence.

Then they came out unexpectedly into low, grey-green scrub without trees, and crisp grey-white soil that crumbled under the hoofs of the horses. There they were, all out in the blue and gold light, with billows of blue-green scrub running away to right and left, towards a rise in front.

" Hold hard there ! " sang out Easu, holding up the whip in his right hand. He held the reins loosely in his left, and with the reins, the leash on which the dogs were pulling. Dogs and horse he held in that left hand.

" I want y' t' divide. Tom, y' lead on a zigzag course down north. Ross, you work south. And this—this fox-hunting gentleman—— " He paused, and Jack felt himself going scarlet.

" Says thank ye, an' hopes he's a gentleman, since y've mentioned it," put in Lennie, in his mild, inconsequential way.

There was a laugh against Red : for there was no mistaking *him* for a gentleman, in any sense of the word. However, he was too much excited by the hunt to persevere.

The fellows were stowing away their pipes in their pockets, and buttoning their coats, ready for the dash. Easu, thrilled by his own unquestioned leadership, gave the orders. All listened closely.

" Call up ! Call up ! Follow my leader and find the trail. Biggest boomer ever ye—— "

" Come ! " cried Tom.

" And I'm here ! " cried Lennie.

Away they went into the gully and through the scrub, riding light but swift, in different directions.

" Let go th' mare's head," yelled Tom over his shoulder. " We're coming to timber, an' she'd best pilot herself."

" Right ! " cried Jack.

" Don't ye kill Lucy," shrieked Lennie. " Because me heart's set on her. Keep y' hands an' y' heel off y' horse, an' y' head on y' shoulders."

The bolt of horsemen through the bush sent parrots screaming savagely over the feathery tree-tops. Jack let Lucy have her way. She was light and swift and surefooted, old steeple-chaser that she was. The slim straight trees slipped past, the motion of the horse surging her own way was exhilarating to a degree.

But Tom had heard something : not the parrots, not the soft thud of the following horses. He must have heard with his sixth sense : perhaps the warning call of the boomer. With face set and eyes burning he swung and urged his horse in a new direction. And like men coming in to supper from different directions, the handful of horsemen came swish-swish through the scrub, toward a centre.

Lucy pricked one ear. Perhaps she too had heard something. Then she gathers herself together and goes like the wind after the twinkling grey quarters of Tom's stallion. Her excitement mounts to Jack's head, and he rides like a projectile on the wind.

Again Tom was reining in, pulling his horse almost on to its haunches. And Jack must hold like a vise with his knees, for Lucy was pawing the air, frantic at being held up.

" Coo-ee ! " came Tom's clear tenor, ringing through the bush. " Coo-ee ! Coo-ee ! Coo-ee ! " A marvellous sound, and Lucy pawing and dancing among the scrub.

" Coo-ee ! Coo-ee ! Coo-ee ! "

It seemed to Jack this sound in the bush was like God. Like the call of the heroic soul seeking its body. Like the call of the bodiless soul, sounding through the immense dead spaces of the dim, open bush, strange and heroic and inhuman. The deep long " coo " mastering the silence, the high summons of the long " eee." The " coo " rising more imperious, and then the " eee ! " thrilling and holding aloft. Then the swift lift and fall : " Coo-eee ! Coo-eee ! Coo-eee ! " till the air rocks with the fierce pulse, as if a

new heart were in motion, and the shriek and scream of the
" eee ! " rips in strange flashes into the far-off, far-off
consciousness.

Much stranger than the weird yelp of the Red Indians'
war-cry was this rocking, ripping noise in the vast grey
bush.

The others were coming in from right and left, like silent
phantoms through the sunny evanescence of the bush, riding hard. Tom is displaced by Red. A few quick words
given and taken. Easu has unleashed the dogs, slashed the
long lash with a resounding crack in the air. The long lean
dogs stretch out—uncannily long, from tip to tip. Tom
lets go and away. Jack lets go and away, and unconsciously his hand goes down for the bow of the slippery
saddle.

Lucy had the situation well in hand, which was more
than Jack had. Thud-thud. Thud-thud. Thud-thud ! Up,
fly ! *Crash !*—Hello ?—All right. A beauty ! a dream of a
jumper, this Lucy. But Jack wished his seat weren't so
slippery.

They were turning into bigger timber : trees further
apart, but much bigger, and with hanging limbs. " Look
out ! Look out f' y' head ! " Jack kept all his eyes open,
till he knew by second sight when to duck. He watched
the twinkling hind quarters of Tom's grey, among the trees.

There was a short yapping of the dogs. Lucy was going
like the wind. Jack was riding light, but she was beginning
to breathe heavily. No longer so young as she was. How
hot the sun was, in the almost shadeless bush. And what
was leading, where was the 'roo ? Jack strained his eyes
almost out of his head, but could see nothing.

They were on the edge of the hills, and the country
changed continually. No sooner were you used to scrub
than it was thin trees. No sooner did you know that Lucy
could manipulate thin trees, than you were among big
timber, with more space and dangerous boughs. Then it
was salty paper-bark country—and back to forest again :
close trees, fallen logs, boody-rat holes and sudden out-
cropping of dark-brown, ancient-looking rocks with little
flat crags, to be avoided. But the other men were going full
speed, and full speed you must follow, watching with all
your eyes, and riding light, and swept along in the run.

Up! That was over an elephant log, and down went a man at Tom's heels. It was Grace's young man. No matter. Jack was going to look over his shoulder when Tom again shouted " Up! ", and Jack and Lennie followed over the fallen timber.

Suddenly they were in a great black blanket of burnt country, clear of undergrowth or scrub, with skeletons of black, charred trees standing gruesome. And there, right under their noses, leapt three kangaroos, swerving across. The baby one, Joey, was first, lithe, light, apparently not a bit afraid, but wildly excited; then the mother doe, all out, panting, anxious-eyed, stiffly jumping; and behind, a long way, with the dogs like needles coming after, ran the Old Man boomer; a great big chap making mighty springs and in varying directions. Yes, he was making a rear-guard action for the safety of his mate and spawn. Leaping with great leaps, as if to the end of the world, leaning forward, his little hands curled in, his immense massive tail straight out behind him like some immense living rudder. And seeming perfectly calm, almost indifferent. With steady, easy, enormous springs he went this way, that way, de-touring, but making for the same ridge his doe and Joey had passed.

The charred ground proved treacherous, holes, smoulder-ing trunks of trees, smouldering hollows where trunks had been. Soon two horses were running loose, with men limp-ing after them. But on went the rest. Thud and crackle went the hoofs of the galloping horses in the charcoal, as after the dogs, after the 'roos they followed, kicking up clouds of grey ash-mounds and red-burnt earth, jumping suddenly over the still-glowing logs.

The chase paused on the ridge, for the drop was sudden and steep, with rocks and boulders cropping out. Down slid the dogs in a cloud, yelping hard, making Easu at all costs turn to try the right, Tom to try the left.

They dropped awkwardly and joltingly down, between rocks, in loose charcoal powder and loose earth.

" Ain't that ole mare a marvel, Jack! " said Tom. " This nag is rode stiff, all-under my knees."

Jack's face was full of wild joy. The stones rattled, the men stood back from the stirrups, the horses seemed to be diving. But Lucy was light and sure.

Down they jolted into the gully. Easu came up swearing—lost the quarry and dogs, Jack pulled Lucy over a boulder to get out of Easu's way : a thing he shouldn't have done. Crack ! went his head against a branch, and Jack was bruising himself on the ground before he knew where he was.

But he was on his feet again, intently chasing Lucy.

" Here y'are ! " It was Herbert who leaned down, picked up the reins of the scampering mare, and threw them to Jack. Jack's face was bleeding. Lennie came up and opened his mouth in dismay. But somebody coo-eed, and the chase was too good to lose. They are all gone.

Jack stiffly mounted, to find himself blinded by trickling blood. Lucy once more was stirring between his knees, stretching herself out, and he had to let her go, fumbling meanwhile for a handkerchief which he pushed under his hat-brim, and pulled down the old felt firmly. Wiping his eyes with his sleeve, he found the wound staunched by the impromptu dressing.

The scene had completely changed. Lucy was whisking him around the side of a huge dark boulder. They were in the dry bed of the gully, on stones.

Lucy stopped dead, practically on her haunches, but her impetus carried her over, and she was slithering down into a loose gravelly hole. Jack jumped off, to find himself face to face with the biggest boomer kangaroo he had ever imagined. It was the Old Man, sitting there at the bottom of the gravel-hole, in the hollow of a barren she-oak, his absurd paws drooping dejectedly before him and his silly dribbling under-jaw working miserably.

" He's trying to get the wind up for another fly," thought Jack, standing there as dazed as the 'roo itself, and feeling himself very much in the same condition. Then he wondered where the doe and Joey were, and where were all the other hunters. He hoped they wouldn't come. Lucy stood by, as calm as a cucumber.

Jack took a step nearer the Old Man 'roo, and instantly brought up his fists as the animal doubled its queer front paws and hit out wildly at him. He wanted to hit back.

" Mind the claws ! " called somebody, with a quiet chuckle, from above.

Jack looked round, and there was Lennie and the heavy

horse, the horse head-down, tail up, feet spread, like a salamander lizard on a wall, slithering down the grade into the hole, Lennie erect in the stirrups. Jack gave a loud laugh.

And the Old Man, either possessed of a sense of humour or terrified to death, seized the nearest thing at hand— which happened to be Jack; grabbed him, gripped him, hugged him in desperate fury, and tried to get up his huge, flail-like hind leg, to rip up the enemy with the toe claw. One stroke of that claw, and Jack was done.

In terror, anger, surprise, Jack jumped at the kangaroo's throat, as far as the animal's grip would let him. The 'roo, trying all the time to use his hind legs, upset, so that the two went rolling on the gravel together. Jack was in horrid proximity to the weird grey fur, clutched by the weird-smelling, violent animal, in a sort of living earthquake, as the kangaroo writhed and bounced to use his great, oar-like hind legs, and Jack clung close and hit at the creature's body, hit, hit, hit. It was like hitting living wire bands. Somebody was roaring, or else it was his own consciousness shouting : " Don't let the hind claw get to work." How horrible a wild thing was, when you were mixed up with it ! The terrible nausea of its powerful, furry, violent-blooded contact. Its unnatural; almost obscene power ! Its different consciousness ! Its overpowering smell !

The others were coming back up the stream-bed, jumping the rocks, towards this place where Jack had fallen and Lennie had come down after him. Esau was calling off the dogs, ferociously. Tom rushed in and got the 'roo by the head.

Lennie was lying on the gravel laughing so hard he couldn't stand on his legs.

iii

Jack wrote a letter to his old friend, the vet. with the " weakness," in England.

" We are out at a place back of beyond, at a place called Gum Tree Valley, so I take up my pen to write as I have time. Tom Ellis is here bossing the clearing gang, and he has a lot of aunts, whom he rightly calls ants. One of them has a place near here, and we go to dinner on Sundays, and

to help when wanted. We stayed all last week and helped
muster in the sheep for the shearing. We rode all round
their paddock boundaries and rounded in the sheep that had
strayed and got lost. They had run off from the main—
about a score of flocks—and were feeding in little herds
and groups miles apart. It's a grand sight to see them all
running before you, their woolly backs bobbing up and down
like brown water. I can tell you I know now the meaning
of the Lost Sheep, and the sort of joy you have in cursing
him when you find him.

" You told me to let you know if I heard any first-hand
news of gold finding. Well, I haven't heard much. But a
man rode into Greenlow's—that's Tom's aunt—place on
Sunday, and he said to Tom : ' Are those the Stirling
Ranges? ' Tom said : ' No, they're not. They're the
Darling Ranges.' He said : ' Are you sure? '—and got very
excited. The black-fellows came and stood by and they
were vastly amused, grinning and looking away. He got
out a compass and said : ' You are wrong, Mr. Ellis, they
are the Stirling Ranges.' Tom said : ' Call 'em what you
choose, chum. We call 'em Darling—and them others
forty mile south-west we call the Stirling.' The man
groaned. Minnie Greenlow called us to come in to tea, and
he came along as well. His manners were awful. He fid-
getted and pushed his hat back on his head and leant forward
and spat in the fire at a long shot, and tipped his cup so that
his tea swobbed in his saucer, then drank it out of the saucer.
Then he pushed the cake back when handed to him, and
leaned his head on his arms on the table and groaned.
You'd have thought he was drunk, but he wasn't, because
he said to Tom : ' Are ye sure them's not the Stirling
Ranges? I can't drink my tea for thinkin' about it.' And
Tom said : ' Sure.'—and then he seemed more distracted
than ever, and blew through his teeth and mopped his head,
and was upset to a degree.

" When we had finished tea and we all went outside he
said : ' Well, I think I'll get back now. It's no use when
the compass turns you down. I'll never find it.' We didn't
know what he was talking about, but when he'd got into
his buggy and drove away the blacks told us : ' Master
lookin' for big lump yellow dirt. He think that very big
fish, an' he bury him longa time. Comin' back no finda

him.' While the boys were talking, who should shout to have the slip rail let down but this same stranger, and he drove right past us and away down the long paddock. When he got to the gate there he turned round and came back and drew up by us muttering, and said : ' Where did you tell me the Stirling Ranges were ? ' Tom pointed it out, and he said : ' So long ! ' and drove off. We didn't see him again. We didn't want to. But Tom is almost sure he found a lump of gold some time back and buried it for safety's sake and now can't find it.

" That's all the gold I've heard about out here.

" Now for news. One day I went out with tucker to old Jack Moss. He's keeping a bit of land warm for the Greenlows, shepherds sheep down there, about forty miles from everywhere. He talked and talked, and when he didn't talk he didn't listen to me. He looked away over the scrub and sucked his cutty. They say he's hoarded wealth but I didn't see any signs. He was in tatters and wore rags round his feet for boots, which were like a gorilla's. Another day we had a kangaroo hunt. We all chased an Old Man for miles and at last he turned and faced us. I was so close I had no time to think and was on him before I had time to pull up. I jumped to the ground and grappled, and we rolled over and over down the gully. They couldn't shoot him because of me, but they fought him off and killed him. And then we saw his mate standing near among the stones, on her hind legs, with her front paws hanging like a helpless woman. Then Tom, who was tying up my cuts, called out : ' Look at her pouch ! It's plum full of little nippers ! ' and so it was. You never saw such a trick. So we let her go. But we got the Old Man.

" Another day we rode round the surveyed area here, which Mr Ellis is taking up for the twins Og and Magog. I asked Tom a lot of questions about taking up land. I think I should like to try. Perhaps if I do you will come out. You would like the horses. There are quite a lot wild. We hunt them in and pick out the best and use them. That's how lots of people raise their horse-flesh. They are called brumbies. Excuse me for not ending properly, the mailman is coming along, he comes once a fortnight. We are lucky.

" JACK."

iv

To his friend, the pugilist, he wrote :

" Dear Pug,
                " You ask me what I think about sending Ned
out here. Well, there's no opening that I can see for a gym.
But work, that's another question, there's more than
enough. I am at work at a place called Gum Tree Valley,
clearing, but we came up to Tom's Aunt's place last week,
to help, and we've been shearing. At least I haven't. I've
been the chap who tars. You splash tar on like paint when
the shearers make a mis-fire and gash the poor brutes and
curse *you*. Lord, don't they curse, if the boss isn't round.
He's got a grey beard and dribbles on it, and the flies get
caught in it and buzz as if it was a spider's web. He
makes everyone work from morn till night like the Devil.
Gosh, if it wasn't that it is only for a short spell, I'd *get*.
Don't you worry, up-country folk know how to get your
tucker's worth out of you all right. To-day, the Sabbath,
we had a rest. I don't think ! We washed our clothes.
Talk about a goodly pile ! Only a rumour. For the old
man fetched along his vests and pants, and greasy overalls
and aprons, his socks, his slimy hanks and night-shirt.
Imagine our horror. He's Tom's Aunt's husband, and has
no sons, only herds of daughters, so we had to do it. We
scrubbed 'em with horse-brushes on the stones. Jinks,
but I rubbed some holes in 'em !

" But cheer up. I'm not grumbling. I like getting
experience as it is called.

" I mean to take up land and have a place of my own
some day, then you and Ned could visit me and we could
have some fun with the gloves. Lennie says I'm like a
kangaroo shaping and punching at nothing, so I got a cow's
bladder and blew it up and tied it to a branch, and I batter
on it. Must have something to hit. You know kangaroos
shape up and make a punch. They are pretty doing that.
We have a baby one, Joey, and it takes a cup in its little
hands and drinks. Honest to God it's got *hands*, you never
saw such a thing.

" Kindest regards to your old woman and Ned. Lord
only knows how I've missed you, and pray that some day

I will be fortunate enough to meet you again. Until then
" Farewell.

" A Merry Xmas and a Glad New Year, by the time you
get this. Think of me in the broiling heat battling with
sheep, their Boss, and the flies, and you'll think of me
true.

" Ever your sincere friend,

" JACK."

v

As the time for returning from camp drew near, Jack
dwelt more and more on this question of the future—of
taking up land. He wished so often that life could always
be a matter of camping, land-clearing, kangaroo hunting,
shearing, and generally messing about. But deep underneath himself he knew it couldn't : not for him at least.
Plenty of fellows lived all their life messing from camp to
camp and station to station. But himself—sooner or later
he would have to bite on to something. He'd have to plunge
into that cold water of responsible living, some time or
other.

He asked Tom about it.

" You must make up y' mind what you want to go in
for, cattle, sheep, horses, wheat, or mixed farming like
us," said Tom. " Then you can go out to select. But it's
no good before you know what you want."

Jack was surprised to find how little information he got
from the men he mixed with.   They knew their jobs :
teamsters knew about teams, and jobs on the mill; the
timber workers knew hauling and sawing; township people
knew trading; the general hands knew about hunting and
bush-craft and axe handling; and farmers knew what was
under their nose, but nothing of the laws of the land, or
how he himself was to get a start.

At last he found a small holder who went out as a hired
man after he had put in the seed on his own land. And
this, apparently, was how Jack would have to start. The
man brought out various grubby Government papers, and
handed them over.

Jack had a bad time with them : Government reports,

blue books, narratives of operations.   But he swotted grimly. And he made out so much :

1. Any reputable immigrant over 21 years could procure fifty acres of unimproved rural Crown land open for selection ; if between the ages of 14 and 21, twenty-five acres.

2. Such land must be held by " occupation certificate," deemed transferable only in case of death, etc.

3. The occupation certificate would be exchanged for a grant at the end of five years, or before that time, providing the land had been enclosed with a substantial fence and at least a quarter cultivated. But if at the end of the five years the above conditions, or any of them, had not been observed, the lots should revert to the Crown.

4. Country land was sub-divided into agricultural and pastoral, either purchasable at the sum of 10s. an acre, or leased : the former for eight years at the nominal sum of 1s. an acre, with the right of purchase, the latter for one year at annual rental of 2s. per hundred acres, with presumptive renewal; or five pounds per 1000 acres with rights.

Jack got all this into his mind, and at once loathed it. He loathed the thought of an " occupation certificate." He loathed the thought of being responsible to the Government for a piece of land. He almost loathed the thought of being tied to land at all. He didn't want to *own* things; especially land, that is like a grave to you as soon as you do own it. He didn't want to own anything. He simply couldn't bear the thought of being tied down. Even his own unpacked luggage he had detested.

But he had started in with this taking-up land business, so he thought he'd try an easy way to get through with it.

" Dear Father,
            " I could take up land on my own account now if you sent a few hundred pounds for that purpose, per Mr George. He would pay the deposit and arrange it for me. I have my eye on one or two improved farms falling idle shortly down this Gum Valley district, which is very flourishing. When they fall vacant on account of

settlers dropping them, they can be picked up very cheap.

" I hope you are quite well, as I am at present.

" Your affec. son,

" JACK."

Jack spent his sixpence on this important document, and forgot all about it. And in the dead end of the hot summer, just in the nick of time, he got this answer.

Sea View Terrace,
Bournemouth,
2/2/'83.

" Dear Jack,

" Thank you for your most comprehensive letter of 30/11/82. It is quite impossible for me to raise several hundreds of pounds, or for the matter of that, one hundred pounds, in this off-hand manner. I don't want to be hard on you, but we want you to be independent as soon as possible. We have so many expenses, and I have no intention of sinking funds in the virgin Australian wild, at any rate until I see a way clear to getting some return for my money, in some form of safe interest accruing to you at my death. You must not expect to run before you can walk. Stay where you are and learn what you can till your year is up, and then we will see about a jackeroo's job, at which, your mother tells me, you will earn £1 a week, instead of our having to pay it for you.

" We all send felicitations.

" Your affectionate father,

" G. B. GRANT."

But this is running ahead. It is not yet Christmas, 1882.

CHAP : VIII. HOME FOR CHRISTMAS

i

It was a red hot Christmas that year—'ot, 'ot, 'ot, all day
long. Good Lord, how hot it was!—till blessed evening.
Sun-down brought blessings in its trail. After six o'clock
you would sense the breeze coming from the sea. Whispering, sighing, hesitating. Then, puff! there it was. Delicious,
sweet, it seemed to save one's life.

It had been splendid out back, but it was nice to get
home again and sit down to regular meals, have clean
clothes and sheets to one's bed. To have your ironing and
cooking done for you, and sit down to dinner at a big table
with fresh, hailstorm-patterned tablecloth on it. There
was a sense almost of glory in a big, white, glossy hailstorm
table-cloth. It lifted you up.

Mr Ellis had taken Gran away for the time, so the place
seemed freer, noisier. There was nothing to keep quiet
for. It was holiday—*pinkie*, the natives called it; the
fierce mid-summer Christmas. Everybody was allowed to
" spell " a great deal.

Tom and Jack were roasted like Red Indians, rather uncouth, and more manly. At first they seemed rather
bumptious, thinking themselves very much men. Jack
could now ride his slippery saddle in fine style, and handle
a rope or an axe, and shoot straight. He knew jarrah,
karri, eucalyptus, sandal, wattle, peppermint, banksia, she-
oaks, pines, paper-back and gum trees; he had learned to
tan a kangaroo hide, pegging it on to a tree; he had looked
far into the wilderness, and seen the beyond, and been
seized with a desire to explore it; he had made excursions
over " likely places," with hammer and pick, looking for
gold. He had hunted and brought home meat, had trapped
and destroyed many native cats and dingoes. He had lain
awake at night and listened to the more-porks, and in the
early morning had heard with delight the warbling of the
timeline and thickhead thrushes that abounded round the
camp, mingled with the noises of magpies, tits, and wrens.
He had watched the manœuvres of willy-wagtails, and of a

brilliant variety of birds : weavers, finches, parrots, honey-eaters, and pigeons. But the banded wrens and blue-birds were his favourites in the bush world.

Well, on such a hero as this, the young home-hussies Monica and Grace had better not look too lightly. He was so grand they could hardly reach him with a long pole.

" An' how many emus did y' see ? " asked Og. For lately at Wandoo they had had a plague of emus, which got into the paddocks and ate down the sheeps' food-stuff, and then got out again by running at the fences and bashing a way through.

Jack had never seen one.

" Never seen an emu ! " Even little Ellie shrilled in derisive amazement. " Monica, he's *never seen an emu !*"

Already they had snipped the tip off the high feather he had in his cap.

But he was still a hero, and Lennie followed him round like a satellite, while the girls were obviously *thrilled* at having Tom and him back again. They would giggle and whisper behind Bow's back, and wherever he was, they were always sauntering out to stand not far off from him. So that, of course, their thrill entered also into Jack's veins, he felt a cocky young lord, a young life-master. This suited him very well.

But there was no love-making, of course. They all laughed and joked together over the milking and pail-carrying and feeding and butter-making and cheese-making and everything, and life was a happy delirium.

They had waited for Tom to come home, to rob the bees. Tom hated the bees and they hated him, but he was staunch. Veils, bonnets, gloves, gaiters were produced, and off they all set, in great joy at their own appearance, with gong, fire, and endless laughter. Tom was to direct from a distance : he stood afar " Smoking them off." Grace and Monica worked merrily among the hives, manipulating the boxes which held the comb, lifting them on to the milk pans to save the honey, and handing the pans to the boys to carry in.

" Oooh," yelled Tom suddenly, " Oooh ! "

A cloud of angry bees was round his head. Down went his fire-protector—a tin full of smouldering chips—down went flappers and bellows as with a shriek he beat the air.

The more he beat the darker the venomous cloud. Crippled with terror, he ran on shaking legs. The girls and youngsters were paralysed with joy. They swarmed after him shrieking with laughter. His head was completely hidden by bees, but his arms like windmills waved wildly to and fro. He dashed into the cubby, but the bees went with him. He appeared at the window for a moment, showing a demented face, then he jumped out, and the bees with him. Leaping the drain gap and yelling in terror, he made for the house. The bees swung with him and the children after. Jack and the girls stood speechless, looking at one another. Monica had on man's trousers with an old uniform buttoned close to her neck, workmen's socks over her shoes and trouser-ends, and a Chinaman's hat with a veil over it, netted round her head like a meat-safe. Jack noticed that she was funny. Suddenly, somehow, she looked mysterious to him, and not just the ordinary image of a girl. Suddenly a new cavern seemed to open before his eyes; the mysterious, fascinating cavern of the female unknown. He was not definitely conscious of this. But seeing Monica there in the long white flannel trousers and the Chinaman's hat meat-safe over her face, something else awoke in him, a new awareness of a new wonder. He had but lately stood on the inward ranges and looked inland into the blue, vast mystery of the Australian interior. And now with another opposite vision he saw an opposite mystery opposing him : the mystery of the female, the young female there in her grotesque garb.

A new awareness of Monica began to trouble him.

"Oooh! Oooh! Ma! Ma! Ma!" Out rushed Tom straight from the kitchen door, the bees still with him. Straight he dashed to the garden, and to the well in the middle. He loosed the windlass and stood on the coping screaming while the bucket clanged and clashed to the bottom. Then Tom seized the rope, and turning his legs round it, slid silently into the hidden, cool, dark depths.

The children shrieked with bliss, Jack and the girls rocked with helpless laughter, convulsed by this last exit.

The bees were puzzled. They poised buzzbee fashion above the well-head, explored the mouth of the shaft, and rose again and hovered. Then they began to straggle away. They melted into the hot air.

And now the girls and Jack drew up from the well a raging
and soaking Tom. Drew him up uncertainly, wobblingly, a
terrible weight on the straining, creaking windlass. Ma
and Ellie took him in hand and daubed him a sublime blue :
like an ancient Briton, Grace said. Then they gave him
bread and jam and a cup of tea.

Then occurred another honey-bee tragedy. Ellie, who
had done nothing at all to the bees, suddenly shrieked
loudly and ran pelting round screaming : " I've got a bee
in my head ! I've got a bee in my head ! " Monica caught
and held her, while Jack took the bee, a big drone, out
of the silky meshes of her honey hair. And as he lifted his
eyes he met the yellow eyes of Monica. And the two
exchanged a moment's look of intimacy and communication
and secret shame, so that they both went away avoiding
one another.

ii

On New Year's Eve there was always a foregathering
of the settlers at the Wandoo homestead. They must fore-
gather somewhere, and Wandoo was the oldest and most
flourishing place. It occupied the banks of the so-called
Avon River, which was mostly just a great dry bed of
stones. But it had plenty of fresh water in the soaks and
wells, among the scorched rocks, and these wells were fed
by underground springs, not brackish, as is so often the
case. Wandoo was therefore a favoured place.

" What am I to wear ? " said Jack aghast, when he
heard of the affair.

" Anything," said Tom.

" Nothing," said Len.

" Your new riding suit," said Monica, who had begun to
assume airs of proprietorship over him. " And you needn't
say anything, young Len," she continued venomously,
" because you've got to wear that new holland suit Ma
got you from England, *and* boots and socks as well."

" It's awful. Oo-er ! It's awful ! " groaned Lennie.

It was. A tight-fitting brown holland suit with pants
halfway down the shin and many pearl-buttons across the
stomach, the coat with a stiff stand-up collar and rigid
seams. Harry had a similar rig, but the twins out-did

Solomon in sailor suits with gold braid and floppy legs. At least they started in glory.

Tom in his father's old tennis-flannels and a neat linen jacket looked quite handsome. But when he saw Jack in his real pukka riding rig, he exclaimed :

" God Almighty, but you've got the goods ! "

" A bit too dashing ? " asked Jack anxiously.

" Not on your life ! You'll do fine. Reds all go in for riding breeks and coats as near sporting dog's yank as they k'n get 'm. There's a couple o' white washing suits o' Dad's as he's grown out of, as I'll plank up in the loft to change into to-night. We can't come in this here cubby again. Once we leave it it'll be jumped by all the women and children from round the country, to put their things in."

" Won't they go into the house ? "

" Hallelujah, no ! Only relations go upstairs. Quality into the dyin' room. Yahoos anywhere, and the ladies always bag our cubby."

" Lor ! "

But it had to be so. For the New Year's chivoo the settlers all saved up, and they all dressed up. By ten o'clock the place was like a fair ground. Horses of all sorts nosing their feed bags ; conveyances of all sorts unhitched ; girls all muslin and ribbon ; boys with hats on at an angle, and boots on ; men in clean shirts and brilliant ties ; mothers in frill and furbelow, with stiffly-starched little children half hidden under sunbonnets ; old dames and ancient patriarchs, young, bearded farmers, and shaven civilians ridden over from York. Children rushing relentlessly in the heat, amid paper bags, orange peel, concertina playing, baskets of victuals and fruit, canvas, rubbish and nuts all over the scorched grass. Christmas !

Tom had asked Jack to organise a cricket eleven to play against the Reds. The Reds were dangerous opponents, and the dandies of the day. In riding breeches made India fashion, with cotton gaiters, and rubber-soled shoes, white shirts, and broad-brimmed hats, they looked a handsome colonial set. And they had a complete eleven.

Tom was sitting on a bat bemoaning his fate. He had only five reliable men.

" Aw, shut up ! " said Lennie. " Somebody'll turn up. Who's comin' in at the gate now ? Ain't it the parson from York, and five gents what can handle a bat. Hell! ain't my name cockadoodle!"

In top hats and white linen suits these gentlemen had ridden their twenty-five miles for a game. What price the Reds now!

Tom's side was in first, Easu and Rosy Ellis bowling. Easu, big, loose, easy, looked strange and *native*, as if he belonged to the natural salt of the earth there. He seemed at home, like an emu or a yellow mimosa tree. He was a bowler of repute. But somehow Jack could not bear to see him palm the ball before he bowled : could not bear to watch it. Whereas fat Ross Ellis, the other bowler, spitting on his hand and rolling the ball in elation after getting the wicket of the best man from York, Jack didn't mind him. But unable to watch Easu, he walked away across the paddock, among the squatting mothers whose terror was the flying leather ball.

" Your turn at the wickets, Mr. Grant," called the excited red-faced parson, who, Lennie declared, " couldn't preach less or act more."

" We're eight men out for twenty-six rounds, so smack at 'em. If ye can get the loose end on Ross, do it. I'll be in t'other end next and stop 'em off Easu. I come in right there as th' useful block."

Jack was excited. And when he was excited, phrases always came up in his mind. He had the sun in his eyes, but the bat felt good.

" If a gentleman sees bad, he ignores it. He——"
Here comes the ball from that devil Easu!
How's that!
" Finds good and fans it to flame—fans it to— "
Joe Low, that stripling, had the other wicket.
Smack! Jack scored the first run off Easu, running for his life.

" You can be a gentleman even if you are a bush-whacker."

Nine wickets had fallen to Easu for twenty-seven runs, and Easu was elated. Then the parson came forth and stood opposite Jack. He at once whacked Ross' ball suc-cessfully, for three. Jack hitched his belt after the run, and hit out for another.

Smack! No need to run that time. It was a boundary.

Lennie's voice outside yelling admiration roused his soul,
as did Easu's yelling angrily to Ross : " You give that
ball to Sam, this over. You blanky idjut ! "

Ross picked up the returning leather, and sent down a
sulky grubber which Jack naturally skied. Herbert, placed
at a point in the shade, came out to catch it, and missed.

Somehow the parson had steadied Jack's spirit. And
when, in a crisis, Jack got his spirit steadied, it seemed to
him he could get a semi-magical grip over a situation.
Almost as if he could alter the swerve of the ball by his pure,
clairvoyant *will*. So it seemed. And keyed up against the
weird, handsome, native Easu, as if by a magic of will
Jack held the wicket and got the runs. It was one of those
subtle battles which are beyond our understanding. And
Jack won.

But Easu got him out in the end. In the first innings,
a terrific full pitch came down crash over his head on to the
middle wicket, when he had made his first half-century;
that was Easu; and Easu stumped him out in the second
innings, for twenty.

Nevertheless the Reds were beaten by a margin of sixteen
runs, before the parson and the gentlemen in top hats set
off for their long and dusty ride to York.

iii

Jack hated the Reds with all the wholesale hatred of
eighteen. There they were, all of them, swaggering round
as if the place belonged to them, taking everything and
giving nothing. Their peculiar air of assertion was particularly maddening, in contrast with the complete lack of
assumption on the part of the other Australians. It was as
if the Reds had made up their minds, all of them, to leave
a bruise on everything they touched. They were all big
men, and all older than Jack. Easu must have been over
thirty, and unmarried, with a bad reputation among the
women of the colony. Yet, apparently, he could always
find a girl. That slow, laconic assurance of his, his peculiar,
meaning smile as he drifted up loose-jointed to a girl,
seemed nearly always to get through. The women watched him out
of the corner of their eye. They didn't *like* him. But they
felt his power. And that was perhaps even more effective.

For he had power. And this was what Jack felt lacking in himself. Jack had quick, intuitive understanding, and a quick facility. But he had not Easu's power. Sometimes Easu could look really handsome, strolling slowly across to some girl with a peculiar rolling gait that distinguished him, and smiling that little, meaningful, evil smile. Then he looked handsome, and as if he belonged to another race of men, men who were like small-headed demons out to destroy the world.

" I'm fighting him," thought Jack. " I wouldn't have a good opinion of myself if I didn't."

For he saw in Easu a malevolent priniciple, a kind of venom.

Ross Ellis, the youngest of the Reds, was old enough to be joining the mounted police force in a few days, and Mr. Ellis had sent up a strong chestnut mount for him, from the coast. Easu, tall, broad, sinewy, with sinewy powerful legs and small buttocks, was sitting close on the prancing chestnut, showing off, his malevolence seeming to smile under his blonde beard, and his blue, rivet eyes taking in everything. All the time he went fooling the simple farmers who had come to the sports, raising a laugh where he could, and always a laugh of derision.

" Tom," said Jack it last, " couldn't you boss it a bit over those Reds? It's *your* place, it's *your* house, not theirs. Go on, put them down a bit, do."

" Aw," said Tom. " They're older'n me, and the place by rights belongs to them : leastways they think so. And they *are* crack sportsmen."

" Why they're not ! Look at Easu parading on that police horse your father sent up from the coast ! And look at all the other cockeys getting ready to compete against him in the riding events. They haven't a chance, and he knows it."

" He won't risk taking that police horse over the jumps, don't you fret."

" No, but he has the pick of your stable, and he'll beat all the others while you stand idling by. Why should *he* be cock of the walk ? "

" Why," cried Lennie breaking in, " I could beat anyfin on Lucy. But Tom won't let me go in against the other chaps, will you, Tom ? "

Tom smiled. He had a plain brick-red face, patient and unchanging, with white teeth, and brown, sensitive eyes. When he smiled he had a great charm. But he did not often smile, and his mouth was marred by the look so many men develop in Australia, facing the bush : that lipless look, which Jack, as he grew more used to it, came to call the suffering look. As if they had bitten and been bitten hard, perhaps too hard.

" Well, Nipper," he said after a moment's hesitation; " if you finds them Waybacks has it between 'em, you stand out. But y'c'n have Lucy if you like, an' if y' beat the *Reds*—y'c'n beat 'em."

" That's what *I* mean all right ! " cried Lennie, capering. " I savvy O.K. I'll give 'em googlies and sneaks an' leg-breaks, y' see if I don't, an' even up for 'em."

iv

Monica came up and took Jack's arm with sudden impulsive affection, on this very public day. Drawing him away, she said :

" Come and sit down a bit under the Bay Fig, Jack. I want to rest. All these people tearing us in two from morning till night."

Jack found himself thrilling to the girl's touch, to his own surprise and disgust. He flushed slowly, and went on stiff legs, hoping nobody was looking at him. Nobody was looking *specially*, of course. But Monica kept hold of his arm, with her light, tense girlish hand, and he found it difficult to walk naturally. And again the queer electric thrills went through him, from that light blade of her hand.

She was very lovely to-day, with a sort of winsomeness, a sort of fierce appeal. As a matter of fact, she had been flirting dangerously with Red Easu, till she was a bit scared. And she had been laughing and fooling with Hal Stockley— otherwise Pink-eye Percy—whom all the girls were mad about, but who didn't affect her seriously. Easu affected her, though. And she didn't really like him. That was why she had come for Jack, whom she liked very much indeed. She felt so safe and happy with him. And she loved his delicate, English, virgin quality, his shyness and his natural purity. He was purer than she was. So she wanted to make him in love with her. She was sure he *was* in love with her. But it was such a shy, unwilling love, she was half annoyed.

So she leaned forward to him, with her fierce young face and her queer, yellow, glowering eyes, not far from his, and she seemed to yearn to him with a yearning like a young leopard. Sometimes she touched his hand, and sometimes, laughing and showing her small, pointed teeth winsomely, she would look straight into his eyes, as if searching for something. And he flushed with a dazed sort of delight, unwilling to be overpowered by the new delight, yet dazed by it, even to the point of forgetting the other people and the party, and Easu on the chestnut horse.

But he made no move. When she touched his hand, though his eyes shone with a queer suffused light, he would not take her hand in his. He would not touch her. He would not make any definite response. To all she said, he answered in simple monosyllables. And there he sat, suffused with delight, yet making no move whatsoever.

Till at last Monica, who was used to defending herself, was niffed. She thought him a muff. So she suddenly rose and left him. Went right away. And he was very much surprised and chagrined, feeling that somehow it wasn't possible, and feeling as if the sun had gone out of the sky.

v

The sun really was low in the heavens. The breeze came at last from the sea and freshened the air and lifted the sweet crushed scent of the trampled dry grass. It was time for the last events of the sports. Everybody was eager, revived by the approach of evening, and Jack felt the drunkenness of new delight upon him. He was still vague, however, and unwilling even to think of Monica, much less seek her out.

The black-boys' event, with unbroken buckjumpers, was finishing down by the river. Joe Low, with a serious face but sparkling eyes, went riding by on a brumby colt he had caught and broken himself. Jack sat alone under a tree, waiting for the flat race, in which he was entered, and feeling sure of himself.

Easu came dancing up on the raw chestnut that had been

sent up from the coast along with the police horse. He
wore spurs, and had a long parrot-feather in his hat.

"Here you, young Pommy Grant," he said to Jack.
"Ketch hold of me bit while I fix me girths a bit tighter,
and then you c'n hold your breath while I show them Cornseeds what."

He had a peculiarly insolent manner towards Jack. The
latter nevertheless held the frothy chestnut while Easu
swung out of the saddle and hitched up the girth. As he
bent there beside the horse, Jack noticed his broad shoulders
and narrow waist and small, hard, tense hips. Yes, he was
a man. But ugh! what an objectionable one! Especially
the slight hateful smile of derision on the red face and in the
light-blue, small-pupilled eyes.

But he clipped into the saddle again, and once more it
was impossible not to admire his seat, his close, fine, clean,
small seat in the saddle. There was no spread about him
there. And the power of the long, muscular thighs. Then
once more he dismounted, leaving Jack to hold the bridle
of the chestnut whilst he himself strolled away.

The other farmers were waiting on their horses, so serious
and quiet : in their patience and unobtrusiveness, so gentlemanly, Jack thought. So unlike the assertive, jeering Easu.

Lennie came up and whipped the pin out of Jack's favour.
It was a rosette of yellow ribbon, shiny as a buttercup, that
Monica had made him.

"Here, what're you doing?" he cried.

"Aw, shut it. Keep still!" said Lennie.

And slipping round, he pushed the pin, point downward,
into the back saddle-pad of the chestnut Jack was holding.
That wasn't fair. But Jack let be.

The judge called his warning, the Cornseeds lined up,
along with Joe Low and a young yellow-faced dairyman and
a slender skin-hunter, and a woolly old stockman. Easu
came and took his chafing horse, but did not mount.

"One!" Easu swung up, standing in his stirrups,
scarce touching the saddle-seat.

"Two! Three!" and the sharp crack of a pistol.

Away went the scraggy brumby and Joe, and, like a
torrent, the dairyman and the skin-hunter and the stockman. But the chestnut had never heard a pistol shot before,
and was jumping round wildly.

" Blood and pace, mark you ! " said the judge, waving towards the chestnut. " Them cockeys does their best on what they got, but watch that chestnut under Red Ellis. It's a pleasure to see good horse-flesh like them Ellises brings up to these parts."

Easu, seeing the field running well and far ahead, wheeled his mount on to the track at that minute, and sat down.

The chestnut sat up, stopped, bucked, threw Easu, and then galloped madly away. It was all so sudden and somehow unnatural, that everybody was stunned. Easu rose and stared, with hell in his face, after the running chestnut. People began to laugh aloud.

" Oh, Gawd my fathers ! " murmured Tom in Jack's ear. " Think of Easu getting a toss ! Easu letting *any* horse get the soft side of him ! Oh, my Gawd, if I'm not sorry for Easu when that crowd o' Reds sets on to him with their tongues to-morrow."

" I'm jolly glad," said Jack complacently.

" So am I," said Lennie. " An' I did it, an' I wish it had killed him. I put a pin under the saddle-crease, Tom. Don't look at me, y'needn't. I've had one up again 'im for a long time, for Jack's sake. D'y' know what he did? He put Jack on that Stampede stallion, when Jack hadn't been on our place a fortnight. So he did. An' if Jack had been killed, who'd ha' called him a murderer? Zah, one of the blacks told *me*. And nobody durst tell you, cos they durstn't."

" On Stampede ! " exclaimed Tom, going yellow, and hell coming into his brown eyes. " An' a new chum my father trusted to him to show him round."

" Oh, well," said Jack.

" The —— ! " said Tom : and that was final.

Then after a moment :

" If the Reds is going over the jumps, you go and get Lucy, Len."

" I likes your sperrit, Tom. I was goin' to anyway, case they get that dark 'oss." Lennie threw off his coat, hat, and tie, then sat on the trodden brown grass to take off his boots and stockings. Thus stripped, he stood up and hitched his braces looser, remarking :

" Jack Grant said he'd bash Easu's head for 'im if he said

anything to me after I beat 'im over the jumps, so I was goin' to risk it anyway."

Jack had said no such thing, but was prepared to take the hint.

The chestnut had been caught and tied up. Down the field they could see Easu persuading Sept to ride a smart piebald filly that had been brought in. Sept was the thinnest of the Reds. The jumping events continued away on the left, the sun was almost setting.

" Hurry up there for the final ! " called the judge.

Sept came up on the delicate piebald filly which they had brought over from their own place. She was dark chestnut, and with flames of pure white, she seemed dazzling.

" That's the dark 'oss I mentioned ! " said Len. " Gosh, but me heart is beatin' ! It'll be a real match between me and him, for that there filly can jump like a 'roo, I've watched 'er."

Joe Low rode up to the jumping yard, and lifted his brumby over. The filly danced down and followed. Lennie was in the saddle like a cat and Lucy went over the rail without effort.

When the rail was at five feet two, Joe Low's brumby was done. Lucy clipped the rail and the filly cleared it. Sept brought his creature round to the judge, with raised eyebrows.

" No y' don't," yelled Lennie, riding down the track hell for leather, and Lucy went over like a swallow. Sept laughed, and came down to the rail that was raised an inch. The filly sailed it, but hit the bar. Lucy baulked. Len swung her round and came again. A perfect over.

Next ! The filly, snorting and frothing, tore down, jibbed, and was sworn at loudly by Easu standing near. Sept whipped and spurred her over.

But at that rail, raised to five feet nine, she would not be persuaded, though Lucy cleared it with a curious casual ease. The filly would not take it.

" Say, Mister ! " called Lennie when he knew he was winner. " Raise that barrier five inches and see us bound it."

He made his detour, brought Lucy along on twinkling feet, and cleared it prettily.

The roar of delight from the crowd sent Easu mad. Jack

kept an eye on him, in case he meant mischief. But Easu
only went away to where the niggers were still trying out
the buckjumpers. Taking hold of a huge rogue of a mare,
he sprang on her back and came bucking all along the track,
apparently to give a specimen of horsemanship. The crowd
watched the queer massive pulsing up and down of the man
and the powerful bucking horse, all in a whirl of long hair,
like some queer fountain of life. And there was Monica
watching Easu's cruel, changeless face, that seemed to have
something fixed and eternal in it, amid all that heaving.

Jack felt he had a volcano inside him. He knew that
Stampede had been caught again, and was being led about
down there, securely roped, as part of the show. Down
there among the outlaws.

Away ran Jack. Anything rather than be beaten by Easu.
But as he ran, he kept inside him that queer little flame of
white-hot calm which was his invincibility.

He patted Stampede's arching neck, and told Sam to
saddle him. Sam showed the whites of his eyes, but obeyed,
and Stampede took it. Jack stood by, intense in his own
cool calmness. He didn't care what happened to him. If
he was to be killed he would be killed. But at the same
time, he was not reckless. He watched the horse with
mystical closeness, and glanced over the saddle and bridle
to see if they were all right.

Then, swift and light, he mounted and knew the joy of
being a horseman, the thrill of being a real horseman. He
had the gift, and he knew it. If not the gift of sheer power,
like Easu, who seemed to overpower his horse as he rode it,
Jack had the gift of adjustment. He adjusted himself to
his horse. Intuitively, he yielded to Stampede, up to a
certain point. Beyond that certain flexible point, there
would be no yielding, none, and never.

Jack came bucking along in Easu's wake, on a much
wilder horse. But though Stampede was wild and wicked,
he never exerted his last efforts. He bucked like the devil.
But he never let himself altogether go. And Jack seemed to
be listening with an inward ear to the animal, listening to
it's passion. After all, it was a live creature, to be mastered,
but not to be overborne. Intuitively, the boy gave way
to it as much as possible. But he never for one moment
doubted his own mastery over it. In his mastery there must

be a living tolerance. This his instinct told him. And the stallion, bucking and sitting up, seemed somehow to accept it.

For, after all, if the horse had gone really wicked, absolutely wicked, it would have been too much for Master Jack. What he depended on was the bit of response the animal was capable of. And this he knew.

He found he could sit the stallion with much greater ease than before. And that strange, powerful life beneath him and between his thighs, heaving and breaking like some enormous alive wave, exhilarated him with great exultance, the exultance in the power of life.

Monica's eyes turned from the red, fixed, overbearing face of Easu, to the queer, abstract, radiant male face of Jack, and a great pang went through her heart, and a cloud came over her brow. The boy balanced on the trembling, spurting stallion, looking down at it with dark-blue, wide, dark-looking eyes, and thinking of nothing, yet feeling so much; his face looking soft and warm with a certain masterfulness that was more animal than human, like a centaur, as if he were one blood with the horse, and had the centaur's superlative horse-sense, its non-human power, and wisdom of hot blood-knowledge. She watched the boy, and her brow darkened and her face was fretted as if she were denied something. She wanted to look again at Easu, with his fixed hard will that excited her. But she couldn't. The queer soft power of the boy was too much for her, she could not save herself.

So they rode, the two men, and all the people watched them, as the sun went down in the wild empty sea westward from hot Australia.

CHAP : IX.   NEW YEAR'S EVE

i

NEW Year's Eve was celebrated Scotch style, at " Wandoo."
It was already night, and Jack and Tom had been round
seeing if the visitors had everything they wanted. Ma and
a few select guests were still in the kitchen. The cold
collation in the parlour still waited majestically. The twins
and Harry were no longer visible : they had subsided on
their stomachs by the wood-pile, in the hot evening, and
found refuge in sleep; for all the world like sailors sunk
dilapidated and demoralised, after a high old spree. But
Ellie and Baby were at their zenith. Having been kept out
of the ruck most carefully upstairs, they were now produced
at their best. Mr. Ellis was again away in Perth, seeing the
doctor.

Tom and Jack went into the loft and changed into clean
white duck. They came forth like new men, jerking their
arms in the stiff starched sleeves. And they proceeded to
light the many chinese lanterns hung in the barn, till the
great place was mellow with soft light. Already in the fore-
noon they had scraped candle ends on to the floor, and
rubbed them in. Now they rubbed in the wax a little more,
to get the proper slipperiness.

The light brought the people, like moths. Of course the
Reds were there, brazen as brass. They, too, had changed
into white suits, tight round the calf and hollow at the
waist, and, for the moment, with high collars rising to their
ears above the black cravats. Also they sported elastic-
sided boots of patent leather, whereas most of the other
fellows were in their heavy hob-nailed boots, nicely blacked,
indeed, but destitute of grace. With their hair brushed
down in a curl over their foreheads, and their beards brushed
apart, their strong sinewy bodies filling out the white duck,
they felt absolutely invincible, and almost they looked it.
For Jack was growing blind to the rustic absurdities,
blinded by the animal force of these Australians.

Jack sat down by Herbert, who was pleasant and mild
after his illness, always a little shy with the English boy.

But the other Reds had taken possession of the place. Their bounce and their brass were astounding. Jack watched them in wonder at their aggressive self-assertion. They were real bounders, more crude and more bouncy than ever the Old Country could produce. But that was Australian. The bulk of the people, perhaps, were dumb and unassuming. But there was always a proportion of real brassy bounders, ready to walk over you and jump in your stomach, if you'd let them.

Easu had constituted himself Master of the Ceremonies, and we know what an important post that is, in a country bean-feast. Wherever he was, he must be in the front, bossing and hectoring other people. He had appointed his brothers " stewards." The Reds were to run the show. There was to be but one will : the will of the big, loose-jointed, domineering Easu, with his reddish blonde beard brushed apart and his keen eyes spying everything with a slight jeer.

Most of the guests, of course, were as they had been all day, in their Sunday suits or new dungarees. Joe Low, trim in a clean cotton jacket, sat by the great open doors very seriously blowing notes out of an old brass cornet, that had belonged to his father, a retired sergeant of the Foot. Near him, a half-caste Huck was sliding a bow up and down a yellow-looking fiddle, while other musicians stood with their instruments under their arms. Outside in the warm night bearded farmers smoked and talked. Mammas sat on the forms round the barn, and the girls, most of them fresh and gay in billowy cotton frocks, clustered around in excitement. It was the great day of all the year.

For the rest, most of the young men were leaning holding up the big timber supports of the barn, or framing the great opening of the sliding doors, which showed the enormous dark gap of the naked night.

Fire-eating Easu waved energetically to Joe, who blew a blast on the cornet. This done, the strong but " common " Australian voice of Easu, shouted effectively :
" Take partners. Get ready for the Grand March."

For of course he plumed himself on doing everything in " style," everything grand and correct, this Australian who so despised the effete Old Country. The rest of the Reds straight away marched to the sheepish ánd awkward fellows who stood propped up against any available prop, seized them by the arm, and rushed them up to some equally sheepish maiden. And, instead of resenting it, the poor clowns were glad at being forced into company. They grinned and blushed and the girls giggled and bridled as they coupled and arranged themselves, two by two, close behind one another.

A blast of music. Easu seized Monica, who was self-consciously waiting on the arm of another young fellow. He just flung his arm around her waist and heaved her to the head of the column. Then the procession set off, Easu in front with his arm round Monica's waist, he shining with his own brass and self-esteem, she looking falsely demure. After them came the other couples, self-conscious but extremely pleased with themselves, slowly marching round the barn.

Jack, who had precipitated himself into the night rather than be hauled into action by one of the Red stewards, stood and looked on from afar, feeling out of it. He felt out in the cold. He hated Easu's common, gloating self-satisfaction, there at the head with Monica. Red cared nothing about Monica, really. Only she was the star of the evening, the chief girl, so he had got her. She was the chief girl for miles around. And that was enough for Easu. He was determined to leave his mark on her.

After the March, the girls went back to their mammas, the youths to their shoulder-supports; and, following a pause, Easu again came into the middle of the floor, and began bellowing instructions. He was so pleased with the sound of his own voice, when it was lifted in authority. Everybody listened with all their ears, afraid of disobeying Easu.

When the ovation was over, the boldest of the young men made a bee-line for the prettiest girls, and there was a hubbub. In a twinkling any girl whom Jack would have deigned to dance with, was monopolised, only the poorest remained. Meanwhile the stewards were busy sorting the couples into groups.

Jack could not dance. He had not intended to dance. But he didn't at all like being left out entirely, in oblivion as if he did not exist. Not at all. So he drifted towards the group of youths in the doorway. But he slid away

again as Ross Ellis plunged in, seized whom he could by
the arm, and led them off to the crude and unprepossessing
maidens left still unchosen.

He felt he would resent intensely being grabbed by the
arm and hustled into a partner by one of the Reds.

What was to be done? He seemed to be marooned in
his own isolation like some shipwrecked mariner : and he
was becoming aware of the size of his own hands and feet.
He looked for Tom. Tom was steering a stout but willing
mother into the swim, and Lennie, like a faithful little tug,
was following in his wake with a gentle but squint-eyed
girl.

Jack became desperate. He looked round quickly. Mrs.
Ellis was sitting alone on a packing-case. At the same
moment he saw Ross Ellis bearing down on him with sardonic satisfaction.

Action was quicker than thought. Jack stood bowing
awkwardly before his hostess.

" Won't you do me the honour, Mrs. Ellis? "

" Oh, dear me! Oh, dear, Jack Grant! But I believe
I will. I never thought of such a thing. But why not?
Yes, I will, it will give me great pleasure. We shall have
to lead off, you know. And I was supposed to lead with
Easu, seeing my husband isn't here. But never mind, we'll
lead off, you and I, just as well."

She rose to her feet briskly, seeming young again. Lately
Jack thought she seemed always to have some trouble on
her mind. For the moment she shook it off.

As for him, he was panic-stricken. He wished he could
ascend into heaven; or at least as high as the loft.

" You'll help me through, marm, won't you? " he said.
" This dance is new to me."

And he bowed to her, and she bowed to him, and it was
horrible. The horrible things people did for enjoyment!

" This dance is new to him," Mrs. Ellis passed over his
shoulder to a pretty girl in pink. " Help him through,
Alice."

Feeling a fool, Jack turned and met a wide smile and a
nod. He bowed confusedly.

" I'm your corner," said the girl. " I'll pass it on to
Monica, she'll be your vis-a-vis."

" Pick up partners," Easu was yelling with his domineering voice. " All in place, please ! One more couple ! One more couple ! " He was at the other end of the barn, coming forward now, looking around like a general. He was coming for his aunt.

" Ah ! " he said when he saw Mrs. Ellis and Jack. " You're dancing with Jack Grant, Aunt Jane ? Thought he couldn't dance."

And he straightway turned his back on them, looking for Monica. Monica was standing with a young man from York.

" Monica, I want you," said Easu. " You can find a girl there," he said, nodding from the young fellow to a half-caste girl with fuzzy hair. The young fellow went white. But Monica crossed over to Easu, for she was a wicked little thing, and this evening she was hating Jack Grant, the booby.

" One more couple not needed," howled Easu. " Top centre. Where are you, Aunt Jane ? Couple from here, lower centre, go to third set on left."

Easu was standing near the top. He stepped backward, and down came his heel on Jack's foot. Jack got away, but an angry light came into his eyes. His face, however, still kept that cherubic expression characteristic of it, and so ill-fitting his feelings. Easu was staring over the room, and never even looked round.

" All in place ? *Music !* " cried the M.C.

The music started with a crash and a bang, Mrs. Ellis had seized Jack's arm and was leading him into the middle of the set.

" Catch hands, Monica," she said.

He loved Monica's thin, nervous, impulsive hands. His heart went hot as he held them. But Monica wouldn't look at him. She looked demurely sideways. But he felt the electric thrill that came to him from her hands, and he didn't want to let go.

She loosed his grasp and pushed him from her.

" Get back to Ma," she whispered. " Corner with Alice."

" Oh, Lor ! " thought Jack. For he was cornered and grabbed and twisted by the girl with the wide smile, before he was let go to fall into place beside Ma, panting with a sort of exasperation.

So it continued, grabbing and twisting and twirling, all

perfectly ridiculous and undignified. Why, oh, why did human beings do it! Yet it was better than being left out. He was half-pleased with himself.

Something hard and vicious dug him in the ribs. It was the elbow of Easu, who passed skipping like a goat.

Was Easu making a dead set at him? The devil's own anger began to rise in the boy's heart, bringing up with it all the sullen dare-devil that was in him. When he was roused, he cared for nothing in earth or heaven. But his face remained cherubic.

" Follow ! " said a gentle voice. Perhaps it was all a mistake. He found himself back by Mrs Ellis, watching other folks prance. There he stood and mopped his brow, in the hot, hot night. He was wet with sweat all over. But before he could wipe his face the pink Alice had caught and twirled him, taking him unawares. He waited alert. Nothing happened. Actually peace for a few seconds.

The music stopped. Perhaps it was over. Oh, enjoyment ! Why did people do such things to enjoy themselves ? Only he would have liked to hold Monica's thin, keen hands again. The thin, keen, wild, wistful Monica. He would like to be near her.

Easu was bawling something. Figure Number Two. He could not listen to instructions in Easu's voice.

They were dancing again, and he knew no more than at first what he was doing. All a maze. A natural diffidence and a dislike of being touched by any casual stranger made dancing unpleasant to him. But he kept up. And suddenly he found himself with Monica folded in his arms, and she clinged to him with sudden fierce young abandon. His heart stood still, as he realised that not only did he want to hold her hands—he had thought it was just that; but he wanted to hold her altogether in his arms. Terrible and embarrassing thought ! He wished himself on the moon, to escape his new emotions. At the same time there was the instantaneous pang of disappointment as she broke away from him. Why could she not have stayed ! And, why, oh, why, were they both doing this beastly dancing !

He received a clean clear kick on the shin as he passed Easu. Dazed with a confusion of feelings, keenest among which perhaps was anger, he pulled up again beside Ma. And there was Monica suddenly in his arms again.

" You always go again," he said in a vague murmur.

" What did you say? " she asked archly, as she floated
from him, just at the moment when Easu jolted him
roughly. Across the little distance she was watching the hot
anger in the boy's confused, dark-blue eyes.

Another pause. More beastly instructions. Different
music. Different evolutions.

" Steady now! " he said to himself, trying to make his
way in the new figure. But what work it was! He tried
to keep his brain steady. But Ma on his arm was heavy
as lead.

And then, with great ease and perfect abandon, in spite
of her years, Ma threw herself on his left bosom and reclined
in peace there. He was overcome. She seemed absolutely
to like resting on his bosom.

" Throw out your right hand, dear boy," she whispered,
and before he knew he had done it, Easu had seized his
hand in a big, brutal, bullying grasp, and was grinding
his knuckles. And then sixteen people began to spin.

The startled agony of it made a different man of him.
For Ma was heavy as a log on his left side, clinging to him
as if she liked to cling to his body. He never quite forgave
her. And Easu had his unprotected right hand gripped in
a vice and was torturing him on purpose with the weight
and the grind. Jack's hands were naturally small, and
Easu's were big. And to be gripped by that great malicious
paw was horrible. Oh, the tension, the pain and rage of
that giddy-go-rounding, first forward, then abruptly backwards. It broke some of his innocence for ever.

But although paralytic with rage when released, Jack's
face still looked innocent and cherubic. He had that sort
of face, and that diabolic sort of stoicism. Mrs Ellis
thought : " What a nice, kind boy! but late waking up to
the facts of life! " She thought he had not even noticed
Easu's behaviour. And again she thought to herself her
husband would be jealous if he saw her. Poor old Jacob!
Aloud she said :

" The next is the last figure. You're doing very well,
Jack. You go off round the ring, now, handing the ladies
first your right and then your left hand."

He felt no desire to hand anybody his hand. But in the
middle of the ring he met Monica, and her slim grasp took

his hurt right hand, and seemed to heal it for a moment.

Easu grabbed his arm, and he saw three others, suffering fools gladly, locked arm in arm, playing soldiers, as they called it. Oh, God! Easu, much taller than Jack, was twisting his arm abominably, almost pulling it out of the socket. And Jack was saving up his anger.

It was over. "That was very kind of you, my dear boy," Mrs Ellis was saying. "I haven't enjoyed a dance so much for years."

Enjoyed! That ghastly word! Why would people insist on enjoying themselves in these awful ways! Why "enjoy" oneself at all? He didn't see it. He decided he didn't care for enjoyment, it wasn't natural to him. Too humiliating, for one thing.

Twenty steps envolved in the black skirts of Mrs Ellis, and he was politely rid of her. She was very nice. And by some mystery she had really enjoyed herself in this awful mélèe. He gave it up. She was too distant in years and experience for him to try to understand her. Did these people never have living anger, like a bright black snake with unclosing eyes, at the bottom of their souls? Apparently not.

ii

There was an interval in the dancing, and they were having games. Red was, of course, still bawling out instructions and directions, being the colonel of the feast. He was in his element, playing top sawyer.

The next game was to be "Modern Proposals." It sounded rotten to Jack. Each young man was to make an original proposal to an appointed girl. Great giggling and squirming even at the mention of it.

Easu still held the middle of the floor. Jack thought it was time to butt in. With his hands in his pockets he walked coolly into the middle of the room.

"You people don't know me, and I don't know you," he found himself announcing in his clear English voice. "Supposing I call this game."

Carried Unanimously!

The young men lined up, and Easu, after standing loose

on his legs for some time just behind Jack, went and sat down somewhat discomfited.

Jack pushed Tom on to his knees before the prettiest girl in the room—the prettiest strange girl, anyhow.   Tom, furiously embarrassed on his knees, stammered :

" I say ! There's a considerable pile o' socks wantin' darning in my ol' camp. I'd go so far as to face the parson, if you'd do 'em for me."

It was beautifully non-committal. For all the Bushies were at heart terrified lest they might by accident contract a Scotch marriage, and be held accountable for it.

Jack was amused by the odd, humorous expression of the young bush-farmers. Joe Low, scratching his head funnily, said : " I'll put the pot on, if you'll cook the stew." But the most approved proposal was that of a well-to-do young farmer who is now a J.P., and head of a prosperous family.

" Me ol' dad an' me ol' lady, they never had no daughters. They gettin' on well in years, and they kind o' fancy one. I've gotter get 'em one, quick an' lively. I've fifteen head o' cattle an' seventy-six sheep, eighteen pigs an 'a fallowin' sow. I've got one hundred an' ninety-nine acres o' cleared land, and ten improved with fruit trees. I've got forty ducks an' hens an' a flock o' geese, an' no one home to feed 'em. Meet me Sunday mornin', eight-forty sharp, at the cross roads, an' I'll be there in me old sulky to drive y'out an' show y'."

And the girl in pink, with a wide smile, answered seriously :

" I will if Mother'll let me, Mr Burton."

The next girl had been looming up like a big coal-barge. She was a half-caste, of course named Lily, and she sat aggressively forwards, her long elbows and wrists much in evidence, and her pleasant swarthy face alight and eager with anticipation. Oh, these Missioner half-castes !

Jack ordered Easu forward.

But Easu was not to be baited. He strode over, put his hand on the fuzzy head, and said in his strong voice :

" Hump y'r bluey and come home."

The laugh was with him, he had won again.

iii

They went down to the cold collation. There Jack found
other arrivals. Mary had come in via York with Gran's
spinster daughters. Also the Greenlow girls from away
back, and they made a great fuss of him. The doctor, too,
turned up. He had been missing all day, but now he strolled
back and forth, chatting politely first to one and then another, but vague and washed-out to a degree.

Jack's anger coiled to rest at the supper, for Monica was
very attentive to him. She sat next to him, found him
the best pieces, and shared her glass with him, in her quick,
dangerous, generous fashion, looking up at him with strange
wide looks of offering, so that he felt very manly and very
shy at the same time. But very glad to be near her. He
felt that it was his spell that was upon her, after all, and
though he didn't really like flirting with her there in the
public supper room, he loved her hand finding his under
the cover of her sash, and her fingers twining into his as if
she were entering into his body. Safely under the cover
of her silk sash. He would have liked to hold her again,
close, close; her agile, live body, quick as a cat's. She was
mysterious to him as some cat-goddess, and she excited him
in a queer electric fashion.

But soon she was gone again, elusive as a cat. And, of
course, she was in great request. So Jack found himself
talking to the little elderly Mary, with her dark animal's
museau. Mary was like another kind of cat : not the panther
sort, but the quiet, dark, knowing sort. She was comfortable to talk to, also, soft and stimulating.

Jack and Mary sat on the edge of the barn, in the hot
night, looking at the trees against the strange, ragged
southern sky, hearing the frogs occasionally, and fighting
the mosquitoes. Mrs Ellis also sat on the ledge not far off.
And presently Jack and Mary were joined by the doctor.
Then came Grace and Alec Rice, sitting a little farther
down, and talking in low tones. The night seemed full of
low, half-mysterious talking, in a starry darkness that
seemed pregnant with the scent and presence of the black
people. Jack often wondered why, in the night, the country
still seemed to belong to the black people, with their strange,
big, liquid eyes.

Where was Easu? Was he talking to Monica? Or to the black half-caste Lily? It might as well be the one as the other. The odd way he had placed his head on Lily's black fuzzy head, as if he were master, and she a sort of concubine. She would give him all the submission he wanted.

But then, why Monica? Monica in her white, full-skirted frock with its moulded bodice, her slender, golden-white arms and throat! Why Monica in the same class with the half-caste Lily?

Anger against Easu was sharpening Jack's wits, and curiously detaching him from his surroundings. He listened to the Australian voices and the Australian accent around him. The careless, slovenly speech in the uncontrolled, slack, caressive voices. At first he had thought the accent awful. And it *was* awful. But gradually, as he got into the rhythm of the people, he began even to sympathise with " Kytie " instead of " Katie." There was an abandon in it all—an abandon of restrictions and confining control. Why have control? Why have authority? Why not let everybody do as they liked? Why not?

That was what Australia was for, a careless freedom. An easy, unrestricted freedom. At least out in the bush. Every man to do as he liked. Easu to run round with Monica, or with the black Lily, or to kick Jack's shins in the dance.

Yes, even this. But Jack had scored it up. He was going to have his own back on Easu. He thought of Easu with his hand on the black girl's fuzzy head. That would be just like Easu. And afterwards to want Monica. And Monica wouldn't really mind about the black girl. Since Easu was Easu.

Sitting there on the barn ledge, Jack in a vague way understood it all. And in a vague way tolerated it all. But with a dim yet fecund germ of revenge in his heart. He was not morally shocked. But he was going to be revenged. He did not mind Easu's running with a black girl, and afterwards Monica. Morally he did not mind it. But physically—perhaps pride of race—he minded. Physically he could never go so far as to lay his hand on the darky's fuzzy head. His pride of blood was too intense.

He had no objection at all to Lily, until it came to actual

physical contact. And then his blood recoiled with old haughtiness and pride of race. It was bad enough to have to come into contact with a woman of his own race; to have to give himself away even so far. The other was impossible.

And yet he wanted Monica. But he knew she was fooling round with Easu. So deep in his soul formed the motive of revenge.

There are times when a flood of realisation and purpose sweeps through a man. This was one of Jack's times. He was not definitely conscious of what he realised and of what he purposed. Yet, there it was, resolved in him.

He was trying not to hear Dr. Rackett's voice talking to Mary. Even Dr. Rackett was losing his Oxford drawl, and taking on some of the Australian ding-dong. But Rackett, like Jack, was absolutely fixed in his pride of race, no matter what extraneous vice he might have. Jack had a vague idea it was opium. Some chemical stuff.

" . . . free run of old George's books? I should say it was a doubtful privilege for a young lady. But you hardly seem to belong to West Australia. I think England is really your place. Do you actually *want* to belong, may I ask?"

" To Western Australia? To the *country*, yes, very much. I love the land, the country life, Dr. Rackett. I don't care for the social life of a town like Perth. But I should like to live all my life on a farm—in the bush."

" Would you now! " said Rackett. " I wonder where you get that idea from. You are the grand-daughter of an earl."

" Oh, my grandfather is further away from me than the moon. You would never know *how* far! " laughed Mary. " No, I am colonial born and bred. Though, of course, there is a fascination about the English. But I hardly knew Papa. He was a tenth child, so there wasn't much of the earldom left to him. And then he was a busy A.D.C. to the Governor-General. And he married quite late in life. And then Mother died when I was little, and I got passed on to Aunt Matilda. Mother was Australian born. I don't think there is much English in me."

Mary said it in a queer complacent way, as if there were some peculiar, subtle antagonism between England and the colonial, and she was ranged on the colonial side. As if she were subtle enemy of the father, the English father in her.

" Queer ! Queer thing to me ! " said Rackett, as if he half felt the antagonism. For he would never be colonial, not if he lived another hundred years in Australia. " I suppose," he added, pointing his pipe-stem upwards, " it comes from those unnatural stars up there. I always feel they are doing something to me."

" I don't think it's the stars," laughed Mary. " I am just Australian, in the biggest part of me, that's all."

Jack could feel in the statement some of the antagonism that burned in his own heart, against his own country, his own father, his own empty fate at home.

" If I'd been born in this country, I'd stick to it," he broke in.

" But since you weren't born in it, what will you do, Grant ? " asked the doctor ironically.

" Stick to myself," said Jack stubbornly, rather sulkily.

" You won't stick to Old England, then ? " asked Rackett.

" Seems I'm a misfit in Old England," said Jack. "And I'm not going to squeeze my feet into tight boots."

Rackett laughed.

" Rather go barefoot like Lennie ? " he laughed.

Jack relapsed into silence, and turned a deaf ear, looking into the alien night of the southern hemisphere. And having turned a deaf ear to Rackett and Mary, he heard, as if by divination, the low voice of Alec Rice proposing in real earnest to Grace : proposing in a low, urgent voice that sounded like a conspiracy.

He rose to go away. But Mary laid a detaining hand on his arm, as if she wished to include him in the conversation, and did not wish to be left alone with Dr. Rackett.

" Don't you sympathise with me, Jack, for wishing I had been a boy, to make my own way in the world, and have my own friends, and size things up for myself ? "

" Seems to me you do size things up for yourself," said Jack rather crossly. " A great deal more than most *men* do."

" Yes, but I can't *do* things as I could if I were a man."

" What *can* a man do, then, more than a woman—that's worth doing ? " asked Rackett.

" He can see the world, and love as he wishes to love, and work."

" No man can love as he wishes to love," said Rackett. " He's nearly always stumped, in the love game."

" But he can *choose!* " persisted Mary.

And Jack with his other ear was hearing Alec Rice's low voice persisting :

" Go on, Grace, you're not too young. You're just right. You're just the ticket now. Go on, let's be engaged and tell your Dad and fix it up. We're meant for one another, you know we are. Don't you think we're meant for one another ? "

" I never thought about it that way, truly."

" But don't you think so now ? Yes, you do."

Silence—the sort that gives consent. And the silence of a young, spontaneous embrace.

Jack was on tenterhooks. He wanted to be gone. But Mary was persisting, in her obstinate voice—he wished she'd shut up, too.

" I wanted to be a sailor at ten, and an explorer at twelve.   At nineteen I wanted to become a painter of wonderful pictures with very noble subjects."   Jack wished she wouldn't say all this.   " And then I had a streak of humility, and wanted to be a gardener. Yet "—she laughed—" not a sort of gardener such as Aunt Matilda hires.   I wanted to grow things and see them come up out of the earth.   And see baby chicks hatched, and calves and lambs born."

She had lifted her hand from Jack's sleeve, to his relief.

" Then marry a farmer like Tom," he said roughly. Mary received this with dead silence.

" And drudge your soul away like Mrs Ellis," said Rackett.   " Worn out before your time, between babies and heavy house-work.   Groping on the earth all your life, grinding yourself into ugliness at work which some animal of a servant-lass would do with half the effort.   Don't you think of it, Miss Mary.   Let the servant lasses marry the farmers.   You've got too much in you.   Don't go and have what you've got in you trampled out of you by marrying some cooky farmer.   Tom's as good as gold, but he wants a brawny lass of his own sort for a wife.   You be careful, Miss Mary.   Women can find themselves in ugly harness, out here in these god-forsaken colonies. Worse harness than any you've ever kicked against."

Monica seemed to have scented the tense atmosphere under the barn, for she appeared like a young witch, in a whirlwind.

"Hello, Mary! Hello, Dr. Rackett! It's just on midnight." And she flitted over to Grace. "Just on midnight, Grace and Alec. Are you coming? You seem as if you were fixed here."

"We're not fixed on the spot, but we're fixed up all right, otherwise," said Alec, in a slight tone of resentment, as he rose from Grace's side.

"Oh, have you and Grace fixed it up!" exclaimed Monica, with a false vagueness and innocence. "I'm awfully glad. I'm awfully glad, Grace."

"I am," said Grace, with a faint touch of resentment, and she rose and took Alec's arm.

They were already like a married couple armed against that witch. Had she been flirting with Alec, and then pushed him over on to Grace? Jack sensed it with the sixth sense which divines these matters.

Monica appeared at his side.

"It's just twelve. Come and hold my hand in the ring. Mary can hold your other hand. Come on! Come on, Alec, as well. I don't want any strangers next to me to-night."

Jack smiled sardonically to himself as she impulsively caught hold of his hand. Monica was " a circumstance over which we have no control," Lennie said. Jack felt that he had a certain control.

They all took hands as she directed, and moved into the barn to link up with the rest of the chain. There, in the soft light of the big chamber, Easu suddenly appeared, without collar or cravat, his hair ruffled, his white suit considerably creased. But he lurched up in his usual aggressive way, with his assertive good humour, demanding to break in between Jack and Monica. Jack held on, and Monica said :

"You mustn't break in, you know it makes enemies."

"Does it!" grinned Easu. And with sardonic good humour he lurched away to an unjoined part of the ring. He carried about with him a sense of hostile power. But Jack was learning to keep within himself another sort of power, small and concentrated and fixed like a stone, the sort of power that ultimately would break through the bulk of Easu's domineering.

The ring complete at last, they all began to sing : " Cheer, boys, cheer ! " and " God Bless the Prince of Wales," " John Brown's Body," and " Britons Never Never Never."

Then Easu bawled : " Midnight !" There was a moment's frightened pause. Joe Low blasted on the cornet, his toe beating time madly all the while. Fiddles, whistles, concertinas, Jew's harps raggedly began to try out the tune. The clasped hands began to rock, and taking Easu's shouting lead, they all began to sing in the ring :

> " Should auld acquaintance be forgot,
> An' never brought to min' ?
> Should auld acquaintance be forgot,
> And the days of auld lang syne ?
>
> For auld lang syne, my dear,
> For auld lang syne,
> We'll tak' a cup o' kindness yet
> For the days of auld lang syne."

They all sang heartily and with feeling. There was a queer Scottish tang in the colony, that made the Scottish emotion dominant. Jack disliked it. There was no auld acquaintance, or auld lang syne, at least for him. And he didn't care for these particular cups of kindness, in one ring with Easu, black Lily, Dr. Rackett, and Monica, and all. He didn't like the chain of emotion and supposed pathetic clanship. It was worse here even than on shipboard.

Why start the New Year like this ? As a matter of fact he wanted to forget most of his own Auld Acquaintance, and start something a little different. And any rate, the emotion was spurious, the chain was artificial, the flow was false.

Monica seemed to take a wicked pleasure in it, and sang more emotionally than anybody, in a sweet but smallish voice. And poor little Mary, with her half audible murmur, had her eyes full of tears and seemed so moved.

Auld lang syne !

Old Long Since.

Why not put it in plain English?

iv

The celebration did not end with Auld Lang Syne. By half-past two most of the ladies had retired, though some ardent dancers still footed the floor, and a chaperone or two, like crumpled rag-bags, slept on their boxes. A good number of young men and boys were asleep with Herbert on the sacks, handkerchiefs knotted round their throats in place of collars. The concertina, the cornet, the fiddles and the rest of the band had gone down to demolish the remains of the cold collation, whilst Tom, Ross, and Ned sat on the barn steps singing as uproariously as they could, though a little hoarse, for the last dancers to dance to. Someone was whistling very sweetly.

Where was Easu? Jack wondered as he wandered aimlessly out into the night. Where was Easu? For Jack had it on his mind that he ought to fight him. Felt he would be a coward if he didn't tackle him this very night.

But it was three o'clock, the night was very still and rich, still warm, rather close, but not oppressive. The strange heaviness of the hot summer night, with the stars thick in clouds and clusters overhead, the moon being gone. Jack strayed aimlessly through the motionless, dark, warm air, till he came to the paddock gate, and there he leaned with his chin on his arms, half asleep. It seemed to be growing cooler, and a dampness was bringing out the scent of the sorched grass, the essence of the earth, like incense. There was a half-wild bush with a few pale pink roses near the gate. He could just get their fragrance. If it were as it should be, Monica would be here, in one of her wistful, her fiercely wistful moments! When she looked at him with her yellow eyes and her fierce, naive look of yearning, he was ready to give all his blood to her. If things were as they should be, she would be clinging to him now like that, and nestling against his breast. If things were as they should be!

He didn't want to go to sleep. He wanted what he wanted. He wanted the night, the young, changeable, yearning Monica, and an answer to his own awake young blood. He insisted on it. He would not go to sleep, he would insist on an answer. And he wanted to fight Easu. He ought to fight Easu. His manhood depended on it.

He could hear the cattle stirring down the meadow. Soon it would begin to be day. What was it now? It was night, dark night towards morning, with a faint breathing of air from the sea. And where was he? He was in Australia, leaning on the paddock gate and seeing the stars and the dim shape of the gum tree. There was a faint scent of eucalyptus in the night. His mother was far away. England was far away. He was alone there leaning on the paddock gate, in Australia.

After all, perhaps the very best thing was to be alone. Better even than having Monica or fighting Easu. Because where you are alone you are at one with your own God. The spirit in you is God in you. And when you are alone you are one with the spirit of God inside you. Other people are chiefly an interruption.

And, moreover, he could never say he was lonely while he was at " Wandoo," while there was Tom and Lennie, and Monica, and all the rest. He hoped he would have them all his life. He hoped he would never, in all his life, say good-bye to them.

No, he would take up land as near this homestead as possible, and build a brick house on it. And he would have a number of fine horses, better than anyone else's, and some sheep that would pay, and a few cows. Always milk and butter with the wheat-meal damper.

What was that? Only a morepork. He laid his head on his arms again, on the gate. He wanted a place of his own, now. He would have it now if he had any money. And marry Monica. Would he marry Monica? Would he marry anybody? He much preferred the whole family. But he wanted a place of his own. If he could hurry up his father. And old Mr George. He might persuade Mr George to be on his side. Why was there never any money? No money! A father ought to have some money for a son.

What was that? He saw a dim white figure stealing across the near distance. Pah! must have been a girl sitting out under the pitosperum tree. When he had thought he was quite alone.

The thought upset him. And he ought to find Easu.

Obstinately he insisted to himself that he ought to find Easu.

He drifted towards the shed near the cubby, where Mr Ellis kept the tools. Somebody unknown and unauthorised had put a barrel of beer inside the shed. Men were there drinking, as he knew they would be.

" Have a pot, youngster ? "

" Thanks."

He sat down on a case beside the door, and drank the rather warm beer. His head began to drop. He knew he was almost asleep.

Easu loomed up from the dark, coatless, hatless, with his shirt front open, asking for a drink. He was thirsty. Easu was thirsty. How could you be angry with a thirsty man ! And he wasn't so bad, after all. No, Easu wasn't so bad after all ! What did it matter ! What did it matter, anyhow ?

Jack slipped to the ground and lay there fast asleep.

CHAP : X. SHADOWS BEFORE

i

But in the morning memory was back, and the unquenched smouldering of passion. Easu had insulted him. Easu had insulted him, and that should never be forgiven. And he had this new, half painful, more than half painful desire to see Monica, to be near her, to touch her hand; a sort of necessity upon him all the while which he was not used to. It made him restless, uneasy, and for the first time in his life, a little melancholy. He was used to feeling angry : a steady, almost blithe sort of anger. And beyond that he had always been able to summon up an indifference to things, cover them with oblivion : to retreat upon himself and insulate himself from contact.

Now he could no longer do this, and it fretted him, made him accessible to melancholy. The hot, hot January days, all dry flaming heat, and flies, and mosquitoes, passed over him, leaving him strange even to himself. There was work, the drudging work of the farm, all the while. And one just sweated. He learned to submit to it, to the sweating all the time during the day, and the mosquitoes at night. It was like a narcotic. The old, English alertness grew darker and darker. He seemed to be moving, a dim consciousness and an unyielding will, in a dark cloud of heat, in a perspiring, dissolving body. He could feel his body, the English cool body of his being, slowly melting down and being invaded by a new tropical quality. Sometimes, he said to himself, he was sweating his soul away. That was how it felt : as if he were sweating his soul away. And he let his soul go, let it slowly melt away out of his wet, hot body.

Any man who has been in the tropics, unless he has kept all his mind and his consciousness focussed homewards, fixed towards the old people of home, will know how this feels. Now, Jack did not turn homewards, back to England. He never wanted to go back. There was in him a slow, abiding anger against this same " home." Therefore he let himself go down the dark tide of the heat. He did not cling on to his old English soul, the soul of an

English gentleman. He let that dissolve out of him, leaving what residuum of a man it might leave. But out of very obstinacy he hung on to his own integrity : a small, dark, obscure integrity.

Usually he was too busy perspiring, panting, and working to think about anything. His mind also seemed dissolving away in perspiration and in the curious eucalyptus solvent of the Australian air. He was too busy and too much heat-oppressed even to think of Monica or of Easu, though Monica was a live wire in his body. Only on Sundays he seemed to come half out of his trance. And then everything went queer and strange, a little uncanny.

Dad was back again for the harvest, but his heart was no better, and a queer frightening cloud seemed over him. And Gran, they said, was failing. Somehow Gran was the presiding deity of the house. Her queer spirit controlled, even now. And she was failing. She adored Lennie, but he was afraid of her.

" Gran's the limit," he asserted. " She's that wilful. Always the same with them women when they gets well on in years. I clear out from her if I can, she's that obstropulous—tells y't'wipe y'nose, pull up y'pants, brush y'teeth, not sniff : golly, I can't stand it ! "

Sunday was the day when you really came into contact with the family. The rule was, that each one took it in turns to get up and make breakfast, while everybody else stayed on in bed, for a much-needed rest. If it was your turn, you rolled out of bed at dawn when Timothy banged on the wall, you slipped on your shirt and pants and went to the " everlasting " fire. Raking the ashes together with a handful of sticks, you blew a blaze and once more smelt the burning eucalyptus leaves. You filled the black iron kettle at the pump, and set if over the flame. Then you washed yourself. After which you carved bread and butter : tiny bits for Gran, moderate pieces for upstairs, and door-steps for the cubby. After which you made the tea, and *holloa'd !* while you poured it out. One of the girls, with a coat over her nighty and her hair in a chinon, would come barefoot to carry the trays, to Gran and to the upstairs. This was just the preliminary breakfast : the Sunday morning luxury. Just tea in bed.

Later the boys were shouting for clean shirts and towels,

and the women were up. Proceeded the hair-cutting, nail-paring, button-sewing, and general murmur, all under the superivision of Ma. Then down to the sand-bagged pool for a dip. After which, clean and in clean raiment, you went to the parlour to hear Dad read the lessons.

The family Bible was carefully kept warm in the parlour, during the week, under a woollen crochet mat. A crochet mat above, and a crochet mat below. Nothing must ever stand on that book, nothing whatever. The children were quite superstitious about it.

Lennie, the Benjamin of his father Jacob, each Sunday went importantly into the drawing-room, in a semi-religious silence, and fetched the ponderous brass-bound book. He put it on the table in front of Dad. Gran came in with her stick and her lace cap, and sat in the arm-chair near the window. Mrs Ellis and the children folded their hands like saints. Mr Ellis wiped his spectacles, cleared his throat, looked again at the little church calendar of the lessons, found the place, and proceeded in a droning voice. Nobody looked at him, except Mrs Ellis. Everybody looked another way. Gran usually gazed sideways at the floor. Tick, tock ! went the clock. It was a little eternity.

Jack knew the Bible pretty well, as a well-brought-up nephew of his aunts. He had no objection to the Bible. On the contrary, it supplied his imagination with a chief stock of images, his ear with the greatest solemn pleasure of words, and his soul with a queer heterogeneous ethic. He never really connected the Bible with Christianity proper, the Christianity of aunts and clergymen. He had no use for Christianity proper : just dismissed it. But the Bible was perhaps the foundation of his consciousness. Do what seems good to you in the sight of the Lord. This was the moral he always drew from Bible lore. And since the Lord, for him, was always the Lord Almighty, Almighty God, Maker of Heaven and Earth, Jesus being only a side issue; since the Lord was always Jehovah the great and dark, for him, one might do as David did, in the sight of the Lord, or as Jacob, or as Abraham or Moses or Joshua or Isaiah, in the sight of the Lord. The sight of the Lord was a vast strange scope of vision, in the semi-dark.

Gran always listened the same, leaning on her stick and looking sideways to the ground, as if she did not quite see the stout and purple-faced Jacob, her son, as the mouth-piece of the Word. As a matter of fact, the way he read Scripture irritated her. She wished Lennie could have read the lessons. But Dad was head of the house, and she was fond of him, poor old Jacob.

And Jack always furtively watched Gran. She frightened him, and he had a little horror of her : but she fascinated him, too. She was like Monica, at the great distance of her years. Her lace cap was snowy white, with little lavendar ribbons. Her face was pure ivory, with fine-shaped features, that subtly arched nose, like Monica's. Her silver hair came over her dead looking ears. And her dry, shiny, blue-veined hand remained fixed over the pommel of her black stick. How awful, how unspeakably awful, Jack felt, to be so old ! No longer human. And she seemed so little inside her clothes. And one never knew what she was thinking. But surely some strange, uncanny, dim non-human thoughts.

Sunday was full of strange, half painful impressions of death and of life. After lessons the boys would escape to the yards, and the stables, and lounge about. Or they would try the horses, or take a gun into the uncleared bush. Then came the enormous Sunday dinner, when everyone ate himself stupid.

In the afternoon Tom and Jack wandered to the loft, to the old concertina. Up there among the hay, they squeezed and pulled the old instrument, till at last, after much practice, they could draw forth tortured hymnal sounds from its protesting internals.

" Ha-a-appy Ho-ome ! Ha-appy Ho-ome !
Oh, Haa-py Ho-me ! Oh, Haa-py Ho-me !
In Paradise with thee ! "

Over and over again the same tune, till Tom would drop off to sleep, and Jack would have a go at it. And this yearning sort of hymn always sent a chill to his bowels. They were like Gran, on the brink of the grave. In fact the word Paradise made him shudder worse than the word coffin. Yet he would grind away at the tune. Till he, too, fell asleep.

And then they would wake in the heat to the silence of

the suspended, fiercely hot afternoon. Only to feel their own sweat trickling, and to hear the horses, the draught-horses which were in stable for the day, chop-chopping underneath. So, in spite of sweat and heat, another go at the fascinating concertina.

ii

One Sunday Jack strolled in an hour early for tea. He had made a mistake, as one does sometimes when one sleeps in the afternoon. Gran was sitting by a little fire in the dark living room. She had to have a little fire to look at. It was like life to her.

" Come here, Jack Grant," she said in her thin imperious voice. He went on reluctant feet, for he had a dread of her years and her strange femaleness. What did she want of him ?

" Did y'hear Mr George get my son to promise to make a will when y'were in Perth ? "

" No, marm," said Jack promptly.

" Well, take it from me, if he promised, he hasn't done it. He never signed a paper in his life, unless it was his marriage register. And but for my driving he'd never have signed that. Sit down ! "

Jack sat on the edge of a chair, his heart in his boots.

" I told you before I'd ha' married your grandfather if he hadn't been married already. I wonder where you'd ha' been then ! Just as well I didn't, for he wouldn't look at me after he took my leg off. Just come here a minute."

Jack got up and went to her side. She put her soft, dry, dead old hand on his face and stroked it, pressing on the cheek-bones.

" Ay," she said. " I suppose those are his bones again. And my bones are in Monica. Don't stand up, lad, take your seat."

Jack sat down in extreme discomfort.

" Well," she resumed, " I was very well off with old Ellis, so I won't complain. But you've got your English father's eyes. You'd have been better with mine. Those bones, those beautiful bones, and my sort of eyes."

Gran's eyes were queer and remote now. But they had

been perhaps like Monica's, only a darker grey, and with a darker, subtler cat look in them.

" I suppose it will be in the children's children," she resumed, her eyes going out like a candle. " For I married old Ellis, though to this day I never quite believe it. And one thing I do know. I won't die in the dying room of this house. I won't do it, not if it was the custom of a hundred families. Not if he was here himself to see me do it. I wouldn't. Though he was kindness itself. But not if he was here himself and had the satisfaction of seeing me do it! A dreadful room! I'd be frightened to death to die in it. I like me sheets sun-kissed, heat or no heat, and no sun ever gets into that room. But it's better for a woman to marry, even if she marries the wrong man. I allus said so. An old maid, especially a decayed gentlewoman, is a blight on the face of the earth."

" Why? " said Jack suddenly. The old woman was too authoritative.

" That's why! What do you know about it?" she said contemptuously.

" I knew a nice old lady in England who'd never been married," he said, thinking of a really beautiful, gentle woman who had kept all her perfume and her charm in spite of her fifty-odd years of single blessedness. But, then, she had a naturally deep and religious nature, not like this pagan old cat of a Gran.

" Did *you*! " said Gran, eyeing him severely. " What do *you* know at your age? I've got three unmarried daughters, and I'm ashamed of them. If I'd married your grandfather I never should have had them. Self-centred, and old as old boots, they are. I'd rather they'd gone wrong and died in the bush, like your aunt who had a child by Mary's father."

Jack made round, English eyes of amazement at this speech. He disapproved thoroughly.

" You've got too much of your English father in you," she said, " and not enough of your hard-hearted grand-father. Look at Lennie, what a beautiful boy he is."

There was a pause. Jack sat in a torment while she baited him. He was full of antagonism towards her and her years.

" But, I tell you, you never realise you're old till you

see your friends slipping away. One by one they go—over the border. *That's* what makes you feel old. I tell you. Nothing else. Annie Brockman died the other day. I was at school with her. She wasn't old, though *you'd* have thought so."

The way Gran said this was quite spiteful. And Jack thought to himself : " What nonsense, she *was* old if she was at school with Gran. If she was as old as Gran, she was awfully old."

" No, she wasn't old—school-girls and fellows laughing in the ball room, or breathing fast after a hard ride. You didn't know Sydney in those days. And men grown old behind their beards for want of understanding; because they're too dense to understand what living means. Men are dense. Are ye listening ?"

The question came with such queer aged force that Jack started almost out of his chair.

" Yes, marm," he said.

" ' Yes, marm ' he says ! " she repeated, with a queer little grin of amusement. " Listen to this grandfather's chit saying ' Yes, marm ! ' to me ! Well, they'll have their way. My friends are nearly all gone, so I suppose I shall soon be going. Not but what there's plenty of amusement here."

She looked round in an odd way, as if she saw ghosts. Jack would have given his skin to escape her.

" Listen," she said with sudden secrecy. " I want ye to do something for me. You love Lennie, don't ye ? "

Jack nodded.

" So do I ! And I'm going to help him." Her voice became sharp with secrecy. " I've put by a stocking for him," she hissed. " At least it's not a stocking, it's a tin box, but it's the same thing. It's up there ! " She pointed with her stick at the wide black chimney. " D'ye understand ? "

She eyed Jack with aged keenness, and he nodded, though his understanding was rather vague. Truth to tell, nothing she said seemed to him quite real. As if, poor Gran, her age put her outside of reason.

" That stocking is for Lennie. Tom's mother was nobody knows who, though I'm not going to say Jacob never married her, if Jacob says he did. But Tom'll get every-

thing. The same as Jacob did. That's how it hits back at
me. I wanted Jacob to have the place, and now it goes to
Tom, and my little Lennie gets nothing. Alice has been a
good woman, and a good wife to Jacob : better than he
deserved. I'm going to stand by her. That stocking in
there is for Lennie because he's her eldest son. In a tin
box. Y'understand ? "

And she pointed again at the chimney.

Jack nodded, though he didn't really take it in. He had
a little horror of Gran at all times ; but when she took on
this witch-like portentousness, and whispered at him in a
sharp, aged whisper, about money, hidden money, it all
seemed so abnormal to him that he refused to take it for
real. The queer aged female spirit that had schemed with
money for the men-folk she chose, scheming to oust those
she had not elected, was so strange and half-ghoulish, that
he merely shrank from taking it in. When she pointed with
her white-headed stick at the wide black mouth of the
chimney, he glanced and looked quickly away again. He
did not want to think of a hoard of sovereigns in a stocking
—or a tin box—secreted in there. He did not want to think
of the subtle, scheming, vindictive old woman reaching up
into the soot to add more gold to the hoard. It was all
unnatural to him and to his generation.

But Gran despised him and his generation. It was as
unreal to her as hers to him.

" Old George couldn't even persuade that Jacob of mine
to sign a marriage settlement," she continued. " And I
wasn't going to force him. Would you believe a man could
be such an obstinate fool ? "

" Yes, marm," said Jack automatically.

And Gran stamped her stick at him in sudden vicious
rage.

The stamping of the stick brought Grace, and he fled.

iii

That evening they were all sitting in the garden. The
drawing-room was thrown open, as usual on Sunday, but
nobody even went in except to strum the piano. Monica
was strumming hymns now. Grace came along calling
Mary. Mary was staying on at " Wandoo."

" Mary, Gran wants you. She feels faint. Come and see to her, will you? "

Ellie came and slipped her fat little hand into Jack's, hanging on to him. Katie and Lennie sat surreptitiously playing cats'-cradle, on the steps : forbidden act, on the Sabbath. The twin boys wriggled their backs against the gate-posts and their toes into the earth, asking each other riddles. Harry as usual aimed stones at birds. It was a close evening, the wind had not come. And they all were uneasy, with that uncanny uneasiness that attacks families, because Gran was not well.

Harry was singing profanely, profaning the Sabbath.

" A blue jay sat on a hickory limb,
He wink at me, I wink at him.
I up with a stone, an' hit him on the shin.
Says he, Little Nigger, don' do that agin !
Clar de kitchen, ol' folk, young folk !
Clar de kitchen, ol' folk, young folk !
An' let us dance till dawn O."

Harry shouted out these wicked words half loud to a tune of his own that was no tune.

Jack did not speak. The sense of evening, Sunday evening, far away from any church or bell, was strong upon him. The sun was slow in the sky, and the light intensely strong, all fine gold. He went out to look. The sunlight flooded the dry, dry earth till it glowed again, and the gum trees that stood up hung tresses of liquid shadow from trunks of gold, and the buildings seemed to melt blue in the vision of light. Someone was riding in from westward, and a cloud of pure gold-dust rose fuming from the earth about the horse and the horseman, with a vast, overwhelming gold glow of the void heavens above. The whole west was so powerful with pure gold light, coming from immense space and the sea, that it seemed like a transfiguration, and another horseman rode fuming in a dust of light as if he were coming, small and Daniel-like, out of the vast furnace-mouth of creation. Jack looked west, into the welter of yellow light, in fear. He knew again, as he had known before, that his day was not the day of all the world, there was a huger sunset than the sunset of his race. There were vaster, more unspeakable gods than the gods of his fathers. The god in this yellow fire was huger than the white men could understand, and seemed to proclaim their doom.

Out of this immense power of the glory seemed to come a proclamation of doom. Lesser glories must crumble to powder in this greater glow, as the horsemen rode trotting in the glorified cloud of the earth, spuming a glory all round them. They seemed like messengers out of the great west, coming with a proclamation of doom, the small, trotting, aureoled figures kicking up dust like sun-dust, and gradually growing larger, hardening out of the sea of light. Like sun-arrivals.

Though, after all, it was only Alec Rice and Tom. But they were gilded men, dusty and sun-luminous, as they came into the yard, with their brown faces strangely vague in shadow, unreal.

The sun was setting, huge and liquid and sliding down at immense speed behind the far-off molten, wavering long ridge towards the coast. Fearsome the great liquid sun was, stooping fiercely down like an enemy stooping to hide his glory, leaving the sky hovering and pulsing above, with a sense of wings, and a sense of proclamation, and of doom. It seemed to say to Jack : I and my race are doomed. But even the doom is a splendour.

Shadow lay very thin on the earth, pale as day, though the sun was gone. Jack turned back to the house. The tiny twins were staggering home to find their supper, their hands in the pockets of their Sunday breeches. The pockets of everyday breeches were, for some mysterious reason, always sewn up, so Sunday alone knew this swagger. Harry was being called in to bed. And Len and Katie, rarely far off at meal times, were converging towards supper too.

Monica was still drumming listlessly on the piano, and singing in a little voice. She had a very sweet voice, but she usually sang " small." She was not singing a hymn, Jack became aware of this. She was singing, rather nervously, or irritably, and with her own queer yearning pathos :

" Oh Jane, Oh Jane, my pretty Jane, Oh Jane
  Ah never, never look so shy.
  But meet me, meet me in the moonlight,
  When the dew is on the rye."

Someone had lighted the piano candles, and she sat there strumming and singing in a little voice, and looking queer and lonely. His heart went hot in his breast, and then started pounding. He crossed silently, and stood just behind her. For some moments she would not notice him, but went on singing the same. And he stood perfectly still close behind her. Then, at last, she glanced upward at him, and his heart stood still again with the same sense of doom the sun had given him. She still went on singing for a few moments. Then she stopped abruptly, and jerked her hand from the piano.

" Don't you want to sing? " she asked sharply.

" Not particularly."

" What do you want then? "

" Let us go out."

She looked at him strangely, then rose in her abrupt fashion. She followed him across the yard in silence, while he felt the curious sense of doom settling down on him.

He sat down on the step of the back-door of the barn, outside, looking southward into the vast, rapidly darkening country, and glanced up at her. She, rather petulantly, sat down beside him. He felt for her cool slip of a hand, and she let it lie in his hot one. But she averted her face.

" Why don't you like me? " she asked petulantly.

" But I love you," he said thickly, with shame and the sense of doom piercing his heart.

She turned swiftly and stared him in the face with a brilliant, oddly triumphant look.

" Sure? " she said.

His heart seemed to go black with doom. But he turned away his face from her glowing eyes, and put his arm round her waist, and drew her to him. His whole body was trembling like a taut string, and she could feel the painful plunging of his heart as he pressed her fast against him, pressed the breath out of her.

" Monica! " he murmured blindly, in pain, like a man who is in the dark.

" What? " she said softly.

He hid his face against her shoulder, in the shame and anguish of desire. He would have given anything, if this need never have come upon him. But the strange fine quivering of his body thrilled her. She put her cheek down caressingly against his hair. She could be very tender, very, very tender and caressing. And he grew quieter.

He looked up at the night again, hot with pain and doom and necessity. It had grown quite dark, the stars were out.

" I suppose we shall have to be married," he said in a dismal voice.

" Why? " she laughed. It seemed a very sudden and long stride to her. He had not even kissed her.

But he did not answer, did not even hear her question. She watched his fine young face in the dark, looking sullen and doomed at the stars.

" Kiss me ! " she whispered, in the most secret whisper he had ever heard. " Kiss me ! "

He turned, in the same battle of unwillingness. But as if magnetised he put forward his face and kissed her on the mouth : the first kiss of his life. And she seemed to hold him. And the fierce, fiery pain of pleasure which came with that kiss sent his soul rebelling in torment to hell. He had never wanted to be given up, to be broken by the black hands of this doom. But broken he was, and his soul seemed to be leaving him, in the pain and obsession of this desire, against which he struggled so fiercely.

She seemed to be pleased, to be laughing. And she was exquisitely sweet to him. How could he be otherwise than caught, and broken.

After an hour of this love-making she blackened him again by saying they must go in to supper. But she meant it, so in he had to go.

Only when he was alone again in the cubby did he resume the fight to recover himself from her again. To be free as he had been before. Not to be under the torment of the spell of this desire. To preserve himself intact. To preserve himself from her.

He lay awake in his bed in the cubby and thanked God he was away from her. Thanked God he was alone, with a sufficient space of loneliness around him. Thanked God he was immune from her, that he could sleep in the sanctity of his own isolation. He didn't want even to think about her.

iv

Gran did not leave her room that week, and Tom talked of fetching the relations.

" What for ? " asked Jack.

" They'd like to be present," said Tom.

Jack felt incredulous.

Lennie came out of her room sniffing and wiping his eyes with his knuckles.

" Poor ol' girl ! " he sniffed. " She do look frail. She's almost like a little girl again."

" You don't think she's dying, do you, Len ? " asked Jack.

" I don't *think*, I knows," replied Len, with utmost scorn. " Sooner or later she's bound to go hence and be no more seen. But she'll be missed, for many a day, she will."

" But, Tom," said Jack. " Do you think Gran will like to have all the relations sniffling round her when she gets worse ? "

" I should think so," replied Tom. " Anyway, *I* should like to die respectable, whether you would or not."

Jack gave it up. Some things were beyond him, and dying respectable was one of them.

" Like they do in books," said Len, seeing that Jack disapproved, and trying to justify Tom's position. " Even ol' Nelson died proper. ' Kiss me, 'Ardy,' he said, an' 'Ardy kissed him, grubby and filthy as he was. He could do no less, though it was beastly."

Still the boys were not sent for the relations until the following Sunday, which was a rest day. Jack went to the Gum Valley Homestead, because he knew the way. He set off before dawn. The terrific heat of the New Year had already passed, and the dawn came fresh and lovely. He was happy on that ride, Gran or no Gran. And that's what he thought would be the happiest : always to ride on at dawn, in a nearly virgin country. Always to be riding away.

The Greenlows seemed to expect him. They had been " warned." After he had been refreshed with a good breakfast, they were ready to start, in the buggy. Jack rode in the buggy with them, his saddle under his seat and the neck rope of the horse in his hand. The hack ran behind, and nearly jerked Jack's arms out of their sockets, with its halts and its disinclination to trot. Almost it hauled him out of the buggy sometimes. He would much rather have ridden the animal, but he had been requested to take the buggy, to spare it.

Mr. and Mrs. Greenlow scarcely spoke on the journey; it would not have been " showing sorrow." But Jack felt they were enjoying themselves immensely, driving in this morning air instead of being cooped up in the house, she cooking and he with the Holy Book. The sun grew furiously hot. But Gum Valley Croft was seven miles nearer to Wandoo than the Ellis' Gum Tree Selection, so they drove into the yard, wet with perspiration, just before the mid-day meal was put on to the table. Mrs. Ellis, aproned and bare-armed, greeted them as they drove up, calling out that they should go right in, and Jack should take the horses out of the buggy.

Quite a number of strange hacks were tethered here and there in the yard, near odd empty vehicles, sulkies dejectedly leaning forward on empty shafts, or buggies and wagonettes sturdily important on four wheels. Yet the place seemed strangely quiet.

Jack came back to the narrow verandah outside the parlour door, where Mrs. Ellis had her fuchsias, ferns, cyclamens and musk growing in pots. A table had been set there, and dinner was in progress, the girls coming round from the kitchen with the dishes. Grace saw Jack hesitate, so she nodded to him. He went to the kitchen and asked doubtfully :

" How is she? "

" Oh, bad ! Poor old dear. They're all in there to say good-bye."

Lennie, who was sitting on the floor under the kitchen window, put his head down on his arms and sobbed from a sort of nervousness, wailing :

" Oh, my poor ol' Gran ! Oh, poor ol' dear ! "

Jack, though upset, almost grinned. Poor Gran indeed, with that ghastly swarm of relations. He sat there on a chair, his nerves all on edge, noticing little things acutely, as he always did when he was strung up : the flies standing motionless on the chopping-block just outside the window,

the smooth-tramped gravel walk, the curious surface of the
mud floor in the kitchen, the smoky rafters overhead, the
oven set in brick below the " everlasting " fire, the
blackness of the pots and kettles above the horizontal
bars. . . .

" Do you mind sitting in the parlour, Jack, in case they
want anything ? " Mrs. Ellis asked him.

Jack minded, but he went and sat in the parlour, like a
chief lackey, or a buffer between all the relations and the
outer world.

The house had become more quiet. Monica had gone
over to the Reds with clean overalls for the little boys, who
had been bundled off there. Jack got this piece of news
from Grace, who was constantly washing more dishes and
serving more relations. A certain anger burned in him as
he heard, but he took no notice. Mary was lying down upstairs : she had been up all night with Gran. Tom was
attending to the horses. Katie and Mrs. Ellis had gone
upstairs with baby and Ellie, and Mr. Ellis was also upstairs. Lennie had slipped away again. So Jack had track
of all the family. He was always like that, wanting to
know where they all were.

Mrs. Greenlow came in from Gran's inner room.

" Mary ? Where's Mary ? " she asked hurriedly.

Jack shook his head, and she passed on. She had left
the door of Gran's room open, so Jack could see in. All
the relations were there, horrible, the women weeping and
perspiring, and wiping tears and perspiration away together,
the men in their waistcoats and shirt-sleeves, perspiring and
looking ugly. A Methodist parson son-in-law was saying
prayers in an important monotone.

At last Mary came, looking anxious.

" Yes, Gran ? Did you want me ? " Jack heard her voice,
and saw her by the bed.

" I felt so overcome with all these people," said Gran,
in a curiously strong, yet frightened voice. " What do
they all want ? "

" They've come to see you. Come "—Mary hesitated—
" to see if they can do anything for you."

" To frighten the bit of life out of me that I've got, but
they're not going to. Get me some beef tea, Mary, and
don't leave me alone with them."

Mary went out for the beef tea. Then Jack saw Gran's white hand feebly beckon.

" Ruth ! " she said. " Ruth ! "

The eldest daughter went over and took the hand, mopping her eyes. She was the parson's wife.

" Well, Ruth, how are you? " said Gran's high, quavering voice, in a conversational tone.

" *I'm* well, Mother. It's how are you? " replied Ruth dismally.

But Gran was again totally oblivious of her. So at length Ruth dropped away embarrassed from the bedside, shaking her head.

Again Gran lifted her head on the pillow.

" Where's Jacob ? "

" Upstairs, Mother."

" The only one that has the decency to leave me alone." And she subsided again. Then after a while she asked, without lifting her head from the pillow, in a distant voice :

" And are the foolish virgins here? "

" Who, Mother? "

" The foolish virgins. You know who I mean."

Gran lay with her eyes shut as she spoke.

There was an agitation among the family. It was the brothers-in-law who pushed the three Miss Ellises forward. They, the poor things, wept audibly.

Gran opened her eyes at the sound, and said, with a ghost of a smile on her yellow, transparent old face :

" I hope virginity is its own reward."

Then she remained unmoved until Mary came with the soup, which she took and slowly sipped as Mary administered it in a spoon. It seemed to revive her.

" Where's Lennie and his mother? " she asked, in a firmer tone.

These also were sent for. Mrs. Ellis sat by the bed and gently patted Gran's arm ; but Lennie, " skeered stiff," shivered at the door. His mother held out her hand to him, and he came in, inch by inch, watching the fragile old Gran, who looked transparent and absolutely unreal, with a fascination of horror.

" Kiss me, Lennie," said Gran grimly : exactly like Nelson.

Lennie shrank away. Then, yielding to his mother's

pressure, he laid his dark smooth head and his brown face on the pillow next to Gran's face, but he did not kiss her.

" There's my precious ! " said Gran softly, with all the soft, cajoling gentleness that had made her so lovely, at moments, to her men.

" Alice, you've been good to my Jacob," she said, as if remembering something. " There's the stocking. It's for you and Lennie." She still managed to say the last words with a caress, though she was fading from consciousness again.

Lennie drew away and hid behind his mother. Gran lay still, exactly as if dead. But the laces of her eternal cap still stirred softly, to show she breathed. The silence was almost unbearable.

To break it the Methodist son-in-law sank to his knees. the others followed his example, and he prayed in a low, solemn, extinguished voice. When he had said *Amen* the others whispered it and rose from their knees. And by one consent they glided from the room. They had had enough deathbed for the moment.

Mary closed the inner door when they had gone, and remained alone in the room with Gran.

v

The sons-in-law all melted through the parlour and out on to the verandah, where they helped themselves from the decanter on the table, filling up from the canvas water-bag that swung in the draught to keep cool. The daughters sat down by the table and wept, lugubriously and rather angrily. The sons-in-law drank and looked afflicted. Jack remained on duty in the parlour, though he would dearly have liked to decamp.

But he was now interested in the relations. They began to weep less, and to talk in low, suppressed, vehement voices. He could only catch bits. " It's a question if he ever married Tom's mother. I doubt if Tom's legitimate. I don't even doubt it, I'm sure. We've suffered from that before. Where's the stocking? Stocking ! Stocking—saved up—bought Easu out. Mother should know better. If she's made a will—Jacob's first marriage. Children to educate and provide for. Unmarried daughters—first claim.

Stocking——" And then quite plainly from Ruth : " It's hard on our husbands if *they* have to support mother's unmarried daughters." This said with dignity.

Jack glanced at the three Miss Ellises, to see if they minded, and inwardly he vowed that if he ever married Monica, for example, and Grace was an unmarried sister, he'd find some suitable way of supporting her, without making her feel ashamed. But the three Miss Ellises did not seem to mind. They were busy diving into secret pockets among their clothing, and fetching out secret little packages. Someone dropped the glass stopper out of a bottle of smelling salts, and spilled the contents on the floor. The pungent odour penetrated throughout the house. Jack never again smelt lavender salts without having a foreboding of death, and seeing mysterious little packets. The three Miss Ellises were surreptitiously laying out bits and tags of black braid, crape, beading, black cloth, black lace; all black, wickedly black, on the table edge. Smoothing them out. For as a matter of fact they kept a little shop. And everybody was looking with interest. Jack felt quite nauseated at the sight of these black blotches, the row of black patches.

Mary came out of Gran's room, going to the kitchen with the cup. She did not pass the verandah, so nobody noticed her. They were all intent on the muttering gloom of their investigation of those scraps of mourning patterns.

Jack felt the door of Gran's room slowly open. Mary had left it just ajar. He looked round and his hair rose on his head. There stood Gran, all white save for her eyes, like a yellow figure of aged female Time, standing with her hand on the door, looking across the parlour at the afternoon and the pre-occupied party on the verandah. Her face was absolutely expressionless, timeless and awful. It frightened him very much. The inexorable female! He uttered an exclamation, and they all looked up, caught.

CHAP : XI. BLOWS

JACK managed to escape. When the rooks were fluttered
by the sight of that ghostly white starling, he just ran. He
ran in disgust from the smell of lavender salts, the tags of
mourning patterns, respectable dying, and these awful
people. Surely there was something rotten at the bottom
of people, he thought, to make them behave as they did.
And again came over him the feeling he had often had, that
he was a changeling, that he didn't belong to the so-called
" normal " human race. Nor, by Jupiter, did he want to.
The " normal " human race filled him with unspeakable
repulsion. And he knew they would kill him if they found
out what he was. Hence that unconscious dissembling of
his innocent face.

He ran, glad to get into a sweat, glad to sweat it all out
of himself. Glad to feel the sun hot on his damp hands,
and then the afternoon breeze, just starting, cool on his
wet skin. When he reached the sand-bagged pool he took
off his clothes and spread them in the sun, while he wallowed
in the luke-warm water. Ay ! if one could wash off one's
associations ! If one could but be alone in the world.

After bathing he sat in the sun awhile to dry, then dressed
and walked off to look at the lower dam pump. Tom had
said it needed attending to. And anyway it led him away
from the house.

The pump was all right. There had been a March shower
that had put water in the dam. So after looking round at
the sheep, he turned away.

Which way ? Not back home. Not yet.

The land breeze had lifted and the sea breeze had come,
clearing the hot dry atmosphere as if by magic, and re-
placing the furnace breath by tender air. Which way ?

At the back of his mind was the thought of Monica not
home yet from the Reds' place, and evening coming on,
another of the full golden evenings, when the light seemed
fierce with declaration of another eternity, a different
eternity from ours.

Last Sunday, on such an evening, he had kissed her. And
162

much as he wanted to avoid her, the desire to kiss her again
drove him as if the great yellowing light were a wind that
blew him, as a butterfly is blown twinkling out to sea. He
drifted towards the trail from the Reds' place. He walked
slowly, listening to the queer evening noise of the magpies,
and the more distant screeching of flying parrots. Someone
had disturbed the parrots beyond the Black Barn gums. So,
as if by intuition, he walked that way, slightly off the trail.

And suddenly he heard the sound his spirit expected to
hear : Monica crying out in expostulation, anger, and fear.
It was the fear in her voice that made his face set. His
first instinct was not to intrude on their privacy. Then
again came the queer, magpie noise of Monica, this time
with an edge of real hatred to her fear. Jack pushed
through the bushes. He could smell the warm horses
already.

Yes, there was Lucy standing by a tree. And Monica,
in a long skirt of pink-sprigged cotton, with a frill at the
bottom, trying to get up into the side-saddle. While Easu,
in his Sunday black reach-me-downs and white shirt and
white rubber-soled cricketing boots, every time she set her
foot in the stirrup, put his hand round her waist and spread
his fingers on her body, and lifted her down again, lifted her
on one hand in a childish and ridiculous fashion, and held
her in a moment's embrace. She in her long cotton riding-
dress with the close-fitting bodice, did indeed look absurd
hung like a child on Easu's hand, as he lifted her down and
held her struggling against him, then let her go once more,
to mount her horse. Lucy was shifting uneasily, and Easu's
big black horse, tethered to a tree, was jerking its head
with a jingle of the bit. The girth hung loose. Easu had
evidently dismounted to adjust it.

Monica was becoming really angry, really afraid, and
really blind with dismay, feeling for the first time her
absolute powerlessness. To be powerless drove her mad,
and she would have killed Easu if she could, without a
qualm. But her hate seemed to rouse the big Easu to a
passion of desire for her. He put his two big hands round
her slender body and compassed her entirely. She gave a
loud, strange, uncanny scream. And Jack came out of the
bushes, making the black horse plunge. Easu glanced
round at the horse, and saw Jack. And at the same time

our hero planted a straight, vicious blow on the bearded chin. Easu, unprepared, staggered up against Lucy, who began to jump, while Monica, tangled in her long skirt, fell to her knees on the ground.

" Quite a picture ! " Jack said it himself. Even he saw himself standing there, like Jack the Giant-killer. And of course he saw Monica on her knees, with tumbled hair and scarlet cheeks, unspeakably furious at being caught, angrily hitching herself out of her long cotton riding-skirt and pressing her cheeks to make them less red. She was silent, with averted face, and she seemed small. He saw Easu in the Sunday white shirt and rather tight Sunday breeches, facing round in unspeakable disgust and fury. He saw himself in a ready-made cotton suit and cheap brown canvas shoes, bought at the local store, standing awaiting an onslaught.

The onslaught did not come. Instead, Easu said, in a tone of unutterable contempt :

" Why, what's up with you, you little sod ? "

Jack turned to Monica. She had got on to her feet and was pushing her hair under her hat.

" Monica," he said, " you'd better get home. Gran's dying."

She looked at him, and a slow, wicked smile of amusement came over her face. Then she broke into a queer hollow laugh, at the bottom of which was rage and frustration. Then her laugh rose higher.

" Ha ! Ha ! Ha ! " she laughed. " Ah, ha-ha-ha-ha-ha ! Ha-ha-ha ! Ah ! ! Ha-ha-ha-ha-ha ! Ha-ha-ha ! Ah ! ! ! Ha-ha-ha-ha-ha-ha-ha ! Ah ! Ha-ha ! Ha ! Ah ! Gran's dying ! Ha-ha-ha ! Is she really ? Oh, ha-ha-ha-ha-ha ! No, I don't mean it. But it seems so funny ! Ah ! Ha-ha-ha-ha-ha ! Ah ! Ha-ha-ha ! "

She smothered herself into a confused bubbling. The two men stood aghast, shuddering at the strange hysterical woman's laughter that went shrilling through the bush. They were horrified least someone else should hear.

Monica in her cotton frock and long sweeping skirt, stood pushing her handkerchief in her mouth and trying in vain to stifle the hysterical laughter that still shook her slender body. Occasionally a strange peal, like mad bells, would break out. And then she ended with a passionate sobbing.

" I know ! I know ! " she sobbed, like a child. " Gran's dying, and you won't let me go home."

" You can go home," Jack said. " You can go home. But don't go with your face all puffed up with crying."

She gradually gained control of herself, and turned away to her horse. Jack went to help her mount. She got into the saddle, and he gave her the reins. She kept her face averted, and Lucy began to move away slowly, towards the home track.

Easu still stood there, planted with his feet apart, his head a little dropped, and a furious, contemptuous, revengeful hate of the other two in his light blue eyes. He had his head down, ready for an attack. Jack saw this, and waited.

" Going to take your punishment? " said Easu, in a nasty voice.

" Ready when you are," said Jack.

Ugh ! How he hated Easu's ugly, jeering, evil eyes, how he would love to smash them out of his head. In the long run, hate was an even keener ecstasy than love, and the battle of hate, the fight with blood in the eyes, an orgasm of deadly gratification keener than any passionate orgasm of love.

Easu slowly threw his hat on the ground. Jack did the same, and started to pull off his coat. Easu glanced round to see if Monica was going. She was. Her back was already turned, and Lucy was stepping gingerly through the bushes. He lifted his chin, unknotted his tie, and threw it in his hat. Then he unbuttoned his shirt cuffs, and pulled off his shirt, and hitched his belt. He was now naked to the waist. He had a very white skin with reddish hair at the breast, and an angular kind of force. His red-haired brawny arms were burnt bright red, as was his neck. For the rest his skin was pure white, with the dazzle of absolute health. Yet he was ugly rather than beautiful. The queer angularity of his brawn, the sense of hostile mechanical power. The sense of the mechanism of power in him made him like some devil fallen into a lower grade.

Jack's torso was rather absurdly marked by the sunburnt scallops of his vest-lines, for he worked a good deal in a vest. Easu always wore a shirt and no vest. And Jack, in spite of the thinness of youth, seemed to have softer lines and a more human proportion, more grace. And there was a warmth in his white skin, making it much less conspicuous than the really dazzling brilliance of Easu. Easu was a good deal bigger, but Jack was more concentrated, and a born fighter. He fought with all his soul.

He shaped up to Easu, and Easu made ready, when they were interrupted by a cry from Monica, in a high, hysterical voice. They looked up. She had reined in her horse among the bushes, and was looking round at them with a queer, sharp, terrified face, from the distance. Her shrill voice cried :

" Don't forget he saved Herbert's life."

Both men faced round and looked at her as if she had committed an indecency. She quailed in her saddle. Easu, with a queer jerk of the head, motioned to her to go. She sank a little forward in her saddle, and hurriedly urged her horse through the bush, out of sight, without ever looking round, leaving the men, as she knew, to their heart's desire.

They waited for a while. Then they lifted their fists again, and drew near. Jack began the light, subtle, harmonious dancing which preceded his attack. He always attacked, no matter whom he fought. He could not fight unless he took the initiative. So now he danced warily, subtly before Easu, and Easu stood ready to side-step. Easu was bigger, harder, much more powerful than Jack, and built in hard mechanical lines : the kind that is difficult to knock out, if you have not much weight behind your blow.

" Are y' insured ? " sneered Easu.

But Jack did not listen. He had always fought with people bigger and older than himself. But he had never before had this strange lust dancing in his blood, the lust of rage dancing for its consummation in blows. He had known it before, as a sort of game. But now the lust bit into his very soul, and he was quivering with accumulated desire, the desire to hit Easu hard, hit him till he knocked him out. He wanted to hit him till he knocked him out.

And he knew himself deficient in brute power. So he must make up in quickness and skill and concentration. When he did strike it must be a fine keen blow that went deep. He had confidence in his power to do it. Only—and this was the disturbing element—he knew there was not much *time*. And he would rather be knocked out himself than have the fight spoiled in the middle.

He moved lightly and led Easu on, ducked, bobbed up again, and began to be consummately happy. Easu could not get at him.

" Come on ! " said Easu thickly.

So suddenly he came on, and bang ! bang ! went his knuckles against that insulting chin. And he felt joy spring in his bowels.

But he did not escape without punishment. Pat !—butt ! Pat !—butt ! went Easu's swinging blows down over his back. But Jack got in two more. Bang ! bang ! He knew by the exquisite pain of his knuckles that he had struck deep, pierced the marrow of the other with pain of defeat.

Pat—butt ! Pat—butt ! came the punishment.

But Jack was out again, dancing softly, electric joy in his bowels. Then suddenly he sprang back at Easu, his arms swinging in strange, vindictive sideways swoops. Ping ! Pong ! Ping ! Pong ! rapid as lightning. Easu fell back a little dazed before this sudden rain of white blows, but Jack followed, followed, followed, nimbly, warily, but with deadly, flickering intent.

Crash ! Easu went down, but caught Jack a heavy smash in the face with his right fist as he fell. Jack reeled away.

And then, poised, waiting, watching, with blood running from bruised cuts on his swelling face, one eye rapidly closing, he stood well forward, fists in true boxing trim, and a deep gratification of joy in his dark belly.

Easu rose slowly, foaming at the mouth ; then, getting to his feet, rushed head down, in a convulsion, at his adversary. Jack stepped aside, but not quite quick enough. He caught Easu a blow with his left under the ear, but not in time to stop the impact. Easu's head butted right where he wanted it to—into his enemy's stomach ; though not full in the pit. Jack fell back winded, and Red also fell again, giving Jack time to throw back his head and whoop for a few mouthfuls of air. So that when Red rushed in again, he was able feebly to fence and stall him off, stepping aside and hitting again, but woefully clipping, smacking only . . .

"Foul! He's winded! Foul!" yelled someone from the bushes. "Time!"

"Not for mine," roared Easu.

He sprang and dashed at his gasping, gulping adversary, whirling his arms like iron piston-rods. Jack dodged the propelled whirl, but stumbled over one of the big feet stuck out to trip him. Easu hit as he fell, and swung a crashing left-right about the sinking, unprotected head. And when Jack was down, kicked the prostrate body in an orgasm of fury.

"Foul, you swine!" screamed Rackett, springing in like a tiger. Easu, absolutely blind with rage and hate, stared hellish and unseeing. Jack lay crumpled on the floor. Dr. Rackett stooped down to him, as Tom and Lennie and Alec Rice ran in. Easu went and dropped on a fallen log, sitting blowing to get his wind and his consciousness back. He was unconscious with fury, like some awful Thing, not like a man.

"My God, Easu!" screamed Rackett, who had lifted the dead head of Jack on to his knees. "If you've done for him I'll have you indicted."

And Easu, slowly, heavily coming back to consciousness, lifted his head, and the blue pupils of his red eyes went ugly with evil fear, his bruised face seemed to have dropped with fear.

He waited, vacant, empty with fear.

At length Jack stirred. There was life in him. And at once the bully Easu began to talk wide.

"Bloody little —— came at me bashing me jaw when I'd never touched him. Had to fight to defend myself. Bloody little ——!"

Jack opened his eyes and struggled to rise.

"Anybody counting?" he said stupidly. But he could not get up.

"It was a foul," said Rackett.

"Foul be blithered!" shouted Easu. "It was a free fight and no blasted umpires asked for. If that bloody bastard wants some more, let him get up. I'm goin' to teach him to come crowin' over an Australian."

But Jack was on his unsteady feet. He would fight now if he died for it.

"Teach me!" he said vaguely, and sprang like a cat

out of a bag on the astonished and rather frightened Easu.

But something was very wrong. When his left fist rang home it caused such an agony that a sheer scream of pain tore from him, clearing the mists from his brain in a strange white light. He was now fully conscious again, super-conscious. He knew he must hit with his right, and hit hard. He heard nothing, and saw nothing. But with a kind of trance vision he was super-awake.

Man is like this. He has various levels of consciousness. When he is broken, killed at one level of consciousness, his very death leaves him on a higher level. And this is the soul in its entirety being conscious, super-conscious, far beyond mentality. It hardly needs eyes or ears. It is clair-voyant and clairaudient. And man's divinity, and his ulti-mate power, is in this super-consciousness of the whole soul. Not in brute force, not in skill or intelligence alone. But in the soul's extreme power of knowing and then will-ing. On this alone hangs the destiny of all mankind.

Jack, uncertain on his feet, incorporate, wounded to horrible pain in his left hand, was now in the second state of consciousness and power. Meanwhile, the doctor was warning Easu to play fair. Jack heard absolutely without hearing. But Easu was bothered by it.

He was flustered by Jack's unexpected uprising. He was weary and wavering, the paroxysm of his ungovernable fury had left him, and he had a desire to escape. His rage was dull and sullen.

Jack was softly swaying. Easu shaped up and waited. And suddenly Jack sprang, with all the weight of his nine stone behind him, and all the mystery of his soul's deadly will, and planted a blow on Easu's astonished chin with his granite right fist. Before there was any recovery he got in a second blow, and it was a knockout. Easu crashed and Jack crashed after him, and both lay still.

Doctor Rackett, watch in hand, counted. Easu stared at the darkening blue, and sat up. An oath came out of his disfigured mouth. Dr. Rackett put the watch in his pocket as Easu got to his feet. But Jack did not move. He lay in a dead faint.

Lennie, the emotional, began to cry when he saw Jack's bruised, greenish-looking face. Dr. Rackett was feeling the pulse and the heart.

" Take the horse and fetch some whiskey and some water, Tom," he said.

Tom turned to Easu, who stood with his head down and his mouth all cut, watching, waiting to depart, undecided. " I'll borrow your horse a minute, Easu," he said. And Easu did not answer. He was getting into his shirt again, and for the moment none of him was visible save the belt of white skin round the waist. Tom pulled up the girth of the black horse, and jumped into the saddle. Lennie slipped up behind him, face still wet with tears. Easu's face emerged, disfigured, out of his white shirt, and watched them go. Rackett attended to Jack, who still gave no signs of life. Alec Rice stood beside the kneeling doctor, silent and impassive.

Easu slowly buttoned his shirt cuffs and shirt collar, with numb fingers. The pain was just beginning to come out, and he made queer slight grimaces with his distorted face. Slowly he got his black tie, and holding up his chin fastened it round his throat, clumsily. He was not the same Easu that had set off so huge and assertive, with Monica.

Lennie came running with a tin of water. He had slipped off the horse at the lower dam, and found the tin which he kept secreted there. Dr. Rackett put a wet handkerchief on Jack's still dead face. Under the livid skin the bruises and the blood showed terrifying, one eye already swollen up. The queer mask of a face looked as if the soul, or the life, had retreated from it in weariness or disgust. It looked like somebody else's altogether.

" He ain't dead, is he? " whimpered Lennie, terrified most of all because Jack, with his swollen face and puffed eye, looked like somebody else.

" No ! But I wish Tom would come with that whiskey."

As he spoke, they heard the crashing sound of the horse through the bushes, and Tom's red, anxious face appeared. He swung out of the saddle and dropped the reins on the ground.

Dr. Rackett pressed the bruised chin, pressed the mouth open, and poured a little liquor down Jack's throat. There was no response. He poured a little more whiskey. There came a slight choking sound, and then the one dark-blue eye opened vacant. It stared in vacancy for some moments, while everybody stood with held breath. Then the whiskey began to have effect. Life seemed to give a movement of itself, in the boy's body, and the wide-open eye took a conscious direction. It stared straight into the eyes of Easu, who stood there looking down, detached, in humiliation, derision and uneasiness. It stared with a queer, natural recognition, and a faint jeering, uneasy grin was the reflex on Easu's disfigured mask.

" Guess he's had enough for once," said Easu, and, turning, he picked up his horse's reins, dropped into the saddle, and rode straight away.

" Feel bad? " Dr. Rackett asked.

" Rotten! " said Jack.

And at last Lennie recognised the voice. He could not recognise the face, especially with that bunged-up eye peering gruesomely through a gradually diminishing slit, Hunlike.

Dr. Rackett smiled slightly.

" Where's your pain? " he asked.

Jack thought about it. Then he looked into Rackett's eyes without answering.

" Think you can stand? " said Rackett.

" Try me."

They got him to his feet. Everything began to swim again. Rackett's arm came round him.

" Did he knock me out? " Jack asked. The question came from his half-consciousness : from a feeling that the battle with Easu was not yet finished.

" No. You knocked him out. Let's get your coat on."

But as he shoved his arm into his coat he knew he was fainting again, and he almost wept, feeling his consciousness and his control going. He thought it was just his stiff, swollen, unnatural face that caused it.

" Can y' walk? " asked Tom anxiously.

" Don't walk on my face, do I? " came the words. But as they came, so did the reeling, nauseous oblivion. He fainted again, and was carried home like a sack over Tom's back.

When he came to, he was on his bed, Lennie was feverishly pulling off his shoes, and Dr. Rackett was feeling him all over. Dr. Rackett smelt of drugs. But now Rackett's face was earnest and attentive, he looked a nice man, only weak.

Jack thought at once of Gran.

" How's Gran? " he asked.

" She's picked up again. The relations put her in a wax, so she came to life again."

" You're the one now, you look an awful sight," said Len.

" Did anybody see me " asked Jack, dim and anxious.

" Only Grace, so far."

Rackett, who was busy bandaging, saw the fever of anxiety coming into the one live eye.

" Don't talk," he said. " Len, he mustn't talk at all. He's got to go to sleep."

After they had got his night-shirt on, they gave him something to drink, and he went to sleep.

ii

When he awoke it was dark. His head felt enormous. It was getting bigger and bigger, till soon it would fill the room. Soon his head would be so big it would fill all the room, and the room would be too small for it. Oh, horror! He was so frightened, he cried out.

" What's amiss? " a quick voice was asking.

" Make a light! Make a light! " cried Jack.

Lennie quickly lit a candle, and to Jack's agonized relief there was the cubby, the bed, the walls, all of natural dimensions, and Tom and Lennie in their night-shirts standing by his bed.

" What's a-matter, ol' dear? " Lennie asked caressively.

" My head! I thought it was getting so big the room couldn't hold it."

" Aw! Go on now! " said Lennie. " Y' face is a bit puffy, but y' head's same as ever it was."

Jack couldn't believe it. He was so sensually convinced that his head had grown enormous, enormous, enormous.

He stared at Lennie and Tom in dismay. Lennie stroked his hair softly.

" There's y' ol' nut! " he said. " 'Tain't no bigger 'n it ever was. Just exactly same life-size."

Gradually Jack let himself be convinced. And at last he let them blow the candle out. He went to sleep.

He woke again with a frenzy working in him. He had

pain, too. But far worse than the pain was the tearing of
the raging discomfort, the frenzy of dislocation. And in
his stiff, swollen head, there was something he remembered
but could not drag into light. What was it? What was it?
In the frenzy of struggle to know, he went vague.
    Then it came to him, words as plain as knives.

> And when I die
> In Hell I shall lie
> With fire and chains
> And awful pains.

The aunts had repeated this to him, as a child, when he
was naughty. And it had always struck a vague terror
into his soul. He had forgotten it. Now it came again.

> In Hell I shall lie
> With fire and chains
> And awful pains.

He had a vivid realisation of this hell. That was where he
lay at that very moment.
    " You must be a good, loving little boy."
    He had never wanted to be a good, loving little boy.
Something in his bowels revolted from being a good, loving
little boy, revolted in nausea. " But if you're not a good,
loving little boy,

> Then when you die
> In hell you will lie——etc.

    " Let me lie in hell, then," the bad and unloving little
boy had answered, to the shocked horror of the aunts.
And the answer had scared even himself.
    And now the hell was on him. And still he was not a
good, loving little boy.
    He remembered his lessons : Love your enemies.
    " Do I love Easu? " he asked himself. And he writhed
over in bed in disgust. He loathed Easu. If he could
crush him absolutely to powder, he would crush him to
powder. Make him extinct.
    " Lord, Lord ! " he groaned. " I loathe Easu. I loathe
him."

What was amiss with him? Did he want to leave off loathing Easu? Was that the root of his sickness and fever?

But when he thought of Easu's figure and face, he knew he didn't want to leave off loathing him. He *did* loathe him, whether he wanted to or not, and the fact to him was sacred. It went right through the core of him.

"Lord! Lord!" he groaned, writhing in fever. "Lord, help me to loathe him properly. Lord, I'll kill him if you want me to; and if you don't want me to, I won't. I'll kill him if you want me to. But if you don't want me to, I won't care any more."

The pledge seemed to soothe him. At the back of Jack's consciousness was always this mysterious Lord, to whom he cried in the night. And this Lord put commands upon him, but so darkly, Jack couldn't easily find out what the commands were. The aunts had always said the command was to be a good, loving little boy. But when he tried being a good, loving little boy, his soul seemed to lose his Lord, and turn wicked. That was what made him fear hell. When he seemed to lose connection with his great, mysterious Lord, with whom he communed absolutely alone, he became aware of hell. And he couldn't share with his aunts that Jesus whom they always commended. At the Sacrament, something in his soul stood still and cold. He knew that Sacrament was no Sacrament to him.

He had his own Lord. And when he could get into communication or communion, with his own Lord, he always felt well and right again.

Now, in his pain and battered fever, he was fighting for his Lord again.

"Lord, I don't love Easu, and I'll kill him if you want me to. But if you don't want me to, I won't. I won't. I won't bother any more."

This pledge and this submission, soothed him strangely. He felt he was coming back to his own Lord. It was a pledge, and he would keep it. He gave no pledge to love Easu. Only not to kill him, if the Lord didn't want it; and to kill him, if the Lord did.

"Lord, I don't love Monica. I don't love her. But if she'd give up to me, I'd love her if you wanted me to."

He thought about this. Somewhere, his soul burned

against Monica. And, somewhere, his soul burned for her.

But she must give up to him. She must give herself up. He demanded this submission, as if it were a submission to his mysterious Lord. She would never submit to the mysterious Lord direct. Like that old demon of a Gran, who knew the Lord, and played with Him, spited Him even. Monica would have first to submit to himself, Jack, in person, before she would really yield before the immense Lord. And yield before the immense Lord she must. Through him.

" Lord ! " he said, invoking the supreme power; " I love Lennie and Tom, and I want always to love them, and I want you to back them."

Then the prickles of pain entered his soul again.

" Lord, I don't love my father, but I don't want to hurt him. Only, I don't love him, Lord. And it's not my fault, though he's a good man, because I wasn't born with love for him in me."

This had been a thorn in his consciousness since he was a child. Best get it out now. Because the fear of *not* loving his father had almost made him hate him. If he ought to love him, and he couldn't love him, then there was nothing to do but hate him, because of the hopeless obligation. But if he *needn't* love him, then he needn't hate him, and they could both be in peace. He would leave it to his Lord.

" Perhaps I ought to love Mary," he continued. " But I don't *really* love her, because she doesn't realise about the Lord. She doesn't realise there is any Lord. She thinks there's only me, and herself. But there is the Lord. And Monica knows. But Monica is spiteful against the Lord. Lord ! Lord ! "

He ended on the old human cry of invocation : a cry which is answered, when it comes from the extreme, passionate soul. The strange, dark comfort and power came back to him again, and he could go to sleep once more, with his Lord.

When he woke in the morning, the fever had left him. Lennie was there at dawn, to see if he wanted anything. The quick little Lennie, who always came straight from the Lord, unless his emotions of pity got the better of him. Then he lost his connections, and became maudlin.

Jack wanted the family not to know. But the twins saw
his disfigured face, with horror. And Monica knew : it was
she who had sent Dr. Rackett and Tom and Alec. And
Grace knew. And soon Ma came, and said : " Dear o' me,
Jack Grant, what d'y'mean by going and getting messed
up like this ! " And Dad came slow and heavy, and said
nothing, but looked dark and angry. They all knew.

But Jack wanted to be left alone. He told Tom and Dr.
Rackett, and Tom and Dr. Rackett ordered the family to
leave him alone.

It was Grace who brought his meals. Poor old Grace,
with her big eyes and rather big nose, she had a gentle
heart, and more real sense than that Monica. Jack only
got to know her while he was sick, and she really touched
his heart. She was so kind, and thought so little of herself,
and had such a sad wisdom at the bottom of her. Who
would have thought it, of the pert, cheeky, nosy Grace ?

Monica slipped in, and stood staring down at him with
her queer, brooding eyes, that shone with widened pupils.
Heaven knows what she was thinking about.

" I was awfully afraid he'd kill you," she said. " I was
so frightened, that's what made me laugh."

" Why should I let him kill me ? " said Jack.

" How could you help it ?   He's much stronger and
crueler than you."

" He may be stronger, but I can match him in other
ways."

She looked at him incredulously. She did not believe
him. He could see she did not believe in that other, inward
power of his, upon which he himself depended. She thought
him in every way weaker, frailer than Easu. Only, of
course, nicer. This made Jack very angry.

" I think I punished him as much as he punished me,"
he said.

" *He's* not laid up in bed," she replied.

Then, with her quivering, exquisite gentleness, she
touched his bandaged hand.

" I'm awfully sorry he hurt you so," she said. " I know
you'll hate *me* for it."

" Why should I ? " he replied coldly.

She took up his bandaged hand and kissed it quickly,
then she looked him long and beseechingly in the eyes : or

the one eye. Somehow she didn't seem to see his caricature
of a face.

" Don't hate me for it," she pleaded, still watching him
with that strange, pleading, watchful look.

The flame leapt in his bowels, and came into his eyes.
And another flame as she, catching the change in his eyes,
softened her look and smiled subtly, suddenly taking his
wrist in a passionate, secret grasp. He felt the hot blood
suffusing him like new life.

" Good-bye ! " she said, looking back at him as she disappeared.

And when she had gone, he remembered the watchfulness
in her eyes, the cat-like watchfulness at the back of all her
winsome tenderness. There it was, like the devil. And he
turned his face to the wall, to his Lord, and two smarting
tears came under his eyes as if they were acid.

The next day Mary came bringing his pap. She was not
going to be kept away any longer. And she would come as
a ministering angel.

He saw on her face that she was startled, shocked, and
a little repelled by his appearance. She hardly knew him.
But she overcame her repulsion at once, and became the
more protective.

" Why, how awful it must be for you ! " she said.

" Not so bad now," he said, manfully swallowing his
pap.

He could see she longed for him to have his own good-
looking face again. She could not bear this strange horror.
She refused to believe this was he.

" I shall never forgive that cruel Easu ! " she said, and
the colour came to her dark cheek. " I hope I never have
to speak to him again."

" Oh, I began it. It was my fault."

" How could it be ? " cried Mary. " That great hulking
brute. How dare he lay a finger on you ! "

Jack couldn't smile, his face was of the fixed sort. But
his one good eye had a gleam.

" He dare, you see," he answered.

But she turned away in smarting indignation.

" It makes one understand why such creatures had
their hands cut off, in the old days," she said, with cold
fierceness.

" How dare he disfigure your beautiful face? How dare he? "

And tears of anger came to her eyes.

A strangled grin caused considerable pain to Jack's beautiful face.

" I suppose he didn' t rightly appreciate my sort of looks," he said.

" The jealous brute," said Mary. " But I hope he'll pay for it. I hope he will. I do hope he hasn't really disfigured you," she ended on a note of agitation.

" No, no ! Besides *that* doesn't matter all the world."

" It matters all the world," she cried, with strange fierceness, " to me."

CHAP : XII.   THE GREAT PASSING

i

JACK soon got better. Soon he was sitting in the old armchair by the parlour fire. There was a little fire, against the damp. This was Gran's place. But Gran did not leave her bed.

He had been in to see her, and she frightened him. The grey, dusky skin round the sunken mouth and sharpened nose, the eyes that were mostly shut, and never really open, the harsh breathing, the hands lying like old translucent stone on the bed-cover : it frightened him, and gave him a horror of dissolution and decay. He wanted terribly to be out again with the healthy Tom, among the horses. But not yet—he must wait yet awhile. So he took his turn sitting by Gran, to relieve Mary, who got little rest. And he became nervous, fanciful, frightened as he had never been before in his life. The family seemed to abandon him as they abandoned Gran. The cold isolation and horror of death.

The first rains had set in. All night the water had thundered down on the slab roof of the cubby, as if the bottom had fallen out of some well above. Outside was cloudy still, and a little chill. A wind was hush-sh-shing round the house. Mary was sitting with Gran, and he was in the parlour, listening to that clock—Tick-tock ! Ticktock ! He sat in the arm-chair with a shawl over his shoulders, trying to read. Curiously enough, in Australia he could not read. The words somehow meant nothing to him.

It was Sunday afternoon, and the smell of roast beef, Yorkshire pudding, cabbage, apple pie and cinnamon custard still seemed to taint the house. Jack had come to loathe Sunday dinners. They seemed to him degrading. They hung so heavy afterwards. And now he was sick, it seemed to him particularly repulsive. The peculiar Sundayness of it. The one thing that took him in revulsion back to England : Sunday dinner. The England he didn't want to be taken back to. But it had been a quiet meal. Monica and Grace, and the little boy twins had all been invited to York, by Alec Rice's parents, and they had gone away from the shadowed house, leaving a great emptiness. It seemed to Jack they should all have stayed, so that their young life could have united against this slow dissolution.

Everything felt very strange. Tom and Lennie were out, Mrs Ellis and the children were upstairs, Mr Ellis had gone to look at some sheep that had got into trouble in the rain. There seemed a darkness, a chill, a deathliness in the air. It is like that in Australia : usually so sunny and absolutely forgetful. Then comes a dark day, and the place seems like an immemorial grave. More gruesome than ever England was, on her dark days. Mankind forever entombed in dissolution, in an endless grave.

Who shall ascend into the hill of the Lord ; or who shall stand in His holy place ?

He that hath clean hands and a pure heart,

Who hath not yielded up himself unto vanity, nor sworn deceitfully.

Jack was thinking over the words Mr Ellis had read in the morning, as near as he remembered them. He looked at his own hands : already they seemed pale and soft and very clean. What had the Lord intended hands for ? So many things hands must do, and still they remain clean. Clean hands ! His left was still discoloured and out of shape. Was it unclean ?

No, it was not unclean. Not unclean like the great paw of Easu's hiking Monica out of the saddle.

Clean hands and a pure heart ! A pure heart ! Jack thought of his own, with two heavy new desires in it : the sudden, shattering desire for Monica, that would rip through him sometimes like a flame. And the slow, smouldering desire to kill Easu. He had to be responsible for them both.

And he was not going to try to pluck them out. They both belonged to his heart, they were sacred even while they were shocking in his blood. Only, driven back on himself, he gave the old pledge : *Lord, if you don't want me to have Monica and kill Easu, I won't. But if you want me to, I will.* Somewhere he was inclined to cry out to be delivered from the cup. But that would be cowardice towards his own blood. It would be yielding himself up to vanity, if he pretended he hadn't got the desires. And if he swore to eradicate them, it would be swearing deceitfully. Sometimes the hands must move in the darkest acts, if they are to remain really clean, not deathly like Gran's now. And the heart must beat hard in the storm of darkest desires, if it is to keep pure, and not go pale-corrupt.

But always subject to the will of the Lord.

" Who shall ascend into the hill of the Lord; or who shall stand in His holy place."

The Seraphim and the Cherubim knew strange, awful secrets of the Lord. That was why they covered their faces with their wings, for the wings of glory also had a dark side.

The fire was burning low. Jack stooped to put on more wood. Then he blew the red coals to make the wood catch. A yellow flame came, and he was glad.

" Forsake me not, Oh God, in mine old age; when I am grey-headed; until I have shown my strength to this generation, and Thy power to all them that are yet to come."

Jack was always afraid of those times when the mysterious sayings of the Bible invaded him. He seemed to have no power against them. And his soul was always a little afraid, as if the walls of life grew thin, and he could hear the great everlasting wind of the mysterious going of the Lord, on the other side.

" Forsake me not, Oh God, in mine old age; when I am grey-headed."

Jack wished Gran would say this, so that the Lord would stay with her, and she would not look so awful. How could Mary *stand* it, sitting with her day after day.

" Until I have shown my strength to this generation, and Thy power to all them that are yet to come."

And again his stubborn strength of life arose. What was he for, but to show his strength to the generation, and a sign of the power of the Lord for all them that were yet to come.

The clock was ticking steadily in the room. But the yellow flames were bunching up in the grate. He wondered where Gran's " stocking " really was? But the thought of stockings, of concealed money, of people hankering for money, always made him feel sick.

" There is one glory of the sun, and another glory of the moon, and another glory of the stars . . . There is a natural body and a spiritual body . . ."

" There is one glory of the sun." But men don't all

realise the same glory. In England the sun had seemed to him to move with a domestic familiarity. It wasn't till he was out here that he had been struck to the soul with the immense assertive vigour and sacred handsomeness of the sun. He knew it now : the wild, immense, fierce, untamed sun, fiercer than a glowing-eyed lion with a vast mane of fire, crouching on the western horizon, staring at the earth as if to pounce on it, the mouse-like earth. He had seen this immense sun, fierce and powerful beyond all human considerations, glaring across the southern sea, as all men may see it if they go there.

" There is one glory of the sun." And it is a glory vast and fierce, of a Lord who is more than our small lives.

" And another glory of the moon." That too he knew. And he had not known, till the full moon had followed him through the empty bush, in Australia, in the night. The immense liquid gleam of the far-south moon, following, following with a great, miraculous, liquid smile. That vast white, liquid smile, so vindictive ! And himself, hurrying back to camp on Lucy, had known a terrible fear. The fear that the broad liquid fire of the cold moon would capture him, capture him and destroy him, like some white demon that slowly and coldly tastes and devours its prey. The moon had that power, he knew, to dissolve him, tissue, heart, body and soul, dissolve him away. The immense, gleaming, liquid, lusting white moon, following him inexorably, and the bush like white charred moon-embers.

" There is another glory of the moon." And he was afraid of it. " The sun is thy right hand, and the moon is thy left hand." The two gleaming, immense living orbs, moving like weapons in the two hands of the Lord.

" And there is another glory of the stars." The strange stars of the southern night, all in unfamiliar crowds and tufts and drooping clusters, with strange black wells in the sky. He never got used to the southern stars. Whenever he stood and looked up at them he felt as if his soul were leaving him, as if he belonged to another species of life, not to man as he knew man. As if there were a metamorphosis, a terrible metamorphosis to take place.

" There is a natural body, and there is a spiritual body." This phrase had haunted his mind from the earliest days. And he had always had a sort of hatred of the thing his aunts, and the parson, and the poets, called The Spirit, with a capital S. It had always, with him, been connected with his Sunday clothes, and best behaviour, and a certain exalted falseness. Part of his natural naughtiness had arisen from his vindictive dislike and contempt of The Spirit, and things of The Spirit.

Now it began to seem different to him. He knew, he always had known, that the Bible really meant something absolutely different from what the aunts and the parson and even the poets meant by the Spirit, or the spiritual body.

Since he had seen the Great God in the roaring of the yellow sun, and the frightening vast smile in the gleaming full-moon following him, the new moon like a delicate weapon-threat in the western sky, and the stars in disarray, like a scattered flock of sheep bunching and communing together in a strange bush, in the vast heavens, he had gradually come to know the difference between the natural body and the spiritual body. The natural body was like in England, where the sun rises naturally to make day, and passes naturally at sunset, owing to the earth's revolving; where the moon " raises her lamp above," on a clear night, and the stars are " candles " in heaven. That is the natural body : all the cosmos just a natural fact. And a man loves a woman so that they can propagate their species. The natural body.

And the spiritual body is supposed to be something thin and immaterial, that can float through a brick wall and subsist on mere thought. Jack had always hated this thin, wafting object. He preferred his body solid. He loved the beautiful weight and transfigured solidity of living limbs. He had no use whatsoever for the gossamer stuff of the supposed " ethereal," or " pure " spirit : like evaporated alcohol. He had a natural dislike of Shelley and vegetarians and socialists and all advocates of " spirit." He hated Blake's pictures, with people waving like the wrong kind of sea-weed, in the sky, instead of underwater. Hated it all. Till hating it had almost made him wicked.

Now he had a new understanding. He had always *known* that the Old Testament never meant any of this Shelley stuff, this Hindu Nirvana business. " There is a natural body, and there is a spiritual body." And his natural body got up in the morning to eat food and tend sheep and earn money and prepare for having a family; to see the sun usefully making day and setting owing to the earth's revolution : the new moon so shapen because the earth's shadow fell on her; the stars being other worlds, other lumps in space, shining according to their various distances, coloured according to their chemical composition. Well and good.

That is man very cleverly finding out all about it, like a little boy pulling his toy to pieces.

But, willy-nilly, in this country he had another sun and another moon. He had seen the glory of the sun and the glory of the moon, and both these glories had had a powerful sensual effect on him. There had been a great passional reaction in himself, in his own body. And as the strange new passion of fear and the sense of gloriousness burned through him, like a new intoxication, he knew that this was his real spiritual body. This glowing, intoxicated body, drunk with the sun and the moon, drunk from the cup in the hand of the Lord, *this* was his spiritual body.

And when the flame came up in him, tearing from his bowels, in the sudden new desire for Monica, this was his spiritual body, the body transfigured with fire. And that steady dark vibration which made him want to kill Easu— Easu seemed to him like the Antichrist—that was his own spiritual body. And when he had hit Easu with his broken left hand, and the white sheet of flame going through him had made him scream aloud, leaving him strange and distant but super-conscious and powerful, this, too, was his spiritual body. The sun in his right hand and the moon in his left hand. When he drank from the burning right hand of the Lord, and wanted Monica in the same fire, it was his body spiritual burning from the right hand of the Lord. And when he knew he must destroy Easu, in the sheet of white pain, it was his body spiritual transfigured from the left hand of the Lord. And when he ate and drank and the food tasted good, it was the dark cup of life he was drinking, drinking the life of the dead ox from the meat. And this was the body spiritual communing with the sacrificed body of natural life : like a tiger glowing at evening and lapping blood. And when he rode after the sheep through the bush, and the horse between his knees went quick and delicate, it was the Lord tossing him in his spiritual body down the maze of living.

But when Easu ground down his horse and shoved it after the sheep, it was the natural body fiendishly subjugating the spiritual body. For the horse, too, is a spiritual body and a natural body, and may be ridden as the one or as the other. And when Easu wanted Monica, it was the natural body malignantly degrading the spiritual body. Monica also half wanted it.

For Easu knew the spiritual body. And like a fallen angel he hated it, he wanted always to overthrow it more, in this day when it is so abjectly overthrown. Monica, too, knew the spiritual body : the body of straight fire. And she, too, seemed to have a grudge against it. It thwarted her " natural " will : which " natural " will is the barren devil of to-day.

Gran, that old witch, she also knew the spiritual body. But she loved spiting it. And she was dying like clay.

Mary, who was so spiritual and so self-sacrificing, she didn't know the body of straight fire at all. Her spirit was all natural. She was so " good," and so heavily " natural," she would put out any fire of the glory of the burning Lord. She was more " natural " even than Easu.

And Jack's father was the same. So good ! So nice ! So kind ! So absolutely well-meaning ! And he would bank out the fire of the burning Lord with shovelfuls of kindness.

They would none of them, none of them let the fire burn straight. None of them. There were no people at all who dared have the fire of the Lord, and drink from the cup of the fierce glory of the Lord, the sun in one hand and the moon in the other.

Only this strange, wild, ash-coloured country with its undiminished sun and its unblemished moon, would allow it. There was a great death between the two hands of the Lord; between the sun and the moon. But let there be a great death. Jack gave himself to it.

He was almost asleep, in the half-trance of inner consciousness, when Dad came in. Jack opened his eyes and made to rise, but Dad waved him to sit still, while he took the chair on the other side of the fire, and sat down inert. He seemed queer. Dad seemed queer. The same dusky look over his face as over Gran's. And a queer, pinched, far-away look. Jack wondered over it. And he could see Dad didn't want to be spoken to. The clock tick-tocked. Jack went into a kind of sleep.

He opened his eyes. Dad was very slowly, very slowly fingering the bowl of his pipe. How quiet it was!

Jack dozed again, and wakened to a queer noise. It was Dad's breathing : and perhaps the falling of his pipe. He had dropped his pipe. And his body had dropped over sideways, very heavy and uncomfortable, and he was breathing hoarsely, unnaturally in his sleep. Save for the breathing it was dreadfully quiet. Jack picked up the pipe and sat down again. He felt tired : awfully tired, for no reason at all.

He woke with a start. The afternoon was passing, there was a shower, the room seemed dark. The firelight flickered on Mr Ellis' watchguard. He wore his unbuttoned waistcoat as ever, with the gold watch-chain showing. He was very stout, and very still. Terribly still and sagging sideways, the hoarse breathing had ceased. Jack would have liked to wake him from that queer position.

How quiet it was! Upstairs someone had dragged a chair and that had made him realise. Far away, very far away, he could hear Harry and Ellie and baby, playing. " There's a quiet of the sun and another quiet of the moon, and another quiet of the stars ; for one star differs from another in quiet. So also is the resurrection of the dead. It is sown a natural body ; it is raised a spiritual body."

Was that Scripture? Or wasn't it? There is a quiet of the sun. This was the quiet of the sun. He was sitting in the cold dead quiet of the sun. For one star differs from another in quiet. The sun had abstained from radiating, this was the quiet of the sun, and the strange, shadowy crowding of the stars' differing quietness seemed to infest the weak daylight.

It is sown a natural body! Oh, bother the words! He didn't want them. He wanted the sun to shine, and everything to be normal. If he didn't feel so weak, and if it weren't raining, he'd go out to the stable to the horses. To the hot-blooded animals.

Mr Ellis' head hung sagging on his chest. Jack wished he would wake up and change his position, it looked horrible.

The inner door suddenly opened, and Mary came swiftly out. She started seeing Mr Ellis asleep in the chair. Then she went to Jack's side and took his arm, and leaned whispering in his ear.

"Jack! She's gone! I think she's gone. I think she passed in her sleep. We shall have to wake uncle."

Jack stood up trembling. There was a queer smell in the room. He walked across and touched the sleeping man on the sleeve.

"Dad!" he said. "Dad! Mr Ellis."

There was no response. They both waited. Then Jack shook the arm more vigorously. It felt very inert. Mary came across and put her hand on her uncle's sunken forehead, to lift his head. She gave a little scream.

"Something's the matter with him," she said, whimpering.

ii

Thank goodness, Dr. Rackett was upstairs. They fetched him and Timothy and Tom, and carried Mr Ellis into the dying room.

"Better leave me alone with him now," said Rackett.

After ten minutes he came out of the dying room and closed the door behind him. Tom was standing there. He looked at Rackett enquiringly. Rackett shook his head.

"Dad's not dead?" said Tom.

Rackett nodded.

Tom's face went to pieces for a moment. Then he composed it, and that Australian mouth of his, almost like a scar, shut close. He went into the dying room.

Someone had to fetch the Methodist son-in-law from York. Jack went in the sulky. Better die in the cart than stop in that house. And he could drive the sulky quietly.

The Methodist son-in-law, though he was stout and wore black and Jack objected to him on principle, wasn't really so bad, in his own home. His wife Ruth, of course, burst into tears and ran upstairs. Her husband kept his face straight, brought out the whiskey tantalus, and poured some for Jack and himself. This they both drank with befitting gravity.

"I must be in chapel in fifteen minutes; that will be

five minutes late," said the parson. " But they can't complain, under the circumstances. Mrs Blogg, of course, will stay at home. Er—is anyone making arrangements out at Wandoo ? "

" What arrangements ? "

" Oh, seeing to things . . . the personal property, too."

" I was sent for you," said Jack. " I suppose they thought you'd see to things."

" Yes ! Certainly ! Certainly ! I'll be out with Mrs Blogg directly after Meeting. Let me see."

He went to a table and laboriously wrote two notes. Twisting them into cocked hats, he handed them one after the other to Jack saying :

" This is to the Church of England parson. Leave it at his house. I've made it Toosday, Toosday at half-past ten. I suppose that'll do. And this—this is to the joiner."

He looked at Jack meaningly, and Jack looked vague.

" Joshua Jenkins, at the joiner's shop. Third house from the end of the road. And you'll find him in the loft over the stable, Sunday or not, if he isn't in the house."

It was sunset and the single bells of the church and chapel were sounding their last ping ! ping ! ping-ping ! as Jack drove slowly down the straggling street of York. People were going to church, the women in their best shawls and bonnets, hurrying a little along the muddy road, where already the cows were lying down to sleep, and the loose horses straggled uncomfortably.   Occasionally a muddy buggy rattled up to the brick Church of England, people passed shadow-shape into the wooden Presbyterian Church, or waited outside the slab Meeting House of the Methodists. The choir band was already scraping fiddles and tooting cornets in the church. Lamps were lighted within, and one feeble lamp at the church gate. It was a cloudy evening. Odd horsemen went trotting through the mud, going out into the country again as night fell, rather forlorn.

Jack always felt queer in York on Sundays. The attempt at Sunday seemed to him like children's make believe. The churches weren't real churches, the parsons weren't real parsons, the people weren't real worshippers. It was a sort of earnest make-belief, where people felt important like actors.   And the pub, with its extra number of lamps, seemed to feel extra wicked. And the men riding home, often tipsy, seemed vague as to what was real, this York acting Sunday, or their dark, rather dreary farms away out, or some other third unknown thing. Was anything quite real? That was what the shadows, the people, the buildings seemed all to be asking. It was like children's games, real and not real, actual and yet unsubstantial, and the people seemed to feel as children feel, very earnest, very sure that they were *very* real, but having to struggle all the time to keep up the conviction. If they didn't keep up the conviction, the dark, strange Australian night might clear them and their little town all away into some final cupboard, and leave the aboriginal bush again.

Joshua Jenkins, the godless, was in the loft with a chisel, working by lantern light. He peered at the twisted note, and his face brightened.

" Two of 'em ! " he exclaimed, with a certain gusto. " Well, think o' that, think o' that ! And I've not had a job o' this sort for over a month. Well, I never, t'be sure ! 'T never rains but it comes down cats and dogs seemingly. Toosday ! Toosday ! Toosday ! Let's see "—and he scratched his head behind the ear. " Pretty quick work that, pretty quick work. But, can be done; oh, yes, can be done. I's'll have t'send somebody t' measure the Boss. How deep should you say he was in the barrel? Never mind, though, I'll send Sam over with the measure, come morning. But I can start right away on the old lady. Let's see ! Let's see ! She wouldn't be-e-e—she wouldn't be over five foot two or three, now, would she ? "

" I don't know," said Jack hoarsely. " Do you mean for her coffin ? " He was filled with horror.

" Well, I should say I do. I should say so. You don't see no sewing-machines here, do you, for sewing her shroud. I suppose I do mean her coffin, being joiner and carpenter, and J.P., and coroner as well, when required."

Jack fled, horrified. But as he lit his sulky candles, and set off at a slow trot out of the town, he laughed a bit to himself. He felt it was rather funny. Why shouldn't it be rather funny ? He hoped it would be a bit funny when he was dead too, to relieve matters. He sat in the easy sulky driving slowly down the washed-out road, in the dark, alien night. The night was dark and strange. An animal ran along the road in front of him, just discernible, at the far edge of the dim yellow candle glow. It was a wild grey thing, running ahead into the dark. On into the dark.

Why should one care? Beyond a certain point, one didn't care about anything, life or death. One just felt it all. Up to a certain point, one had to go through the mill, caring and feeling bad. One had to cry out to the Lord, and fight the ugly brutes of life. And then for a time it was over, and one didn't care, good or bad, Lord or no Lord. One paid one's whack of caring and then one was let off for a time. When one was dead, one didn't care any more. And that was death. But life too had its own indifference, its own deep, strong indifference : as the ocean is calm way down, under the most violent storm.

When he got home, Tom came out to the sulky. Tom's face was set with that queer Australian look, as if he were caught in a trap, and it wasn't any use complaining about it. He unharnessed the horse in a rough, flinging fashion. Jack didn't know what to say to him, so he thought he'd better keep quiet.

Lennie came riding in on Lucy. He slid to the ground and dragged the mare's bridle roughly.

" Come on, yer blasted old idjut, can't ye ! " he blubbed, dragging her to the stable door. " Blasted idjut, my Uncle Joe ! " he continued, between the sniffs and gulps of his blubbing. " Questions ! Questions ! How c'n I answer questions when I don't know myself ! " A loud blub as he dragged the saddle down on top of himself, in his frenzy of untackling Lucy. " Rackett says to me, ' Len,' he says," blub and a loud sniff—" ' y' father's took bad and pore ol' Gran's gone,' he says "—blub ! blub ! blub. " ' Be off an' fetch y' Uncle Joe an' tell him to come at onst '—an' he can go to *hell*." Lennie ended on a shout of defiance as he staggered into the stable with the saddle. And from the dark his voice came : " An' when I ask our Tom what's amiss wi' m' Dad," blub ! blub ! " blasted idjut looks at me like a blasted owl—like a blasted owl ! " And Lennie sobbed before he sniffed and came out for the bridle.

" Don't y' cry, Lennie," said Jack, who was himself crying for all he was worth, under the cover of the dark.

" I'm not crying, y' bloomin' fool, you ! " shouted Len. " I'm goin' in to see Ma, I am. Get some sense outta *her*."

He walked off towards the house, and then came back.

" Why don' *you* go in, Tom, an' see ? " he cried. " What d'yer stan' there like that for, what *do* yer ? "

There was a dead and horrible silence, outside the stable door in the dark. A silence that went to the core of the night, having no word to say.

The lights of a buggy were seen at the gate. The three waited. It was the unmarried aunts. One of them ran and took Len in her arms.

" Oh, you poor little lamb ! " she cried. " Oh, your poor Ma ! Your Ma ! Your poor Ma ! "

" Ma's not bad ! She's all right," yelped Len in a new fear. Then there was a pause, and he became superconscious. Then he drew away from the aunts.

" Is Dad dead ? " he asked in a queer, quizzical little voice, looking from Tom to Jack, in the dim buggy light. Tom stood as if paralysed.

Lennie at last gave a queer, animal " Whooo," like a dog dazed with pain, and flung himself into Tom's arms. The only sounds in the night were Tom's short, dry sobs, as he held Lennie, and the whimpering of the aunts.

" Come to your poor Mother, come to comfort her," said one of the aunts gently.

" Tom ! Tom ! " cried Lennie. " I'm skeered ! I'm skeered, Tom, o' them two corpses ! I'm skeered of 'em, Tom." Tom, who was a little skeered too, gave a short, dry bark of a sob.

" They won't hurt you, precious ! " said the aunt. " They won't hurt you. Come to your poor Mother."

" No-o-o ! " wailed Lennie in terror, and he flung away to Timothy's cabin, where he slept all night.

When the horses were fixed up, Tom and Jack went to the cubby. Tom flung himself on the bed without undressing, and lay there in silence. Jack did the same. He didn't know what else to do. At last he managed to say :

" Don't take it too hard, Tom ! Dad's lived his life, and he's got all you children. We have to live. We all have to live. An' then we've got to die."

There was unresponsive silence for a time.

" What's the blasted use of it all, anyhow ? " said Tom.

" There's no such thing as *use*," said Jack. " Dad lived, and he had his life. He had his life. You'll have yours.

And I shall have mine. It's just your life, and you live it."

" What's the *good* of it ? " persisted Tom heavily.

" Neither good nor bad. You live your life because it's your own, and nobody can live it for you."

" What good is it to me ? " said Tom dully, drearily. " I don't care if people live their lives or not."

Jack felt for the figure on the bed.

" Shake hands though, Tom," he said. " You *are* alive, and so am I. Shake hands on it."

He found the hand and got a faint response, sulky, heavy. But for very shame Tom could not withhold all response.

Tim came in the morning with tea and bread and butter, saying Tom was wanted inside, and would Jack go with him to attend to the grave. Poor Tim was very much upset, and wept and wailed unrestrainedly. Which perhaps was good, because it spared the others the necessity to weep and wail.

They hitched up the old buggy, and set off with a pick and a couple of spades. Old black Timothy on the driving-box occasionally startled Jack by breaking forth into a new sudden wail, like a dog suddenly remembering again. It was a fine day. The earth had already dried up, and a hot, dry, gritty wind was blowing from inland, from the east. They drove out of the paddocks and along an overgrown trail, then they crossed the river, heaving and floundering through the slough, for at this season it was no more. The excitement of the driving here made Timothy forget to wail.

Rounding a steep little bluff, they came to a lonely, forlorn little enclosed graveyard, which Jack had never seen. Tim wailed, then asked where the grave should be. The sun grew very hot. They nosed around the little, lonely, parched acre.

Jack could not dig, so he unharnessed the outfit and put a box of chaff before the horses. Tim flung his spade over against a little grey headstone, and climbed in with the pick. Even then they weren't quite sure how big to make the grave, so Jack lay on the ground while Tim picked out a line around him. They got a straight line with a rope.

The soil was as hard as cement. Tim toiled and moiled, and forgot all wailing. But he made little impression on the cement-like earth.

" What we goin' to do ? " he asked, scratching his sweating head. " What'n hell's name we goin' t' do, sir ? Gotta bury 'm Toosday, gotta." And he looked at the blazing sun. " Gotta dig him hole sevenfut deep grave, gotta do 't."

He set to again. Then two of the Reds came, sent to help. But the work was killing. The day became so hot, you forgot it, you passed into a kind of spell. But that work was heart-breaking.

Jack went off for dynamite, and Rackett came along, with Lennie, who would never miss a dynamiting show. Tim wrung his wet hair like a mop. The Reds, in their vests, were scarlet, and the vests were wet and grimy.

Much more fun with dynamite. Boom ! Bang ! Then somebody throwing out the dirt. Somebody going for a ladder. Boom ! Bang ! The explosions seemed enormous.

" Oh, for the love o' Mike ! " cried the excited Lennie. " Ye'll blow me ol' grandfather sky high, if y' don't mind. For the love of Mike, don't let me see his bones."

But the grandfather Ellis was safe in the next grave. Rackett laid another fuse. They all stood back. Bang ! Boom ! Pouf ! went the dust.

iii

Jack would have done anything to escape the funeral, but Timothy, for some reason, kept hold of him. He wanted him to help replace the turf : moral support rather than physical assistance.

The two of them hid behind the pinch. At last they saw the cortege approaching. Easu Ellis held the reins of the first team, and chewed the end of the whip. Beside him sat Joshua Jenkins, as a mute, fearful in black, and like a scarecrow with loose danglings of crape. In the buggy behind them, on the floor-boards, was Gran's coffin, shaking woefully, covered with a black cloth. Joe Low drove the second buggy, which was the second hearse, and he looked strained and anxious as the heavy coffin bumped when the buggy dropped into holes on the track. Then came the family shay with the chief male mourners. Then a little crowd on foot.

The horses were behaving badly, not liking the road. It was hot, the vile east wind was blowing. Easu's horse jibbed at the slough of the stream : would not take it. He was afraid they would jump, and toss the coffin out of the buggy. He had to get bearers to carry Gran's poor remains across the mud and up the pinch to their last house. The bearers sunk almost to their knees in mud. The whole cortége was at a standstill.

Joe Low's horses, mortally frightened, were jumping round till they were almost facing the horses in the mourners' shay. Easu ran to their heads. More bearers, strong men, came forward to lift out Dad's heavy coffin. Everybody watched in terror as they staggered through the slough of the stream with that unnatural burden. Was it going to fall ?

No, they were through. Men were putting branches and big stones for the foot-mourners to cross, everybody sweating and sweltering. The sporting parson, his white surplice waving in the hateful, gritty hot wind, came striding over, holding his book. Then Tom, with a wooden, stupid face. Then Lennie, cracking nuts between his teeth and spitting out the shells, in an agony of nervousness. Then the other mourners, some carrying a few late, weird bush-flowers, picking their way over like a train of gruesome fowls, staggering and clutching on the stones and boughs, landing safe on the other bank. Jack watched from a safe distance above.

There were two coffins, one on either side of the grave. Some of the uncles had top hats with dangling crape. Nearly everybody was black. Poor Len, what a black little crow he looked ! The sporting parson read the service manfully. Then he announced hymn number 225.

Jack could feel the hollow place below, with the black mourners, simmer with panic, when the parson in cold blood asked them to sing a hymn. But he read the first verse solemnly, like an overture :

> " Oh sweet and blessed country
> The home of God's elect !
> Oh sweet and blessed country
> That eager hearts expect . . ."

There was a deadly pause. There was going to be no answer from the uncomfortable congregation, under that hot sun.

But Uncle Blogg was not to be daunted. He struck up in a rather fat, wheezy, Methodist voice, and Aunt Ruth piped feebly. The maiden aunts, who had insisted on following their mother, though women were not expected to attend, listened to this for an awful minute or two, then they waveringly " tried " to join in. It was really only funny. And Tom, in all his misery, suddenly started to laugh. Lennie looked up at him with wide eyes, but Tom's shoulders shook, shook harder, especially when Aunt Minnie " tried " to sing alto. That alto he could not bear.

The Reds were beginning to grin sheepishly and to turn their heads over their shoulders, as if the open country would not object to their grins. It was becoming a scandal.

Lennie saved the situation. His voice came clear and pure, like a chorister's, rising above the melancholy " trying " of the relations, a clear, pure singing, that seemed to dominate the whole wild bush.

> " Oh sweet and blessed country
> That eager hearts expect.
>
> Jesu in mercy bring us
> To that dear land of rest;
> Who art with God the Father,
> And Spirit ever blessed."

At the sound of Lennie's voice, Tom turned white as a sheet, and looked as if he were going to die, too. But the boy's voice soared on, with that pure quality of innocence that was sheer agony to the elder brother.

iv

Jack, who was looking sick again, was sent away to the Greenlow's next day. And he was glad to go, thankful to be out of it. He loathed death, he loathed death, and Wandoo had suddenly become full of death.

The first cool days of the year, golden and blue, were at hand. The Greenlow girls made much of him. He rode with them after sheep, inspecting fences, examining far-off wells. They were not bad girls at all. They taught him to play solitaire at evening, to hold worsted, even to spin. Real companionable girls, thankful to have a young man in the house, spoiling him completely. Pa was home after the first day, and acted as a sort of hairy chimpanzee chaperone, but looking over his spectacles and hissing through his teeth was his severest form of reproof. He didn't set Jack to wash that Sunday, but even gave him tit-bits from the joint, so that our young hero almost knew what it was to have a prospective father-in-law.

Jack left Gum Tree Croft with regret. For he knew his life at Wandoo was over. Now Dad was dead, everything was going to break up. This was bitter to him, for it was the first place he had ever loved, ever wanted to stay in, for ever and ever. He loved the family. He couldn't bear to go away from them.

" Never mind ! " he said to himself. " I shall always have them in some way or other, all my life."

Things seemed different when he got back. There wasn't much real difference, except a bit of raking and clearing up had been done for the funeral. But Wandoo itself seemed to have died. For the meantime the homestead was as if dead.

Grace and Monica looked unnatural in black frocks. They felt unnatural.

Jack was told that Mr George was having a conclave in the parlour, and that he was to go in.

Tom, Mrs Ellis, and Mr George and Dr. Rackett were there, seated round the table, on which were some papers. Jack shook hands, and sat uneasily in an empty chair on Dr. Rackett's side of the table. Mr George was explaining things simply.

Mr Ellis left no will. But the first marriage certificate had been found. Tom was to inherit Wandoo, but not till he came legally of age, in a year and a half's time. Meanwhile, Mrs Ellis could continue on the place, and carry on as best she might, on behalf of herself and all the children. For a year and a half.

She heard in silence. After a year and a half she would be homeless : or at least dependent on Tom, who was not her son. She sat silent in her black dress.

Tom cleared his throat and stared at the table. Then he looked up at Jack, and, scarlet in the face, said :

" I've been thinking, Ma, I don't want the place. You have it, for Len. I don't want it. You have it, for Len an' the kids. I'd rather go away. Best if that certificate hadn't never been found, if you're going to feel you're turned out."

He dropped his head in confusion. Mr George held up his hand.

" No more of that heroic talk," he said. " When Jacob Ellis stored up that marriage certificate at the bottom of that box, he showed what he meant. And you may feel as you say to-day, but two years hence you might repent it."

Tom looked up angrily.

" I don't believe Tom would ever regret it," put in Mrs Ellis. " But I couldn't think of it. Len wouldn't let me, even if I wanted to."

" Of course not," said Mr George. " We've got to be sensible, and the law's the law. You *can't* alter it yet, my boy, even if you want to. You're not of age yet.

" So you listen to me. My plan is for you and Jack to go out into the colony and get some experience. Sow your wild oats, if you've got any to sow, or else pick up a bit of *good* oat-seed. One or the other.

" My idea is for you and Jack to go up for a year to Lang's Well station, out Roeburne way. Lang'll give you your keep and a pound a week each, and your fare refunded if you stay a year.

" The Rob-Roy sails from Geraldton about a month from now ; you can get passages on her. And I thought it would be just as well, Tom, if you and Jack rode up through that midland country. You've a hundred connections to see, who'll change y'r horses for y'. And you'll see the country. And y'll be men of travel. We want men of experience, men of a wide outlook. Somebody's got to be the head-piece of this colony when men like me and the rest of us are gone. It'll be a three hundred mile ride, but ye've nigh on a month to do it.

" Now, what do you say, my boy? Your mother will stop on here with the children. I'll see she gets a good man to run the place. And meanwhile she'll be able to fix some-thing up for herself. Oh, we shall settle all right. I'll see your mother through all right. No fear of that. And no fear of any deterioration to the place. I'll watch that. You bet I will."

Tom twisted his fingers, white at the gills, and mumbled his thanks vaguely.

"Jack," said Mr George. "I know you're game. And you will look after Tom."

Dr. Rackett said he thought it a wise plan, and further, that if Mrs Ellis would consent, he would like to bear the expenses of sending Lennie to school in England for the next three years.

Mrs Ellis woke from her dream to say quickly :

"Although I thank you kindly, Dr. Rackett, I think you'll understand if I say No."

Her decision startled everybody.

"Prrh! Bah!" snorted Mr George. "There's one thing. I doubt if we could make Lennie go. But, with your permission Alice, we'll ask him. Jack, find Lennie for us."

"I'll not say a word," said Mrs Ellis, nervously clutching the edge of the table. "I won't influence him. But if he goes it'll be the death of me. Poor old Lennie! Poor old Lennie!"

"Prrh! Bah! That's nonsense! Nonsense!" said Mr George angrily. "Give the boy his chance, leave your fool emotions out, d'ye hear, Alice Ellis."

Mrs Ellis sat like a martyr stubborn at the stake. Jack brought the mistrustful Len, who stood like a prisoner at the bar. Mr George put the case as attractively as possible.

Len slowly shook his head, with a grimace of distaste.

"No, I *don't* think!" he remarked. "Not fer mine, you bet! I stays alongside my pore ol' Ma, here in Western Austrylia."

Mr George adjusted his eyeglasses severely.

"Your mother is neither poor nor old," he said coldly.

"I never!" broke out Lennie.

"And this country, thank God, is called Australia, not Austrylia. When you open your mouth you give proof enough of your need for education. I should like to hear different language in your mouth, my son, and see different ideas working in your head."

Lennie, rather pale and nervous, stared with wide eyes at him.

" You never," he said, " you never ketch me talkin' like Jack Grant, not if y' skin me alive." And he shifted from one foot to the other.

" I wouldn't take the trouble to skin you, alive or dead. Your skin wouldn't be worth it. But come. You're an intelligent boy. You *need* education. You *need* it. Your nature needs it, child. Your mother ought to see that. Your nature needs you to be educated, well educated. You'll be wasted afterwards—you will. And you'll repent it. Mark me, you'll repent it, when you're older, and your spirit, which should be trained and equipped, is all clumsy and half-baked as any other cornseed's. You'll be a fretful, uneasy, wasted man, you will. Your mother ought to see that. You'll be a half-baked, quarter-educated bush-whacker, instead of a well-equipped man."

Len looked wonderingly at his mother. But she still sat like an obstinate martyr at the stake, and gave him no sign.

" Don't *he* educate me ? " asked Len, pointing to Rackett.

" As much as you'll let him," said Mr George. " But—— "

Lennie's face crumpled up with irritation.

" Oh, what for do you *want* me to be educated ! " he cried testily. " I don't want to be like Uuncle Blogg. I don' wantter be like Dr. Rackett even." He wrinkled his nose in distaste. " 'N I don't wantter be like Jack Grant, neither. I don' wantta. I don' wantta, I tell y' I don' wantta."

" Do you think they would want to be like *you*? " asked Mr George.

Lennie looked from him to Rackett, and then to Jack.

" Jack's not so *very* diff'rent," he said slowly. And he shook his head. " But can't y' believe me," he cried. " I don' wantta go to England. I don' wantta talk fine and be like them. Can't ye see I don't ? I don' wantta. What's the good ! What's the mortal use of it, anyhow ? Aren't I right as I am ? "

" What *do* you want to do ? "

" I wants to work. I wants to milk an' feed, and plough and reap and lay out irrigation, like Dad. An' I wants to look after Ma an' the kids. An' then I'll get married and be on a place of me own with kids of me own, an' die, like Dad, an' be done for. That's what I wants. It is."

He looked desperately at his mother.

Mr George slowly shook his head, staring at the keen, beautiful, but reluctant boy.

"I suppose that's what we've come to," said Rackett.

"Didn't you learn me!" cried Lennie defiantly. And striking a little attitude, like a naive earnest actor, he repeated :

"Here rests, his head upon the lap of earth,
A youth to fortune and to fame unknown.
Fair science frowned not on his humble birth,
And melancholy marked him for her own.

Large was his bounty, and his soul sincere,
Heaven did a recompense as largely send.
He gave to misery all he had, a tear,
He gained from heaven, 'twas all he wished, a
    friend."

"There," he continued. "That's me! An' I've got a friend already."

"You're a little fool," said Mr George. "Much mark of melancholy there is on you! And do you think Misery is going to thank you for your idiotic tear? As for your friend, he's going away. And you're a fool, putting up a headstone to yourself while you're alive still. Damn you, you little fool, and be damned to you."

Mr George was really cross. He flounced his spectacles off his nose. Len was frightened. Then he said, rather waveringly, turning to his mother :

"We're all right, Ma, ain't we?"

Mrs Ellis looked at him with her subtlest, tenderest smile. And in Lennie's eyes burned a light of youthful indignation against these old men.

CHAP : XIII. TOM AND JACK RIDE TOGETHER

i

THESE days Monica was fascinating to Jack's eyes. She wore a black dress, and her slimness, her impulsive girlishness under this cloud were wistful, exquisite. He would have liked to love her, soothingly, protectively, passionately. He would have liked to cherish her, with passion. Always he looked to her for a glance of intimacy, looked to see if she wouldn't accept his passion and his cherishing. He wanted to touch her, to kiss her, to feel the eternal lightning of her slim body through the cloud of that black dress. He wanted to declare to her that he loved her, as Alec Rice had declared to Grace; and he wanted to ask her to marry him. To ask her to marry him at once.

But mostly he wanted to touch her and hold her in his arms. He watched her all the time, hoping to get one of the old, long looks from her yellow eyes, from under her bended brows. Her long, deep, enigmatic looks, that used to worry him so. Now he longed for her to look at him like that.

Or better still if she would let him see her trouble and her grief, and love her so, with a passionate cherishing.

But she would do neither. She kept her grief and her provocation both out of sight, as if neither existed. Her little face remained mute and closed, like a shut-up bud. She only spoke to him with a vague distant voice, and she never really looked at him. Or if she did glance at him, it was in a kind of anger, and pain, as if she did not want to be interfered with; didn't want to be pulled down.

He was completely puzzled. Her present state was quite incomprehensible to him. She had nothing to reproach him with, surely. And if she had loved him, even a little, she could surely love him that little still. If she had so often taken his hand and clutched it, surely she could now let him take her hand, in real sympathy.

It was as if she were angry with *him* because Dad had died. Jack hadn't wanted Dad to die. Indeed, no. He was cut up by it as if he had been one of the family. And it was as bad a blow to his destiny as to hers. He was as

201

sore and sorry as anybody. Yet she kept her face shut against him, and avoided him, as if *he* were to blame.

Completely puzzled, Jack went on with his preparations for departure. He had no choice. He was under orders from Mr George, and with Mrs Ellis' approval, to quit Wandoo, to ride with Tom up to Geraldton, and to spend at least a year on the sheep station up north. It had to be. It was the wheel of fate. So let it be.

And as the last day drew near, the strange volcano of anger which slumbered at the bottom of his soul—a queer, quiescent crater of anger which churned its deep hot lava invisible—threw up jets of silver rage, which hardened rapidly into a black, rocky indifference. And this was characteristic of him : an indifference which was really congealed anger, and which gave him a kind of innocent, remote, childlike quietness.

This was his nature. He was himself vaguely aware of the unplumbed crater of silent anger which lay at the bottom of his soul. It was not anger against any particular thing, or because of anything in particular. It was just generic, inherent in him. It was himself. It did not make him hate people, individually, unless they were hateful. It did not make him hard or cruel. Indeed he was too yielding rather than otherwise, too gentle and mindful of horses and cattle, for example, unmindful of himself. Tom often laughed at him for it. If Lucy had a will of her own, and a caprice she wanted to execute, he always let her go ahead, take her way, as far as was reasonable. If she exceeded her limits his anger roused and there was no doing any more with him. But he very rarely, very rarely got really angry. Only then in the long, slow accumulation of hostility, as with Easu.

But anger ! A deep, fathomless well-head of slowly-moving, invisible fire. Somewhere in his consciousness he was aware of it, and in this awareness it was as if he belonged to a race apart. He never felt identified with the great humanity. He belonged to a race apart, like the race of Cain. This he had always known.

Sometimes he met eyes that were eyes of his own outcast race. As a tiny boy it had been so. Fairs had always fascinated him because at the Fairs in England he met the eyes of gipsies who, in a glance, understood him. His own people *could* not understand. But in the black eyes of a gipsy woman he had seen the answer, even as a boy of ten. And he had thought : I ought to go away with her, run away with her.

It was the anger, the deep, burning *life-anger* which was the kinship. Not a deathly, pale, nervous anger. But an anger of the old blood. And it was this which had attracted him to grooms, horsey surroundings, and to pugilists. In them was some of this same deep, generous anger of the blood. And now in Australia, too, he saw it like a secret away at the bottom of the black, full, strangely shining eyes of the aborigines. There it lay, the secret, like an eternal, brilliant snake. And it established at once a kind of free-masonry between him and the blacks. They were curiously aware of him, when he came : aware of his coming, aware of his going. As if in him were the same great Serpent of their anger. And they were downcast now he was going away, as if their strength were being taken from them. Old Tim, who had taken a great fancy to Jack, relapsed into a sort of glumness as if he, too, now, were preparing to die.

Since Jack had come back from the Greenlow's farm, Monica had withdrawn to a distance, a kind of luminous distance, and put a chasm between herself and Jack. She moved mute and remote on the shining side of the chasm. He stood on the dark side, looking across the blackness of the gulf at her as if she were some kind of star. Surely the gulf would close up. Surely they both would be on natural ground again.

But, no ! always that incomprehensible little face with fringed lashes, and mouth that opened with a little smile, a vulnerable little smile, as if asking them all to be kind to her, to be pitiful towards her, and not try to touch her.

" Well, good-bye, Monica, for the present," he said, as he sat in the saddle in the yard, and Tom started away riding towards the gate, leading the bulky-looking packhorse.

" Good-bye. Come back ! " said Monica, looking up with a queer, hard little question come into her eyes, but her face remote as ever.

Jack kicked his horse and started.

" I'll come back," he said over his shoulder. But he

didn't look round at her. His heart had gone hard and hot in his breast. He was glad to be going.

Lennie had opened the gate. He stood there as Jack rode through.

" Why can't I never come? " he cried.

Jack laughed and rode on, after the faithful Tom. He was glad to go. He was glad to leave Wandoo. He was glad to say no more good-byes, and to feel no more pain. He was glad to be gone, since he was going, from the unlucky place. He was glad to be gone from its doom. There was a doom over it, a doom. And he was glad to be gone.

The morning was still orange and green. Winter had set in at last, the rains had begun to be heavy. They might have trouble with drenchings and boggings, but that, Tom said, was better than drought and sunstrokes. And, anyhow, the weather this morning was perfect.

The dark forest of Karri that ran to the left of Wandoo away on the distant horizon, cut a dark pattern on the egg-green sky. Good-bye! Good-bye! to it. The sown fields they were riding through glittered with tender blades of wheat. Good-bye! Good-bye! Somebody would reap it. The bush was now full of sparks of the beautiful, uncanny flowers of Western Australia, and bright birds started and flew. Sombre the bush was in itself, but out of the heavy dullness came sharp scarlet, flame-spark flowers, and flowers as lambent gold as sunset, and wan white flowers, and flowers of a strange, darkish rich blue, like the vault of heaven just after sundown. The scent of rain, of eucalyptus, and of the strange brown-green shrubs of the bush!

They rode in silence, Tom ahead with the pack-horse, and they did not draw near, but rode apart. They were travelling due west from York, along a bush track toward Paddy's Crossing. And as they went they drew nearer and nearer to the dark, low fringe of hills behind which, for the last twelve months, Jack had seen the sun setting with its great golden glow. Trees grew along the ridge of the hills, scroll-like and mysterious. They had always seemed to Jack like the bar of heaven.

By noon the riders reached the ridge, and the bar of heaven was the huge Karri trees which went up aloft so magnificently. But the Karri forest ended here with a jerk. Beyond, the earth ran away down long, long slopes

covered with scrub, down the greyness and undulation of
Australia, towards the great dimness where was the coast.
The sun was hot at noon. Jack was glad when Tom called
a halt under the last trees, facing the great, soft, open
swaying of the land seaward, and they began to make
tea.

They had hardly sat down to drink their tea, when they
heard a buggy approaching. It was the mysterious Dr.
Rackett, driven by the grinning Sam. Rackett said nothing,
just greeted the youths, pulled his tin mug and tucker from
under the buggy seat, and joined in, chatting casually as
if it had all been pre-arranged.

Tom was none too pleased, but he showed nothing. And
when the tea was finished, he made good by handing over
the beast of a pack-horse to Sam. Poor Sam sat in the
back of the vehicle lugging the animal along, jerking its
reluctant neck. Rackett drove in lonely state on the driving seat. Tom and Jack trotted quickly ahead, on the
down-slope, and were soon out of sight. They were thankful to ride free.

Over the ridge they felt Wandoo was left behind, and
they were in the open world again, away from care. Whenever man drives his tent-pegs deep, to stay, he drives them
into underlying water of sorrow. Best ride tentless. So
thought the boys.

They were going to a place called Paddy's Crossing, a
settlement new to Jack, but well known to Tom as the
placewheremenwentwhentheywantedaprivatejamboree.

What a jamboree was, Jack, being a gentleman—that is,
not a lady—would learn in due course.

As the ground came to a rolling hollow, Tom set off at a
good pace, and away they went, galloping beautifully along
the soft earth trail, galloping, galloping, putting the miles
between them and Wandoo and women and care. They
both rode in a kind of passion for riding, for hurling themselves ahead down the new road. To be men out alone in
the world, away from the women and the dead stone of
trouble.

They reached the river hours before Rackett's turn-out.
Fording, they rode into the mushroom settlement, a string
of slab cabins with shingle roofs and calico window-panes—
or else shuttered-up windows. The stoves were outside

the chimney-less cabins, under brush shelters. One such " kitchen," a fore-runner, had already a roof of flattened-out, rusty tin cans.

But it was a cosy, canny nook, homely, nestling down in the golden corner of the earth, the mimosa in bloom by the river. And it was beautifully ephemeral. As transient, as casual as the bushes themselves.

Jack for the moment had a dread of solid houses of brick and stone and permanence. There was always horror some-where inside them.

He wanted the empty, timeless Australia, with nooks like this of flimsy wooden cabins by a river with a wattle bush.

There was one older, white-washed cabin with vine trellises.

" That's Paddy's," said Tom. " He grows grapes, and makes wine out of the little black ones. But the muscats is best. I'm not keen on wine anyhow. Something a drop more warming."

Jack was amazed at the good Tom. He had never known him to drink.

" There's nobody about," said Jack, as they rode up the incline between the straggling cabins.

" All asleep," said Tom.

It was not so, however, because as they crested the slope and looked into the little hollow beyond, they saw a central wooden building, hall or mission or church, and people crowding like flies.

But Tom turned up to Paddy's white inn, up the side slope. He was remorseful about having galloped the horses at the beginning of such a long trip. The inn seemed deserted. Tom Coo-eeed ! but there was no answer.

" All shut up ! " he said. " What's that paper on the door ? "

Jack got down and walked stiffly to the door, for the ride had been long and hard and downhill, and his knees were hurting. " Gone to the wedin be ome soon P. O. T." he read. " What is P. O. T. ? " he asked.

" What I stand in need of," said the amazing Tom.

They were just turning their horses towards the stable when, with a racket and a canter, an urchin drove round from the yard in a pitch-black wicker chaise, a bone-white, careworn horse slopping between the shafts.

" You two blokes," yelled the urchin, " 'd better get onta th' trail for th' church, elst Father Prendy 'll be on y' tail, I tell y'."

" What's up ? " shouted Tom.

" I'm just off fer th' bride. Ol' Nick 'ere 'eld me up runnin' away from me in the paddock."

Tom grinned, the outfit swept past. Our heroes took their horses to the stable and settled them down conscientiously. Then they set off, glad to be on foot, down to the church.

The crowd was buzzing. It was half-past three. Father Prendy, the old mission priest, who looked like a dusty old piece of furniture from a loft, was peering up the road. The black wicker buggy still made no appearance with the bride.

" Two o'clock's the legal limit for marriages," said Father Prendy. " But, praise God, we've half an hour yet."

And he showed his huge watch, which said half-past one, since he had slipped away for a moment to put back the fingers.

The slab-building, hall, school, and church—was now a church, though the oleographs of the Queen and the Prince Consort in robes still glowed on the walls, and a black-board stood with its face to the wall, and one of those wire-things with coloured beads poked out from behind, and the globe of the world could not be hidden entirely by the eucalyptus boughs.

But it was a church. A table with a white cloth and a crucifix was the altar. Crimson-flowering gum-blossom embowered the walls, the blackboard, the windows, but left the Queen and Prince Consort in full isolation. Forms were ranked on the mud floor, and these forms were densely packed with settlers dressed in all kinds of clothes. It was not only a church, it was a wedding. Just inside the door, like a figure at Madame Tussaud's, sat an elderly creature in greenish evening suit with white waistcoat, and copper-toed boots, waiting apparently for the Last Trump. On the other side was a brown-whiskered man in frock-coat, a grey bell-topper in his hand, leaning balanced on a stick. He was shod in white socks and carpet slippers. Later on this gentleman explained to Jack : " I suffer from corns, and shouldn't be happy in boots."

There was a great murmuring and staring and shuffling and shifting as Jack and Tom came up, as though one of them was the bride in disguise. The wooden church buzzed like a cocoanut shell. A red-faced man seized Tom's arm as if Tom were a long-lost brother, and Jack was being introduced, shaking the damp, hot, trembling hand of the red-faced man, who was called Paddy.

" It's fair come over me, so ut has !—praise be to the saints an' may the devil run away with them two young turmagants ! Father Prendy makin' them come to this pass all at onst ! For, mark my words, in his own mind he's thinkin' the wrong they've done, neither of them speakin' to confess, till he was driven to remark on the girl's unnatural figure. And not a soul in the world, mark you, has seen 'em speak a word to one another for the last year in or out. But she says it's he, an' Danny Mackinnon, he payin', I'll be bound, that black priest of a Father Prendy to come over me an' make me render up my poor innocent Pat to the hussy, in holy matrimony. May the saints fly away with 'em."

He wiped away his sweat, speechless. And Danny Mackinnon, the hussy's father—it could be no other than he—in moth-eaten scarlet coat and overall trousers, and top-boots slashed for his bunions, and forage-cap slashed for his increased head, stood bulging on the other side of the door, compressed in his youthful uniform, and scarlet in the face with the compression. He was a stout man with a black beard and a fixed, fierce, solemn expression. Creator of this agitated occasion, he was almost bursting with wrathful agitation as that hussy of a daughter of his still failed to appear. By his side stood an ancient man with a long grey beard, anciently clad.

Patrick, the bridegroom to be, lurked near his father. He was a thin, pale, freckled, small-faced youth with broad brittle shoulders and brittle limbs, who would, no doubt, in time fill out into a burly fellow. As it was, he was agitated and unlovely in a new ready-made suit and a black bomb of a hard hat that wouldn't stay on, and new boots that stank to heaven of improperly-dressed kangaroo hide : one of the filthiest of stinks.

Poor Paddy, the father of the bridegroom, was a tall, thin, well set-up man with trembling hands and a face like beetroot, garbed in a blue coat with brass buttons, mole trousers, leggings, and a sideways-leaning top hat. His tie was a flowing red with white spots. His eyes were light blue and wickedly twinkling behind their slight wateriness.

" What's that yer sayin' about me? " said Father Prendy, coming up rubbing his hands, bowing to the strangers, beaming with a cheerfulness that could outlast any delay under the sun.

" 'Twas black I was callin' ye, Father Prendy," said Paddy. " For the fine pair of black eyes ye carry, why not? Isn't it a good drink ye'll be havin' on me afore the day is out, eh? Isn't it a pretty penny ye're costin' me, with your marryin' an' givin' in marriage? An' why isn't it Danny what pays the wedding breakfast, eh? "

" Hold your peace, Paddy, my dear. I see a wagon comin', don't I? "

Sure enough the black wicker buggy rattling down hill, the white horse seeming to swim, the urchin standing up, feet wide apart, elbows high up, bending forward and urging the bone-white steed with curses unnameable.

" What now! What now! " murmured the priest, feeling in his pocket for his stole. " What now! "

" Where's Dad? " yelled the urchin, pulling the bone-white steed on to its bony haunches, in front of the church.

Dad had gone round the corner. But he came bustling and puffing and bursting in his skin-tight scarlet coat, that almost cut his arms off, his own ancient father, with a long grey beard, pushing him irritably, propelling him towards the slippery boy. As if this family, generation by generation, got more and more behind-hand in its engagements.

" Gawd's sake ! " blowed the scarlet Dad, as the old grey grand-dad shoved him.

" Hold ye breath, Dad, 'n come 'ome ! " said the urchin, subsiding comfortably on to the seat and speaking as if he enjoyed utmost privacy. " Sis can't get away. She's had a baby. An' Ma says I was to tell Mr. O'Burk as it's a foine boy, an' would Father Prendy step up, and Pat O'Burk can come 'n see with his own eyes."

CHAP : XIV.   JAMBOREE

i

" Let's get along," said Jack uncomfortably in Tom's ear.

" Get ! Not for mine ! We're in luck's way, if ever we were."

" There's no fun under the circumstances."

" Oh, Lord my, ain't there ! What's wrong? They're all packing into the buggy. Father Prendy's putting his watch back a few more minutes. He'll have 'em married before you can betcher life. It's a wedding this is, boy ! "

The people now came crowding, nudging, whispering, giggling, stumbling out of the church. The gentleman in the carpet slippers rakishly adjusted his grey bell-topper over his left brow, and came swaggering forward.

" Major Brownlee—Mr. Jack Grant," Tom introduced them.

" Retired and happy in the country," the Major explained, and he continued garrulously to explain his circumstances, his history and his family history. This continued all the way to the inn : a good half-hour, for the Major walked insecurely on his tender feet.

When they arrived at Paddy's white, trellised house, all was in festivity. Paddy had thrown open the doors, disclosing the banquet spread in the bar parlour. Large joints of baked meat, ham, tongue, fowls, cakes and bottles and bunches of grapes and piles of apples : these Jack saw in splendid confusion.

" Come along in, come along in ! " cried Paddy, as the Major and his young companions hesitated under the vine-trellis. " I guess ye're the last. Come along in—all welcome !—an' wet the baby's eye. Sure she's a clever girl to get a baby an' a man the same fine afternoon. A fine child, let me tell you. Father Prendy named him for me, Paddy O'Burk Tracy, on the spot, the minute the wedding was tied up. So yer can please yerselves whether it's a christening ye're coming to, or a wedding. I offer ye the choice. Come in."

" P. O. T.," thought Jack. He still did not feel at ease.

210

Perhaps Paddy noticed it. He came over and slapped him on the back.

" It's yerself has brought good luck to the house, sir. Sit ye down an' help y'self. Sit ye down an' make y'self at home."

Jack sat down along with the rest of the heterogeneous company. Paddy went round pouring red wine into glasses.

" Gentlemen ! " he announced from the head of the table. " We are all here, for the table's full up. The first toast is : *The stranger within our gates !* "

Everybody drank but Jack. He was uncomfortably uncertain whether the baby was meant, or himself. At the last moment he hastily drank, to transfer the honour to the baby.

Then came " The Bride ! ", then " The Groom ! ", then " The Priest ! Father Prendy, that black limb o' salvation ! " Dozens of toasts, it didn't seem to matter to whom. And everybody drank and laughed and made clumsy jokes. There were no women present, at least no women seated. Only the women who went round the table, waiting. One ! Two ! Three ! Four ! Five ! Six ! Seven ! Westminster chimes from the grandfather's clock behind Jack. Seven o'clock ! He had not even noticed them bring in the lights. Father Prendy was on his feet blessing the bride : " at the moment absent on the high mission of motherhood." He then blessed the bridegroom, at the moment asleep with his head on the table.

The table had been cleared, save for bottles, fruit, and terrible cigars. The air was dense with smoke, bitter in the eyes, thick in the head. Everything seemed to be turning thick and swimmy, and the people seemed to move like living oysters in a natural, live liquor. A girl was sitting on Jack's chair, putting her arm surreptitiously round his waist, sipping out of his glass. But he pushed her a little aside, because he wanted to watch four men who had started playing euchre.

" There's a bright moon, gentlemen. Let's go out and have a bit o' sparrin'," said Paddy swimmingly from the head of the table.

That pleased Jack a lot. He was beginning to feel shut in.

He rose, and the girl—he had never really looked at her—followed him out. Why did she follow him? She ought to stay and clear away dishes.

The yard, it seemed to Jack, was clear as daylight : or clearer, with a big, flat white moon. Someone was sizing up to a little square man with long thick arms, and the little man was probing them off expertly. Hello! Here was a master, in his way.

The girl was leaning up against Jack, with her hand on his shoulder. This was a bore, but he supposed it was also a kind of tribute. He had still never looked at her.

" That's Jake," she said. " He's champion of these parts. Oh, my, if he sees me leanin' on y' arm like this, he'll be after ye ! "

" Well, don't lean on me, then," said Jack complacently.

" Go on, he won't see me. We're in the dark right here."

" I don't care if he sees you," said Jack.

" You *do* contradict yourself," said the girl.

" Oh, no, I don't ! " said Jack.

And he watched the long-armed man, and never once looked at the girl. So she leaned heavier on him. He disapproved, really, but felt rather manly under the burden.

The little, square, long-armed man was oldish; with a grey beard. Jack saw this as he danced round, like a queer old satyr, half gorilla, half satyr, roaring, booing, fencing with a big yahoo of a young bushman, holding him off with his unnatural long arms. Over went the big young fellow sprawling on the ground, causing such a splother that everyone shifted a bit out of his way. They all roared delightedly.

The long-armed man, looking round for his girl, saw her in the shadow leaning heavily and laughingly on Jack's young shoulder. Up he sprang, snarling like a gorilla, his long hairy arms in front of him. The girl retreated, and Jack, in a state of semi-intoxicated readiness, opened his arms and locked them round the little gorilla of a man. Locked together, they rolled and twirled round the yard under the moon, scattering the delighted onlookers like a wild cow. Jack was laughing to himself, because he had got the grip of the powerful long-armed old man. And there

was no real anger in the tussle. The gorilla was an old
sport.

Jack was sitting in a chair under the vine, with his head
in his hands and his elbows on his knees, getting his wind.
Paddy was fanning him with a bunch of gum-leaves, and
congratulating him heartily.

" First chap as ever laid out Long-armed Jake."

" What'd he jump on me for? " said Jack. " I said
nothing to him."

" What y' sayin'? " ejaculated Paddy coaxingly.
"Didn't ye take his girl, now? "

" Take his girl? I? No! She leaned on *me*, I didn't
take her."

" Arrah! Look at that now! The brazenness of it!
Well, be it on ye! Take another drink. Will ye come an'
show the boys some o' ye tricks, belike? "

Jack was in the yard again, shaking hands with Long-
armed Jake.

" Good on ye'! Good on y'! " cried old Jake. " Ye're
a cock bird in fine feather! What's a wench between two
gentlemen! Shake, my lad, shake! I'm Long-armed Jake,
I am, an' I set a cock bird before any whure of a hen."

They rounded up, sparred, staved off, showed off like two
amiable fighting-cocks, before the admiring cockeys. Then
they had good-natured turns with the young farmers, and
mild wrestling bouts with the old veterans. Having another
drink, playing, gassing, swaggering . . .

Tom came bawling as if he were deaf :

" What about them 'osses! "

" What about 'em! " said Jack.

" See to 'm! " said Tom. And he went back to where
he came from.

" All right, Mister, we'll see to 'm! " yelled the admiring youngsters. " We'll water 'm an' feed 'm."

" Water? " said Jack.

" Yes. Show us how to double up, Mister, will y'? "

" A' right! " said Jack, who was considerably tipsy.
" When—when I've—fed—th'osses."

He set off to the stables. The admiring youngsters ran
yelling ahead. They brought out the horses and led them
down to the trough. Jack followed, feeling the moon-lit
earth sway a little.

He shoved his head in between the noses of the horses, into the cool trough of water. When he lifted and wrung out the shower from his hair, which curled when it was wet, he saw the girl standing near him.

" Y' need a towel, Mister," she said.

" I could do with one," said he.

" Come an' I'll get ye one," she said.

He followed meekly. She led him to an outside room, somewhere near the stable. He stood in the doorway.

" Here y' are ! " she said, from the darkness inside.

" Bring it me," he said from the moon outside.

" Come in an' I'll dry your hair for yer." Her voice sounded like the voice of a wild creature in a black cave. He ventured, unseeing, uncertain, into the den, half reluctant. But there was a certain coaxing imperiousness in her wild-animal voice, out of the black darkness.

He walked straight into her arms. He started and stiffened as if attacked. But her full, soft body was moulded against him. Still he drew fiercely back. Then feeling her yield to draw away and leave him, the old flame flew over him, and he drew her close again.

" Dearie ! " she murmured. " Dearie ! " and her hand went stroking the back of his wet head.

" Come ! " she said. " And let me dry your hair."

She led him and sat him on a pallet bed. Then she closed the door, through which the moonlight was streaming. The room had no window. It was pitch dark, and he was trapped. So he felt as he sat there on the hard pallet. But she came instantly and sat by him and began softly, caressingly to rub his hair with a towel. Softly, slowly, caressingly she rubbed his hair with a towel. And in spite of himself, his arms, alive with a power of their own, went out and clasped her, drew her to him.

" I'm supposed to be in love with a girl," he said, really not speaking to her.

" Are you, dearie ? " she said softly. And she left off rubbing his hair and softly put her mouth to his.

Later—he had no idea what time of the night it was— he went round looking for Tom. The place was mostly dark. The inn was half dark. Nobody seemed alive. But there was music somewhere. There was music.

As he went looking for it, he came face to face with **Dr. Rackett.**

" Where's Tom ? " he asked.

" Best look in the barn."

The dim-lighted barn was a cloud of half-illuminated dust, in which figures moved. But the music was still martial and British. Jack, always tipsy, for he had drunk a good deal and it took effect slowly, deeply, felt something in him stir to this music. They were dancing a jig or a horn-pipe. The air was all old and dusty in the barn. There were four crosses of wooden swords on the floor. Young Patrick, in his shirt and trousers, had already left off dancing for Ireland, but the Scotsman, in a red flannel shirt and a reddish kilt, was still lustily springing and knocking his heels in a haze of dust. The Welshman was a little poor fellow in old shirt and trousers. But the Englishman, in costermonger outfit, black bell-bottom trousers and lots of pearl buttons, was going well. He was thin and wiry and very neat about the feet. Then he left off dancing, and stood to watch the last two.

Everybody was drunk, everybody was arguing, according to his nationality, as to who danced best. The Englishman in the bell-bottom trousers *knew* he danced best, but spent his last efforts deciding between Sandy and Taffy. The music jigged on. But whether it was " British Grenadiers " or " Campbells are Coming," Jack didn't know. Only he suddenly felt intensely patriotic.

" I am an Englishman," he thought, with savage pride. " I am an Englishman. That is the best on earth. Australian is English, English, English, she'd collapse like a balloon but for the English in her. British means English first. I'm a Britisher, but I am an Englishman ! God ! I could crumple the universe in my fist, I could. I'm an Englishman, and I could crush everything in my hand. And the women are left behind. I'm an Englishman."

Voices had begun to snarl and roar, fists were lifted.

" Mussen quarrel !—my weddin' ! Mussen quarrel ! " Pat was drunkenly saying, sitting on a box shaking his head.

Then suddenly he sprang to his feet, and quick and sharp as a stag, rushed to the wooden swords and stood with arms uplifted, smartly showing the steps. The fellow had spirit, a queer, staccato spirit.

Somebody laughed and cheered, and then they all began to laugh and cheer, and Pat pranced faster, in a cloud of dust, and the quarrel was forgotten.

Jack went to look for Tom. " I'm an Englishman," he thought, " I'd better look after him."

He wasn't in the barn. Jack looked and looked.

He found Tom in the kitchen, sitting in a corner, a glass at his side, quite drunk.

" It's time to go to bed, Tom."

" G'on, ol' duck. I'm waiting for me girl."

" You won't get any girl to-night. Let's go to bed."

" Shan't I get——? Yes shall! Yes shall! "

" Where shall I find a bed? "

" Plenty 'r flore space."

And he staggered to his feet as a short, stout, red-faced, black-eyed, untidy girl slipped across the kitchen and out of the door, casting a black-eyed, meaningful look at the red-faced Tom, over her shoulder as she disappeared. Tom swayed to his feet and sloped after her with amazing quickness. Jack stood staring out of the open door, dazed. They both seemed to have melted.

Himself, he wanted to sleep—only to sleep. " Plenty of floor space," Tom had said. He looked at the floor. Cockroaches running by the dozen, in all directions : those brown, barge-like cockroaches of the south, that trail their huge bellies and sheer off in automatic straight lines and make a faint creaking noise, if you listen. Jack looked at the table : an old man already lay on it. He opened a cupboard : babies sleeping there.

He swayed, drunk with sleep and alcohol, out of the kitchen in some direction : pushed a swing door : the powerful smell of beer and sawdust made him know it was the bar. He could sleep on the seat. He could sleep in peace.

He lurched forward and touched cloth. Something snored, started, and reared up.

" What y' at? "

Jack stood back breathless—the figure subsided—he could beat a retreat.

Hopeless, he looked in on the remains of the breakfast.

Table and every bench occupied. He boldly opened another door. A small lamp burning, and what looked like dozens of dishevelled elderly women's awful figures heaped cross-wise on the hugest double bed he had ever seen.

He escaped into the open air. The moon was low. Someone was singing.

CHAP : XV.   UNCLE JOHN GRANT

i

IT was day. The lie was hard. He didn't want to wake.
He turned over and was asleep again, though the lie was
very hard.

Someone pushing him. Tom, with a red, blank face was
saying :

" Wake up ! Let's go before Rackett starts."

And the rough hands pushing him crudely. He hated it.

He sat up. He had been lying on the bottom of the
buggy, with a sack over him. No idea how he got there.
It was full day.

" Old woman's got some tea made. If y' want t' change
y' bags hop over 'n take a dip in the pool. Down th'
paddock there. Here's th' bag. I've left soap 'n comb
on th' splash board, an' I've seen to th' 'osses. I'm goin'
f'r a drink while you get ready."

Tom had got a false dawn on him. He had wakened
with that false energy which sometimes follows a "drunk,"
and which fades all too quickly. For he had hardly slept at
all.

So when Jack was ready, Tom was not. His stupor was
overcoming him. He was cross—and half-way through his
second pewter mug of beer.

" I'm not coming," said Tom.

" You *are*," said Jack. For the first time he felt that
old call of the blood which made him master of Tom.
Somewhere, in the night, the old spirit of a master had
aroused in him.

Tom finished his mug of beer slowly, sullenly. He put
down the empty pot.

" Get up ! " said Jack. And Tom got slowly to his feet.

They set off, Jack leading the pack-horse. But the beer
and the " night before " had got Tom down. He rode like
a sack in the saddle, sometimes semi-conscious, sometimes
really asleep. Jack followed just behind, with the beast
of a pack-horse dragging his arm out. And Tom ahead,
like a sot, with no life in him.

Jack himself felt hot inside, and dreary, and riding was a

cruel effort, and the pack-horse dragging his arm from its socket was hell. He wished he had enough saddle-tree to turn the rope round : but he was in his English saddle.

Nevertheless, he had decided something, in that Jamboree. He belonged to the blood of masters, not servants. He belonged to the class of those that are sought, not those that seek. He was no seeker. He was not desirous. He would never be desirous. Desire should not lead him humbly by the nose. Not desire for anything. He was of the few that are masters. He was to be desired. He was master. He was a real Englishman.

So he jogged along, in the hot, muggy day of early winter. Heavy clouds hung over the sky, lightning flashed beyond the purple hills. His body was a burden and a weariness to him, riding was a burden and a weariness, the pack-horse was hell. And Tom, asleep on his nag, like a dead thing, was hateful to have ahead. The road seemed endless.

Yet he had in him his new, half savage pride to keep him up, and an isolate sort of resoluteness.

At mid-day they got down, drank water, camped, and slept without eating. Thank God, the rain hadn't come. Jack slept like the dead till four o'clock.

He woke sharp, wondering where he was. The clouds looked threatening. He got up. Yes, the horses were there. He still felt bruised, and hot and dry inside, from the Jamboree. Why, in heaven, did men want Jamborees ?

He made a fire, boiled the billy, prepared tea, and set out some food, though he didn't want any.

" Get up there ! " he shouted to Tom, who lay like a beast.

" Get up ! " he shouted. But the beast slept.

" Get up, you beast ! " he said, viciously kicking him. And he was horrified because Tom got up, without any show of retaliation at all, and obediently drank his tea.

They ate a little food, in silence. Saddled in silence, each finding the thought of speech repulsive. Watched one another to see if they were ready. Mounted, and rode in repulsive silence away. But Jack had left the pack-horse to Tom this time. And it began to rain, softly, seepily.

And Tom was cheering up. The rain seemed to revive him wonderfully. He was one who was soon bowled over by a drink. Consequently he didn't absorb much, and he recovered sooner. Jack absorbed more, and it acted much more slowly, deeply, and lastingly on him. On they went, in the rain.

Tom began to show signs of new life. He swore at the pack-horse. He kicked his nag to a little trot, and the packs flap-flapped like shut wings, on the rear pony. Presently he reined up, and sat quite still for a minute. Then he broke into a laugh, lifting his face to the rain.

" Seems to me we're off the road," he said. " We haven't passed a fence all day, have we ? "

" No," said Jack. " But you were asleep all morning."

" We're off the road. Listen ! "

The rain was seeping down on the bush; in the grey evening the warm horses smelt of their own steam. Jack could hear nothing except the wind and the increasing rain.

" This track must lead somewhere. Let's get to shelter for the night," said Jack.

" Agreed ! " replied Tom magnanimously. " We'll follow on, and see what we shall see."

They walked slowly, pulling at the pack-horse, which was dragging at the rope, tired with the burden that grew every minute heavier with the rain.

Tom reined in suddenly.

" There *is* somebody behind," he said. " It's *not* the wind."

They sat there on their horses in the rain, and waited. Twilight was falling. Then Jack could distinguish the sound of a cart behind. It was Rackett in the old shay rolling along in the lonely dusk and rain, through the trees, approaching. Black Sam grinned mightily as he pulled up.

" Thought I'd follow, though you are on the wrong road," said Rackett from beneath his black waterproof. " Sam showed me the turning two miles back. You missed it. Anyhow, we'd better camp in on these people ahead here."

" Is there a place ahead ? " asked Jack.

" Yes," replied Rackett. " Even a sort of relation of yours, that I promised Gran I would come and see. Hence my following on your heels."

" Didn't know I'd any relation hereabout," said Tom sulkily. He couldn't bear Rackett's interfering in the family in any way.

" You haven't. I meant Jack. But we'll get along, shall we ? "

" We're a big flood," remarked Tom. " But if they'll give us the barn, we'll manage. It's getting wet to sleep out."

They pressed ahead, the pack-horse trotting, but lifting up his head like a venomous snake, in unwillingness. They had come into the open fields. At last in the falling dark they saw a house and buildings. A man hove in sight, but lurked away from them. Rackett hailed him. The man seemed to oppose their coming further. He was a hairy, queer figure, with his untrimmed beard.

" Master never takes no strangers," he said.

Rackett slipped a shilling in his hand, and would he ask his master if they might camp in the barn, out of the rain.

" Y' ain't the police, now, by any manner of means ? " asked the man.

" God love you, no," said Rackett.

" We're no police," said Tom. " I'm Tom Ellis, from Wandoo, over York way."

" Ellis : I heared th' name. Well, master's sick, an' skeered to death o' th' police. They're ready to drop in on the place, that they are, rot 'em, the minute he breathes his last. And he's skeered he's dyin' this time. Oh, he's skeered o't. So I have me doubt of all strangers. I have me doubts, no matter what they be. Master he've sent a letter to his only relation upon earth, to his nephew, which, thank the Lord, he's writ for to come an' lay hold on the place, against he dies. If there's no one to lay hold, the police steps in, without a word. That's how they do it. They lets the places in grants like—lets a man have a grant —and when the poor man dies, his place is locked up by the Government. They takes it all."

" Gawd's sake ! " murmured Tom aside, " the man's potty ! "

" Bush mad," supplemented Rackett, who was sitting in the buggy with his chin in his hand, intently listening to the queer, furtive, garrulous individual.

" Say, friend," he added aloud. " Go and ask your master if we harmless strangers can camp in the barn out of the wet."

" What might your names be, Mister ? " asked the man.

" Mine's Dr Rackett. This is Tom Ellis. And this is
Jack Grant. And no harm in any of us."

" D'y'say Jack Grant ? Would that be Mr John Grant ?"
asked the man, galvanised by sudden excitement.

" None other ! " said Rackett.

" Then he's come ! " cried the man.

" He certainly has," replied Rackett.

" Oh, Glory, Glory ! Why didn't ye say so afore ? Come
in. Come in all of ye, come in ! Come in, Mr Grant !
Come in ! "

They got down, gave the reins to Sam, and were ready
to follow the bearded man, looking one another in the face
in amazement, and shaking their heads.

" Gawd Almighty, I'd rather keep out o' this ! " murmured Tom, standing by his horse and keeping the rope
of the pack-horse.

" Case of mistaken identity," said Rackett coolly.
" Hang on, boys. We'll get a night's shelter."

A woman came out of the dilapidated stone house, clutching her hands in distress and agitation.

" Missus ! Missus ! Here he is at last. God be praised !"
cried the bearded man. She ran up in sudden effusion of
welcome, but he ordered her into the house to brighten up
the fire, while he waved the way to the stables, knowing
that horse comes before man, in the bush.

When they had shaken down in the stable, they left Sam
to sleep there, while the three went across to the house.
Tom was most unwilling.

The man was at the door, to usher them in.

" I've broke the news to him, sir ! " he said in a mysterious voice to Jack, as he showed them into the parlour.

" What's your master's name ? " asked Rackett.

" Don't y' know y're at your destination ? " whispered
the man. " This is Mr John Grant's. This is the place
ye're looking for."

A melancholy room ! The calico ceiling drooped, the
window and front door were hermetically sealed, an ornate
glass lamp shone in murky, lonely splendour upon a wool
mat on a ricketty round table. Six chairs stood against
the papered walls. Nothing more.

Tom wanted to beat it back to the kitchen, through which
they had passed to get to this sarcophagus, and where a

fire was burning and a woman was busy. But the man was tapping at another door, and listening anxiously before entering.

He went into the dark room beyond, where a candle shone feebly, and they heard him say :

" Your nephew's come, Mr Grant, and brought a doctor and another gentleman, the Lord be praised."

" The Lord don't need to be praised on my behalf, Amos," came a querulous voice. " And I ain't got no nephew, if I *did* send him a letter. I've got nobody. And I want no doctor, because I died when I left my mother's husband's house."

" They're in the parlour."

" Tell 'em to walk up."

The man appeared in the doorway. Rackett walked up, Jack followed, and Tom hung nervously and disgustedly in the rear.

" Here they are ! Here's the gentry," said Amos.

In the candle-light they saw a thin man in a red flannel night-cap with a blanket round his shoulders, sitting up in bed under an old green cart-umbrella. He was not old, but his face was thin and wasted, and his long colourless beard seemed papery. He had cunning shifty eyes with red rims, and looked as mad as his setting.

Rackett had shoved Jack forward. The sick man stared at him and seemed suddenly pleased. He held out a thin hand. Rackett nudged Jack, and Jack had to shake. The hand seemed wet and icy, and Jack shuddered.

" How d'you do ! " he mumbled. " I'm sorry, you know; I'm not your nephew."

" I know ye're not. But are y' Jack Grant ? "

" Yes," said Jack.

The man under the umbrella seemed hideously pleased.

Jack heard Tom's ill-suppressed, awful chuckle from behind.

The sick man peered irritably at the other two. Then he nodded slowly, under the green baldachino of the old cart-umbrella.

" Jack Grant ! Jack Grant ! Jack Grant ! " he murmured to himself. He was surely mad, obviously mad.

" I'm right glad you've come, cousin," he said suddenly,

looking again very pleased. " I'm surely glad you've come in time. I've a nice tidy place put together for you, Jack, a small proposition of three thousand acres, five hundred cleared and cropped, fifty fenced—dog-leg fences, broke MacCullen's back putting 'em up. But I'll willingly put in five hundred more for a gentleman like young master. Meaning old master will soon be underground. Well, who cares, now young master's come to light, and the place doesn't go out of the family ! I am determined the place shall not go out of the family, Cousin Jack. Aren't you pleased ? "

" Very," said Jack soothingly.

" Call me Cousin John. Or Uncle John, if you like. I'm more like your uncle, I should think. Shake hands, and say, *Right you are, Uncle John.* Call me Uncle John."

Jack shook hands once more, and dutifully, as to a crazy person, he said :

" Right you are, Uncle John."

Tom, in the background, was going into convulsions. But Rackett remained quite serious.

Uncle John closed his eyes, muttering, and fell back under the cart-umbrella.

" Mr Grant," said Dr. Rackett, " I think Jack would like to eat something after his ride."

" All right, let him go to the kitchen with yon buck wallaby as can't keep a straight face. Stop with me a minute yourself, Mister, if you will."

The two boys bundled away into the kitchen. The woman had a meal ready, and they sat down at the table.

" I thank my stars," said Tom impressively, " he's not *my* Uncle John."

" Shut up," said Jack, because the woman was there.

They ate heartily, the effects of the jamboree having passed. After the meal they strolled to the door to look out, away from that lugubrious parlour and bedroom. They found a stiff wind blowing, the sky clear with running clouds and vivid stars in the spaces.

" Let's get ! " said Tom. It was his constant craving.

" We can't leave Rackett."

" We can. He pushed us in. Let's get. Why can't we ? "

" Oh, well, we can't," said Jack.

Rackett had entered the kitchen, and was eating his meal.
He asked the woman for ink.

" There's no ink," she said.

" Must be somewhere," said Amos, her husband. " Jack
Grant's letter was written in ink."

" I never got a letter," said Jack, turning.

" Eh, hark ye! How like old master over again! Ye've
come, haven't ye? "

" By accident," said Jack. " I'm not Mr Grant's
nephew."

" Hark ye! Hark ye! It runs in the family, father to
son, uncle to nephew. All right! All right! Have it your
own way," cried Amos. He had been struggling with crazy
contradictions too long.

Tom was in convulsions. Rackett put his hand on Jack's
shoulder. " It's all right," he said. " Don't worry him.
Leave it to me." And to the woman he said, if there was
no ink she was to kill a fowl and bring it to him, and he'd
make ink with lamp-black and gall.

" You two boys had better be off to bed," he said.
" You have to be off in good time in the morning."

" Oh, not going, not going so soon, surely. The young
master's not going so soon! Surely! Surely! Master's
so weak in the head and stomach, we can't cope with him
all by ourselves," cried the old man and woman.

" Perhaps I'll stay," said Rackett. " And Jack will
come back one day, don't you worry. Now, let me make
that ink."

The boys were shown into a large, low room—the fourth
room of the house—that opened off the kitchen. It contained a big bed with clean sheets and white crochet quilt.
Jack surmised it was the old couple's bed, and wanted to
go to the barn. But Tom said, since they offered it, there
was nothing to do but to take it.

Tom was soon snoring. Jack lay in the great feather
bed feeling that life was all going crazy. Tom was already
snoring. He cared about nothing. Out of sight, out of
mind. But Jack had a fit of remembering. His head was
hot, and he could not sleep. The wind was blowing, it was
raining again. He could not sleep, he had to remember.

It was always so with him. He could go on careless and
unheeding, like Tom, for a while. Then came these fits of

reckoning and remembering.   Life seemed unhinged in Australia.   In England there was a strong central pivot to all the living.   But here the centre pin was gone, and the lives seemed to spin in a weird confusion.

He felt that for himself.   His life was all unhinged.   What was he driving at?   What was he making for?   Where was he going?   What was his life, anyhow?

In England, you knew.   You had your purpose.   You had your profession and your family and your country. But out here you had no profession.   You didn't do anything for your country except boast of it to strangers and leave it to get along as best it might.   And as for your family, you cared for that, but in a queer, centreless fashion.

You didn't really care for anything.   The old impetus of civilisation kept you still going, but you were just rolling to rest.   As Mr. Ellis had rolled to rest, leaving everything stranded.   There was no grip, no hold.

And yet, what Jack had rebelled against in England was the tight grip, the fixed hold over everything.   He liked this looseness and carelessness of Australia.   Till it seemed to him crazy.   And then it scared him.

To-night everything seemed to him crazy.   He didn't pay any serious attention to Uncle John Grant : he was obviously out of his mind.   But then everything seemed crazy.   Mr. Ellis' death, and Gran's death, and Monica and Easu Ellis—it all seemed as crazy as crazy.   And the jamboree, and that girl who called him Dearie !   And the journey, and this mad house in the rain.   What did it all mean?   What did it all stand for?

Everything seemed to be spinning to a darkness of death. Everybody seemed to be dancing a crazy dance of death. He could understand that the blacks painted themselves like white bone skeletons, and danced in the night like skeletons dancing, in their corrobees.   That was how it was. The night, dark and fleshly, and skeletons dancing a clickety dry dance in it.

Tom, so awfully upset at his father's death !   And now as careless as a lark, just spinning his way along the road, in a sort of weird dance, dancing humorously to the black verge of oblivion.   That was how it was.   To dance humorously to the black verge of oblivion.   The children of death.

With a sort of horror of death around them. " Wandoo "
suddenly grim and grisly with the horror of death.

Death, the great end and goal. Death the black, void,
pulsating reality which would swallow them all up, like a
black lover finally possessing them. The great black fleshli-
ness of the end, the huge body of death reeling to swallow
them all. And for this they danced, and for this they
loved and reared families and made farms : to provide good
meat and white, pure bones for the black, avid horror of
death.

Something of the black, aboriginal horror came over
him. He realised, to his amazement, the actuality of the
great, grinning black demon of death. The vast infinite
demon that eats our flesh and cracks our bones in the last
black potency of the end. And for this, for this demon one
seeks for a woman, to lie with her and get children for the
Moloch. Children for the Moloch ! Lennie, Monica, the
twins Og and Magog ! Children for the Moloch.

One God or the other must take them at the end. Either
the dim white god of the heavenly infinite. Or else the
great black Moloch of the living death. Devoured and
digested in the living death.

Satan, Moloch, Death itself, all had been unreal to him
before. But now, suddenly, he seemed to see the black
Moloch grinning huge in the sky, while human beings danced
towards his grip, and He gripped and swallowed them into
the black belly of death. That was their end.

Dance ! Dance ! Death has its deep delights ! And
ever-recurring. Be careless, ironical, stoical and reckless.
And go your way to death with a will. With a dark handsomeness and a dark lustre of fatality and a splendour of
recklessness. Oh, God, the Lords of Death ! The big,
darkly-smiling, heroic men who are Lords of Death ! And
they too go on splendidly towards death, the great goal
of unutterable satisfaction, and consummated fear.

" I am going my way the same," Jack thought to himself. " I am travelling in a reckless, slow dance, darker
and darker, into the black, hot belly of death, where is my
end. Oh, let me go gallantly, let me have the black joy of
the road. Let me go with courage and a bit of splendour
and dark lustre, down to the great depths of death, that I
am so frightened of, but which I long for in the last con-

summation. Let death take me in a last black embrace.
Let me go on as the niggers go, with the last convulsion
into the last black embrace. Since I am travelling the
dark road, let me go in pride. Let me be a Lord of Death,
since the reign of the white Lords of Life, like my father,
has become sterile and a futility. Let me be a Lord of
Death. Let me go that other great road, that the blacks
go."

The bed was soft and hot, and he stretched his arms
fiercely. If he had Monica! Oh, if he had Monica! If
that girl last night had been Monica!

That girl last night! He didn't even know her name.
She had stroked his head—like—like—Mary! The association flashed into his mind. Yes, like Mary. And Mary
would be humble and caressive and protective like that. So
she would. And dark! It would be dark like that if one
loved Mary. And brief! Brief! But sharp and good in
the briefness. Mary! Mary!

He realised with amazement it was Mary he was now
wanting. Not Monica. Or was it Monica? Her slim keen
hand. Her slim body like a slim cat, so full of life. Oh,
it was Monica! First and foremost, most intensely, it was
Monica, because she was really his, and she was his destiny.
He dared not think of her.

He rolled in the bed in misery. Tom slept unmoving.
Oh, why couldn't he be like Tom, slow and untormented.
Why couldn't he? Why was his body tortured? Why was
he travelling this road? Why wasn't Monica there like a
gipsy with him? Why wasn't Monica there?

Or Mary! Why wasn't Mary in the house? She would
be so soft and understanding, so yielding. Like the girl of
the long-armed man. The long-armed man didn't mind
that he had taken his girl, for once.

Why was he himself rolling there in torment? Pug had
advised him to " punch the ball," when he was taken with
ideas he wanted to get rid of. There was no ball to punch.
" Train the body hard, but train the mind hard too." Yes,
all very well. He could think, now for example, of fighting
Easu, or of building up a place and raising fine horses. But
the moment his mind relaxed for sleep, back came the other
black flame. The women! The women! The women!
Even the girl of last night.

What was a man born for? To find a mate, a woman, isn't it? Then why try to think of something else? To have a woman—to make a home for her—to have children. And other women in the background, down the long, dusky, strange years towards death. So it seemed to him. And to fight the men that stand in one's way. To fight them. Always a new one cropping up, along the strange dusky road of the years, where you go with your head up and your eyes open and your spine sharp and electric, ready to fight your man and take your woman, on and on down the years, into the last black embrace of death. Death that stands grinning with arms open and black breast ready. Death, like the last woman you embrace. Death, like the last man you die fighting with. And he beats you. But somehow you are not beaten, if you are a Lord of Death.

Jack hoped he would die a violent death. He hoped he would live a defiant, unsubmissive life, and die a violent death. A bullet, or a knife piercing home. And the women he left behind—his women, enveloped in him as in a dark net. And the children he left, laughing already at death.

And himself! He hoped never to be downcast, never to be melancholy, never to yield. Never to yield. To be a Lord of Death, and go on to the black arms of death, still laughing. To laugh, and bide one's time, and leap at the right moment.

CHAP : XVI. ON THE ROAD

i

" My dear nephew, I haven't sent you a letter since the last one which I never wrote, yet you have come in answer to the one you never got. I wrote because I wanted you to come and receive the property, and I never posted it because I didn't know your address, and you couldn't come if I did, because you don't exist. Yet here you are and I think you look very pleased to receive the property which you haven't got yet. I was so afraid I should die sudden after this long lingering illness, but it's you who has come suddenly and the illness hasn't begun yet. So here am I speechless, but you are doing a lot of talking to your dear uncle who never had a nephew. What does it matter to me if you are Jack Grant because I am not, but took the name into the grant of land given me on the land grant system at a shilling an acre. So, like a bad shilling, the name turns up again on the register, so that the land goes back to the grant, and the Grant to the land. But a better-looking nephew I never wish to see, being as much like me as an ape is like meat. So when I'm dead I won't be alive to trouble you, and I'll trouble no further about you since you might as well be dead for all I care."

In this vein Tom ranted on the next morning, when they had set out in the glorious early dawn. Tom never wearied of the uncle under the umbrella. He told the tale to everybody who would listen, and wore out Jack's ears with these long and facile pleasantries.

They were both glad to get away from the crazy, lugubrious place. Jack refused to give it a thought further, though he felt vaguely, at the back of his mind, that he knew something about it already. Something somebody had told him.

Rackett had stayed behind, so they made no very good pace, leading the pack-horse. But they pushed on, being already overdue at the homestead of one of Tom's aunts, who was expecting them.

Once on horseback and in the open morning, Jack wished for nothing more. Women, death, skeletons, the dance

into the darkness, the future, the past, love, home, and
sorrow all disappeared in the bright well of the daylight,
as if they'd dropped into a pool. He wanted nothing more
than to ride, to jog along the track on the rather wet road,
through bush and scrub still wet with rain, in a pure
Westralian air that was like a clean beginning of everything, seeing the tiny bushman's flowers sparking and gild-
ing eerily in the dunness of the world.

By mid-day they reached the highway to Geraldton, via
Gingin, and camped at the Three-mile Government well in
perfect good spirits. Everything was gone, everything was
forgotten except the insouciance of the moment. They
knew the uselessness of thinking and remembering and
worrying. When worry starts biting like mosquitoes, then,
if it bites hard enough, you've *got* to attend. But it's like
illness, avoid it, beat it back if you can.

They found the high road merely a bush-track after all.
If it was near a settlement, or allotments, or improved
lands, it might run well for miles. But, for the most part,
it was exceedingly bad, full of holes of water, and beginning
in places to be a bog.

Tom was now at his best, out in the bush again. All his
bush lore came back to him, and he was like an animal in
its native surroundings. His charm came back, too, and
his confidence. He went ahead looking keenly about, like
a travelling animal, pointing out to Jack first this thing and
then the other, initiating him into bush wisdom, teaching
him the big cipher-book of the bush. And Jack learned
gladly. It was so good, so good to be away from home-
steads, and women, and money, watching the trees and the
land and the marks of wild life. And Tom, a talker once
he was wound up, told the histories of settlers, their failures
and successes, and their peculiarities. It seemed to Jack
there was a surplus of weird people out there. But, then,
Tom said, the weird ones usually came first, and they got
weirder in the wild.

They passed an enormous hollow tree, from which issued
an old man with a grey beard that came to his waist, dressed
in rags. A grey-haired, very ragged woman also came out,
carrying a baby. Other children crawled around. The
travellers called Good-day! as they passed.

Tom said the woman's baby was the youngest of seventeen children. The eldest son was already grown up, a prosperous young man trading in sandal wood. But Dad and Mum liked the bush, and would accept nothing for their supposed welfare, either from their sons or anyone else.

In the middle of the afternoon they passed a sundowner trekking with a cartful of produce down to Middle Swan. At four o'clock they camped for half an hour, to drink a billy of tea. Before the water boiled they saw two tramps coming down the road. The slouchers came straight up and greeted the boys, eyeing them curiously up and down.

" Wot cheer, mate ? " said one, a ruffianly mongrel.

" Good O ! How's the goin' Gingin way ? " asked Tom.

" Plenty grass an' water this time o' the year. But look out for the settlers this side. They ain't over hopeful." He turned to stare at Jack. Then he continued, to Tom : " 'Ow's it y' got y' baby out ? "

" New chum," explained Tom. He spoke quietly, but his mouth had hardened. " You blokes want anything of us ? "

" Yessir," said the spokesman, coming in close. " We wants bacca."

" Do you ? " said Tom pleasantly, and he pulled out his pouch. " I've only got three plugs. That's one apiece for me an' the baby an' you can have the other to do as you likes with. But chum here doesn't keer much for smokin', so he might give you his."

There was a tone of finality in Tom's voice.

" You've surely got more blasted cheek than most kids," said the fellow. " What've ye got planted away in y' swags ? " He glanced at his mate. " We don't want to use no bally persuasion, does we, Bill ? "

Bill was of villainous but not very imposing appearance. He had weak eyes, a dirty, hairy face, and a purple mouth showing unbecomingly through his whiskers.

Tom calmly filled his pipe, and waving to the first tramp, gave him sufficient to fill his cutty. The fellow took it, ignoring his mate, and began to fill up eagerly. He sat down by the fire and, taking a hot ember, lit up, puffing avidly.

" The other can have my share, if he wants it," said Jack.

" Thank you kindly," said the other with a sneer. And as he stuffed it in his pipe : " It'll do for a start." But he was puffing almost before he could finish his words.

They smoked in silence round the fire for some time. Then Tom rose and went over to the pack, as if he were going to give in to the ruffians. One swaggy rose and followed him.

The other tramp, taking not the slightest notice of the boy sitting there, reached out his filthy hand and began to fill his pockets with everything that lay near the fire : the packet of tea, a spoon, a knife.

He had got as far as the spoon when the astonished Jack said : " Drop it ! " as if he were speaking to a dog.

The man turned with a snarl, and made to cuff him. Jack seized his wrist and twisted it cruelly, making him drop the spoon and shout with pain. The other swaggy at once ran on Jack from the rear, and fell over him. Tom rushed on the second swaggy and fell, too. Over they all went in a heap. Jack laughed aloud in the scrimmage, as he gripped the swaggy's wrist with one hand and with the other emptied out the contents of the pocket again. He brought out two knives, one which didn't belong to him. Dropping the lot for safety, he got to his feet. Tom and the second swaggy were rolling and unlocking. That villain spied the open knife, seized it and sprang to his feet, snarling and brandishing.

" Come on, ye pair of . . ."

Jack gave another twist to the wrist of the prisoner, who howled, and then he kicked him three yards away. But his heart smote him, for the kick was so bony, the tramp was thin and frail. Then, full of the black joy of scattering such wastrels, he sprang unexpectedly on the other tramp. The swaggy gave a yell, and fled. For a minute or two the couple of ragged, wretched, despicable figures could be seen bolting like running vermin down the trail. Then they were out of sight.

Tom and Jack sat by the fire and roared with laughter, roared and roared till the bush was startled.

They were just packing up when someone else came down the road. It was a young woman in a very wide skirt on a very small pony, riding as if she were used to it. This was not the figure they expected to see.

"Why!" cried Tom, staring, "I do believe it's Ma's niece grown up."

It was. She was quite pleasant, but her hands were stub-fingered and work-hardened, and her voice was common.

"Y' didn't come along yesterday as Ma expected," she explained, "So I just took Tubby to see if y' was coming to-day. How's the twins? How's Monica and Grace? I do wish they'd come."

"They're all right," said Tom.

"We heard about your Dad and your Gran. Fancy! But I wish Monica had come with you. She was such a little demon at school. I'm fair longing to see her."

"She's not the only one of you that's a demon!" said Tom, in the correct tone of banter, putting over his horse and drawing to the girl's side and becoming very manly for her benefit. "An' what's wrong with us, that you aren't glad to see us?"

"Oh, you're all right," said the cousin. "But a girl of your own age is more fun, you know."

"Well, I don't happen to be a girl of your own age," said Tom. "Just by accident, I'm a man. But, come on. There's some roughs about. We might just as well get out of their way."

He trotted alongside the damsel, leaving Jack to bring the pack-horse. Jack didn't mind.

ii

So they went on, receiving a rough and generous hospitality from one or another of Tom's or Jack's relations, of whom there were astonishingly many, along the grand bush track to Geraldton. If they weren't direct relations they were relations by marriage, and it served just as well. There were the Brockmans, there were the Browns, the Gales, and Davises, Edgars and Conollys, Burgesses, Cooks, Logues, Cradles, Morrises, Fitzgeralds and Glasses. Families united by some fine-drawn connection or other; and very often much more divided than united, by some very plain-drawn feud. Their names like brooks trickled across the land, and you crossed and re-crossed. You would lose a name entirely: like the Brockman name. Then suddenly it re-appeared as Brackman, and " Oh, yes, we're cousins ! "

" Who isn't cousin ! " thought Jack.

Some of them had huge tracts of land fenced in. Some had little bits of poor farms. Sometimes there were deserted farms.

" And to think," said Tom, " that none of them is my *own* mother's relations. All Dad's, or else Ma's. Mostly Ma's."

It was queer the way he hankered after his own real mother. Jack, for his part, didn't care a straw who was his mother's relation and who wasn't. But you would have thought Tom lived under a Matriarchy, and derived everything from a lost mother.

It was not wet enough yet to be really boggy, though camping out was damp. However, they mostly got a roof. If it wasn't a relation's, it was a barn, or the " Bull and Horns " by Gingin. And to the boys, all that mattered was whether they were on the right road : often a very puzzling question : or if the heavy rain would hold off : if there was plenty of grub : if the horses seemed tired or not quite fit : if they were going to get through a boggy place all right : if the packs were fast : if they made good going. The inns were " low " in every sense of the word, including the low-pitched roof. And full of bed-bugs, however new the country. With red-nosed, grassy-whiskered landlords who thumbed the glasses when there were any glasses to thumb. And there were always men at these inns, almost always the same kind of brutal, empty roughs.

" Look here," said Jack, " wherever we go there are these roughs, and more roughs, and more. Where the devil do they come from, and how do they make a living? Apart from farm labourers, I mean."

" A lot of them are shearers," said Tom, " drifting from job to job, according to climate. When shearing season's over here, they work on to the south-west, where it's cooler. And then there are kangaroo and 'possum snarers. That young fellow we saw rooked of all his sugar last night was a skin hunter. They get half-a-crown apiece for good 'roo skins, and it's quite a trade. The others last night were mostly sandal-wood getters. There's quite a lot of men make money collecting bark for export, and manna-gum. That rowdy lot playing fifty-three were a gang of well-sinkers. Then what with timber-workers, haulers, teamsters, junkers—oh, there's all sorts. But they're mostly one sort, swabs, rough and rowdy, an' can't keep their pants hitched up enough to be decent. You've seen 'em. They're mostly like the dirty old braces they wear. All the snap gone out of 'em, all the elastic perished. They just work and booze and loaf and work and booze. I hope I'll never get so that I don't keep myself spruce. I hope I never will. But that's the worst o' the life out here. Nobody hardly keeps spruce."

Jack kept this well in mind. He, too, hated a man slouching along with a discoloured face and trousers slopping down his insignificant legs. He loathed that look which tramps and ne'er-do-wells usually have, as if their legs weren't there, inside their beastly bags. Despicable about the rear and the legs. The best of the farmers, on the contrary, had strong, sinewy legs, full of life. Easu was like that, his powerful legs holding his horse. And Tom had good, live legs. But poor Dad had not been very alive, inside his pants.

" Whatever I do, I'll never go despicable and humiliated about the legs and seat," said Jack to himself, as he pressed the stirrups with his toes and felt the powerful elasticity of his thighs, holding the live body of the horse between his muscles in permanent grip. And it seemed as if the powerful animal life of the horse entered into him, through his legs and seat, and made him strong.

" What's a junker, Tom ? "

" A low, four-wheeled log hauler, with a long pole."

" I thought it was a man. A swab is a man ? "

" Yes. He's any old drunk."

" But a swaggy is a tramp ? "

" It is. It is one who humps it. If he's got a pack, it's his swag. If he's only got a blanket and a billy, it's his bluey and his drum. And if he's got nothing, it's Waltzing Matilda."

" I suppose so," said Jack. " And his money is his sugar ? "

" Right-O, son ! "

" And Chink is Chinaman ? "

" No, sir. That's Chow. Chink means prison. An' a

lag is a ticketer : one who's out on lease. Now, what more Child's Guide to Knowledge do you want? "

" I'm only getting it straight. Jam and dog both mean ' side '? "

" Verily. Only dog is sometimes same as bully tinned meat."

" And what's *stosh*? "

" Landin' him one."

Jack rode on, thinking about it.

" What's a remittance man, really, Tom? "

" A waster. A useless bird shipped out here to be kept south o' the line, because he's a disgrace to England. And his family soothes their conscience by sending him so much a month, which they call his remittance, 'stead o' letting him starve, or work. Like Rackett. Plenty o' money sent out to him to stink on."

" Why don't you like Rackett? "

" I fairly despise him, an' his money. He's absolutely useless baggage, rotting life away. I can't abear to see him about. Old George gave me the tip he was leaving our place, else I'd never have gone and left him loose there."

" He is no harm."

" How do you know? If he hasn't got a disease of the body, he's got a disease of the soul."

" What disease? "

" Dunno."

" Does he take drugs? "

" I reckon that's about his figure. But he's an eyesore to me, loafin', loafin'. An' he's an eyesore to Ma, save for the bit he teaches Lennie. An' when he starts talkin' on the high fiddle, like he does to Mary the minute she comes down, makes you want to walk on his face."

Poor Rackett! Jack marvelled that Tom had always been so civil.

The two jogged along very amicably together. Tom was hail-fellow well-met with everybody. At the same time, he was in his own estimation a gentleman, and a person of consideration. It was " thus far " with him.

But whoever came along, they all drew up.

" Hello, mate! How's goin'? " . . . Well, so long! "

One youth was walking to Fremantle to take a job

offered by his uncle, serving in a grocery shop. The lad was in tatters. His blanket was tied with twine, his battered billy hung on to it. But he was jubilant. And now he is one of Australia's leading lights. Even it is said of him that he never forgot the kindness he received on the road.

But most of the trailers were sundowners, sloping along anyhow, subsisting anyhow, but ready with the ingenious explanation that they " chopped a bit," or " fenced a bit," or " trapped a bit." Perhaps they never realised how much bigger was the bit they loafed.

They were not bad. The bad ones were the scoundrels down from the Never-Never, emerging in their rags and moral degradation after years on the sheep runs or cattle stations, years of earnings spent in drink and squalid, beastly debauchery. Some were hoarding their cheques for coast-town consumption, like the first two rogues, and cadging and stealing their way.

But then there were families driving to the nearest settlement to do a bit of shopping, or visit their relations, or fetch the doctor to " fix up Teddy's little leg." Once there was a posse of mounted police, very important and gallant, with horses champing and chains clinking. They were out after a criminal supposed to have been landed on the coast by a dago boat " from the other side." Then there was an occasional Minister of the Gospel, on a pony, dressed in black. Jack's heart always sank when he saw that black. He decided that priests should be white, or in orange robes, like the Buddhist priests he had seen in Colombo, or in a good blue, like some nuns.

Gradually the road became a home : more a home than any homestead.

" Let's get ! " was Tom's perpetual cry, when they were fixed up in the house of some relation, or in some inn. He only felt happy on the road. Sometimes they went utterly lonely for many miles. Sometimes they passed a deserted habitation. But there were always signs of life near a well. And often there were mile-stones.

" Fifty-seven miles to where ? "

" I don't know. We're leagues from Gingin. Certainly fifty-seven miles to nowhere of any importance on the face of this earth."

" Wonder what Gingin means ? "

" Better not ask. You never know what these natives'll be naming places after. Usually something vile. But *gin* means a woman, whatever Gingin is."

Gradually they got further and further, geographically, mentally, and emotionally, from Wandoo and all permanent associations. Jack was glad. He loved the earth, the wild country, the bush, the scent. He wanted to go on for ever. Beyond the settlements—beyond the ploughed land—beyond all fences. That was it—beyond all fences. Beyond all fences, where a man was alone with himself and the untouched earth.

Man escaping from Man ! That's how it is all the time. The passion men have to escape from mankind. What do they expect in the beyond ? God ?

They'll never find the same God ! Never again. They are trying to escape from the God men acknowledge, as well as from mankind, the acknowledger.

The land untouched by man. The call of the mysterious, vast, unoccupied land. The strange inaudible calling, like the far-off call of a kangaroo. The strange, still, pure air. The strange shadows. The strange scent of wild, brown, aboriginal honey.

Being early for the boat, the boys camped for twenty-four hours in a perfectly lonely place. And in the utterly lonely evening Jack began craving again : for Monica, for a woman, for some object for his passion to settle on. And he knew again, as he had always known, that nowhere is free, so long as man is passionate, desirous, yearning. His only freedom is to find the object of his passion, and fulfil his desires and satisfy his yearning, as far as his life can succeed. Or else, which is more difficult, to harden himself away from all desire and craving, to harden himself into pride, and refer himself to that other God.

Yes, in the wild bush, God seemed another God. God seemed absolutely another God, vaster, more calm and more deeply, sensually potent. And this was a profound satisfaction. To find another, more terrible, but also more deeply-fulfilling God stirring subtly in the uncontaminated air about one. A dread God. But a great God, greater than any known. The sense of greatness, vastness, and newness, in the air. And the strange, dusky, grey eucalyptus-smelling sense of depth, strange depth in the air, as of a great deep well of potency, which life had not yet tapped. Something which lay in a man's blood as well—and in a woman's blood—in Monica's—in Mary's—in the Australian blood. A strange, dusky, gum-smelling depth of potency that had never been tapped by experience. As if life still held great wells of reserve vitality, strange unknown wells of secret life-source, dusky, of a strange, dim, aromatic sap which had never stirred in the veins of man, to consciousness and effect. And if he could take Monica and set the dusky, secret, unknown sap flowing in himself and her, to some unopened life consciousness—that was what he wanted. Dimly, uneasily, painfully he realised it.

And then the bush began to frighten him, as if it would kill him, as it had killed so much man-life before, killed it before the life in man had time to come to realisation.

He was glad when the road came down to the sea. There, the great, pale-blue, strange empty sea, on new shores, with new strange sea-birds flying, and strange rocks sticking up, and strange blue distances up the bending coast. The sea that is always the same, always a relief, a vastness and a soothing. Coming out of the bush, and being a little afraid of the bush, he loved the sea with an English passion. It made him feel at home in the same known infinite of space.

Especially on a windy day, when the track would curve down to a greeny-grey opalescent sea that beat slowly on the red sands, like a dying grey bird with white wing feathers. And the reddish cliffs with sage-green growth of herbs, stood almost like flesh.

Then the road went inland again, through a swamp, and to the bush. To emerge next morning in the sun, upon a massive deep indigo ocean, infinite, with pearl-clear horizon; and in the nearness, emerald-green and white flashing unspeakably bright on a pinkish shore, perfectly world-new.

They were nearing the journey's end. Nearing the little port, and the ship, and the world of men.

CHAP : XVII.   AFTER TWO YEARS

i

A SKY with clouds of white and grey, and patches of blue. A green sea flecked with white, and shadowed golden brown. On the horizon, the sense of a great open void, like an open valve, as if the bivalve oyster of the world, sea and sky, were open away westward, open into another infinity, and the people on land, inside the oyster of the world, could look far out to the opening.

They could see the bulk of near islands. Farther off, a tiny white sail coming down fast on the fresh great sea-wind, emanating out of the north-west. She seemed to be coming from the beyond, slipping into the slightly-open, living oyster of our world.

The men on the wharf at Fremantle, watching her black hull emerge from the flecked sea, as she sailed magically nearer, knew she would be a cattle-boat coming in from the great Nor' West. They watched her none the less.

As she hesitated, turning to the harbour, she was recognised as the old fore-and-aft schooner " Venus "; though if Venus ever smelled like that, we pity her lovers. Smell or not, she balanced nicely, and with a bit of manoeuvring ebbed her delicate way up the wharf.

There they are ! There they are, Tom and Jack, though their own mothers wouldn't know them ! Looking terribly like their fellow-passengers : stubby beards, long hair, greasy dirty dungarees, and a general air of disreputable outcasts. But, no doubt, with cheques of some sort in their pockets.

Two years, nearer three years have gone by, since they set out from Wandoo. It is more than three years since Jack landed fresh from England, in this very Fremantle. And he is so changed, he doesn't even trouble to remember.

They don't trouble to remember anything : not yet. Back in the Never-Never, one by one the ties break, the emotional connections snap, memory gives out, and you come undone. Then, when you have come undone from the great past, you drift in an unkempt nonchalance here and there, great distances across the great hinterland country, and there is nothing but the moment, the instantaneous moment. If you are working your guts out, you are working your guts out. If you are rolling across for a drink, you are rolling across for a drink. If you are just getting into a fight with some lump of a brute, you are just getting into a fight with some lump of a brute. If you are going to sleep in some low hole, you are going to sleep in some low hole. And if you wake feeling dry and hot and hellish, why, you feel dry and hot and hellish till you leave off feeling dry and hot and hellish. There's no more to it. The same if you're sick. You're just sick, and stubborn as hell, till your stubbornness gets the better of your sickness.

There are words like home, Wandoo, England, mother, father, sister, but they don't carry very well. It's like a radio message that's so faint, so far off, it makes no impression on you; even if you can hear it in a shadowy way. Such a faint, unreal thing in the broadcast air.

You have moved outside the pale, the pale of civilisation, the pale of the general human consciousness. The human consciousness is a definitely limited thing, even on the face of the earth. You can move into regions outside of it. As in Australia. The broadcasting of the vast human consciousness can't get you. You are beyond. And since the call can't get you, the answer begins to die down inside yourself, you don't respond any more. You don't respond, and you don't correspond.

There is no past : or if there is, it is so remote and ineffectual it can't work on you at all. And there is no future. Why saddle yourself with such a spectre as the future ? There is the moment. You sweat, you rest, the bugs bite you, you thirst, you drink, you think you're going to die, you don't care, and you know you won't die, because a certain stubbornness inside you keeps the upper hand.

So you go on. If you've got no work, you either get a horse or you tramp it off somewhere else. You keep your eyes open that you don't get lost, or stranded for water. When you're damned, infernally and absolutely sick of everything, you go to sleep. And then if the bugs bite you, you are beyond that too.

But at the bottom of yourself, somewhere, like a tiny seed, lies the knowledge that you're going back in a while.

That all the unreal will become real again, and this real will become ureal. That all that stuff, home, mother, responsibility, family, duty, etc., it all will loom up again into actuality, and this, this heat, this parchedness, this dirt, this mutton, these dying sheep, these roving cattle that take the flies by the million, these burning tin gold-camps—all this will recede into the unreal, it will cease to be actual.

Some men decide never to go back, and they are the derelicts, the scarecrows and the warning. " Going back " was a problem in Jack's soul. He didn't really want to go back. All that which lay behind, society, homes, families, he felt a deep hostility towards. He didn't want to go back. He was like an enemy, lurking outside the great camp of civilisation. And he didn't want to go into camp again.

Yet neither did he want to be a derelict. A mere derelict he would never be, though temporary derelicts both he and Tom were. But he saw enough of the real waster, the real out-and-out derelict, to know that this he would never be.

No, in the end he would go back to civilization. But the thought of becoming a part of the civilized outfit was deeply repugnant to him. Some other queer hard resolve had formed in his soul. Something gradually went hard in the centre of him. He couldn't yield himself any more. The hard core remained impregnable.

They had dutifully spent their year on the sheep-run Mr. George had sent them to. But after that, it was shift for yourself. They had stuck at nothing. Only they had stuck together.

They had cashed their cheques in many a well-known wooden " hotel " of the far-away coast. Oh, those wooden hotels with their uneasy verandahs, flies, flies, flies, flies, flies, their rum or whisky, their dirty glasses, their flimsy partitions, their foul language, their bugs and dirt and desolation. The brutal foul-mouthed desolation of them, with the horses switching their tails at the hitching posts, the riders slowly soaking, staring at the blue heat and the silent world of dust, too far gone even to speak. Gone under the heat, the drought, the Never-Neverness of it, the unspeakable hot desolation. And evening coming, with men already drunk, already ripe for brawling, obscenity, and swindling gambling.

They had gone away chequeless, mourning their chequelessness, back on their horses to the cable station. Then following the droves miles and miles through the tropical, or semi-tropical bush, and over the open country, camping by water for a week at a time, and going on.

Then they had chucked cattle, wasted their cheques, footed it for weary, weary miles, like the swaggies they had so despised. Clothes in rags, boots in holes, another job; away in out-back camps with horsemen prospectors, with well-contractors; shepherding again, with utter wastrels of shepherds camping along with them, chucking the job, chucking the blasted rich aristocratic squatters with all their millions of acres and sheep and fence and blasted outfit, all so dead bent on making money as quick as possible, all the machinery of civilization, as far as possible, starting to grind and squeak there in the beyond. They had gone off with well-sinkers, and laboured like navvies. Chucked that, taken the road, spent the night at mission stations, watched the blacks being saved, and got to the mining camps.

Poor old Tom had got into deep waters. Even now he more than thought that he was legally married to a barmaid, far away back in the sublimest town you can imagine, back there in the blasting heat which so often burns a man's soul away even before it burns up his body. It had burned a hole in Tom's soul, in that town away back in the blasting heat, a town consisting of a score or so of ready-made tin houses got up from the coast in pieces, and put together by anybody that liked to try. There they stood or staggered, the tin ovens that men and women lived in; houses leaning like drunken men against stark tree-trunks, others looking strange and forlorn with some of their parts missing, said parts being under the seas, or elsewhere mislaid. But the absence of one section of a wall did not spoil the house for habitation. It merely gave you a better view of the inside happenings. Many of the tin shacks were windowless, and even shutterless : square holes in the raw corrugated erection. One was entirely wall-less, and this was the pub. It was just a tin roof reared on saplings against an old tree, with a sacking screen round the bar, through which sacking screen you saw the ghost of the landlady and her clients, if you approached from the back. The front view was open.

Here sat the motionless landlady, in her cooking hot

shade, dispensing her indispensable grog, while her boss or husband rolled the barrels in. He had a team with which he hauled up the indispensable from the coast.

The nice-mannered Miss Snook took turns with her mamma in this palace of Circe. She was extremely " nice " in her manners, for the " boss " owned the team, the pub, and the boarding-house at which you stayed so long as you could pay the outrageous prices. So Miss Snook, never familiarized into Lucy, for she wouldn't allow it, oscillated between the closed oven of the boarding-house and the open oven of the pub.

Father—or the " boss "—had been a barber in Sydney. Now he cooked in the boarding-house, and drove the team. " Mother " had been the high-born daughter of a chemist; she had ruined all her prospects of continuing in the eastern " swim " by running away with the barber, now called " boss." However, she took her decline in the social scale with dignity, and allowed no familiarities. Her previous station helped her to keep up her prices.

" We're not, y'understand, Mr. Grant, a Provident concern, as some foot-sloggers seem to think us. We're doing out best to provide for Lucy, against she wants to get married, or in case she doesn't."

She and Lucy did the washing and cleaning between them, but their efforts were nominal. Boss's cooking left everything to be desired. The place was a perfect paradise.

" We know a gentleman when we see one, Mr. Grant, and we're not going to throw out only child away on a penniless waster."

Jack wanted loudly to proclaim himself a penniless waster. But Tom and he had a pact, not to say *anything* about themselves, or where they came from. They were just " looking round."

And in that heat, the plump, perspiring, cotton-clad Lucy thought that Tom seemed more amenable than Jack. Poor Tom seemed to fall for it, and Jack had to look on in silent disgust. There was even a ghastly, gruesome wedding. Neither of the boys could bear to think of it. Even in the stupefaction of that heat, when the brain seems to melt, and the will degenerates, and nothing but the most rudimentary functions of the organism called man, continue to function, even then a sense of shame overpowered them.

Tom continued in the trance for about a week after his so-called marriage. Then he woke up from the welter of perspiration, rum, and Lucy in an amazed horror, and the boys escaped.

The nightmare of this town—it was called " Honey-suckle "—was able to penetrate Tom's most nonchalant mood, even when he was hundreds of trackless miles away. The young men covered their tracks carefully. The Snooks knew nothing but their names. But a name, alas, is a potent entity in the wilds.

They covered their tracks and disappeared again. But even so, an ancient letter from Wandoo followed them to a well-digging camp. It was from Monica to Tom, but it didn't seem to mean much to either boy.

For almost a year Tom and Jack had never written home. There didn't seem any reason. In his last letter, Tom, suddenly having some sort of qualm, had sent his cheque to his maiden aunts in York, because he knew, now Gran and Dad were gone, they'd be in shallow water. This off his conscience, he let Wandoo go out of his mind and spirit.

But now wandered in a letter from Aunt Lucy—dreaded name ! It was a " thank you, my dear nephew," and went on to say that though she would be the last to repeat things she hoped trouble was not hanging over Mrs. Ellis' head.

Tom looked at Jack.

" We'd best go back," said Jack, reading his eyes.

" Seems like it."

So—the time had come. The " freedom " was over. They were going back. They caught the old ship " Venus," going south with cattle.

To come back in body is not always to come back in mind and spirit. When Jack saw the white buildings of Fremantle he knew his soul was far from Fremantle. But nothing to be done. The old ship bumped against the wharf, and was tied up. Nothing to do but to step ashore.

They loafed off that ship with a gang of similar unkempt, unshaved, greasy, scoundrelly returners.

" Come an' 'ave a spot ! "

" What about it, Tom ? "

" Y'know I haven't a bean above the couple o' dollars to take me to Perth."

" Oh, dry it up," cried the mate. " What y'come ashore

for? You're not goin' without a spot. It's on me. My shout."

" Shout it back in Perth, then."

" Wot'll y'ave? "

And through the swing doors they went.

" Best an' bitter's mine."

ii

Jack had not let himself be cleaned out entirely, as Tom had. Tom seemed to *want* to be absolutely stumped. But Jack, with deeper sense of the world's enmity, and his own need to hold his own against it, had posted a couple of cheques to Lennie to hold for him. Save for this he too was cleaned out.

The same little engine of the same little train of four years ago shrieked her whistle. The North-West crowd drifted noisily out of the hotel and down the platform, packing into the third class compartment, in such positions as happily to negotiate the spittoons.

" Let's go forward," said Jack. " We might as well have cushions, if we're not smoking."

And he drew Tom forward along the train. They were going to get into another compartment, but seeing the looks of terror on the face of the woman and little girl already there, they refrained and went farther.

Aggressively they entered another smoking compartment. A couple of fat tradesmen and a clergyman glowered at them. One of the tradesmen pulled out a handkerchief, shook it, and pretended to wipe his nose. There was perfume in the air.

" Oh, my aunt! " said Tom, putting his hand on his stomach. " Turns me right over."

" What? " asked Jack.

" All this smell o' scent."

Jack grinned to himself. But he was back in civilization, and he involuntarily stiffened.

" Hello! There's Sam Ellis! " Tom leaned out of the door. " Hello, Sam! How's things, eh? "

The young fellow addressed looked at Tom, grinned sicklily, and turned away. He didn't know Tom from Adam.

" Let's have another drink ! " said Tom, flabbergasted, getting out of the train.

Jack followed, and they started down the platform, when the train jogged, jerked, and began to pull away. Instantly they ran for it, caught the rail of the guard's van, and swung themselves in. The interior was empty, so they sat down on the little boxes let in at the side. Then the two eyed each other self-consciously, uncomfortably. They felt uncomfortable and aware of themselves all at once.

" Of all the ol' sweeps ! " said Tom. " Tell you what, you look like a lumper, absolutely nothing but a lumper."

" And what do you think you look like, you distorted scavenger ! "

Tom grinned uncomfortably.

They got out of the station at Perth without having paid any railway fare.

The first place they went to was Mr. George's office. Jack pushed Tom through the door, and stood himself in the doorway fingering his greasy felt hat. Tom dropped his, picked it up, hit it against his knee.

Mr. George, neat in pale grey suit and white waistcoat, glared at them briefly.

" Now then, my men, what can I do f' ye ? "

" Why—" began Tom, grinning sheepishly.

" Trouble about a mining right ? Mate stolen half y' gold dust ? Want stake a claim on somebody else's reserve ? Come, out with it. What d' you want me to do for ye, man ? "

" Why— " Tom began, more foolishly grinning than ever. Mr. George looked shrewdly at him, then at Jack. Then he sat back smiling.

" Well, if you're not a pair ! " he said. " So it was mines for the last outfit ? How'd it go ? "

" About as slow as it could," said Tom.

" So you've not come back millionaires ? " said Mr. George, a little bit disappointed.

" Come to ask for a fiver," said Tom.

" You outcast ! " said Mr. George. " You had me, completely. But look here, lads, I'll stand y' a fiver apiece if y'll stop around Perth like that all morning, an' nobody spots ye."

" Easy ! " said Tom.

" A bigger pair o' blackguards I've seldom set eyes on.
But you have dinner with me at the club to-night, I'll hear
all about y' then. Six-thirty sharp. An' then I'll take ye
to the Government House. Y' can wear that evening suit
in the closet at my house, Jack, that you've left there all
this time. See you six-thirty then."

iii

Dismissed, they bundled into the street.

" Outcasts on the face value of us ! " said Jack.

Tom stopped to roar with laughter, and bumped into a
pedestrian.

" Hold hard ! Keep a hand on the reins, can't you? "
exclaimed the individual, pushing Tom off.

Tom looked at him. It was Jimmie Short, another sort
of cousin.

" Stow it, Jimmie. Don't y' know me? "

Jimmie took him firmly by the coat lappels and pulled
him into the gutter.

" 'F course I know ye," said Jimmie in a conciliatory
tone, as to a drunk. " Meet me in half an hour at the
Miners' Refuge, eh ? Three steps and a lurch and there y'
are ! Come, matey "—this to Jack—" take hold of y' pal's
arm. See ye later."

Tom was weak with laughter at Jimmie's benevolent
attitude. They were not recognised at all, as they lurched
across the road.

They had a drink, and strolled down the long principal
street of Perth, looking in at the windows of all the shops,
and in spite of the fact that they had no money, buying
each a silk handkerchief and a cake of scented soap. The
excitement of this over, they rolled away to the river-side,
to the ferry. Then again back into the town.

At the corner of the Freemason's Hotel they saw Aunt
Matilda and Mary; Aunt Matilda huge in a tight-fitting,
ruched dress of dark purple stuff, and Mary in a black-and-
white striped dress with a tight bodice and tight sleeves
with a little puff at the top, and a long skirt very full
behind. She wore also a little black hat with a wing. And
Jack, with a wickedness brought with him out of the North

West, would have liked to rip these stereotyped clothes and corsets off her, and make her walk down Hay Street *in puris naturalibus*. She went so trim and exact behind the huge Mrs. Watson. It would have been good to unsheathe her.

" Hello ! " cried Tom. " There's Aunt Matilda. We've struck it rich."

The two young blackguards followed slowly after the two women, close behind them. Mary carried a book, and was evidently making for the little bookshop that had a lending library of newish books.

" Well, Mary, while you go in there I'll go and see if the chemist can't give me something for my breathing, for it's awful ! " said Mrs Watson, standing and puffing before the book-shop.

" Shall I come for you or you for me ? " asked Mary.

" I'll sit and wait for you in Mr Pusey's," panted Aunt Matilda, and she sailed forward again, after having glanced suspiciously backward at the two ne'er-do-wells who were hesitating a few yards away.

Mary, with her black hair in a huge bun, her hat with a wing held on by steel pins, was gazing contemplatively into the window of the book-shop at the newest books. " The Book-lovers' Latest ! " said a cardboard announcement.

" Can you help a poor chap, Miss ? " said Tom, dropping his head and edging near.

Mary started, looked frightened, glanced at the first tramp and then at the second, in agitation, began to fumble for her purse, and dropped her book, spilling the loose leaves.

Jack at once began to gather up the scattered pages of the book : an Anthony Trollope novel. Mary, with black kid-gloved fingers, was fumbling in her purse for a penny. Tom peeped into the purse.

" Lend us the half a quid, Mary," he said.

She looked at his face, and a slow smile of amusement dawned in her eyes.

" I should never have known you ! " she said.

Then as Jack rose, shoving the leaves together in the book, she looked into his blue eyes with her brown, queer shining eyes.

She held out her hand to him without saying a word,

only looked into his eyes with a look of shining meaning. Which made him grin sardonically inside himself. He shook hands with her silently.

" You look something like you did after you'd been fighting with Easu Ellis," she said. " When are you going to Wandoo? "

" To-morrow, I should think," said Tom. " Everybody O.K. down there? "

" Oh, I think so! " said Mary nervously.

" What do you men want? " came a loud, panting voice. Aunt Matilda sailing up, purple in the face.

" Lend us half a quid, Mary," murmured Tom, and hastily she handed it over. Jack had already commenced to beat a retreat. Tom sloped away as the large lady loomed near.

" Beggars! " she panted. " Are they begging? How much—how much did you give him? The disgraceful—— !"

" He made me give him half-a-sovereign, Aunt."

Mrs Watson had to stagger into the shop for a chair.

The boys had a drink, and set off to the warehouse to look up Jack's box, in which were his white shirts and other forgotten garments.

Back in town, Jack felt a slow, sinister sense of oppression coming over him, a sort of fear, as if he were not really free, as if something bad were going to happen to him.

" How am I going to get dressed to dine with Old George to-night? " grumbled the still careless Tom, who was again becoming tipsy. " Wherever am I goin' to get a suit to sport? "

" Oh, some of yer relations 'll fix you up."

Jack had an undefinable, uncomfortable feeling that he might suddenly come upon Monica, and she might see him in this state. He wouldn't like the way she'd look at him. No, he wouldn't be looked at like that, not for a hundred ponies.

They turned their backs on the beautiful river, with its Mount Eliza headland and wide sweeps and curves twinkling in the sun, and they walked up William Street looking for an adventure.

A man whom they knew from the north, in filthy denins, came out of a boot-shop and hailed them.

" Come an' stop one on me, maties."

" Righto ! But where's Lukey? He stood us one this morning. Seen him? "

" Yes, I seen him—but, 'arf a mo' ! "

Scottie turned into the pawnbroker's, under the three balls, and the boys followed.

" If y' sees what y' didn't oughta see, keep y' mouth shut."

" As a dead crab," assented Jack.

" Now, then, Uncle ! What'll y' advance on that pair o' bran new boots I've just bought? "

" Two bob."

" Glory be. An' I just give twenty for 'em. Ne' mind, gimme th' ticket."

This transaction concluded, Jack wondered what he could pawn. He pulled out a front tooth, beautifully set in a gold plate. It had been a parting finish to his colonial outfit, the original tooth having been lost in a football scrum.

" Father Abraham," he said, holding up the tooth, " I'm a gentleman whether I look it or not. So is my friend, this gentleman. He needs a dress suit for to-night, though you wouldn't believe it. He needs a first-class, well-fitting dress suit for this evening."

" I have first-class latest fashion gents' clothes upstairs. But a suit like that is worth five pound to me."

" Let me try the jacket on."

Abraham was doubtful. But at length Tom was hustled shamefacedly into a rather large tail-coat. It looked awful, but Jack said it would do. The man wouldn't take a cent less than two quid deposit, and ten bob for the loan of the suit. The boys said they would call later.

" What'll you give me on this tooth? " asked Jack. "There's not a more expensive tooth in Western Australia."

" I'll lend y' five bob on that, pecos y' amuth me."

" And we'll come in later for the dress suit. Alright, Aaron. Hang on to that tooth, it's irreplaceable. Treat it like a jewel. Give me the five bob and the ticket."

In the Miners' Refuge Jack flung himself down on a bench beside an individual who looked tidy but smelt strongly of rum, and asked :

" Say mate, where can y' get a wash an' a brush-up for two ?—local ? "

The fellow got up and lurched surlily to the counter, refusing to answer.

Jack sat on, while Tom drank beer, and a heavy depression crept over his spirit. He had been hobnobbing with riff-raff so long, it had almost become second nature. But now a sense of disgust and impending disaster came over him. He would soon have to make an angry effort, and get out. He was becoming angry with Tom, for sitting there so sloppily soaking beer, when he knew his head was weak.

They began to eat sandwiches, hungrily standing at the bar. Another slipshod waster, eyeing the denin man as if he were a fish, sidled over to him and muttered.

" Sorry," said Scottie, with a mournful expression, pulling out the pawn-ticket, " I've just had to pawn me boots. Can't be done."

Jack grinned. The waster then came sloping over to him.

" Y' axed me mate a civil question just now, lad, an' I'd 'ave answered it for 'im, but I just spotted a racin' pal o' mine an' was onter him ter get a tip he'd promised—a dead cert f' Belmont to-morrer.

" Y' might ha' seen him lettin' me inter th' know," he breathed. " Hev' a drink, lad ! "

" Thanks ! " said Jack. " This is my mate. I'll take the shout, an' one back, an' then we must be off. Going up country to-morrer morning."

This seemed to push the man's mind on quicker.

" Just from up North, aren't ye ? Easy place to knock up a cheque. How'd y' like to double a fiver ? "

" O.K.", said Tom.

" Well, here's a dead cert. Take it from me, and don't let it past yer. I got it from a racin' pal wots in the know. Not straight for the punters, maybe—but straight as a die f'r me 'n my pals. Double y' money ? Not 'arf ! Multiply it by ten. 'S a dead cert."

" Name ? "

" Not so quick. Not in 'ere. Come outside, 'n I'll whisper it to y'."

Jack paid for the drinks, and winking warningly to Tom, followed the man outside.

" The name o' the 'oss," the fellow said, "—but tell yer

wot, I'll put ye on the divvy with a book I know—or y' c'n come wi' me. He keeps a paper-shop in Hay Street."

" We don't know the name of the horse yet."

" Comin' from up North you don't know the name o' none of 'em, do yer? He's a rank outsider. Y' oughter get twenties on 'im."

" We've only got a quid atween us," said Tom.

" Well, that means a safe forty—after th' race."

" Bob on! " said Tom. " Where's the book-shop? "

" How can we go in an' back a hoss without knowin' his name? " said Jack.

" Oh, I'll tip it y' in 'ere."

They entered a small paper-shop, and the man said to the fellow behind the counter :

" These two gents 's pals o' mine. How much did y' say y'd lay, mates? "

" Out with the name o' th' hoss first," said Tom, confidentially.

" This shop's changed hands lately," said the fat fellow behind the counter, " I don't make books. Got no licence."

Didn't that look straight? But the boys were no greenhorns. They walked out of the shop again.

In the road the stranger said :

" The name o' th' 'oss is Double Bee. If y'll give me th' money I'll run upstairs 'ere t' old Josh—everyone knows him for a sound book."

" The name o' th' hoss," said Jack, " is Boots-two-Bob. An' a more cramblin' set o' lies I never heard. Get outter this, or I'll knock y' head off."

The fellow went off with a yellow look.

" Gosh! " said Tom. " We're back home right enough, what? "

" Bon soir, as Frenchy used to say? "

Rolling a little drearily along, they saw Jimmie Short standing on the pavement watching them.

" Hello, mates! " he said. " Still going strong? "

" Fireproof! " said Tom.

" Remember barging into me this morning? And my best girl was just coming round the corner with her Ma! Had to mind my company, eh, boys? But come an' have a drink now. I seem to have seen you before to-day, haven't I? Where was it? "

" Don't try and think," said Tom. " Y' might do us out of a pony."

" Right-o! old gold dust! Step over on to the Barparlour mat."

" I'm stepping," said Tom. " 'N I'm not drunk."

" No, he's not," said Jack.

" You bet he's not," said Jimmy. He was eyeing them curiously, as if his memory pricked him.

" My name," said Tom, " is Ned Kelly. And if yours isn't Jimmie Miller, what is it? "

" Why, it's Short. Well, I give it up. I can't seem to lay my finger on you, Kelly."

Tom roared with laughter.

" What time is it? " he asked.

" Ten past twelve."

" We've won a pony off Old George! " said the delighted Tom. " I'm Tom Ellis and he's Jack Grant. *Now* do you know us, Jimmie? "

Jack was glad to get washed and barbered and dressed. After all, he was sick of wasters and roughs. They were stupider than respectable people, and much more offensive physically and morally. To hell with them all. He wouldn't care if some tyrant would up and extirpate the breed.

Anyhow he stepped clean out of their company.

CHAP : XVIII. THE GOVERNOR'S DANCE

THREE gentlemen in evening dress passing along by the low brick wall skirting the Government House. One of the gentlemen portly and correct, two of the gentlemen young, with burnt brown faces that showed a little less tan below the shaving line, and limbs too strong and too rough to fit the evening clothes. Jack's suit was on the small side, though he'd scarcely grown in height. But it showed a big piece of white shirt-cuff at the wrists, and seemed to reveal the muscles of his shoulders unduly. As for Tom's quite good and quite expensive suit from the pawn-shop, it was a little large for him. If he hadn't been so bursting with life it would have been sloppy. But the crude animal life came so forcibly through the black cloth, that you had to overlook the anomaly of the clothes. Both boys wore socks of fine scarlet wool, and the new handkerchiefs of magenta silk inside their waistcoats. The scarlet, magenta, and red-brown of their faces made a gallant pizzicato of colour against the black and white. Anyhow, they fancied themselves, and walked conceitedly.

Jack's face was a little amusing. It had the kind of innocence and half-smile you can see on the face of a young fox, which will snap holes in your hand if you touch it. He was annoyed by his father's letter to him for his twenty-first birthday. The general had retired, and hadn't saved a sou. How could he, given his happy, thriftless lady. So it was a case of " My dear boy, I'm thankful you are at last twenty-one, because now you must look out for yourself. I have bled myself to send you this cheque for a hundred pounds, but I know you think I ought to send you something so take it, but don't expect any more, for you won't get it if you do."

This was not really the text of the General's letter, but this was how Jack read it. As for his mother, she sent him six terrible neckties and awful silver-backed brushes which he hated the sight of, much love, a few tears, a bit of absurd fond counsel, and a general wind-up of tender doting which Jack felt was really meant, like the Harry Smith letter, " for 'appy Jack wot went up Cossack way."

He was annoyed, because he had expected some sort of real assistance in setting out like a gentleman on his life's career, now he had attained his majority. But the hundred quid was a substantial sop.

Mr George had done them proud at the Weld Club, and got them invitations to the ball from the Private Secretary. Oh, yes, he was proud of them, handsome upstanding young fellows. So they were proud of themselves. It was a fine, hot evening, and nearly everybody was walking to the function, showing off their splendour. For few people possessed private carriages, and the town boasted very few cabs indeed.

Mr George waited in the porch of the Government House for Aunt Matilda and Mary. They had not long to wait before they saw the ladies in their shawls, carrying each a little holland bag with scarlet initials, containing their dancing slippers, slowly and self-consciously mounting the steps.

The boys braced themselves to face the introduction to the Representation. They were uneasy. Also they wanted to grin. In Jack's mind a picture of Honeysuckle, that tin town in the heat, danced as on heat-waves, as he made his bows and his murmurs. He wanted to whisper to Tom : " Ain't we in Honeysuckle ? " But it would have been too cruel.

Clutching their programmes as drowning men clutch straw, they passed on. The primary ordeal was over.

" Oh, Lord, I'm sweating already," said Tom with a red-faced grin. " I'm off to get me bill-head crammed."

" Take me with you, for the Lord's sake," said Jack.

" Y're such an owl of a dancer. An' y' have to do it proper here. You go to Mr George."

" Don't desert me, you swine."

" Go on ! Want me to take you back to Auntie ? Go on ! I'm goin' to dance an' sit out an' hold their little white hands."

Tom pulled a droll face as he took his place in the line of glove-buttoning youths who made a queue on the Governor's left hand, where his daughter stood booking up duty dances. Jack, galvanised by the advent of the A.D.C., ducked through the crowd to Aunt Matilda's side.

He was always angry that he couldn't dance. The fact

was, he would never learn. He could never bring himself
to go hugging promiscuous girls round the waist and
twiddling through dances with them. Underneath all his
carelessness and his appearance of " mixing," there was a
savage physical reserve which prevented his mixing at all.
He could not bear the least physical intimacy. Something
inside him recoiled and stood savagely at a distance, even
from the prettiest girl, the moment she seemed to be
" coming on." To take the dear young things in his arms
was repugnant to him, it offended a certain aloof pride and
a subtle arrogance in him.   Even with Tom, intimate
though they were, he always kept a certain unpassable space
around him, a definite *noli me tangere* distance which gave
the limit to all approach. It would have been difficult to
define this reserve. Jack seemed absolutely the most open
and accessible individual in the world, a perfect child. He
seemed to lay himself far too open to anybody's approach.
But those who knew him better, like Mrs Ellis or his mother,
knew the cold inward reserve, the savage unwillingness to
be touched, which was central in him, as in a wolf-cub.
There was something reserved, fierce and untouched at the
very centre of him. Something, at the centre of all his
openness and his seeming softness, that was cold, overbearing, and a little angry. This was the old overweening
English blood in him, which would never really yield to
promiscuity, or to vulgar intimacy. He seemed to mix in
with everybody at random, but, as a matter of fact, he had
never finally mixed in with anybody, not even with his own
father and mother, not even with Tom. And certainly not
with any casual girl. Essentially, he kept himself a stranger
to everybody.

Aunt Matilda was in green satin with a tiara of diamonds.
" The devil you know is better than the devil you don't
know," was Jack's inward comment as he approached her.

Aloud he said :

" Would it be right if I asked you to let me have the
pleasure of taking you in to supper later, Marm ? "

" Oh, you dear boy ! " simpered Aunt Matilda, " So
like y' dear father. But, you see, I'm engaged on these
occasions. We have to go in in order of rank and pre-
cedence. But you can take Mary. She says she has hurt
her foot and can't dance much."

Mary took his arm, and they went out on to the terrace. There was clear moonlight, and trees against a shadowy, green-blue sky, and a dark perfume of tropical flowers. Jack felt the beauty of it and it moved him. He waited for his soul to melt. But his soul would never melt. It was hard and clear as the moon itself.

" It is much better here," he said, looking at the sky.

" Oh, it's beautiful ! " said Mary. " I wanted so much to sit quietly and talk to you. It seems so long, and you looked so wild and different this morning. I've been so frightened, reading so much about the natives murdering people."

Mary was different, too, but Jack didn't know wherein.

" I don't believe there's much more danger in one place than in another," he said. " So long as you keep yourself in hand. Shall we sit down and have a real wongie ? "

They found a seat under the overspreading tree, and sat listening to the night-insects.

" You're not *very* glad to be back, are you ? " asked Mary.

" Yes I am," he assented, without a great deal of vigour. " What has been happening to you all this time, Mary ? "

" The little things that are nothing," she said. " The only thing "—she hesitated—" is that they want me to marry. And I lie awake at night wondering about it."

" Marry who ? " asked Jack, his mind running at once to Rackett.

They were sitting under a magnolia tree. Jack could make out the dark shape of a great flower against the moon, among black leaves. And the perfume was magnolia flowers.

" Do you want me to talk about it ? " she said.

" I do."

Jack was glancing rather fiercely down the slope of the black-and-white garden, that sloped its lawns to the river. Mary sat very still beside him, in a cream lace dress.

" It's a Mr Boyd Blessington. He is a widower with five children, but he is an interesting man. He's got a black beard."

" Goodness ! " said Jack. " Have you accepted him ? "

" No. Not yet."

" Why do you think of marrying him? Do you like him? "

" For some things. He is a good man, and he wants me in a good way. He has a beautiful library. And as he is a man of the world, there seems to be a big world round him. Yes, he is quite somebody. And Aunt Matilda says it is a wonderful opportunity for me. And I know it is."

Jack mused in silence.

" It may be," he said, " but I hardly fancy you kissing a widower of fifty, with a black beard and five children. Lord! "

" He's only thirty-seven. And he's a *man*."

Jack thought about Monica. He wanted Monica. But he also couldn't bear to let Mary go. This arrogance in him made him silent for some moments. Then he turned to Mary, his head erect, and looked down sternly on her small, sinking figure in the pale lace dress.

" Do you *want* him? " he asked in a subtle tone of authority and passion.

Mary was silent for some moments.

" No-o! " she faltered. " Not—not—— "

Her hands lay inert in her lap. They were small, soft, dusky hands. The flame went over him, over his will. By some curious destiny she really belonged to him. And Monica? He wanted Monica, too. He wanted Monica first. But Mary also was his. Hard and savage he accepted this fact.

He took her two hands and lifted them to his lips, and kissed them with strange, blind passion. When the flame went over him, he was blind. Mary gave a little cry, but did not withdraw her hands.

" I thought you cared for Rackett," he said suddenly, looking at her closely. She shook her head, and he saw she was crying.

He put his arm round her and gathered her in her lace dress to his breast. She was small, but strangely heavy. Not like that whip-wire of a Monica. But he loved her heaviness, too. The heaviness of a dark magnetic stone. He wanted that, too.

And in his mind he thought, " Why can't I have her, too? She is naturally mine."

His soul was hard and unbending. " She is naturally

mine ! " he said to himself. And he kissed her softly, softly, kissed her face and her tears. And all the while Mary knew about Monica. And he, his soul fierce, would not yield in either direction. He wanted to marry her, and he wanted to marry Monica. Something was in Mary that would never be appeased unless he married her. And something in him would never be appeased unless he married Monica. His young, clear instinct saw both these facts. And the inward imperiousness of his nature rose to meet it. " Why can't I have both these women ? " he asked himself. And his soul, hard in its temper like a sword, answered him : " You can if you will."

Yet he was wary enough to know he must go cautiously. Meanwhile, determined that one day he would marry Monica and Mary both, he held the girl soft and fast in his arms, kissing her, wanting her, but wanting her with the slow knowledge that he must wait and travel a long way before he could take her, yet take her he would. He wanted Monica first. But he also wanted Mary. The soft, slow weight of her as she lay silent and unmoving in his arms.

They could hear the music inside.

" I must go in for the next dance," she said in a muted tone. He kissed her mouth and released her. Then he escorted her back to the ball-room. She went across to Aunt Matilda, as the dance ended. And in her lace dress, the small, heavy, dusky Mary was like a lode-stone passing among flimsy people. She had a certain magnetic heaviness of her own, and a certain stubborn, almost ugly kind of beauty which in its heavy quietness, seemed like a darkish, perhaps bitter flower that rose from a very deep root. You were sensible of a deep root going down into the dark.

A tall, thin, rather hollow-chested man in perfect evening suit and with orders on his breast, was speaking to her. He, too, had a faint air of proprietorship. He had a black beard and eyeglasses. But his face was sensitive, and delicate in its desire. It was evident he loved her with a real, though rather social, uneasy desirous love, as if he wanted all her answer. He was really a nice man, a bit frail and sad. Jack could see that. But he seemed to belong so entirely to the same world as the general, Jack's father.

He belonged to the social world, and saw nothing really outside.

Mary, too, belonged almost entirely to the social world, her instinct was strongly social. But there was a wild tang in her. And this Jack depended on. Somewhere deep in himself he hated his father's social world. He stood in the doorway and watched her dancing with Blessington. And he knew that as Mrs Blessington, with a thoughtful husband and a good position in society, she would be well off. She would forfeit that bit of a wild tang.

If Jack let her. And he wasn't going to let her. He was hard and cool inside himself. He took his impetus from the wild sap that still flows in most men's veins, though they mostly choose to act from the tame sap. He hated his father's social sap. He wanted the wild nature in people, the unfathomed nature, to break into leaf again. The real rebel, not the mere reactionary.

He hated the element of convention and slight smugness which showed in Mary's movements as she danced with the tall, thin reed of a man. Anything can become a convention, even an unconventiality, even the frenzied jazzing of the modern ballroom. And then the same element of smugness, very repulsive, is evident, evident even in the most scandalous jazzers. This is curious, that as soon as any movement becomes accepted in the public consciousness, it becomes ugly and smug, unless it be saved by a touch of the wild individuality.

And Mary dancing with Mr Blessington was almost smug. Only the downcast look on her face showed that she remembered Jack. Blessington himself danced like a man neatly and efficiently performing his duty.

The dance ended. Aunt Matilda was fluttering her fan at him like a ruffled cockatoo. There was a group : Mary, Blessington, Mr George, Mr James Watson, Aunt Matilda's brother-in-law, and Aunt Matilda. Mr Blessington, with the quiet assurance of his class, managed to eclipse Mr George and Jim Watson entirely, though Jim Watson was a rich man.

Jack went over and was introduced. Blessington and he bowed at one another. " Stay in your class, you monkey !" thought Jack, with some of the sensual arrogance he had brought with him from the North-west.

Mr Blessington introduced him to a thin, nervous girl, his daughter. She was evidently unhappy, and Jack was sorry for her. He took her out for refreshments, and was kind to her. She made dark-grey, startled round eyes at him, and looked at him as if he were an incalculable animal that might bite. And he, in manner, if not in actuality, laughed and caressed the frail young thing to cajole some life into her.

Mary danced with Tom, and then with somebody else. Jack lounged about, watching with a set face that still looked innocent and amiable, keeping a corner of his eye on Mary, but chatting with various people. He wouldn't make a fool of himself, trying to dance.

When Mary was free again—complaining of her foot—he said to her :

" Come outside a bit."

And obediently she came. They went and sat under the same magnolia tree.

" He's not a bad fellow, your Blessington," he said.

" He's not my Blessington," she replied. " Not yet, anyhow. And he never would be *really* my Blessington."

" You never know. I suppose he's quite rich."

" Don't be horrid to me."

" Why not—I wish I was rich. I'd do as I liked. But you'll never marry him."

" Why shan't I ? "

" You just won't."

" I shall if Aunt Matilda makes me. I'm absolutely dependent on her—and do you think I don't feel it ? I want to be free. I should be much freer if I married Mr Blessington. I'm tired of being as I am."

" What would you really like to do ? "

She was silent for a time. Then she answered :

" I should like to live on a farm."

" Marry Tom," he said maliciously.

" Why are you so horrid ? " she said, in hurt surprise.

He was silent for a time.

" Anyhow, you won't marry Boyd Blessington."

" Why are you so sure. Aunt Matilda is going to England in April. And I won't travel with her. Travel with *her* would be unspeakable. I want to stay in Australia."

" Marry Tom," he said again, in malice,

" Why," she asked in amazement, " do you say that to me ? "

But he didn't know himself.

" A farm "—he was beginning, when a figure sailed up in the moonlight. It was Aunt Matilda. The two young people rose to their feet. Jack was silent and rather angry. He wanted to curl his nose and say : "It isn't done, Marm !" But he said nothing. Aunt Matilda did the talking.

" I though it was *your* voices," she said coldly. " Why do you make yourself conspicuous, Mary ? Mr Blessington is looking for you in all the rooms."

Mary was led away. Jack followed. Aunt Matilda had no sooner seen Mary led out by Mr Blessington for the Lancers, than she came full sail upon Jack, as he stood lounging in the doorway.

" Come for a little walk on the terrace, dear boy," she said.

" Can't I have the pleasure of piloting you through this set of Lancers, Marm ? " he retorted.

She stood and smiled at him fixedly.

" I've heard of y'r dancing, dear boy," she said, " and your father was a beautiful dancer. This governor is very particular. He sent his A.D.C. to stop Jimmy Short reversing, right at the beginning of the evening." She eyed him with a shrewd eye.

" Surely worse form to hurt a gentleman's feelings, than to reverse, Marm ! " retorted Jack.

" It wasn't bad form, it was bad temper. The Governor can't reverse himself. Ha-ha-ha ! Neither can I go through a set of Lancers with you. So come and take me out a minute."

They went in silence down the terrace.

" Lovely evening ! Not at all too hot," he said.

She burst into a sputter of laughter.

" Lor ! m'dear. You are amusin' ! " she said. " But you won't get out of it like that, young man. What have y' t'say f' y'self, running off with Mary like that, *twice !* "

" You told me I could take her, Marm."

" I didn't ask you to keep her out and get her talked about, m'dear. I'm not a fool, my dear boy, and I'm not going to let her lose the chance of a life-time. You want her y'self for *one night !* " She slapped her fan crossly. " *You* leave well alone, we don't want *another* scandal in the family. Mr Blessington is a good man for Mary, a Godsend. For she's heavy, she's heavy for any man to take up with.'' Aunt Matilda said this almost spitefully. '' Mr Blessington's the very man for her, and a wonderful match. She's got her family. She's the granddaughter of Lord Haworth. And he has position. Besides, they're *suited* for one another. It's the very finger of Heaven. Don't you dare make another scandal in the family.''

She stopped under a lamp, and was leaning forward peering at him. Her large person exhaled a scent of artificial perfume. Jack hated perfume, especially in the open air. And her face, with its powder and wrinkles, in the mingled light of the lamp and the moon, made him think of a lizard.

'' D'you want Mary yourself? '' she snapped, like a great lizard. '' It's out of the question. You've got to make your way. She'd have to go on waiting for years. And you'd compromise her.''

'' God forbid ! '' said Jack ironically.

'' Then leave her alone,'' she said. '' If you compromise her, *I'll* do no more for her, mind that.''

'' Just exactly what do you mean, compromise her? '' he asked.

'' Get her talked about—as you're trying to do,'' she snapped.

He thought it over. He must, anyhow, appear to yield to circumstances.

'' All right,'' he said. '' I know what you mean.''

'' See you do,'' she retorted. '' Now take me back to the ballroom.''

They returned, in a silence that was safe, if not golden. He was inwardly more set than ever. His appearance, however, was calm and innocent. She was much more ruffled. She wondered if she had said too much or too little, if he were merely stupid, or really dangerous.

He politely steered a way back to the reception room, placed her in a chair and turned to disappear. One thing he could not stand, and that was her proximity.

But as she sat down, she clutched his sleeve, cackling her unendurable laugh.

'' Sit down then,'' she said. '' We're friends now, aren't

we ? " And she tapped his tanned cheek, that still had a
bit of the peach-look, with her feathery black fan.

" On the contrary, Marm," he said, bowing but not
taking a seat.

" Lor', but you are an amusin' boy, m'dear ! " she said,
and she let go his sleeve as she turned to survey the field.

In that instant he slipped away from her disagreeable
presence.

He slipped behind a stout judge from Melbourne, then
past a plumed woman, apparently of fashion, and was gone.

What he had to do was to reconnoitre his own position.
He wanted Monica first. That was his fixed determination.
But he was not going to let go of Mary either. Not in
spite of battalions of Aunt Matildas, or correct social
individuals. It was a battle.

But he had to gauge Mary's disposition. He saw how
much she was a social thing : how much, even, she was
Lord Haworth's grand-daughter. And how little she was
that other thing.

But it was a battle, a long, slow, subtle battle. And he
loved a fight, even a long, invisible one.

In the ball-room the A.D.C. pounced on him.

When he was free again, he looked round for Mary. It
was the sixteenth dance, and she was being well nursed.
When the dance was over, he went calmly and sat between
her and Aunt Matilda, on a red gilt sofa. Things were a
little stiff. Even Mary was stiff.

He looked at her programme. The next dance was a
polka, and she was not engaged.

" You are free for this dance ? " he said.

" Yes, because of my foot," she said firmly. He could
see she too was on Aunt Matilda's side, for the moment.

" I can dance a polka. Come and dance it with me," he
said.

" And my foot ? "

He didn't answer, merely looked her in the face. And
she rose.

They neither of them ever forgot that absurd, jogging
little dance.

" I must speak to you, Mary," he said.

" What about ? "

" Would you really like to live on a farm ? "

" I *think* I should."

The conversation was rather jerky and breathless.

" In two years I can have a farm," he said.

She was silent for some time. Then she looked into his eyes, with her queer, black, humble-seeming eyes. She was thinking of all the grandeur of being Mrs. Boyd Blessington. It attracted her a great deal. At the same time, something in her soul fell prostrate, when Jack looked straight into her. Something fell prostrate, and she couldn't help it. His eyes had a queer power in them.

" In two years I can have a farm—a good one," he said.

She only gazed into his eyes with her queer, black, fascinated gaze.

The dance was over. Aunt Matilda was tapping Jack's wrist with her fan and saying :

" Yes, Mr. Blessington, do be so good as to take Mary down to supper."

Supper was over. It was the twentieth dance. Jack had been introduced to a sporting girl in her late twenties. She treated him like a child, and talked quite amusingly. Tom called her a " barrack hack."

Mr. Blessington went by with Mary on his arm.

" Mary," said Jack, " do you know Miss Brackley."

Mary stopped and was smilingly introduced. Miss Brackley at once pounced amusingly upon Mr. Blessington.

" I want to speak to you," Jack said once more to Mary. " Behind the curtain of the third window."

He glanced at the red, ponderous plush curtain he meant. Mary looked frightened into his eyes, then glanced too. Mr Blessington, extricating himself, walked on with Mary.

Jack looked round for Tom. That young man was having a drink, at the supper extra. Jack left the Barrack Hack for a moment.

" Tom," he said. " Will you stand by me in anything I say or do ? "

" I will," said the glistening, scarlet-faced Tom, who was away on the gay high seas of exaltation.

" Get up a rubber of whist for Aunt Matilda. I know she'd like one. Will you ? "

" Before you c'n say Wiggins," replied Tom, laughing as he always did when the was tipsy.

" And I say, Tom, you care for Mary, don't you? Would you provide a home for her if she was wanting one? "

" I'd marry Mary if she'd 'ave me 'n I hadn't got a wife."

" Shut up! "

Tom broke into a laugh.

" Don't go back on me, Tom."

" Never, s'elp me bob."

" Get a move on then, and arrange that whist."

He sent him off with the Barrack Hack. And then he watched Mary. She still was walking with Mr. Blessington. They were not dancing. She knew Jack was watching her, and she was nervous. He watched her more closely.

And at the third window she fluttered, staggered a little, left go Mr. Blessington's arm, and turned round to gather up her skirt behind. She pretended she had torn a hem. She pretended she couldn't move without a pin. She asked to be steered into the alcove. She sent Mr. Blessington away into the ladies' dressing-room, for a pin.

And when he came back with it, she was gone.

Jack, outside in the night, was questioning her.

" Has Mr. Blessington proposed to you yet? "

" No."

" Don't let him. Would you really be happy on a farm? Even if it was rather hard work? "

He had to look down on her very steadfastly as he asked this. And she was slow in answering, and the tears came into her eyes before she murmured :

" Yes."

He was touched, and the same dominating dark desire came over him again. He held her fast in his arms, fast and silent. The desire was dark and powerful and permanent in him.

" Can you wait for me, even two years? " he asked.

" Yes," she murmured faintly.

His will was steady and black. He knew he could wait.

" In two years I shall have a farm for you to live on," he said. And he kissed her again, with the same dark, permanent passion.

Then he sent her off again.

He went and found Mr. George, in the card room. There was old Aunt Matilda, playing for her life, her diamonds twinkling but her fan laid aside.

" We're going to Wandoo to-morrow morning, sir," said Jack.

" That's right, lad," said Mr. George.

" I say, sir, won't you do Tom a kindness? " said Jack. " You're coming down yourself one day this week, aren't you? "

" Yes, I shall be down on Wednesday or Thursday."

" Bring Mary down with you. Make her Aunt Matilda let her come. Tom's awfully gone on her, and when he sees her with Boyd Blessington he straightway goes for a drink. I don't think she's suited for Mr. Blessington; do you, sir? He's nearly old enough to be her father. And Tom's the best fellow in the world, and Mary's the one he cares for. If nothing puts him out and sends him wrong, there's not a better fellow in the world."

Mr. George blew his nose, prrhed! and bahed! and was in a funk. He feared Aunt Matilda. He was very fond of Mary, might even have married her himself, but for the ridicule. He liked Tom Ellis. He didn't care for men like Blessington. And he was an emotional old Australian.

" That needs thinking about! That needs thought! " he said.

Not the next day, but the day following that, the boys drove away from Perth in a new sulky, with a horse bought from Jimmy Short. And Mr. George had promised to come on the coach the day after, with Mary.

CHAP : XIX.   THE WELCOME AT WANDOO

" Things change," said Jack, as he and Tom drove along in the sulky, " and they never go back to what they were before."

" Seems like they don't," said Tom uneasily.

" And men change," continued Jack. " I have changed, and I shall never go back to what I was before."

" Oh, dry up," said the nervous Tom. " You're just the blanky same."

Both boys felt a load on their spirits, now they were actually on the road home. They hated the load too.

" We're going to make some change at Wandoo," said Tom. " I wish I could leave Ma on the place. But Mr. George says she absolutely refuses to stay, and he says I've not got to try an' force her. He sortta winked at me, and told me I should want to be settlin' down myself. I wondered what 'n hell he meant. Y'aven't let on nothing about that Honeysuckle trip, have y'? I don't mean to insult you by askin', but it seemed kinder funny like."

" No," said Jack. " I've not breathed Honeysuckle to a soul, and never will. You get it off your mind—it's nothing."

" Well, then I dunno what he meant. I told him I hadn't made a bean anyhow. An' I asked him what 'n hell Ma was goin' ter live on. He seemed a bit down in the mouth about 'er himself, old George did. Fair gave me the bally hump. Wisht I was still up north; strike me lucky, I do.

" We've been gone over two years, yet I feel I've never been away, an' yet I feel the biggest stranger in th world, comin' back to what's supposed to be me own house. I hate havin' ter come, because o' the bloomin' circumstances. Why 'n hell couldn't Ma have had the place for while she lived, an' me be comin' back to her and the kids. Then I shouldn't feel sortta sick about it. But as it is—it fair gets me beat. Lennie'll resent me, an' Katie an' Monica'll hate havin' ter get inter a smaller house, an' the twins an' Harry an' the little ones don' matter so much, but I do worry over pore ol' Ma."

There he was with a blank face, driving the pony homewards. He hadn't worried over pore ol' Ma till this very minute, on the principle ' out of sight, out of mind.' Now he was all strung up.

" Y' know, Jack," he said, " I kinder don' want Wandoo. I kinder don' want to be like Dad, settlin' down with a heap o' responsibilities an' kids an' all that. I kinder don' want it."

" What do you want ? " said Jack.

" I'd rather knock about with you for me mate, Jack; I'd a sight rather do that."

" You can't knock about for ever," said Jack.

" I don' know whether you can or you can't. I only know I never knew my own mother. I only know *she* never lived at Wandoo. *She* never raised me there. I bet she lugged me through the bush. An' when all comes to all, I'd rather do the same. I don' want Dad's property. I don' want that Ellis property. Seems ter me bad luck. What d' yer think ? "

" I should think it depends on you," said Jack.

" I should think it does. Anyhow, shall you stop on with me, an' go shares in the blinkin' thing ? "

" I don't know," said Jack.

He was thinking that soon he would see Monica. He was wondering how she would be. He was wondering if she was ready for him, or if she would have a thousand obstacles around her. He was wondering if she would want him to plead and play the humble and say he wasn't good enough for her. Because he wouldn't do it. Not if he never saw her again. All that flummery of love he would not subscribe to. He would not say he adored her, because he didn't adore her. He was not the adoring sort. He would not make up to her, and play the humble to her, because it insulted his pride. He didn't feel like that, and he never would feel like that, not towards any woman on earth. Even Mary, once he had declared himself, would fetch up her social tricks and try to bring him to his knees. And he was not going down on his knees, not for half a second, not to any woman on earth, nor to any man either. Enough of this kneeling flummery.

He stood fast and erect on his two feet, that had travelled many wild miles. And fast and erect he would continue to stand. Almost he wished he could be clad in iron armour,

inaccessible. Because the thought of women bringing him
down and making him humble himself, before they would
give themselves to him, this turned his soul black.

Monica ! He didn't love her. He didn't feel the slightest
bit of sentimental weakening towards her. Rather when
he thought of her his muscles went stiffer and his soul
haughtier. It was not he who must bow the head. It was
she.

Because he wanted her. With a deep, arrowy desire, and
a long, lasting dark desire, he wanted her. He wanted to
take her apart from all the world, and put her under his
own roof.

But he didn't want to plead with her, or weep before her,
or adore her, or humbly kiss her feet. The very thought of
it made his blood curdle and go black. Something had
happened to him in the Never-Never. Before he went over
the border, he might have been tricked into a surrender to
this soft and hideous thing they called love. But now, he
would have love in his own way, haughtily, passionately,
and darkly, with dark, arrowy desire, and a strange,
arrowily-submissive woman : either this, or he would not
have love at all.

He thought of Monica, and sometimes the thought of her
sent him black with anger. And sometimes, as he thought
of her wild, delicate, reckless, lonely little profile, a hot
tenderness swept over him, and he felt he would envelop
her with a fierce and sheltering tenderness, like a scarlet
mantle.

So long as she would not fight against him, and strike
back at him. Jeer at him, play with Easu in order to
insult him. Not that, my God, not that.

As for Mary, a certain hate of her burned in him. The
queer heavy stupid conceit with which she had gone off to
dance with Boyd Blessington, because he was an important
social figure. Mary, wanting to live on a farm, but at the
same time absolutely falling before the social glamour of a
Blessington, and becoming conceited on the strength of it.
Inside herself, Mary thought she was very important,
thought that all sorts of eternal destinies depended on *her*
choice and *her* actions. Even Jack was nothing more than
an instrument of her divine importance.

He had sensed this clearly enough. And it was this that

made Aunt Matilda a bit spiteful against her, when she said Mary was " heavy " and wouldn't easily get a man.

But there was also the queer black look in Mary's eyes, that was outside her conceit and her social importance. The queer, almost animal dark glisten, that was full of fear and wonder, and vulnerability. Like the look in the eyes of a caught wild animal. Or the look in the shining black eyes of one of the aborigines, especially the black woman looking askance in a sort of terror at a white man, as if a white man was a sort of devil that might possess her.

Where had Mary got that queer aboriginal look, she the grand-daughter of an English earl?

" Y're real lively to-day, aintcher, Jack? Got a hundred quid for your birthday, and my, some talk !"

" Comes to that," said Jack, rousing himself with difficulty, " we've come fifteen or twenty miles without you opening your mouth either."

Tom laughed shortly and relapsed into silence.

" Well," he said, " let's wake up now, there's the out-lying paddock." He pointed with his whip. " And there's the house through the dip in the valley." Then suddenly in a queer tone : " Say, matey, don't it look lovely from here, with all that afternoon sun falling over it like snow . . . You think I've never seen snow : but I have, in my dream."

Jack's heart contracted as he jumped down to open the first gate. For him, too, the strange fulness of the yellow afternoon light was always unearthly, at Wandoo. But the day was still early, just after dinner-time, for they had stayed the night half way.

" Looks in good trim, eh ? " said Jack.

" So it does ! A.1. ! " replied Tom. " Mr George says Ma done wonders. Made it pay hand over fist. Y'remember that fellow, Pink-eye Percy, what came from Queensland and had studied agriculture an' was supposed to be a bad egg an' all that ? At that 'roo hunt, you remember ? Well, he bought land next to Wandoo, off-side from the Reds. An' Ma sortta broke wi' the Reds over something, an' went in wi' him, and t' seems they was able to do wonders. Anyway, Old George says Ma's been able to buy a little place near her own old home in Beverley, to go to. But seems to me—— "

" What ? "

" Funny how little anyone *tells* you, Jack."

" How ? "

" I felt I couldn't get to th' bottom of what Old George was tellin' me. I took no notice then. But it seems funny now. An' I say—— "

" What ? "

" You'd 'a thought Monica or Katie might ha' driven to the Cross Roads for us, like we used to in Dad's days."

" Yes. I thought one of them would have been there."

The boys drove on, in tense silence, through the various gates. They could see the house ahead.

" There's Timothy," said Tom.

The old black was holding open the yard gate. He seemed to have almost forgotten Jack, but the emotion in his black, glistening eyes was strange, as he stared with strange adoration at the young master. He caught Tom's hand in his two wrinkled dark hands, as if clinging to life itself.

The twins ran out, waved, and ran back. Katie appeared, looking bigger, heavier, more awkward than ever. Tom patted Timothy's hands again, then went across and kissed Katie, who blushed with shyness.

" Where's Ma, Katie ? "

" In the parlour."

Tom broke away, leaving Katie blushing in front of Jack. Jack was thinking how queer and empty the house seemed. And he felt an outsider again. He stayed outside, sat down on the bench.

A boy much bigger than Harry, but with the same blue eyes and curly hair, appeared chewing a haystalk, and squatted on a stone near by. Then Og and Magog, a bit taller, but no thinner, came and edged on to the seat. Then Ellie, a long-legged little girl, came running to his knees. And then what had been baby, but was now a fat, toddling little girl, came racing out, fearless and inconsequential as the twins had been.

" Where's Len ? " said Jack.

" He's in the paddock seein' to th' sheep," said Harry.

There was a queer tense silence. The children seemed to cling round Jack for male protection.

" We're goin' t' live nearer in to th' township now," said Harry, " in a little wee sortta house."

He stared with bold, blue eyes, unwinking and yet not easy, straight into Jack's eyes.

" Well, Harry," said Jack, " you've grown quite a man."

" I hev so ! " said Harry, " quite the tyke ! I ken kill birds for Ma to put in th' pot. I ken skin a kangaroo. I ken—— "

But Jack didn't hear what else, because Tom was calling him from the doorway. He went slowly across.

" Say, mate," said Tom in a low tone, " stand by me. Things is not all right." Aloud he said : " Ma wants t' see ye, Jack."

Jack followed through the back premises, down the three steps into the parlour. It all seemed forlorn.

Ma sat with her face buried in her hands. Jack knitted his brows. Tom put his hand on her shoulder.

" What is it, Ma ? What is it ? I wouldn't be anything but good to yer, Ma, ye know that. Here's Jack Grant."

" Ye were always a good boy, Tom. I'm real glad t' see ye back. And Jack," said Ma, through her hands.

Tom looked at Jack in dismay. Then he stooped and kissed her hair.

" You look to me," he said. " We'll fix everything all right, for Lennie, 'n everybody."

But Ma still kept her face between her hands.

" There's nothing t' worry about, Ma, sure there isn't," persisted the distracted Tom. " I want y' t' have everything you want, I do, you an' Lennie an' the kids."

Mrs Ellis took her hands from her face. She looked pale and worn. She would not turn to the boys, but kept her face averted.

" I know you're as good a boy as ever lived," she faltered. Then she glanced quickly at Tom and Jack, the tears began to run down her face, and she threw her apron over her head.

" God's love ! " gasped the bursting Tom, sinking on a chair.

They all waited in silence. Mrs Ellis suddenly wiped her face on her apron and turned with a wan smile to the boys.

" I've saved enough to buy a little place near Beverley, which is where I belong," she said. " So me and the children are all right. And I've got my eye, at least Lennie's got *his* on a good selection east of here, between this and

my little house, for Lennie. But we want cash for that,
I'm afraid. Only it's not that. That's not it."

" Lennie's young yet to take up land, Ma ! " Tom
plunged in. " Why won't he stop here and go shares with
me ? "

" He wants to get married," said the mother wanly.

" Get married ! Len ! Why, he's only seventeen ! "

At this very natural exclamation, Ma threw her apron
over her head, and began to cry once more.

" He's been so good," she sobbed. " He's been so good !
And his Ruth is old enough and sensible enough for two.
Better anything "—with more sobbing—" than another
scandal in the family."

Tom rubbed his head. Gosh ! it was no joke being the
head of a family !

" Well, Ma, if you wish it, what's the odds. But I'm
afraid it'll have to wait a bit. Jack'll tell you I haven't
any cash. Not a stiver, Ma ! Blown out ! It takes it
outter yer up North. We never struck it rich."

Mrs Ellis, under her apron, wept softly.

" Poor little Lennie ! Poor little Lennie ! He's been so
good, Tom, working day and night. And never spending a
shilling. All his learning gone for nought, Tom, and him
a little slave, at his years, old and wise enough to be his
father, Tom. And he wants to get married. If we could
start him out fair ! The new place has only four rooms
and an out-kitchen, and there's not enough to keep him,
much less a lady wife. She's a lady earning her bread
teaching. He could go to Grace's. Alec Rice would have
him. But—— "

She had taken her apron off her face, and was staring
averted at the door leading into Gran's old room.

The two boys listened mystified and a little annoyed.
Why all this about Lennie ? Jack was wondering where
Monica was. Why didn't she come ? Why wasn't she
mentioned ? And why was Ma so absolutely downcast, on
the afternoon of Tom's home-coming ? It wasn't fair on
Tom.

" Where is Monica ? " asked Jack shyly at last.

But Mrs Ellis only shook her head faintly and was mute,
staring across at Gran's door.

" Lennie married ! " Tom was brooding. " Ye'll have

to put it out of y'r mind for a bit, Ma. Why, it wouldn't hardly be decent."

" Let him marry if he's set on it—an' the girl's a good girl," said Mrs Ellis, her eyes swamping with tears again and her voice breaking as she rocked herself again.

" Yes, if we could afford it," Tom hastily put in. And he raised his stunned eyes to Jack. Jack shrugged, and looked in the empty fireplace, and thought of the little fires Gran used to have.

Money ! Money ! Money ! The moment you entered within four walls it was the word money, and your mouth full of ashes.

And then again something hardened in his soul. All his life he had been slipping away from the bugbear of money. It was no good. You had to turn round and get a grip on the miserable stuff. There was nothing else for it. Though money nauseated him, he now accepted the fact that he must have control over money, and not try just to slip by.

He began to repent of having judged Gran. That little old witch of a Gran, he had hated the way she had seemed to hoard money and gloat in the secret possession of it. But perhaps she knew, *somebody* must control it, somebody must keep a hand over it. Like a deadly weapon. Money ! Property ! Gran fighting for them, to bequeath them to the man she loved.

Perhaps she too had really hated money. She wouldn't make a will. Neither would Dad. Their secret repugnance for money and possessions. But you *had* to have property, else you were down and out. The men you loved had to have property, or they were down and out. Like Lennie !

Poor old plucky Gran, fighting for her men. It was all a terrible muddle anyhow. But he began to understand her motive.

Yes, if Lennie had got a girl into trouble and wanted to marry her, the best thing he could do would be to have money and buy himself a little place. Otherwise, heaven knows what would happen to him. With their profound indifference to the old values, these Australians seemed either to exaggerate the brutal importance of money, or they wanted to waste money altogether, and themselves along with it. This was what Gran feared : that her best male heirs would go and waste themselves, as Jacob had begun to waste himself. The generous ones would just waste themselves, because of their profound mistrust of the old values.

Better rescue Lennie for the little while it was still possible to rescue him. Jack's mind turned to his own money. And, then, looking at that inner door, he seemed to see Gran's vehement figure, pointing almost viciously with her black stick. She had tried so hard to drive the wedge of her meaning into Jack's consciousness. And she had failed. He had refused to take her meaning.

But now with a sigh that was almost a groan, he took up the money burden. The " stocking " she had talked about, and which he had left in the realms of unreality, was an actuality. That witch Gran, with her uncanny, hateful second sight, had put by a stocking for Lennie, and entrusted the secret of it to Jack. And he had refused the secret. He hated those affairs.

Now he must assume the mysterious responsibility for this money. He got up and went to the chimney, and peered into the black opening. Then he began to feel carefully along the side of the chimney stack inside, where there was a ledge. His hand went deep in soot and charcoal and grey ash.

He took off his coat and rolled up his sleeve.

" Gone off y'r bloomin' nut, Jack? " asked Tom, mystified.

" Gran told me she had put a stocking for Len in here," said Jack.

" Stocking be blowed ! " said Tom testily.   " We've heard that barm-stick yarn before. Leave it alone, boy."

He was looking at Jack's bare, brown, sinewy arm. It reminded him of the great North-West, and the heat, and the work, and the absolute carelessness. This money and stocking business was like a mill-stone round his neck. He felt he was gradually being drowned in soot, as Jack continued to fumble up inside the chimney, and the soot poured down over the naked arm.

" Oh, God's love, leave it alone, Jack ! " he cried.

" Let him try," said Mrs Ellis quietly.   " If Gran told him, I wonder he didn't speak before."

" I never really thought about it," said Jack.

" Don't think about it now ! " shouted Tom.

Jack could feel nothing in the chimney. He looked contemplatively at the fireplace. Something drew him to the place near Gran's arm-chair. He began feeling, while the other two watched him in a state of nervous tension. Tom hated it.

" She pointed here with her stick," said Jack.

There was a piece of tin fastened over the side of the fire-place, and black-leaded.

" Mind if we try behind this? " he asked.

" Leave it alone! " cried Tom.

But Jack pulled it out, and the ash and dirt and soot poured down over the hearth. Behind the sheet of thin iron was the naked stone of the chimney-piece. Various stones were loose : that was why Gran had had the tin sheet put over.

He got out of the cavity behind the stones, where the loose mortar had all crumbled, a little square dusty box that had apparently been an old tea-caddy. It was very heavy for its size, and very dirty. He put it on the table in front of Mrs Ellis. Tom got up excitedly to look in. He opened the lid. It was full to the brim of coins, gold coins and silver coins and dust and dirt, and a sort of spider filament. He shook his head over it.

" Isn't that old Gran to a T! " he exclaimed, and poured out the dust and the money on the table.

Ma began eagerly to pick out the gold from the silver, saying :

" I remember when she made Dad put that iron plate up. She said insects came out and worried her."

Ma only picked out the gold pieces, the sovereigns and half sovereigns. She left Tom to sort the silver crowns and half-crowns into little piles. Jack watched in silence. There was a smell of soot and old fire-dust, and everybody's hands were black.

Mrs Ellis was putting the sovereigns in piles of ten. She had a queer sort of satisfaction, but her gloom did not really lift. Jack stayed to know how much it was. Mentally he counted the piles of gold she made : the pale, washy gold of Australia, most of it. She counted and counted again.

" Two hundred and fourteen pounds! " she said in a low voice.

" And ten in silver," said Tom.

" Two hundred and twenty-four pounds," she said.

" It's not the world," said Tom, " but it's worth having. It's a start, Ma. And you can't say *that* isn't Lennie's."

Jack went out and left them. He listened in all the rooms downstairs. What he wanted to know about was Monica. He hated this family and family money business, it smelled to him of death. Where was Monica? Probably, to add to the disappointment, she was away, staying with Grace.

The house sounded silent. Upstairs all was silent. It *felt* as if nobody was there.

He went out and across the yard to the stable. Lucy whinnied. Jack felt she knew him. The nice, natural old thing : Tom would have to christen her afresh. At least *this* Lucy wouldn't leave a stocking behind her when she was dead. She was much too clean. Ah, so much nicer than that other Lucy with her unpleasant perspiration, away in Honeysuckle.

Jack stood a long while with the sensitive old horse. Then he went round the out-buildings, looking for Lennie. He drifted back to the house, where Harry was chopping something with a small hatchet.

" Where's Monica, Harry? " he asked.

" She's not home," said Harry.

" Where's she gone? "

" Dunno."

And the resolute boy went on with his chopping.

Tom came out, calling : " I'm going over to have a word wi' th' Reds, Jack. Comin' with me? "

Tom didn't care for going anywhere alone, just now. Jack joined him.

" Where's Monica, Tom? " he asked.

" Ay, where is she? " said Tom, looking round as if he expected her to appear from the thin air.

" She's not at home, anyhow," said Jack.

" She's gone off to Grace's, or to see somebody, I expect," said Tom, as they walked across the yard. " And Len is out in the paddocks still. He don't seem in no hurry to come an' meet us, neither. The little cuss ! Fancy that nipper wantin' to be spliced ! Gosh ! I'll bet he's old for his age, the little old wallaby. An' that bloomin' teacher woman, Ruth, why, she's older'n me. She oughtta be ashamed of herself, kidnappin' that nipper."

The two went side by side across the pasture, almost as if they were free again. They came to a stile.

" Gosh ! " said Tom. " They've blocked up this gate, 'n put a stile over, see ! Think o' that ! "

They climbed the stile and continued their way.

" God's love, boy, didn't we land in it over our heads ! Ever see Ma like that ? I never. Good for you, Jack, lad, findin' that tea-caddy. That's how the Ellises are—ain't it the devil ! 'Spect I take after my own mother, f'r I'm not in the tea-caddyin' line. Ma's cheered up a bit. She'll be able to start Lennie in a bit of a way now, 'n the twins can wait for a bit, thank goodness ! My, but ain't families lively ! Here I come back to be boss of this bloomin' place, an' I feel as if I was goin' to be shot. Say, boy, d'ye think I'm really spliced to that water-snake in Honeysuckle ? Because I s'll have to have somebody on this outfit. Alone I will not face it. Say, matey, promise me you won't leave me till I'm fixed up a bit. Give me your word you'll stand by me here for a time, anyhow."

" I'll stay for a time," said Jack.

" Right O ! an' then if I'm not copped by the Honey- suckle bird—'appen Mary might have me, what d'you think ? I shall have to have somebody. I simply couldn't stand this place all by my lonesome. What d'you think about Mary ? D'you think she'd like it, here ? "

" Ask her," said Jack grimly.

CHAP : XX.   THE LAST OF EASU

i

THEY knew that Easu was married, but they were hardly prepared for the dirty baby crawling on the verandah floor. Easu had seen them come through the gate, and was striding across to meet them, after bawling something in his bullying way to someone inside the house : presumably his wife.

Outwardly, he was not much altered. Yet there was an undefinable change for the worse. He was one of those men whom marriage seems to humiliate, and to make ugly. As if he despised himself for being married.

Easu ignored the baby as if it were not there, striding past into the house, leading the newcomers into the parlour. It was darkened in there, to keep out the flies; but he pulled up the blind : " t'see their blanky fisogs." And he called out to the missus to bring glasses.

The parlour was like most parlours. Enlarged photographs of Mr. and Mrs. Ellis, the Red parents, in large pine frames, on the wall. A handsome china clock under a glass case on the mantelpiece, with flanking vases to match, on fawn-and-red woollen crochet mats. An oval, rather curvy table in the middle of the room, with the family Bible, and the meat under a fly-proof wire cover. The parlour was the coolest place for the meat.

Easu shifted the red obnoxity, wire cover and all, to the top of a cupboard where some cups and saucers were displayed, and drew forth a demijohn of spirit from the back of the horsehair sofa, in front of the window.

Mrs. Easu came in with the glasses. She was a thin, pale-faced young woman with big dark eyes and her hair in huge curling pins, and a hostile bearing. She took no notice of the visitors : only let her big what-do-*you*-want eyes pass over them with distaste beneath her bald forehead. It was her fixed belief that whoever came to the house came to *get* something, if they could. And they were not going to get it out of *her*. She made an alliance with Easu so far.

But her rather protruding teeth and her vindictive mouth showed that Easu would get as many bites as kisses.

She set the glasses from her hands on to the table and looked down at Easu under her pale lashes.

" What else d'ye want ? " she asked rudely.

" Nothing. If I want anything I'll holloa."

They seemed to be on terms of mutual rudeness. She had been quite an heiress : brought Easu a thousand pounds. But the way she said it—a tharsand parnds—as if it was something absolutely you couldn't get beyond, made even Easu writhe. She was common, to put it commonly. She spoke in a common way, she thought in a common way, and acted in a common way. But she had energy, and even a vulgar *suffisance*. She thought herself as good as anybody, and a bit better, on the strength of the tharsand parnds !

" 'S not eddication as matters, it's munney ! " she said blatantly to Lennie. " At your age y'ought t'ave somethink in th' bank."

He of course hated the sight of her after that. She had looked at him with a certain superciliousness and contempt in her conceited brown eyes, because he had no money and was supposed to be clever. He never forgave her.

But what did she care ? She jerked up her sharp-toothed mouth, and sailed away. She wasn't going to be put down by any penniless snobs. The Ellises ! Who were the Ellises ? Yes, indeed ! They thought themselves so superior. Could *they* draw a tharsand parnd ? Pah !

She felt a particularly spiteful, almost vindictive scorn of Jack. He was somebody, was he ? Ha ! What was he *worth?* That was the point. How much *munney* did he reckon he'd got ? " If yer want me ter think anythink of yer, yer mun show me yer bank-book," she said.

Easu listened and grinned, and said nothing to all this. But she had a fiery temper of her own, and they went for one another like two devils. She wasn't to be daunted, she wasn't. She had her virtues too. She had no method, but she was clean. The place was forever in a muddle, but she was always cleaning it, almost vindictively, as if the shine on the door-knob reflected some of the tharsand parnd. Even the baby was turned out and viciously cleaned once a day. But in the intervals it groped where it would. As for herself, she was a sight this morning, with her hair in huge iron waving-pins, and her forehead and her teeth both sticking out. She looked a sight to shudder at. But wait. Wait till she was dressed up and turning out in the buggy, in a coat and skirt of thick brown cord silk with orange and black braiding, and a hugely feathered hat, with huge floating ostrich feathers, an orange one and a brown one. And her teeth sticking out and a huge brooch of a lump of gold set with pearls and diamonds, and a great gold chain. And the baby, in a silk cape with pink ribbons, and a frilled silk bonnet of alternate pink and white ruches, mercilessly held against her chains and brooches ! Wait !

Therefore, when Jack glanced at her from a strange distance, she tossed her bald forehead with the curling irons, and thought to herself : " You can look, Master Jack Nobody. And you can look again, next Sunday, when I've got my proper things on. *Then* you'll see who's got the munney ! "

She seemed to think that her Sunday gorgeousness absolutely obliterated the grimness of her week of curling pins. " Six days shalt thou labour in thy curling irons." She lived in them. They kept her hair out of the way and saved her having to do it up all the time.

And it may be that Easu never really looked at her in her teeth and pins. That was not the real Sarah Ann. The real Sarah Ann swayed with ostrich feathers; brown silk, brown and orange feathers, reddish hair, brown eyes, pale skin, and a stiff, militant, vulgar bearing that wasn't going to let *anybody* put it over *her*. " They can't put *me* down, whoever they are ! " she asserted. " I consider myself equal to the best, and perhaps a little better."

This Easu heard and saw with curious gratification. This was his Sarah Ann.

None the less, he was no fool. He saw the baffled, surprised look Jack turned upon this grisly young woman in curlers and teeth, as if he could not quite enter her in the class of human beings. And Easu was enough of an Ellis to know what that look meant. It was a silent " Good God ! " And no man, when his wife enters the room, cares to hear another man's horrified ejaculation : " Good God ! " at the sight of her.

Easu wanted his wife to be common. Nevertheless, with

the anomalousness of human beings, it humiliated him and
put acid in his blood.

" Have a jorum ! " said Easu to Tom.

" I s'd think you're not goin' to set down drinkin' at
this time of day," she said, in her loud, common, interfering voice.

" What's the time of the day to you? " asked Easu
acidly, as he filled Tom's glass.

" We can't stop. Ma'll be expecting us back," said Tom.

Easu silently filled Jack's glass, and the wife went out,
banging the door. Immediately she fell upon the baby and
began to vituperate the little animal for its dirt. The men
couldn't hear themselves speak.

But Easu lifted up his chin and poured the liquor down
his throat. He had shaved his beard, and had only three
days of yellowish stubble. He smacked his lips as he set
down his glass, and looked at the two boys with a sarcastic,
gloating look.

" Find a few changes, eh? " he observed.

" Just a few."

" How's the place look? "

" All right."

" Make a pile up North? "

" No."

Easu grinned slowly.

" Thought you didn't need to, eh?" he asked maliciously.

" Didn't worry myself," said Tom.

" Jack Grant come in for a fortune? " Easu asked,
looking at Jack.

" No," said Jack coldly. There was something about
Easu's vulgar, taunting eyes, which he couldn't stand.

" Oh, you 'aven't ! " The pleased sneer was unbearable.

" How's Ma ? " asked Easu.

" All right," said Tom, surprised.

" Don't see much of her now," said Easu.

" No, I saw the gate was blocked up," said Tom.

" Looks like she blocked the wrong gate up."

" How ? "

" How ? Well, don't you think she'd better have blocked
up the gate over to Pink-eye Percy's place? " Easu was
smiling with thin, gloating lips.

" Why? "

" Why ?   Don't y' know ? "

" What ? "

" Don't ye know about Monica ? "

Jack's blood stood still for a moment, and death entered his soul again, to stay.

" No.   What ? "

" Didn't Old George say nothing to y' in Perth ? "

" No ! " said Tom, becoming sullen and dangerous.

" Well, that's funny now !   And Aunt Alice said nothing ? "

" No !   What about ? "

Easu was smiling gloatingly, in silence, as if he had something very good.

" Well, that's funny now !   Think of your getting right here, and not having heard a thing !   I shouldn't have thought it possible."

Tom was going white under his tan.

" What's amiss, Red ? " he said curtly.

" To think as you haven't heard !   Why it was the talk of the place.   Ross heard all about it in Perth.   Didn't you come across him there ?   He's been in the Force quite a while now."

" No !   What was it he heard about ? "

" Why, about Monica."

" What about her ? "

" D'y' mean to say you don't know ? "

" I tell you I don't know."

" Well ! " and Easu smiled with a curious, poisonous satisfaction.   " I don't know as I want to be the one to tell you."

There was a moment's dead silence.   The sun was setting.

" What have you got to say ? " asked Tom, his face set and blank, and his mouth taking on the lipless, Australian look.

" Funny thing nobody has told you.   Why, it happened six or seven months since."

This was received in dead silence.

" She went off with Percy when the baby was a month old."

Again there was nothing but dead silence.

" Mean she married Pink-eye Percy ? " asked Tom, in a muffled tone.

" I dunno about marryin' him. They say he's got a wife or two already : legal and otherwise. All I know is they cleared out a month after the baby was born, and went down south."

Still dead silence from the other two. The room was full of golden light. Jack was looking at the fly-dirts and the lamp-black on the ceiling. He was sitting in a horse-hair arm-chair, and the broken springs were uncomfortable, and the horse-hair scratched his wrist. Otherwise he felt vacant, and, in a deathly way, remote.

" You're minding what you're saying? " came Tom's empty voice.

" Minding what I'm saying! " echoed Easu cunningly. " *I* didn't want to tell you. It was you who asked me."

" Was the baby Percy's baby? " asked Jack.

" I should say so," Easu replied, stumbling. " I never asked her, myself. They were all thick with Percy at that time, and I was married with a family of my own. Why, I've not been over to Wandoo for—for—for close on two years, I should think."

" That's what was wrong with Ma! " Tom was saying, in a dull voice, to himself.

" I wonder Old George or Mary didn't prepare ye," said Easu. " They both came down before the baby came. But seemingly Old George couldn't do nothing, Percy confessing he was married, and trying to say he wasn't to blame. However, he's run off with Monica all right. Ma had a letter from her from Albany, to say there was no need to worry, Percy was playin' the gentleman."

" She never cared for him," Jack cried.

" I dunno about that. Seems she's been mad about him all the time. Maybe she waited for you to come back. I dunno! I tell you, I've never been over to Wandoo for nigh on two years."

Jack could not bear any more. The golden light had gone out of the room, the sun was under that ridge— that ridge—

" Let's get, Tom! " said Jack rising to his feet.

They stumbled out of the house, and went home in silence, through the dusk. Again the world had caved in, and they were walking through the ruins.

Ma was upstairs when they got home, but Katie had

got the tea on the table, and Lennie was in. He was a tall, thin, silent, sensitive youth.

" Hello, you two wanderin' Jews ! " he said.

" Hello, Len ! "

" Come an' 'ave y' teas."

Lennie was like the head of the house. They ate their meal in silence.

ii

Tom and Jack and Lennie still slept in the cubby, but Og and Magog had moved indoors. The three of them lay in the dark, without sleeping.

" Say, young Len," said Tom at length, " What was you after, letting Monica get mixed up with that Pink-eyed Percy ? "

" Me ? What was I after ? How could I be after 'er every minute. She snapped my 'ead off if I looked at 'er. What for did you an' Jack stop away all that time, an' never write a word to nobody ? Blame me, all right ! But you go 'avin' 'igh jinks in the Never-Never, and nobody says a word to you. *You* never did nothing wrong, did you ? An' *you* kep' an eye on the fam'ly, didn't you ? An' it's only me to blame. 'F course ! 'Twould be ! But what about yourselves ? "

This outburst was received in silence. Then a queer, sullen snake reared its head haughtily in Jack's soul.

" I shouldn't have thought she'd have cared for Percy," said he.

" No more would nobody," replied Len. " You never know what women's up to. Give me a steady woman, Lord, I pray. Because for the last year Monica wasn't right in 'er mind, that's what I say. It wasn't Percy's fault. It was she made 'im. She made 'im as soft as grease about 'er. Percy's not bad, he's not. But women can make him as soft as grease. An' I knows what that means myself. Either there shouldn't be no men an' women, or they should be kept apart till they're pitched into the same pen, to breed."

Tom, with Honeysuckle Lucy on his conscience, said never a word.

" Is it true that Percy's got a wife already out east ? " asked Jack.

" He says he has. But he wrote to find out if she was
dead. At first he said he wasn't to blame. Then he said
he was but he couldn't marry her. An' Monica like a wild
cat at us all. She would let nobody write an' tell you. She
went over to Reds, but Easu had just got married, an'
Sarah Ann threatened to lay her out. Then she turned on
Percy. I tell you, she skeered me. The phosphorus came
out of her eyes like a wild cat's. She's bewitched or something. Or else possessed of a devil. That's what I think
she is. Though I needn't talk, for maybe I am myself.
Oh, mates, leave me alone, I'm sick of it all. Lemme go
to sleep."

" What did she go over to Easu's for ? "

" God knows. She'd been nosing round with Easu, till
Ma got mad and put a stop to it. But that's a good while
since. A good while afore Easu married the lovely Sarah
Ann, with her rows o' cartridges on her forehead. Oh,
Cripes, *marriage !* Leave m'alone, I tell you."

" Funny she should go to Easu's, if she was struck on
Percy," said Jack.

" Don't make me think of it, sonny ! " came Len's voice.
" She went round like a cat who's goin' t' have kittens,
an' nobody knew what was amiss with her. Oh, Jehosaphat !
Talk about bein' born in sin. I should think we are. But
say, Jack ! Do you suppose the Lord gets awful upset,
whether Monica has a baby or not? I don't believe He
does. An' I don't believe Jesus either turns a hair. I
don't believe he turns half a hair. Yet we get into all this
stew. Tell you what, makes a chap sick of bein' a humin
bein'. Wish I grew feathers, an' was an emu."

" Don't you bother," said Jack.

" Not me," said Len. " I don't bother ! Anyhow, I
know all about the parsley bed, 'n I don't care, I'd rather
know an' have done with it. 'S got to come some time.
I'm a collar horse, I am, like ol' Rackett said. All right,
let me_be one. Let me be one, an' pull me guts out.
Might just as well do that, as be a sick outlaw like Rackett,
or a softy like Percy. Leave m'alone ! I've got the collar
on, an' the load behind, an' I'll pull it out if I pulls me
guts out. That's the past, present an' future of Lennie."

" Where is Rackett ? "

" Hanged if I know. Don't matter where he is. He

wanted to educate me an' make a gentleman of me. Else I'd be nothing but a cart-'oss, he said. Well, I am nothing but a cart-'oss. But if I enjoys pullin' me guts out, let me. I enjoys it all right."

Tom lay in silence in the dark, and felt scared. He hated having to face things. He hated taking a long view. Sufficient unto the day is the evil thereof, was his profound conviction. He hated even to look round the next corner.

" Say, Jack," came Lennie's voice again. " You always turns up like a silver lining. I got your cheques all right. Fifty-seven pound. That's only a pair o' socks, that is, compared to Gran's store. I had to have a laugh over that stockin', you're the angel that stood in Jacob's doorway an' looked like a man, you are. I'd love it if you'd come an' live with me an' Ruthie."

But Jack was thinking his own thoughts. It had come over him that it was Easu who had betrayed Monica. The picture of her wandering across like a cat that is going to have kittens, to the Red's place, and facing that fearful, common Sarah Ann, and Easu grinning and looking on, made his spirit turn to steel. Pink-eye Percy was not the father of that baby. Percy was as soft as wax. Monica would never have fallen for him. She had simply made use of him. The baby was Easu's.

" Was the baby a girl or a boy ? " he asked.

" A girl."

" Did it look like Percy ? "

" Not it. It didn't have any of Percy's goo-goo brown eyes or anything. Ma said it was the spitten image of Harry when he was born."

iii

Jack decided what he would do. In the morning he would take the new horse and set off south, to Albany. He would see Monica and ask her. Anyhow, he would see her.

He was up at dawn, saddling his horse. He told Tom of his plan, and Tom merely remarked :

" It's up to you, mate."

Tom was relapsing at once into the stiff-faced, rather

taciturn Australian he had been before. The settled life
on the farm at once pulled him to earth, the various
calamities had brought him down with a bump.

So Jack rode off almost unnoticed, with a blanket
strapped behind his saddle, and a flat water-bottle, a pistol
in his belt, and a hatchet and a little bag of food tied to
the front saddle strings. Something made him turn his
horse past the place where he had fought Easu, and along
the bush trail to the Reds' place.

The sun had come up hot out of a pink, dusty dawn. In
an hour it would be blazing like a fiend out of the bare blue
heavens. Meanwhile it was still cool, there was still a faint
coolness on the parched dry earth, whose very grass was
turning into yellowish dust. Jack jogged along slowly, at
a slow morning jog-trot. He was glad to be in the saddle
again.

As he came down the track, he saw the blue smoke rising
out of the chimneys of Easu's house, and a dark movement
away in one of the home paddocks. He got down for the
gates, then rode on, over to the paddock fence, and sat
there on his horse, watching Easu and Herbert and three
blacks, sorting out some steers from a bunch of about thirty
cattle. They were running the steers through a gate to a
smaller enclosure.

There was a good deal of yelling and shouting and running and confusion, as the bunch of young cattle, a mixed
little mob of all colours, blacks and black-and-white and
red and red-and-white, tossed and swayed, the young cows
breaking away and running nimbly on light feet, excited by
the deep, powerful lowing of the stock bull, which had
wandered up to the outer corner of the fence under a group
of ragged gum-trees, and there stood bellowing at the excitement that was going on in the next paddock.

Jack kept an eye on the bull, as he sat on his uneasy
horse outside the shut gate, watching. Near by, two more
horses stood saddled and waiting. One of them was Easu's
big black mare with the two white forefeet. The other was
a thin roan, probably Herbert's horse.

Herbert was quite a man now : tall and thin and broad,
with a rather small red face and dull fairish hair that stood
up straight from his brow. He was the only one of the
brothers left with Easu. He was patient and didn't pay any

attention to that scorpion of a Sarah Ann. Sam and Ross had cleared out at the first sight of her.

It was Herbert who did most of the running. Easu, who stood with his feet apart, did most of the bossing—he was never happy unless he was bossing, and finding fault with somebody—and the blacks did most of the holloaing. Easu didn't move much. He seemed to have gone heavier, and where he stood, with his feet apart and his bare arm waving, he seemed stuck, as if he were inert. This was unlike him. He was always stiffish, but he used to be quick. Now he seemed slow and wooden in his movements, his body had gone inert, the life had gone out of it, and he could only shout and jeer. He used to have a certain flame of life, that made him handsome, even if you hated him. A certain conceit and daring, inside all his bullying. Now the flame had gone, the conceit and daring had sunk, he was only ugly and defeated, common, and a little humiliated. He was getting fat, and it didn't suit him at all.

He had glanced round, when Jack rode up, and it was evident that he hated the intrusion. Herbert had waved his arm. Herbert still felt a certain gratitude—and the blacks had all stopped for a moment to stare. But Easu shouted them on.

At last the sorting out was done, and the bars put up. The bull went bellowing along the far fence. Herbert came striding to the gate, his smallish red face shining, and Jack got down to greet him. The two shook hands, and Herbert said :

" Glad to see you back."

He was the first to say he was glad to see Jack back. Even Len had not said it. The two men stood exchanging awkward sentences beside the horse.

Easu, too, came through the gate. He looked grudgingly at Jack and at Jack's horse. Jack thought how ugly he was, now his face had gone fatter and his mouth with its thin, jeering line looked mean. The alert bird-look had gone, he was heavy, and consumed with grudging. His very healthiness looked heavy, a bit dead. His light blue eyes stared and pretended to smile, but the smile was a grudging sneer.

" Where 'd you get y' 'oss ? "

" From Jimmy Short, in Perth."

" Bit long in the barrel. Making a trip, are y' ? "

And Easu looked with his pale blue eyes straight and sneering into Jack's eyes, and smiled with his grudging, mean mouth.

Jack noticed that Easu had begun to belly, inside his slack black trousers. He was no longer the spruce, straight fellow. Easu saw the glance, and was again humiliated. He himself hated his growing bulk. He looked a second time, into Jack's eyes, furtively, before he said :

" Find out if it was right what I was tellin' y' ? "

Jack was ready for the insult, and did not answer. He turned to Herbert, asking about Joe Low, who had been a pal of Herbert's. Joe Low also was married, and had gone down Busselton way. Jack asked for his directions, saying perhaps he might be able to call on him.

" What, are y' goin' south ? " put in Easu.

Jack looked at him. It was impossible not to see the slack look of defeat in Easu's face. Something had defeated him, leaving him all sneering and acid and heavy. Again Jack did not answer.

" What did you say ? " Easu persisted, advancing a little insolently.

" What about ? "

" I asked if y' was goin' south."

" That's my business, where I'm going."

" Of course it is," said Easu with a sneer and a grin. " You don't think anyone wants to get ahead of you, do you ? " He stood with a faint, sneering smile on his face, malevolent with impotence. " You'll do Percy a lot o' hurt, I'll bet. I wouldn't like to be Percy when you turn up." And he looked with a grin at Herbert. Herbert grinned faintly in echo.

" I should think, whatever Percy is, he wouldn't want to be you," said Jack, going white at the gills with anger, but speaking with calm superiority, because he knew that enraged Easu most.

" What's that ? " cried Easu, the grin flying out of his face at once, and leaving it stiff and dangerous.

" I should think Percy wouldn't want to be you, let him be what he may in himself," said Jack, in the cold, clear, English voice which he knew infuriated Easu unbearably.

Easu searched Jack's face intently with his pale blue eyes.

" How's that ? " he asked curtly.

Jack stared at the red, heavy face with the smallish eyes and thought to himself : " You pig ! You intolerable white-fat pig ! " But aloud he said nothing.

Easu smiled a defeated grin, and strode away heavily to his horse. He unhitched, swung heavily into the saddle, and moved away, then at a little distance reined in to hear what Jack and Herbert were talking about. He couldn't go.

Herbert was giving Jack directions, how to find Joe Low down Busselton way. Then he sent various items of news to his old pal. But he asked Jack no questions, and was careful to avoid any kind of enquiry concerning Jack's business.

Easu sat on his black horse a little way off, listening. He had a rope and an axe tied to his saddle. Presumably he was going into the bush. Herbert was asking questions about the North-West, about the cattle stations and the new mines. He talked as if he would like to talk all day. And Jack answered freely, laughing easily and making a joke of everything. They spoke of Perth, and Jack told how Tom and he had been at the Governor's ball a few night ago, and what a change it was from the North-West, and how Tom had enjoyed himself. Herbert listened, impressed.

" Gosh ! That's something to rag old Tom about ! " he said.

" *When you've done gassing there !* " called Easu.

Jack turned and looked at him.

" You don't have to wait," he said easily, as if to a servant.

There was really something about Easu now that suggested a servant. He went suddenly yellow with anger.

" What's that ? " he said, moving his horse a few paces forward.

And Jack, also white at the gills, but affecting the same ease, repeated distinctly and easily, as if to a man servant :

" We're talking, you don't have to wait."

There was no answer to this insult. Easu remained stock motionless on his horse for a few moments. Was he going to have to swallow it ?

Jack turned laughing to Herbert, saying :
" I've got several things to tell you about old Tom."

But he glanced up quickly. Easu was kicking his horse, and it was dancing before it would take a direction. Herbert gave a loud, inarticulate cry. Jack turned quickly to his own horse, to put his foot in the stirrup. Just as quickly he refrained, swung round, drew his pistol, and cocked it. Easu, once more a horseman, was kicking his restive horse forward, holding the small axe in his right hand, the reins in his left. His face was livid, and looked like the face of one returning from the dead. He came bearing down on Jack and Herbert, like Death returning from the dead, the axe held back at arm's length, ready for the swing, half urging, half holding his horse, so that it danced strangely nearer. Jack stood with the pistol ready, his back to his own horse, that was tossing its head nervously.

" Look out ! " cried Herbert, suddenly jumping at the bit of Jack's horse, in terror, and making it start back, with a thudding of hoofs.

But Jack did not move. He stood with his pistol ready, his eyes on Easu. Easu's horse was snaffling and jerking, twisting, trying to get round, and Easu was forcing it slowly forward. He had on his death face. He held the axe at arm's length, backward, and with his pale-blue, fixed death eyes he watched Jack, who stood there on the ground. So he advanced, waiting for the moment to swing the axe, fixing part of his will on the curvetting horse, which he forced on.

Jack, in a sort of trance, fixed Easu's death-face in the middle of the forehead. But he was watching with every pore of his body.

Suddenly he saw him begin to heave in the stirrups, and on that instant he fired at the mystic place in Easu's forehead, under his old hat, at the same time springing back. And in that self-same instant he saw two things : part of Easu's forehead seemed to shift mystically open, and the axe, followed by Easu's whole body, crashed at him as he sprang back. He went down in the universal crash, and for a moment his consciousness was dark and eternal. Then he wriggled to his feet, and ran, as Herbert was running, to the black horse, which was dancing in an agony of terror, Easu's right foot having caught in the stirrup, the body rolling horribly on the ground.

He caught the horse, which was shying off from Herbert, and raised his right hand to take the bridle. To his further horror and astonishment, he saw his hand all blood, and his fore finger gone. But he clutched the bridle of the horse with his maimed hand, then changed to his left hand, and stood looking in chagrin and horror at the bloody stump of his finger, which was just beginning, in a distant sort of way, to hurt.

" My God, he's dead ! " came the high, hysterical yell from Herbert, on the other side of the horse, and Jack let go the bridle again, to look.

It was too obvious. The big, ugly, inert bulk of Easu lay crumpled on the ground, part of the forehead shot away. Jack looked twice, then looked away again. A black had caught his horse, and tied it to the fence. Another black was running up. A dog came panting excitedly up, sniffing and licking the blood. Herbert, beside himself, stood helpless, repeating : " He's dead ! He's dead ! My God, he's dead ! He is."

Then he gave a yell, and swooped at the dog, as it began to lick the blood.

Jack, after once more looking round, walked away. He saw his pistol lying on the ground, so he picked it up and put it in his belt, although it was bloody, and had a cut where the axe had struck it. Then he walked across to his horse, and unhitched the bridle from the fence. But before he mounted, he took his handkerchief and tied it round his bleeding hand, which was beginning to hurt with a big aching hurt. He knew it, and yet he hardly heeded it. It was hardly noticeable.

He got into the saddle, and rode calmly away, going on his journey southward just the same. The world about him seemed faint and unimportant. Inside himself was the reality and the assurance. Easu was dead. It was a good thing.

He had one definite feeling. He felt as if there had been something damning life up, as a great clot of weeds will dam a stream and make the water spread marshily and dead over the surrounding land. He felt he had lifted this clod out of the stream, and the water was flowing on clear again.

He felt he had done a good thing. Somewhere inside himself he felt he had done a supremely good thing. Life could flow on to something beyond. Why question further?

He rode on, down the track. The sun was very hot, and his body was re-echoing with the pain from his hand. But he went on calmly, monotonously, his horse travelling in a sort of sleep, easy in its single-step. He didn't think where he was going, or why; he was just going.

CHAP : XXI. LOST

AT evening he was still riding. But his horse lagged, and would not be spurred forward. Darkness came with swift persistence. He was looking anxiously for water, a burning thirst had made him empty his bottle.

As if directed by God, he felt the horse rousing up and pressing eagerly forward. In a few minutes it stopped. Darkness had fallen. He found the horse nosing a timber-lined Government well.

He got down and awkwardly drew water, for the well was low. He drank and the horse drank. Then, with some difficulty, he unsaddled, tied the reins round a sapling and removed the bit. The horse snorted, nosed round, and began to crop in the dark. Jack sat on the ground and looked up at the stars. Then he drank more water, and ate a piece of bread and dry cheese.

Then he began to go to sleep. He saw Easu coming at him with the axe. Ugh, how good it was Easu was dead. Dead, to go in the earth to manure the soil. Hadn't Old George said it ? The land wanted dead men dug into it, to manure it. Men like Easu, dead and turned to manure. And men like old Dad Ellis. Poor old Dad.

Jack thought of Monica. Monica with her little flower-face. All messed up by that nasty dog of an Easu. He should be twice dead. Jack felt she was a little repulsive, too. To let herself be pawed over and made sticky by that heavy dog of an Easu ! Jack felt he could never follow where Easu had been messing. Monica was no good now. She had taken on some of Easu's repulsiveness.

Aunt Matilda had said, " Another scandal in the family ! " Well, the death of Easu should make a good scandal.

How lonely it was in the bush ! How big and weapon-like the stars were. One great star very flashing.

" I have dipped my hand in blood ! " he thought to himself. And looking at his own bloody, hurting hand, in the starlight, he didn't realise whether it was Easu's blood or his own.

" I have dipped my hand in blood ! "

" So be it. Let it be my testament."

And he lifted up his hand to the great flashing star, his wounded hand, saying aloud :

" Here ! Here is my hand in blood ! Take it, then. There is blood between us forever."

The blood was between him and his mysterious Lord, for ever. Like a sort of pledge, or baptism, or a sacrifice : a bond between them. He was speaking to his mysterious Lord.

" There is blood between us for ever," he said to the star.

But the sound of his own hoarse, rather deep voice, reminded him of his surroundings. He looked round. He heard his horse, and called to it. It nickered in the loneliness, still cropping. He started up to see if it was all right, to stroke it and speak to it. The bush was very lonely.

" Hello, you ! " he said to it. " In the midst of life we are in death. There's death in the spaces between the stars. But somehow it seems all right. I like it. I like to be Lord of Death. Who do they call the Lords of Death. I am a Lord of Death."

He patted the horse's neck as he talked.

" I can't bear to think of Monica messy with Easu," he said. " But I suppose it's my destiny. I suppose it means I am a lord of death. I hope if I have any children they'll have that look in their eyes, like soldiers from the dark kingdom. I don't want children that aren't warriors. I don't want little love children for my children. When I beget children I want to sow dragon's teeth, and warriors will spring up. Easu hadn't one grain nor spark of a warrior in him. He was absolutely a groping civilian, a bully. That's why he wanted to spoil Monica. She is the wife for a fighting man. So he wanted to spoil her. . . . Funny, my father isn't a fighting man at all. He's an absolute civilian. So he became a general. And I'm not a civilian. I know the spaces of death between the stars, like spaces in an Egyptian temple. And at the end of life I see the big black door of death, and the infinite black labyrinth beyond. I like to think of going in, and being at home and one of the masters in the black halls of death, when I am dead. I hope I die fighting, and go into the black halls of death as a master : not as a scavenger servant, like Easu, or a sort of butler, like my father. I don't want to be a servant in the black house of death. I want to be a master."

He sat down again, with his back to the tree, looking at the sharp stars, and the fume of stars, and the great black gulfs between the stars. His hand and arm were aching and paining a great deal. But he watched the gulfs between the stars.

" I suppose my Lord meant me to be like this," he said. " Think if I had to be tied up and a gentleman, like that Blessington. Or a lawyer like Old George. Or a politician dropping his aitches, like that Mr Watson. Or empty and important like that A.D.C. Or anything that's successful and goes to church and sings hymns and has supper after church on the best linen table-cloth ! What Lord is it that likes these people? What God can it be that likes success and Sunday dinners. Oh, God ! It must be a big, fat, reesty sort of God.

" My God is dark and you can't see him. You can't even see his eyes, they are so dark. But he sits and bides his time and smiles, in the spaces between the stars. And he doesn't know himself what he thinks. But there's deep, powerful feelings inside him, and he's only waiting his time to upset this pigsty full of white fat pigs. I like my Lord. I like his dark face, that I can't see, and his dark eyes, that are so dark you can't see them, and his dark hair, that is blacker than the night, on his forehead, and the dark feelings he has, which nobody will ever be able to explain. I like my Lord, my own Lord, who is not Lord of pigs."

He slept fitfully, feverishly, with dreams, and rose at daylight to drink water, and dip his head in water. His horse came, he tended it, and with great difficulty got the saddle on. Then he left it standing, and when he came again, it wasn't where he had left it.

He called, and it whinnied, so he went into the scrub for it. But it wasn't where the sound of whinnying came from. He went a few more steps forward, and called. The scrub wasn't so very thick, either, yet you couldn't see that horse. He was sure it was only a couple of yards away. So he went forward, coaxing, calling. But nothing . . . Queer !

He looked round. The track wasn't there. The well wasn't there. Only the silent, vindictive, scattered bush.

He couldn't be lost. That was impossible. The homestead wasn't more than twenty miles away—and the settlement.

Yet, as he tramped on, through the brown, heath-like undergrowth, past the ghost-like trunks of the scattered gum-trees, over the fallen, burnt-out trunks of charred trees, past the bushes of young gum-trees, he gradually realised he *was* lost. And yet it was impossible. He would come upon a cabin, or pick up the track of a wood cutter, or a 'roo hunter. He was so near to everywhere.

There is something mysterious about the Australian bush. It is so absolutely still. And yet, in the near distance, it seems alive. It seems alive, and as if it hovered round you to maze you and circumvent you. There is a strange feeling, as if invisible, hostile things were hovering round you and heading you off.

Jack stood still and coo-eed! long and loud. He fancied he heard an answer, and he hurried forward. He felt lightheaded. He wished he had eaten something. He remembered he had no water. And he was walking very fast, the sweat pouring down him. Silly this. He made himself go slower. Then he stood still and looked around. Then he coo-eed again, and was afraid of the ringing sound of his own cry.

The changeless bush, with scattered, slender tree-trunks everywhere. You could see between them into the distance, to more open bush : a few brown rocks : two great dead trees as white as bone : burnt trees with their core charred out : and living trees hanging their motionless clusters of brown, dagger-like leaves. And the permanent soft blue of the sky overhead.

Nothing was hidden. It was all open and fair. And yet it was haunted with a malevolent mystery. You felt yourself so small, so tiny, so absolutely insignificant, in the still, eternal glade. And this again is the malevolence of the bush, that it reduces you to your own absolute insignificance, go where you will.

Jack collected his wits and began to make a plan.

" First look at the sky, and get your bearing." Then

he would go somewhere straight west from the Reds. The sun had been in his eyes as he rode last evening.

Or had he better go east, and get back? There were scores of empty miles, uninhabited, west. It was settled, he would go east. Perhaps someone would find his horse, and come to look for him.

He walked with the sun straight bang in his eyes. It was very hot, and he was tired. He was thirsty, his arm hurt and throbbed. Why did he imagine he was hungry. He was only thirsty. And so hot! He took off his coat and threw it away. After a while his waistcoat followed. He felt a little lighter. But he was an intolerable burden to himself.

He sat down under a bush and went fast asleep. How long he slept he did not know. But he woke with a jerk, to find himself lying on the ground in his shirt and trousers, the sun still hot in the heavens, and the mysterious bush all around. The sun had come round and was burning his legs.

What was the matter? Fear, that was the first thing. The great, resounding fear. Then, a second, he was terribly thirsty. For a third, his arm was aching horribly. He took off his shirt and made a sling of it, to carry his arm in.

For a fourth thing, he realised he had killed Easu, and something was gnawing at his soul.

He heard himself sob, and this surprised him very much. It even brought him to his senses.

" Well! " he thought. " I have killed Easu." It seemed years and years ago. " And the bush has got me, Australia has got me, and now it will take my life from me. Now I am going to die. Well, then so be it. I will go out and haunt the bush, like all the other lost dead. I shall wander in the bush throughout eternity, with my bloody hand. Well, then, so be it. I shall be a lord of death hovering in the bush, and let the people who come beware."

But suddenly he started to his feet in terror and horror. The face of death had really got him this time. It was as if a second wakening had come upon him, and his life, which had been sinking, suddenly flared up in a frenzy of struggle and fear. He coo-eed! again and again, and once more plunged forward in mad pursuit of an echo.

He might certainly run into a 'roo hunters' camp any minute. The place was alive with them, great big boomers! Their silly faces! Their silly complacency, almost asking to be shot. There were a lot of wallabies out here, too. You might make a fortune hunting skins.

Christ! how one could want water.

But no matter. On and on! His soul dropped to its own sullen level. If he was to die, die he would. But he would hold out through it all.

On and on in a persistent dogged stupor. Why give in?

Then suddenly he dropped on a log, in weariness. Suddenly he had thought of Monica. Why had she betrayed him? Why had they all betrayed him, betrayed him and the thing he wanted from life? He leaned his head down on his arms and wept hoarsely and dryly, and went silent again even as he sat, realising the futility of weeping. His heart, the heart he wept from, went utterly dark. He had no more heart of torn sympathy. That was gone. Only a black, deep, male volition. And this was all there was left of him. He would carry the same into death. Young or old, death sooner or later, he would carry just this one thing into the further darkness, his deep, black, undying male volition.

He must have slept. He was in great misery, his mouth like an open sepulchre, his consciousness dull. He was hardly aware that it was late afternoon, hot and motionless. The outside things were all so far away. And the blackness of death and misery was thick, but transparent, over his eyes.

He went on, still obstinately insisting that ahead there was something, perhaps even water, though hope was dead in him. It was not hope, it was heavy volition that insisted on water.

The sling dragged on his neck, he threw it away, and walked with his hand against his breast. And his braces dragged on him. He didn't want any burden at all, none at all. He stopped, took off his braces and threw them away, then his sweat-soaked under-vest. He didn't want these things. He didn't want them. He walked on a bit.

He hesitated, then came for a moment to his senses. He was going to throw away his trousers, too. But it came to him : " Don't be a fool, and throw away your clothes, man. You know men do it who are lost in the bush, and then they are found naked, dead."

He looked vaguely round for the vest and braces he had just thrown away. But it was half an hour since he had flung them down. His consciousness tricked him, obliterating the interval. He could not believe his eyes. They had ghostlily disappeared.

So he rolled his trousers on his naked hips, and pressed his hurt hand on his naked breast, and set off again in a sort of fear. His hat had gone long ago. And all the time he had this strange desire to throw all his clothes away, even his boots, and be absolutely naked, as when he was born. And all the time something obstinate in him combatted the desire. He wanted to throw everything away, and go absolutely naked over the border. And, at the same time, something in him deeper than himself obstinately withstood the desire. He wanted to go over the border. And something deeper even than his consciousness refused.

So he went on, scarcely conscious at all. He himself was in the middle of a vacuum, and pressing round were visions and agonies. The vacuum was perhaps the greatest agony, like a death-tension. But the other agonies were pressing on its border : his dry, cardboard mouth, his aching body. And the visions pressed on the border, too. A great lake of ghostly white water, such as lies in the valleys where the dead are. But he walked to it, and it wasn't there. The moon was shining whitely.

And on the edge of the aching void of him, a wheel was spinning in his brain like a prayer-wheel.

" Petition me no petitions, sir, to-day;
Let other hours be set apart for business.
To-day it is our pleasure to be drunk
And this our queen . . ."

Water ! Water ! Water ! Was water only a visionary thing of memory, something only achingly, wearyingly, thought and thought and thought, and never substantiated ?

" A Briton even in love should be
A subject not a slave . . ."

The wheel of words went round, the wheel of his brain, on the edge of the vacuum. What did that mean? What was a Briton?

> " A Briton even in love should be
> A subject not a slave . . ."

The words went round and round and were absolutely meaningless to him.

And then out of the dark another wheel was pressing and turning.

> " How fast has brother followed brother
> From sunshine to the sunless land."

Away on the hard dark periphera of his consciousness the wheel of these words was turning and grinding.

His mind was turning helplessly, but his feet walked on. He realised in a weird, mournful way that he was shut groping in a dark, unfathomable cave, and that the walls of the cave were his own aching body. And he was going on and on in the cave, looking for the fountain, the water. But his body was aching, ghastly, jutting walls of the cave. And it made this weary grind of words on the outside. And he had need to struggle on and on.

In little flickers he tried to associate his dark cave-consciousness with his grinding body. Was it night, was it day?

But before he had decided that it was night, the two things had gone apart again, and he was groping and listening to the grind.

> " But hushed be every thought that springs
> From out the bitterness of things.
> Those obstinate questionings
> Of sense and outward things
> Falling from us, vanishing."

He was so weary of the outward grind of words. He was stumbling as he walked. And waiting for the walls of the cave to crash in and bury him altogether. And the spring of water did not exist.

" Blank misgivings of a creator moving about in a world not realised."

This phrase almost united his two consciousnesses. He was going to crash into this creator who moved about unrealised. Other people had gone, and other things. Monica, Easu, Tom, Mary, Mother, Father, Lennie. They were all like papery, fallen leaves blowing about outside in some street. Inside here there were no people at all, none at all. Only the Creator moving around unrealised. His Lord.

He stumbled and fell, and in the white flash of falling knew he hurt himself again, and that he was falling for ever.

CHAP : XXII. THE FIND

i

THE subconscious self woke first, roaring in distant wave-beats unintelligible, unmeaning, persistent, and growing in volume. It had something to do with birth. And not having died. " I have not let my soul run like water out of my mouth."

And as the roaring and beating of the waves increased in volume, tiny little words emerged like flying-fish out of the black ocean of consciousness. " Ye must be born again," in little, silvery, twinkling spurts, like flying-fish which twinkle silver and spark into the utterly dark sea again. They were gone and forgotten before they were realised. They had merged deep in the sea again. And the roar of dark consciousness was the roar of death. The kingdom of death. And the lords of death.

" Ye must be born again." But the twinkling words had disappeared into the lordly powerful darkness of death. And the baptism is the blackness of death between the eyes, that never lifts, forever, neither in life nor death. You may be born again. But when you emerge, this time you emerge with the darkness of death between your eyes, as a lord of death.

The waves of dark consciousness surged in a huge billow, and broke. The boy's eyes were wide open, and his voice was saying :

" Is that you, Tom ! "

The sound of his voice paperily rustling these words, was so surprising to him that he instantly went dark again, He heard no answer.

But those surging dark waves pressed him again and again, and again his eyes were open. They recognised nothing. Something was being done to him on the outside of him. His own throat was moving. And life started again with a sharp pain.

" What was it ? "

The question sparked suddenly out of him. Someone was putting a metal rim to his lips, there was liquid in his mouth.

He put it out. He didn't want to come back. His soul sank again like a dark stone.

And at the very bottom it took a command from the Lord of Death, and rose slowly again.

Someone was tilting his head, and pouring a little water again. He swallowed with a crackling noise and a crackling pain. One had to come back. He recognised the command from his own Lord. His Lord was the Lord of Death. And he, Jack, was dark-anointed and sent back. Returned with the dark unction between his brows. So be it.

He saw green leaves hanging from a blue sky. It was still far off. And the dark was still better. But the dark green leaves were also like a triumphal banner. He tries to smile, but his face is stiff. The faintest irony of a smile sets in its stiffness. He is forced to swallow again, and know the pain and tearing. Ah! He suddenly realised the water was good. He had not realised it the other times. He gulped suddenly, everything forgotten. And his mind gave a sudden lurch towards consciousness.

" Is that you, Tom."

" Yes.   Feel better? "

He saw the red mistiness of Tom's face near. Tom was faithful. And this time his soul swayed, as if it too had drunk of the water of faithfulness.

He drank the water from the metal cup, because he knew it came from Tom's faithfulness.

Gradually Jack revived. But his burning bloodshot eyes were dilated with fever, and he could not keep hold of his consciousness. He realised that Tom was there, and Mary, and somebody he didn't for a long time recognise as Lennie; and that there was a fire, and a smell of meat, and night was again falling. Yes, he was sure night was falling. Or was it his own consciousness going dark? He didn't know. Perhaps it was the everlasting dark.

" What time is it? " he asked.

" Sundown," said Tom. " Why? "

But he was gone again. It was no good trying to keep a hold on one's consciousness. The ache, the nausea, the throbbing pain, the swollen mouth, the strange feeling of cracks in his flesh, made him let go.

Tom was there and Mary. He would leave himself to Tom's faithfulness and Mary's tenderness, and Lennie's watchful intuition. The mystery of death was in that bit of deathless faithfulness which was in Tom. And Mary's tenderness, and Lennie's intuitive care, both had a touch of the mystery and stillness of the death that surrounds us darkly all the time.

ii

They got Jack home, but he was very ill. His life would seem to come back. Then it would sink away again like a stone, and they would think he was going. The strange oscillation. Several times, Mary watched him almost die. Then, from the very brink of death, he would come back again, with a strange, haunted look in his blood-shot eyes.

" What is it, Jack ? " she would ask him. But the eyes only looked at her.

And Lennie, standing there silently watching, said :

" He's had about enough of life, that's what it is."

Mary, blenched with fear, went to find Tom.

" Tom," she said, " he's sinking again. Lennie says it's because he doesn't want to live."

Tom silently threw down his tool, and walked with her into the house. It was obvious he was sinking again.

" Jack ! " said Tom in a queer voice, bending over him. " Mate ! Mate ! " He seemed to be calling him into camp.

Jack's expressionless, fever-dilated, blood-shot eyes opened again. The whites were almost scarlet.

" Y' aren't desertin' us, are y' ? " said Tom, in a gloomy, reproachful tone. " Are y' desertin' us, Mate ? "

It was the Australian, lost but unbroken on the edge of the wilderness, looking with grim mouth into the void, and calling to his mate not to leave him. Man for man, they were up against the great dilemma of white men, on the edge of the white man's world, looking into the vaster, alien world of the undawned era, and unable to enter, unable to leave their own.

Jack looked at Tom and smiled faintly. In some subtle way, both men knew the mysterious responsibilities of living. Tom was almost fatalistic-reckless. Yet it was a reckless-ness which knew that the only thing to do was to go ahead, meet death that way. He could see nothing but meeting death ahead. But since he was a man, he would go ahead to meet it, he would not sit and wait.

Jack smiled faintly, and the courage came back to him. He began to rally.

The next morning he turned to Mary and said :

" I still want Monica."

Mary dropped her head and did not answer. She recognised it as one of the signs that he was going to live. And she recognised the unbending obstinacy in his voice.

" I shall come for you, too, in time," he said to her, looking at her with his terrible scarlet eyes.

She did not answer, but her hand trembled as she went for his medicine. There was something prophetic and terrible in his sallow face and burning, blood-shot eyes.

" Be still," she murmured to him. " Only be still."

" I shan't ever really drop you," he said to her. " But I want Monica first. That's my way."

He seemed curiously victorious, making these assertions.

CHAP : XXIII.   GOLD

i

THE boy Jack never rose from that fever. It was a man who got up again. A man with all the boyishness cut away from him, all the childishness gone, and a certain unbending recklessness in its place.

He was thin, and pale, and the cherubic look had left his face forever. His cheeks were longer, leaner, and when he got back his brown-faced strength again, he was handsome. But it was not the handsomeness, any more, that would make women like Aunt Matilda exclaim involuntarily : " Dear boy ! " They would look at him twice, but with misgiving, and a slight recoil.

It was his eyes that had changed most. From being the warm, emotional dark blue eyes of a boy, they had become impenetrable, and had a certain fixity. There was a touch of death in them, a little of the fixity and changelessness of death. And with this, a peculiar power. As if he had lost his softness in the other world of death, and brought back instead some of the relentless power that belongs there. And the inevitable touch of mockery.

As soon as he began to walk about, he was aware of the change. He walked differently, he put his feet down differently, he carried himself differently. The old drifting, diffident careless bearing had left him. He felt his uprightness hard, bony. Sometimes he was aware of the skeleton of himself. He was a hard skeleton, built upon the solid bony column of the back-bone, and pitched for balance on the great bones of the hips. But the plumb-weight was in the cage of his chest. A skeleton !

But not the dead skeleton. The living bone, the living man of bone, unyielding and imperishable. The bone of his forehead like iron against the world, and the blade of his breast like an iron wedge held forward. He was thin, and built of bone.

And inside this living, rigid man of bone, the dark heart heavy with its wisdom and passions and emotions and its correspondences. It, too, was living, softly and intensely living. But heavy and dark, plumb to the earth's centre.

311

During his convalescence, he got used to this man of bone which he had become, and accepted his own inevitable. His bones, his skeleton was isolatedly itself. It had no contact. Except that it was forged in the kingdom of death, to be durable and effectual. Some strange Lord had forged his bones in the dark smithy where the dead and the unborn came and went.

And this was his only permanent contact : the contact with the Lord who had forged his bones, and put a dark heart in the midst.

But the other contacts, they were alive and quivering in his flesh. His passive but enduring affection for Tom and Lennie, and the strange quiescent hold he held over Mary. Beyond these, the determined molten stirring of his desire for Monica.

And the other desires. The desire in his heart for master-hood. Not mastery. He didn't want to master anything. But to be the dark lord of his own folk : that was a desire in his heart. And the concurrent knowledge that, to achieve this, he must be master, too, of gold. Not gold for the having's sake. Not for the spending's sake. Nor for the sake of the power to hire services, which is the power of money. But the mastery of gold, so that gold should no longer be like a yellow star to which men hitched the wagon of their destinies. To be Master of Gold, in the name of the dark Lord who had forged his bones neither of gold nor silver nor iron, but of the white glisten of life. Master-hood, as a man forged by the Lord of Hosts, in the inner-most fires of life and death. Because, just as a red fire burning on the hearth is a fusion of death into what was once live leaves, so the creation of man in the dark is a fusion of life into death, with the life dominant.

The two are never separate, life and death. And in the vast dark kingdom of afterwards, the Lord of Death is Lord of Life, and the God of Life and creation is Lord of Death.

But Jack knew his Lord as the Lord of Death. The rich, dark mystery of death, which lies ahead, and the dark sumptuousness of the halls of death. Unless Life moves on to the beauty of the darkness of death, there is no life, there is only automatism. Unless we see the dark splendour of death ahead, and travel to be lords of darkness at last, peers in the realms of death, our life is nothing but a petu-

lant, pitiful backing, like a frightened horse, back, back to
the stable, the manger, the cradle. But onward ahead is
the great porch of the entry into death, with its columns of
bone-ivory. And beyond the porch is the heart of darkness,
where the lords of death arrive home out of the vulgarity of
life, into their own dark and silent domains, lordly, ruling
the incipience of life.

ii

At the trial Jack said, in absolute truth, he shot Easu
in self-defence. He had not the faintest thought of shooting him when he rode up to the paddock; nor of shooting
anybody. He had called in passing, just to say good-day.
And then he had fired at Easu because he knew the axe
would come down in his skull if he didn't.

Herbert gave the same deposition. The shot was entirely
in self-defence.

So Jack was free again. There had been no further
mention of Monica, after Jack had said he was riding south
to see her, because he had always cared for her. No one
hinted that Easu was the father of her child, though Mrs
Ellis knew, and Old George knew.

Afterwards, Jack wondered why he had called at the
Reds' place that morning. Why had he taken the trail
past where he and Easu had fought? He had intended to
see Easu, that was why. But for what unconscious purpose who shall say? The death was laid at the door of the
old feud between Jack and Red. Only Old George knew
the whole, and he, subtle and unafraid, pushed justice as
it should go, according to his own sense of justice, like a
real Australian.

Meanwhile he had been corresponding with Monica and
Percy. They were in Albany, and on the point of sailing
to Melbourne, where Percy would enter some business or
other, and the two would live as man and wife. Monica
was expecting another child. At this news, Mr George
wanted to let them go, and be damned to them. But he
talked to Mary, and Mary said Jack would want Monica,
no matter what happened.

" When he wants a thing really, he can't change," said
Mary gloomily. " He is like that."

" An obstinate young fool that's never had enough lickings," said Old George. " Devil's blood of his mother's devil of an obstinate father. But very well then, let him have her, with a couple of babies for a dowry. Make himself the laughing stock of the colony."

So he wrote to Monica : " If you care about seeing Jack Grant again, you'd better stop in this colony. He sticks to it he wants to see you, being more of a fool than a knave, unlike many people in Western Australia."

She, being obstinate like the rest, stayed on in Albany, though Percy, angry and upset, sailed on to Melbourne. He said she could join him if she liked. He stayed till her baby was born, then went because he didn't want to face Jack.

Jack arrived by sea. He was still not strong enough to travel by land. He got a vessel going to Adelaide, that touched at Albany.

Monica, thinner than ever, with a little baby in her arms, and her flower-face like a chilled flower, was on the dock to meet him. He saw her at once and his heart gave a queer lurch.

As he came forward to meet her, their eyes met. Her yellow eyes looked straight into his, with the same queer, panther-like scrutiny, and the eternal question. She was a question, and she had got to be answered. It made her fearless, almost shameless, whatever she did.

But with Percy, the fear had nipped her, the fear that she should go forever unanswered, as if life had rejected her.

This nipped and her strange yellow flare of question as she peered at him under her brows, like a panther, made Jack's cheeks slowly darken, and the life-blood flow into him stronger, heavier. He knew his passion for her was the same. Thank God he met her at last.

" You're awfully thin," she said.

" So are you," he answered.

And she laughed her quick, queer, breathless little laugh, showing her pointed teeth. She had seen the death-look in his eyes and it was her answer, a bitter answer enough. She stopped to put straight the tiny bonnet over her little baby's face, with a delicate, remote movement. He watched her in silence.

" Where do you want to go ? " she asked him, without looking at him.

" With you," he said.

Then she looked at him again, with the dry-eyed question. But she saw the unapproachable death-look there in his eyes, at the back of their dark-blue, dilated emotion and passion. And her heart gave up. She looked down the pier, as if to walk away. He carried his own bag. They set off side by side.

She lived in a tiny slab cottage in a side lane. But she called first at a neighbour's house, for her other child. It was a tiny, toddling thing with a defiant stare in its pale-blue eyes. Monica held her baby on one arm, and led this tottering child by the other. Jack walked at her side in silence.

The cottage had just two rooms, poorly furnished. But it was clean, and had bright cotton curtains and sofa-bed, and a pale-blue convolvulus vine mingling with a passion vine over the window.

She laid the baby down in its cradle, and began to take off the bonnet of the little girl. She had called it Jane.

Jack watched the little Jane as if fascinated. The infant had curly reddish hair, of a lovely fine texture and a beautiful tint, something like raw silk with threads of red. Her eyes were round and bright blue, and rather defiant, and she had the delicate complexion of her kind. She fingered her mother's brooch, like a little monkey touching a bit of glittering gold, as Monica stooped to her.

" Daddy gone ! " she said in her chirping, bird-like, quite emotionless tone.

" Yes, Daddy gone ! " replied Monica, as emotionlessly.

The child then glanced with unmoved curiosity at Jack. She kept on looking and looking at him, sideways. And he watched her just as sharply, her sharp pale-blue eyes.

" Him more Daddy ? " she asked.

" I don't know," replied Monica, who was suckling her baby.

" Yes," said Jack in a rather hard tone, smiling with a touch of mockery. " I'm your new father."

The child smiled back at him, a faint, mocking little grin, and put her finger in her mouth.

The day passed slowly in the strange place, Monica busy all the time with the children and the house. Poor Monica, she was already a drudge. She was still careless and hasty

in her methods, but clean, and uncomplaining. She kept
herself to herself, and did what she had to do. And Jack
watched, mostly silent.

At last the lamp was lighted, the children were both in
bed. Monica cooked a little supper over the fire.

Before he came to the table, Jack asked :

" Is Jane Easu's child ? "

" I thought you knew," she said.

" No one has told me. Is she ? "

Monica turned and faced him, with the yellow flare in
her eyes, as she looked into his eyes, challenging.

" Yes," she said.

But his eyes did not change. The remoteness at the back
of them did not come any nearer.

" Shall you hate her ? " she asked, rather breathlessly.

" I don't know," he said slowly.

" Don't ! " she pleaded, in the same breathlessness.
" Because I rather hate her."

" She's too little to hate," said Jack.

" I know," said Monica rather doubtfully.

She put the food on the table. But she herself ate nothing.

" Aren't you well ? You don't eat," he asked.

" I can't eat just now," she said.

" If you have a child to suckle, you should," he replied.

But she only became more silent, and her hands hung
dead in her lap. Then the baby began to cry, a thin, poor,
frail noise, and she went to soothe it.

When she came back, Jack had left the table and was
sitting in Percy's wooden arm-chair.

" Percy's child doesn't seem to have much life in it," he
said.

" Not *very* much," she replied. And her hands trembled
as she cleared away the dishes.

When she had finished, she moved about, afraid to sit
down. He called her to him.

" Monica ! " he said, with a little jerk of his head, meaning she should come to him.

She came rather slowly, her queer, pure-seeming face
looking like a hurt. She stood with her thin hands hanging
in front of her apron.

" Monica ! " he said, rising and taking her hands. " I

should still want you if you had a hundred children. So we won't say any more about that. And you won't oppose me when there's anything I want to do, will you? "

She shook her head.

" No, I won't oppose you," she said, in a dead little voice.

" Let me come to you, then," he said. " I should have to come to you if you had gone to Melbourne or all round the world. And I should be glad to come," he added whimsically, with the warmth of his old smile coming into his eyes; " I suppose I should be glad to come, if it was in hell."

" But it isn't hell, is it? " she asked, wistfully and a little defiantly.

" Not a bit," he said. " You've got too much pluck in you to spoil. You're as good to me as you were the first time I knew you. Only, Easu might have spoiled you."

" And you killed him," she said quickly, half in reproach.

" Would you rather he'd killed me? " he asked.

She looked a long time into his eyes, with that watchful, searching look that used to hurt him. Now it hurt him no more.

She shook her head, saying :

" I'm glad you killed him. I couldn't bear to think of him living on, and sneering,—sneering.—I was always in love with you, really."

" Ah, Monica! " he exclaimed softly, teasingly, with a little smile. And she flushed, and flashed with anger.

" If you never knew, it was your own fault ! " she jerked out.

" *Really*," he said, quoting and echoing the word as she had said it, and smiling with a touch of raillery at her, before he added :

" You always loved me *really*, but you loved the others as well, unreally."

" Yes," she said, baffled, defiant.

" All right, that day is over. You've *had* your unreal loves. Now come and have your real one."

In the next room Easu's child was sleeping in its odd little way, a sleep that was neither innocent nor not innocent, queer and naïvely " knowing," even in its sleep. Jack watched it as he took off his things : this little inheritance

he had from Easu. An odd little thing. With an odd,
loveless little spirit of its own, cut off and not daunted.
He wouldn't love it, because it wasn't loveable. But its
odd little dauntlessness and defiance amused him, he would
see it had fair play.

And he took Monica in his arms, glad to get into grips
with his own fate again. And it was good. It was better,
perhaps, than his passionate desirings of earlier days had
imagined. Because he didn't lose and scatter himself. He
gathered, like a reaper at harvest gathering.

And Monica, who woke for her baby, looked at him as he
slept soundly and she sat in bed suckling her child. She
saw in him the eternal stranger. There he was, the eternal
stranger, lying in her bed sleeping at her side. She rocked
her baby slightly as she sat up in the night, still rocking
in the last throes of rebellion. The eternal stranger, she
must fear him, because she could never finally know him,
and never entirely possess him. He would never *belong*
to her. This had made her rebel so dangerously against
the thought of him. Because *she* would have to belong to
him. Now he had arrived again before her like a doom,
a doom she still stiffened herself against, but could no longer
withstand. Because the emptiness of the other men, Percy,
Easu, all the men she knew, was worse than the doom of
this man who would never give her his ultimate intimacy,
but who would be able to hold her till the end of time.
There was something enduring and changeless in him. But
she would never hold *him* entirely. Never! She would
have to resign herself to that.

Well, so be it. At least it relieved her of the burden
of responsibility for life. It took away from her her own
strange, fascinating female power, which she couldn't bear
to part with. But at the same time she felt saved, because
her own power frightened her, having brought her to a
brink of nothingness that was like a madness. The nothingness that fronted her with Percy was worse than submitting
to this man. After all, this man was magical.

She put her child in its cradle, and returning waked the
man. He put out his hand quickly for her, as if she were
a new, blind discovery. She quivered and thrilled, and left
it to him. It was his mystery, since he would have it so.

iii

They were married in Albany, and stayed there another
month waiting for a ship. Then they sailed away, all the
family, away to the North West. They did not go to Perth;
they did not go to Wandoo. Only Jack saw Mr. George
in Fremantle, and waved to him good-bye as the ship proceeded north.

Then came two months of wandering, a pretty business
with a baby and a toddling infant. The second month,
Percy's baby suddenly died in the heat, and Monica hardly
mourned for it. As Jack looked at its pinched little dead
face, he said : " *You are better dead.*" And that was
true.

The little Jane, however, showed no signs of dying. The
knocking about seemed to suit her. Monica remained very
thin. It was a sort of hell-life to her, this struggling from
place to place in the heat and dust, no water to wash in,
sleeping anywhere like a lost dog, eating the food that came.
Because she loved to be clean and good-looking and in
graceful surroundings. What fiend of hell had ordained
that she must be a sort of tramp woman in the back of
beyond ?

She did not know, so it was no good asking. Jack seemed
to know what he wanted. And she was his woman, fated to
him. There was no more to it. Through the purgatory of
discomfort she had to go. And he was good to her, thoughtful for her, in material things. But at the centre of his
soul he was not thoughtful for her. He just possessed her,
mysteriously owned her, and went ahead with his own
obsessions.

Sometimes she tried to rebel. Sometimes she wanted to
refuse to go any farther, to refuse to be a party to his will.
But then he suddenly looked so angry, and so remote,
looked at her with such far-off, cold, haughty eyes, that she
was frightened. She was afraid he would abandon her, or
ship her back to Perth, and put her out of his life forever.

Above all things, she didn't want to be shipped back to
Perth. Here in the wild she could have taken up with
another man. She knew that. But she knew that if she
did, Jack would just put her out of his life altogether.
There would be no return. His passion for her would just

take the form of excluding her forever from his being. Because passion can so reverse itself, and from being a great desire that draws the beloved towards itself, it can become an eternal revulsion, excluding the once-beloved forever from any contact at all.

Monica knew this. And whenever she tried to oppose him, and the deathly anger rose in him, she was pierced with a fear so acute she had to hold on to some support, to prevent herself sinking to the ground. It was a strange fear, as if she were going to be cast out of the land of the living, among the unliving that slink like pariahs outside.

Afterwards she was puzzled. Why had he got this power over her? Why couldn't she be a free woman, to go where she chose, and be a complete thing in herself?

She caught at the idea. But it was no good. When he went away prospecting for a week or more at a time, she would struggle to regain her woman's freedom. And it would seem to her as if she had got it : she was free of him again. She was a free being, by herself.

But then, when he came back, tired, sunburnt, ragged, and still unsuccessful : and when he looked at her with desire in his eyes, the living desire for her; she was so glad, suddenly, as if she had forgotten, or as if she had never known what his desire of her meant to her. She was so glad, she was weak with gladness instead of fear. And if, in perverseness, she still tried to oppose him, in the light of her supposedly regained freedom ; and she saw the strange glow of desire for her go out of his eyes, and the strange loveliness, to her, of his wanting to have her near, in the room, giving him his meal or sitting near him outside in the shade of the evening; then, when his face changed, and took on the curious look of aloofness, as if he glistened with anger looking down on her from a long way off; then, she felt all her own world turn to smoke, and her own will mysteriously evaporate, leaving her only wanting to be wanted again, back in his world. Her freedom was worth less than nothing.

Still often, when he was gone, leaving her alone in the little cabin, she was glad. She was free to spread her own woman's aura round her, she was free to delight in her own woman's idleness and whimsicality, free to amuse herself, half-teasing, half-loving that little odd female of a Jane.

And sometimes she would go to the cabins of other women, and gossip. And sometimes she would flirt with a young miner or prospector who seemed handsome. And she would get back her young, gay liveliness and freedom.

But when the man she flirted with wanted to kiss her, or put his arm round her waist, she found it made her go cold and savagely hostile. It was not as in the old days, when it gave her a thrill to be seized and kissed, whether by Easu, by Percy or Jack or whatever man it was she was flirting with. Then, there had been a spark between her and many a man. But now, alas, the spark wouldn't fly. The man might be never so good-looking and likeable, yet when he touched her, instead of the spark flying from her to him, immediately all the spark went dead in her. And this left her so angry, she could kill herself, or so wretched, she couldn't even cry.

That little goggle-eyed imp of a Jane, in spite of her one solitary year of age, seemed somehow to divine what was happening inside her mother's breast, and she seemed to chuckle wickedly. Monica always felt that the brat knew, and that she took Jack's side.

Jane always wanted Jack to come back. When he was away, she would toddle about on her own little affairs, curiously complacent and impervious to outer influences. But if she heard a horse coming up to the hut, she was at the door in a flash. And Monica saw with a pang, how steadily intent the brat was on the man's return. Somehow, from Jane, Monica knew that Jack would go with other women. Because of the spark that flashed to him from that brat of a baby of Easu's.

And at evening, Jane hated going to bed if Jack hadn't come home. She would be a real little hell-monkey. It was as if she felt the house wasn't safe, wasn't real, till he had come in.

Which annoyed Monica exceedingly. Why wasn't the mother enough for the child?

But she wasn't. And when Jane was in bed, Monica would take up the uneasiness of the manless house. She would sit like a cat shut up in a strange room, unable to settle, unable really to rest, and hating the night for having come and surprised her in her empty loneliness. Her loneliness might be really enjoyable during the day. But after nightfall it was empty, sterile, a mere oppression to her. She wished he would come home, if only so that she could hate him.

And she felt a flash of joy when she heard his footstep on the stones outside, even if the flash served only to kindle a great resentment against him. And he would come in, with his burnt, half-seeing face, unsuccessful, worn, silent, yet not uncheerful. And he spoke his few rather low words, from his chest, asking her something. And she knew he had come back to her. But where from, and what from, she would never know entirely.

She had always known where Percy had been, and what he had been doing. She felt she would always have known, with Easu. But with Jack she never knew. And sometimes this infuriated her. But it was no good. He would tell her anything she asked. And then she felt there was something she couldn't ask about.

The months went by. He staked his claim, and worked like a navvy. He *was* a navvy, nothing but a navvy. And she was a navvy's wife, in a hut of one room, in a desert of heat and sand and grey-coloured bush, sleeping on a piece of canvas stretched on a low trestle, eating on a tin plate, eating sand by the mouthful when the wind blew. Percy's baby was dead and buried in the sand : another sop to the avid country. And she herself was with child again, and thin as a rat. But it was his child this time, so she had a certain savage satisfaction in it.

He went on working at his claim. It was now more than a year he had spent at this game of looking for gold, and he had hardly found a cent's worth. They were very poor, in debt to the keeper of the store. But everybody had a queer respect for Jack. They dared not be very familiar with him, but they didn't resent him. He had a good aura. The other men might jeer sometimes at his frank but unapproachable aloofness, his subtle sort of delicacy, and his simple sort of pride. Yet when he was spoken to, his answer was so much in the spirit of the question, so frank, that you couldn't resent him. In ordinary things he was gay and completely one of themselves. The self that was beyond them he never let intrude. Hence their curious respect for him.

Because there was something unordinary in him. The

biggest part of himself he kept entirely to himself, and a curious sombre steadfastness inside him made shifty men uneasy with him. He could never completely mix in, in the vulgar way, with men. He would take a drink with the rest, and laugh and talk half an hour away. Even get a bit tipsy and talk rather brilliantly. But always, always at the back of his eyes was this sombre aloofness, that could never come forward and meet and mingle, but held back, apart, waiting.

They called him, after his father, the General. But never was a General with so small an army at his command. He was playing a lone hand. The mate he was working with suddenly chucked up the job and travelled away, and the General went on alone. He moved about the camp at his ease. When he sat in the bar drinking his beer with the other men, he was really alone, and they knew it. But he had a good aura, so they felt a certain real respect for his loneliness. And when he was there they talked and behaved as if in the aura of a certain blood-purity, although he was in rags, for Monica hated sewing and couldn't bear, simply couldn't bear to mend his old shirts and trousers. And there was no money to buy new.

He held on. He did not get depressed or melancholy. When he got absolutely stumped, he went away and did hired work for a spell. Then he came back to the gold field. He was now nothing but a miner. The miner's instinct had developed in him. He had to wait for his instinct to perfect itself. He knew that. He knew he was not a man to be favoured by blind luck. Whatever he won, he must win by mystic conquest.

If he wanted gold he must master it in the veins of the earth. He knew this. And for this reason he gave way neither to melancholy nor to impatience. " If I can't win," he said to himself, " it's because I'm not master of the thing I'm up against."

" If I can't win, I'll die fighting," he said to himself. " But in the end I will win."

There was nothing to do but to fight, and fight on. This was his creed. And a fighter has no use for melancholy and impatience.

He saw the fight his boyhood had been, against his aunts, and school and college. He didn't want to be made *quite* tame, and they had wanted to tame him, like all the rest. His father was a good man and a good soldier : but a tame one. He himself was not a soldier, nor even a good man. But also he was not tame. Not a tame dog, like all the rest.

For this reason he had come to Australia, away from the welter of vicious tameness. For tame dogs are far more vicious than wild ones. Only they can be brought to heel.

In Australia, a new sort of fight. A fight with tame dogs that were playing wild. Easu was a tame dog, playing the wolf in a mongrel, back-biting way. Tame dogs escaped and became licentious. That was Australia. He knew that.

But they were not all quite tame. Tom, the safe Tom, had salt of wild savour still in his blood. And Lennie had his wild streak. So had Monica. So, somewhere had the à terre Mary. Some odd freakish wildness of the splendid, powerful, wild, old English blood.

Jack had escaped the tamers : they couldn't touch him now. He had escaped the insidious tameness, the slight degeneracy, of Wandoo. He had learned the tricks of the escaped tame dogs who played at licentiousness. And he had mastered Monica, who had wanted to be a domestic bitch playing wild. He had captured her wildness, to mate his own wildness.

It was no good *playing* wild. If he had any real wildness in him, it was dark, and wary, and collected, self-responsible, and of unbreakable steadfastness : like the wildness of a wolf or a fox, that knows it will die if it is caught.

If you had a tang of the old wildness in you, you ran with the most intense wariness, knowing that the good tame dogs are really turning into licentious, vicious tame dogs. The vicious tame dogs, pretending to be wild, hate the real clean wildness of an unbroken thing much more than do the respectable tame people.

No, if you refuse to be tamed, you have to be most wary, most subtle, on your guard all the time. You can't afford to be licentious. If you are, you will die in the trap. For the world is a great trap set wide for the unwary.

Jack had learned all these things. He refused to be tamed. He knew that the dark kingdom of death ahead had no room for tame dogs. They merely were put into earth as carrion. Only the wild, untamed souls walked on after death over the border into the porch of death, to be lords of death and masters of the next living. This he knew. The tame dogs were put into the earth as carrion, like Easu and Percy's poor little baby, and Jacob Ellis. He often wondered if that courageous old witch-cat of a Gran had slipped into the halls of death, to be one of the ladies of the dark. The lords of death, and the ladies of the dark! He would take his own Monica over the border when she died. She would sit unbroken, a quiet, fearless bride in the dark chambers of the dead, the dead who order the goings of the next living.

That was the goal of the afterwards, that he had at the back of his eyes. But meanwhile here on earth he had to win. He had to make room again on earth for those who are not unbroken, those who are not tamed to carrion. Some place for those who know the dark mystery of being royal in death, so that they can enact the shadow of their own royalty on earth. Some place for the souls that are in themselves dark and have some of the sumptuousness of proud death, no matter what their fathers were. Jack's father was tame, as kings and dukes to-day are almost mongrelly tame. But Jack was not tame. And Easu's weird baby was not tame. She had some of the eternal fearlessness of the aristocrat whose bones are pure. But a weird sort of aristocrat.

Jack wanted to make a place on earth for a few aristo-crats-to-the-bone. He wanted to conquer the world.

And first he must conquer gold. As things are, only the tame go out and conquer gold, and make a lucrative tameness. The untamed forfeit their gold.

" I must conquer gold! " said Jack to himself. " I must open the veins of the earth and bleed the power of gold into my own veins, for the fulfilling of the aristocrats of the bone. I must bring the great stream of gold flowing in another direction, away from the veins of the tame ones, into the veins of the lords of death. I must start the river of wealth of the world rolling in a new course, down the sombre, quiet, proud valleys of the lords of death and the ladies of the dark, the aristocrats of the afterwards."

So he talked to himself, as he wandered alone in his search, or sat on the bench with a pot of beer, or stepped into Monica's hot little hut. And when he failed he knew it was because he had not fought intensely enough, and subtly enough.

The bad food, the climate, the hard life gave him a sort of fever and an eczema. But it was no matter. That was only the pulp of him paying the penalty. The powerful skeleton he was was powerful as ever. The pulp of him, his belly, his heart, his muscle seemed not to be able to affect his strength, or at least his power, for more than a short time. Sometimes he broke down. Then he would think what he could do with himself, do for himself, for his flesh and blood. And what he *could* do, he would do. And when he could do no more, he would go and lie down in the mine, or hidden in some shade, lying on the earth, alone, away from anything human. Till the earth itself gave him back his power. Till the powerful living skeleton of him resumed its sway and serenity and fierce power.

He knew he was winning, winning slowly, even in his fight with the earth, his fight for gold. It was on the cards he might die before his victory. Then it would be death, he would have to accept it. He would have to go into death, and leave Monica and Jane and the coming baby to fate.

Meanwhile, he would fight, and fight on. The baby was near, there was no money. He had to stay and watch Monica. She, poor thing, went to bed with twins, two boys. There was nothing hardly left of her. He had to give up everything, even his thoughts, and bend his whole life to her, to help her through, and save her and the two quite healthy baby boys. For a month he was doctor and nurse and housewife and husband, and he gave himself absolutely to the work, without a moment's failing. Poor Monica, when she couldn't bear herself, he held her hips together with his arm, and she clung to his neck for life.

This time he almost gave up. He almost decided to go and hire himself out to steady work, to keep her and the babies in peace and safety. To be a hired workman for the rest of his days.

And as he sat with his eyes dark and unchanging, ready to accept this fate, since this his fate must be, came a letter from Mr George with an enclosure from England and a cheque for fifty pounds, a legacy from one of the aunts who had so benevolently died at the right moment. He

decided his dark Lord did not intend him to go and hire
himself out for life, as a hired labourer. He decided Monica
and the babies did not want the peace and safety of a hired
labourer's cottage. Perhaps better die and be buried in
the sand and leave their skeletons like white messengers in
the ground of this Australia.

So he went back to his working. And three days later
struck gold, so that there was gold on his pick-point. He
was alone, and he refused at first to get excited. But his
trained instinct knew that it was a rich lode. He worked
along the vein, and felt the rich weight of the yellow-
streaked stuff he fetched out. The light-coloured softish
stuff. He sat looking at it in his hand, and the glint of it
in the dark earth-rock of the mine, in the light of the
lamp. And his bowels leaped in him, knowing that the
white gods of tameness would wilt and perish as the pale
gold flowed out of their veins.

There would be a place on earth for the lords of death.
His own Lord had at last spoken.

Jack sent quickly for Lennie to come and work with him.
For Lennie, with a wife and a child, was struggling very
hard.

Len and Tom both came. Jack had not expected Tom.
But Tom lifted his brown eyes to Jack and said :

" I sortta felt I couldn't stand even Len being mates
with you, an' me not there. I was your first mate, Jack.
I've never been myself since I parted with you."

" All right," laughed Jack. " You're my first
mate."

" That's what I am, General," said Tom.

Jack had showed Monica some of the ore, and told her
the mine seemed to be turning out fairly. She was getting
back her own strength, that those two monstrous young
twins had almost robbed from her entirely. Jack was very
careful of her. He wanted above all things that she should
become really strong again.

And she, with her rare vitality, soon began to bloom once
more. And as her strength came back she was very much
taken up with her babies. These were the first she had
enjoyed. The other two she had never really enjoyed. But
with these she was as fussy as a young cat with her kittens.
She almost forgot Jack entirely. Left him to be busy with

Tom and Lennie and his mine. Even the gold failed to excite her.

And she had rather a triumph. She was able to be queenly again with Tom and Lennie. As a girl she had always been a bit queenly with the rest of them at Wandoo. And she couldn't bear to be humiliated in their eyes.

Now she needn't. She had the General for her husband, she had his twins. And *he* had gold in his mine. Hadn't she a perfect right to be queenly with Tom and Lennie? She even got into the habit, right at the beginning, of speaking of Jack as " the General " to them.

" Where's the General? Didn't he come down with you? " she would snap at them, in her old, sparky fashion.

" He's reviewing his troops," Lennie sarcastically answered.

Whereupon Jack appeared in the door, still in rags. And it was Lennie who mended his shirt for him, when it was torn on the shoulder and showed the smooth man underneath. Monica still couldn't bring herself to these fiddling jobs.

CHAP : XXIV. THE OFFER TO MARY

i

THEY worked for months at the mine, and still it turned out richly. Though they kept as quiet as possible, the fame spread. They had a bonanza. They were all three going to be rich, and Jack was going to be very rich. In the light of his luck, he was " the General " to everybody.

And in the midst of this flow of fortune, came another, rather comical windfall. Again the news was forwarded by Mr George, along with a word of congratulation from that gentleman. The forwarded letter read :

" Dear Sir,
This come hopping to find you well as it leaves me at prisent thanks be to almity God. Your dear uncle Passed Away peaceful on Satterday nite And though it be not my place to tell you of it i am Grateful to have the oppertunity to offer my umble Respecs before the lord and Perlice I take up my pen with pleashr to inform you that He passed without Pain and even Drafts as he aloud the umberrela to be put down and the Book read.

" The 24 salm and i kep the ink and paper by to rite of his sudden dismiss but he lingered long years after the bote wint so was onable to Inform you before he desist the doctor rote a butiful certicket of death saying he did of sensible decay but I don no how he brote himself to rite it as the pore master was wite as driven snow and no blemish. And being his most umble and Dutiful servants we could not ave brout ourself to hever ave rote as he was sensible Pecos god knows the pore sole was not. be that as it may we burried him proud under the prisent arrangements of town council the clerk was prisent xpects the doctors will he mad up the nite you was hear in the cimetary and pending your Return Holds It In Bond as Being rite for us we are Yor Respectable servants to Oblige Hand Commend

EMMA and AMOS LEWIS."

Jack and Tom roared with laughter over this epistle, that brought back so vividly the famous trip up north.

" Gloryanna, General, you've got your property at Coney Hatch all right," said Tom.

There was a letter from Mr George saying that the defunct John Grant was the son of Jack's mother's elder sister, that he had been liable all his life to bouts of temporary insanity, but that in a period of sanity he had signed the will drawn up by Dr. Rackett, when the two boys called at the place several years before, and that the will had been approved. So that Jack, as legal heir and nearest male relative, could now come down and take possesion of the farm.

" I don't want that dismal place," said Jack. " Let it go to the Crown. I've no need of it now."

" Don't be a silly cuckoo ! " said Tom. " You saw it of a wet night with Ally Sloper in bed under a green cart-umbrella. Go an' look at it of a fine day. An' then if you don't want it, sell it or lease it, but don't let the Crown rake it in."

So in about a fortnight's time Jack rather reluctantly left the mine, with its growing heaps of refuse, and departed from the mining settlement which had become a sort of voluntary prison for him, and went west to Perth. He was already a rich man and notorious in the colony. He rode with two pistols in his belt, and that unchanging aloof look on his face. But he carried himself with pride, rode a good horse, wore well-made riding breeches and a fine bandanna handkerchief loose round his neck, and looked, with a silver studded band round his broad felt hat, a mixture of gold miner, a gentleman settler, and a bandit chief. Perhaps he felt a mixture of them all.

Mr George received him with a great welcome. And Jack was pleased to see the old man. But he refused absolutely to go to the club or to the Government House, or to meet any of the responsible people of the town.

" I don't want to see them, Mr George. I don't want to see them."

And poor old George, his nose a bit out of joint, had to submit to leaving Jack alone.

Jack had his old room in Mr George's house. The Good Plain Cook was still going. And Aunt Matilda, rather older, stouter, with more lines in her facce, came to tea with Mary and Miss Blessington. Mary had not married Mr Blessington. But she had remained friends with the odd daughter, who was now a self-contained young woman, shy, thin, well-bred, and delicate. Mr Blessington had not married again. In Aunt Matilda's opinion, he was still waiting for Mary. And Mary had refused Tom's rather doubtful offer. Tom was still nervous about Honeysuckle. So there they all were.

When Jack shook hands with Mary he had a slight shock. He had forgotten her. She had gone out of his consciousness. But when she looked up at him with her dark, clear, waiting eyes, as if she had been watching and waiting for him afar off, his heart gave a queer, dizzy lurch. He had forgotten her. They say the heart has a short memory. But now, as a dark hotness gathered in his heart, he realised that his blood had not forgotten her. He had only forgotten her with his head. His blood, with its strange submissiveness and its strange unawareness of time, had kept her just the same.

The blood has an eternal memory. It neither forgets nor moves on ahead. But it is quiescent and submits to the mind's oversway.

He had a certain blood-connection with Mary. He had utterly forgotten it, in the stress and rage of other things. And now, the moment she lifted her eyes to him, and he saw her dusky, quiet, heavy, permanent face, the dull heat started in his breast again, and he remembered how he had told her he would come for her again.

Since his twins were born and he had been so busy with the mine, and he had Monica, he had not given any thought to women. But the moment he saw Mary and met her eyes, the dark thought struck home in him again : I want Mary for my other woman. He didn't want to displace Monica. Monica was Monica. But he wanted this other woman, too.

Aunt Matilda " dear-boyed " him more than ever. But now he was not a dear boy, he didn't feel a dear boy, and she was put out.

" Dear boy ! and how does Monica stand that trying climate ? "

" She is quite well again, Marm."

" Poor child ! Poor child ! I hope you will bring her into a suitable home here in Perth, and have the children suitably brought up. It is so *fortunate* for you your mine is so successful. Now you can build a home here by the river, among us all, and be charming company for us, like you dear father.''

Mary was watching him with black eyes, and Miss Blessington with her wide, quick, round, dark-grey eyes. There was a frail beauty about that odd young woman; frail, highly-bred, sensitive, with an uncanny intelligence.

'' No, Marm,'' said Jack cheerfully. '' I shall not come and live in Perth.''

'' Dear boy, of course you will. You won't forsake us and take your money and your family and your attractive self far away to England? No, don't do that. It is just what your dear father did. Robbed us of one of our sweetest girls, and never came back.''

'' No, I shan't go to England, either,'' smiled Jack.

'' Then what will you do? ''

'' Stay at the mine for the time being.''

'' Oh, but the mine won't last for ever. And, dear boy, don't waste your talents and your charm mining, when it is no longer necessary ! Oh, do come down to Perth, and bring your family. Mary is pining to see your twins : and dear Monica. Of course we all are.''

Jack smiled to himself. He would no longer give in a hair's breadth to any of these dreary world-people.

'' A la bonne heure ! '' he said, using one of his mother's well-worn tags. But then his mother could rattle bad colloquial French, and he couldn't.

Mary asked him many questions about the mine and Monica, and Hilda Blessington listened with lowered head, only occasionally fixing him with queer, searching eyes, like some odd creature not quite human. Jack was something of a hero. And he was pleased. He wanted to be a hero.

But he was no hero any more for Aunt Matilda. Now that the cherub look had gone for ever, and the shy, blushing, blurting boy had turned into a hard-boned, healthy young man with a half haughty aloofness and a little reckless smile that made you feel uncomfortable, she was driven to venting some venom on him.

'' That is the worst of the colonies,'' she said from her bluish powdered face. '' Our most charming, cultured young men go out to the back of beyond, and they come home quite—quite—— "

" Quite what, Marm ? "

" Why, I was going to say uncouth, but that's perhaps a little strong."

" I should say not at all," he answered. He disliked the old lady, and enjoyed baiting her. Great stout old hen, she had played cock-o'-the-walk long enough.

" How many children have you got out there ? " she suddenly asked, rudely.

" We have only the twins of my own," he answered. " But, of course, there is Jane."

" Jane ! Jane ! Which is Jane ? "

" Jane is Easu's child. Monica's first."

Everybody started. It was as if a bomb had been dropped in the room. Miss Blessington coloured to the roots of her fleecy brown hair. Mary studied her fingers, and Aunt Matilda sat in a Queen Victoria statue pose, outraged.

" What is she like ? " asked Mary softly, looking up.

" Who, Jane ? She's a funny little urchin. I'm fond of her. I believe she'd always stand by me."

Mary looked at him. It was a curious thing to say.

" Is that how you think of people—whether they would always stand by you or not ? " she asked softly.

" I suppose it is," he laughed. " Courage is the first quality in life, don't you think ? and fidelity the next."

" Fidelity ? " asked Mary.

" Oh, I don't mean automatic fidelity. I mean faithful to the living spark," he replied a little hastily.

" Don't you try to be too much of a spark, young man," snapped Aunt Matilda, arousing from her statuesque offence in order to let nothing pass by her.

" I promise you I won't try," he laughed.

Mary glanced at him quickly—then down at her fingers.

" I think fidelity is a great problem," she said softly.

" Pray why," bounced Aunt Matilda. " You give your word, and you stick to it."

" Oh, it's not just simple word-faithfulness, Mrs Watson," said Jack. He had Mary in mind.

" Well, I suppose I have still to live and learn," said Aunt Matilda

" What's that you have still to live and learn, Matilda? "
said Mr George, coming in again with papers.

" This young man is teaching me lessons about life.
Courage is the first quality in life, if you please."

" Well, why not? " said Old George amiably. " I like
spunk myself."

" Courage to do the right thing ! " said Aunt Matilda.

" And who's going to decide which is the right thing? "
asked the old man, teasing her.

" There's no question of it," said Aunt Matilda.

" Well," said the old lawyer rubbing his head, " there
often is, my dear woman, a very big question ! "

" And fidelity is the second virtue," said Mary, looking
up at him with trustful eyes, enquiringly.

" A man's no good unless he can keep faith," said the
old man.

" But what is it one must remain faithful to? " came the
quiet, cool voice of Hilda Blessington.

" Do you know what old Gran Ellis said? " asked Jack.
" She said a man's own true self is God in him. She was
a queer old bird."

" His *true* self," said Aunt Matilda. " His true self !
And I should say old Mrs Ellis was a doubtful guide to
young people, judging from her own family."

" She made a great impression on me, Marm," said Jack
politely.

Mr George had brought the papers referring to the new
property. Jack read various documents, rather absently.
Then the title deeds. Then he studied a fascinating little
green-and-red map, " delineating and setting forth," with
" easements and encumbrances," whatever they were.
There was a bank-book showing a balance of four hundred
pounds nineteen shillings and sixpence, in the West
Australian Bank.

Jack told about his visit to Grant farm, and the man
under the umbrella. They all laughed.

" The poor fellow had a bad start," said Mr George.
" But he was a good farmer and a good business man, in
his right times. Oh, he knew who he was leaving the place
to, when Rackett drew up that will."

" Gran Ellis told me about him," said Jack. " She told
me about all the old people. She told me about my mother's

old sister. And she told me about the father of this crazy man as well, but—— ''

Mr George was looking at him coldly and fiercely.

'' The poor fellow's father,'' the old man said, '' was an Englishman who thought himself a swell, but wasn't too much of a high-born gentleman to abandon a decent girl and go round to the east side and marry another woman, and flaunt round in society with women he hadn't married.''

Jack remembered. It was Mary's father : seventh son of old Lord Haworth. What a mix up ! How bitter old George sounded !

'' It seems to have been a mighty mix-up out here, fifty years ago, sir,'' he said mildly.

'' It was a mix-up then—and is a mix-up now.''

'' I suppose,'' said Jack, '' if the villain of a gentleman had never abandoned my aunt—I can't think of her as an aunt—he'd never have gone to Sydney, and his children that he had there would never have been born.''

'' I suppose not,'' said Mr George drily. But he started a little and involuntarily looked at Mary.

'' Do you think it would have been better if they had never been born ? '' Jack asked pertinently.

'' I don't set up to judge,'' said the old man.

'' Does Mrs Watson ? ''

'' I certainly think it would be better,'' said Mrs Watson, '' if that poor half-idiot cousin of yours had never been born.''

'' I've got Gran Ellis on my mind,'' said Jack. '' She was funny, what she condemned and what she didn't. I used to think she was an old terror. But I can understand her better now. She was a wise woman, seems to me.''

'' Indeed ! '' said Aunt Matilda. '' I never put her and wisdom together.''

'' Yes, she was wise. I can see now. She knew that sins are as vital a part of life as virtues, and she stuck up for the sins that are necessary to life.''

'' What's the matter with you, Jack Grant, that you go and start moralising ? '' said Old George.

'' Why, sir, it must be that my own sinful state is dawning on my mind,'' said Jack, '' and I'm wondering whether to take Mrs Watson's advice and repent and weep, etc., etc.

Or whether to follow old Gran Ellis' lead, and put a sinful feather in my cap."

" Well," said Old George, smiling, " I don't know. You talk about courage and fidelity. Sin usually means doing something rather cowardly, and breaking your faith in some direction."

" Oh, I don't know, sir. Tom and Lennie are faithful to me. But that doesn't mean they are not free. They are free to do just what they like, so long as they are faithful to the spark that is between us. As I am faithful to them. It seems to me, sir, one is true to one's *word* in *business*, in affairs. But in life one can only be true to the spark."

" I'm afraid there's something amiss with you, son, that's set you off arguing and splitting hairs."

" There is. Something is always amiss with most of us. Old Gran Ellis was a lesson to me, if I'd known. Something is always wrong with the lot of us. And I believe in thinking before I act."

" Let us hope so," said Mr George. " But it sounds funny sort of thinking you do."

" But," said Hilda Blessington, with wide, haunted eyes, " what is the spark that one must be faithful to? How are we to be sure of it? "

" You just feel it. And then you act upon it. That's courage. And then you always live up to the responsibility of your act. That's faithfulness. You have to keep faith in all kinds of ways. I have to keep faith with Monica, and the babies, and young Jane, and Lennie, and Tom, and dead Gran Ellis : and—and more—yes, more."

He looked with clear, hard eyes at Mary, and at the young girl. They were both watching him, puzzled and perturbed. The two old people in the background were silent but hostile.

" Do you know what I am faithful to? " he said, still to the two young women, but letting the elders hear. " I am faithful to my own inside, when something stirs in me. Gran Ellis said that was God in me. I know there's a God outside of me. But he tells me to go my own way, and never be frightened of people and the world, only be frightened of him. And if I felt I really wanted two wives, for example, I would have them and keep them both. If I really wanted them, it would mean it was the God outside me bidding me, and it would be up to me to obey, world or no world."

" You describe exactly the devil driving you," said Aunt Matilda.

" Doesn't he ! " laughed Mr George, who was oddly impressed. " I only hope there isn't a streak of madness in the family."

" No there's not. The world is all so tame, it's like an idiot to me, a dangerous idiot. So that if I do want two wives—or even three—well, I *do*. Why listen to the Idiot."

" Sounds like *you'd* gone cracked out there in that mining settlement," said Mr George.

" If I said I wanted two fortunes instead of one," said Jack, with a malicious smile, " you wouldn't think it cracked."

" No, only greedy," said Old George.

" Not if I could use them. And the same if I can really value two wives, and use them—or even three "—Jack glanced with a queer, bright grin at Hilda Blessington— " Well, three wives would be three fortunes for my blood and spirit."

" For your wickedness," said Aunt Matilda. " You are not allowed to say such things, even in joke."

" Surely I may say them in dead earnest," persisted Jack mischievously. He was aware of Mary and Hilda Blessington listening, and he wanted to throw a sort of lasso over them.

" You'll merely find yourself in gaol for bigamy," said Mr George.

" Oh," said Jack, " I wouldn't risk that. It would really be a Scotch marriage. Monica is my legal wife. But what I pledged myself to, I'd stick to, as I stick to Monica. I'd stick to the others the same."

" I won't hear any more of this nonsense," said Aunt Matilda, rising.

" Nonsense it is," said Old George testily.

Jack laughed. Their being bothered amused him. He was a little surprised at himself breaking out in this way. But the sight of Mary, and the sense of a new, different responsibility, had struck it out of him. His nature was ethical, inclined to be emotionally mystical. Now, however, the sense of foolish complacency, and empty assurance in Aunt Matilda, and in all the dead-certain people of this world struck out of him a hard, sharp, non-emotional opposition. He felt hard and mischievous, confronting them. Who were they, to judge and go on judging? Who was Aunt Matilda, to judge the dead fantastic soul of the fierce Gran? The Ellises, the Ellises they all had some of Gran's fierce pagan uneasiness about them, they were all a bit uncanny. That was why he loved them so.

And Mary! Mary had another slow, heavy, mute mystery that waited and waited for ever, like a lode stone. And should he therefore abandon her, abandon her society and a sort of sterility? Not he. She was his to fertilise. His, and no other man's. She knew it herself. He knew it. Then he would fight them all. Even the good old George. For the mystery that was his and Mary's.

Let it be an end of popular goodness. Let there be another deeper, fiercer, untamed sort of goodness, like in the days of Abraham and Samson and Saul. If Jack was to be good he would be good with these great old men, the heroic fathers, not with the saints. The christian goodness had gone bad, decayed almost into poison. It needed again the old heroic goodness of untamed men, with the wild great God who was for ever too unknown to be a paragon.

Old George was a little afraid of Jack, uneasy about him. He thought him not normal. The boy had to be put in a category by himself, like a madman in a solitary cell. And at the same time, the old man was delighted. He was delighted with the young man's physical presence. Bewildered by the careless, irrational things Jack would say, the old bachelor took off his spectacles and rubbed his tired eyes again and again, as if he were going blind, and as if he were losing his old dominant will.

He had been a dominant character in the colony so long. And now this young fellow was laughing at him and stealing away his power of resistance.

"Don't make eyes at me, sir," said Jack laughing. "I know better than you what life means."

"You do, do you? Oh, you do?" said the old man. And he laughed too. Somehow it made him feel warm and easy. "A fine crazy affair it would be if it were left to you." And he laughed loud at the absurdity.

ii

Jack persuaded Mary to go with Mr George and himself to look at Grant Farm. Mary and the old lawyer went in a buggy, Jack rode his own horse. And it seemed to him to be good to be out again in the bush and forest country. It was rainy season, and the smell of the earth was delicious in his nostrils.

He decided soon to leave the mine. It was running thin. He could leave it in charge of Tom. And then he must make some plans for himself. Perhaps he would come and live on the Grant farm. It was not too far from Perth, or from Wandoo, it was in the hills, the climate was balmy and almost English, after the gold-fields, and there were trees. He really rejoiced again, riding through strong, living trees.

Sometimes he would ride up beside Mary. She sat very still at Mr George's side, talking to him in her quick, secret-seeming way. Mary always looked as if the things she was saying were secrets.

And her upper lip with its down of fine dark hair, would lift and show her white teeth as she smiled with her mouth. She only smiled with her mouth : her eyes remained dark and glistening and unchanged. But she talked a great deal to Mr George, almost like lovers, they were so confidential and so much in tune with one another. It was as if Mary was happy with an old man's love, that was fatherly, warm and sensuous, and wise and talkative, without being at all dangerous.

When Jack rode up she seemed to snap the thread of her communication with Mr George, her ready volubility failed, and she was a little nervous. Her eyes, her dark eyes, were afraid of the young man. Yet they would give him odd, bright, corner-wise looks, almost inviting. So different from the full, confident way she looked at Mr George. So different from Monica's queer yellow glare. Mary seemed almost to peep at him, while her dark face, like an animal's muzzle with its slightly heavy mouth, remained quite expressionless.

It amused him. He remembered how he had kissed her, and he wondered if she remembered. It was impossible, of course, to ask her. And when she talked, it was always so seriously. That again amused Jack. She was so voluble, especially with Mr George, on all kinds of deep and difficult subjects. She was quite excited just now about authoritarianism. She was being drawn by the Roman Catholic Church.

" Oh," she was saying, " I am an authoritarian. Don't you think that the whole natural scheme is a scheme of authority, one rank having authority over another ? "

Mr George couldn't quite see it. Yet it tickled his paternal male conceit of authority, so he didn't contradict her. And Jack smiled to himself. " She runs too much to talk," he thought. " She runs too much in her head." She seemed, indeed, to have forgotten quite how he kissed her. It seemed that " questions of the day " quite absorbed her.

They came through the trees in the soft afternoon sunshine. Jack remembered the place well. He remembered the Jamboree, and that girl who had called him Dearie ! His first woman ! And insignificant enough : but not bad. He thought kindly of her. She was a warm-hearted soul. But she didn't belong to his life at all. He remembered, too, how he had kicked Tom. The faithful Tom ! Mary would never marry Tom, that was a certainty. And it was equally certain Tom would never break his heart.

Jack was thinking to himself that he would build a new house on this place, and ask Mary to live in the old house. That was a brilliant idea.

But as he drove up he thought : " The first money you spend on this place, my boy, will be on a brand new five-barred white gate."

Emma and Amos came out full of joy. They, too, were a faithful old pair. Jack handed Mary down. She wore a dark blue dress and white silk gloves. It was so like her to put on white silk gloves. But he liked the touch of them, as he handed her down. Her small, short, rather passive hands.

He and she walked round the place, and she was very much interested. A new place, a new farm, a new undertaking always excited her, as if it was she who was making the new move.

" Don't you think *that* will be a good place for the new house ? " he was saying to her. " Down there, near that jolly bunch of old trees. And the garden south of the trees. If you dig in that flat you'll find water, sure to."

She inspected the place most carefully, and uttered her mature judgments.

" You'll have to help think it out," he said. " Monica's as different as an opossum. Would you like to build yourself a house here, and tend to things? I'll build you one if you like. Or give you the old one."

She looked at him with glowing eyes.

" Wouldn't that be splendid ! " she said. " Oh, wouldn't that be splendid ! If I had a house and a piece of land of my own ! Oh, yes ! "

" Well, I can easily give it you," he said. " Just whatever you like."

" Isn't that lovely ! " she exclaimed.

But he could tell she was thinking merely of the house and the bit of land, and herself a sort of Auntie to his and Monica's children. She was fairly jumping into old-maiddom, both feet first. Which was not what he intended. He didn't want her as an Auntie for his children.

They went back to the house, and inspected there. She liked it. It was a stone one-storey house with a great kitchen and three other rooms, all rather low and homely. The dead cousin had wanted his house to be exactly like the houses of the other respectable farmers. And he had not been prevented.

The place was a bit tumble-down, but clean. Emma was baking scones, and the sweet smell of scorched flour filled the house. Mary lit the lamp in the little parlour, and set it on the highly-polished but rather ricketty rose-wood table, next the photograph album. The family Bible had been removed to the bed-room. But the old man had a photograph album, like any other respectable householder.

Mary drew up one of the green-rep chairs, and opened the book. Jack, looking over her shoulder, started a little as he saw the first photograph : an elderly lady in lace cap and voluminous silken skirts was seated reading a book, while negligently leaning with one hand on her chair was a gentleman with long white trousers and old fashioned coat and side whiskers, obviously having his photograph taken.

This was the identical photograph which held place of honour in Jack's mother's album; the photograph of her father and mother.

" See ! " said Jack. " That's my grandfather and grandmother. And he must have been the man who took Gran Ellis' leg off. Goodness ! "

Mary gazed at them closely.

" He looks a domineering man ! " she said. " I hope you're not like him."

Jack didn't feel at all like him. Mary turned over, and they beheld two young ladies of the Victorian period. Somebody had marked a cross, in ink, over the head of one of the young ladies. They must be his own aunts, both of them many years older than his own mother, who was a late arrival.

" Do you think that was his mother ? " said Mary, looking up at Jack, who stood at her side. " She was beautiful."

Jack studied the photograph of the young woman. She looked like nobody's mother on earth, with her hair curiously rolled and curled, and a great dress flouncing round her. And her beauty was so photographic and abstract, he merely gazed seeking for it.

But Mary, looking up at him, saw his silent face in the glow of the lamp, his rather grim mouth closed ironically under his moustache, his open nostrils, and the long, steady, self-contained look of his eyes under his lashes. He was not thinking of her at all, at the moment. But his calm, rather distant, unconsciously imperious face was something quite new and startling, and rather frightening to her. She became intensely aware of his thighs standing close against her, and her heart went faint. She was afraid of him.

In agitation she was going to turn the leaf. But he put his work-hardened hand on the page, and turned back to the first photograph.

" Look ! " he said. " *He* "—pointing to his grandfather —" disowned her "—turning to the aunt marked with a cross—" and she died an outcast, in misery, and her son burrowed here, half crazy. Yet their two faces are rather alike. Gran Ellis told me about them."

Mary studied them.

" They are both a bit like yours," she said, " their faces."

" Mine ! " he exclaimed. " Oh, no ! I look like my father's family."

He could see no resemblance at all to himself in the handsome, hard-mouthed, large man, with the clean face and the fringe of fair whiskers, and the black cravat, and the overbearing look.

" Your eyes are set in the same way," she said. " And your brows are the same. But your mouth is not so tight."

" I don't like what I heard of him, anyhow," said Jack. " A puritanical surgeon ! Turn over."

She turned over and gave a low cry. There was a photograph of a young elegant with drooping black moustachios, and mutton-chop side whiskers, and large, languid, black eyes, leaning languidly and swinging a cane. Over the top was written, in a weird hand-writing :

The Honourable George Rath, blasted father of

This skull and cross-bones was repeated on the other sides of the photograph.

" Oh ! " said Mary, covering her face with her hands.

Jack's face was a study. Mary had evidently recognised the photograph of her father as a young man. Yet Jack could not help smiling at the skull and cross-bones, in connection with the Bulwer Lytton young elegant, and the man under the green umbrella.

" My God ! " he thought to himself. " All that happens in a generation ! From that sniffy young dude to that fellow here who made this farm, and Mary with her face in her hands ! "

He could not help smiling to himself.

" Had you seen that photograph before ? " he asked her. She, unable to answer, kept her face in her hands.

" Don't worry," he said. " We're all more or less that way. We're none of us perfect."

Still she did not answer. Then he went on, almost without thinking, as he studied the rather fetching young gentleman with the long black hair and bold black eyes, and the impudent, handsome, languid lips :

" You're a bit like *him*, too. You're a bit like him in the look of your eyes. I bet he wasn't tall either. I bet he was rather small."

Mary took her hands from her face and looked up fierce and angry.

" You have no feeling," she said.

" I have," he replied, smiling slightly. " But life seems to me too rummy to get piqued about it. Think of him

leaving a son like the fellow I saw under the umbrella!
Think of it! Such a dandy! And that his son! And then
having you for a daughter when he was getting quite on in
years. Do you remember him? "

" How can you talk to me like that? " she said.

" But why? It's life. It's how it was. Do you remember your father? "

" Of course I do."

" Did he dye his whiskers? "

" I won't answer you."

" Well, don't then. But this man under the umbrella
here—you should have seen him—was your half-brother
and my cousin. It makes us almost related."

Mary left the room. In a few minutes Mr George came
in.

" What's wrong with Mary? " he asked, suspiciously,
angrily.

Jack shrugged his shoulders, and pointed to the photograph. The old man bent over and stared at it: and
laughed. Then he took the photograph out of the book, and
put it in his pocket.

" Well, I'm damned! " he said. " Signs himself skull
and cross-bones! Think of that, now! "

" Was the Honourable George a smallish built man? "
asked Jack.

" Eh? " The old man started. Then startled, he began
to remember back. " Ay! " he said. " He was. He was
smallish built, and the biggest little dude you ever set eyes
on. Something about his backside always reminded me of
a woman. But all the women were wild about him. Ay,
even when he was over fifty, Mary's mother was wild in
love with him. And he married her because she was going
to be a big heiress. But she died a bit too soon, an' he
got nothing, nor Mary neither, because she was *his*
daughter." The old man made an ironic grimace. " He
only died a few years back, in Sydney," he added. " But
I say, that poor lass is fair cut up about it. We'd always
kept it from her. I feel bad about her."

" She may as well get used to it," said Jack, disliking
the old man's protective sentimentalism.

" Eh? Get used to it! Why? How can she get used
to it? "

" She's got to live her own life some time."

" How d'y' mean, live her own life? She's never going to live *that* sort of a life, as long as I can see to it." He was quite huffed.

" Are you going to leave her to be an old maid? " said Jack.

" Eh? Old maid? No! She'll marry when she wants to."

" You bet," said Jack with a slow smile.

" She's a child yet," said Mr George.

" An elderly child—poor Mary !"

" Poor Mary! Poor Mary! Why poor Mary? Why so? "

" Just poor Mary," said Jack slowly smiling.

" I don't see it. Why is she poor? You're growing into a real young devil, you are." And the old man glanced into the young man's eyes in mistrust, and fear, and also in admiration.

They went into the kitchen, the late tea was ready. It was evident that Mary was waiting for them to come in. She had recovered her composure, but was more serious than usual. Jack laughed at her, and teased her.

" Ah, Mary," he said, " do you still believe in the Age of Innocence? "

" I still believe in good feeling," she retorted.

" So do I. And when good feeling's comical, I believe in laughing at it," he replied.

" There's something wrong with you," she replied.

" Quoth Aunt Matilda," he echoed.

" Aunt Matilda is very often right," she said.

" Never, in my opinion. Aunt Matilda is a wrong number. She's one of life's false statements."

" Hark at him ! " laughed Old George.

As soon as the meal was over, he rose, saying he would see to his horse. Mary looked up at him as he put his hat on his head and took the lantern. She didn't want him to go.

" How long will you be? " she asked.

" Why, not long," he answered, with a slight smile.

Nevertheless he was glad to be out and with his horse. Somehow those others made a false atmosphere, Mary and Old George. They made Jack's soul feel sarcastic. He lingered about the stable in the dim light of the lantern, preparing himself a bed. There were only two bedrooms in the house. The old couple would sleep on the kitchen floor, or on the sofa. He preferred to sleep in the stable. He had grown so that he did not like to sleep inside their fixed, shut-in houses. He did not mind a mere hut, like his at the camp. But a shut-in house with fixed furniture made him feel sick. He was sick of the whole pretence of it.

And he knew he would never come to live on this farm. He didn't want to. He didn't like the atmosphere of the place. He felt stifled. He wanted to go North, or West, or North-west once more.

Suddenly he heard footsteps : Mary picking her way across.

" Is your horse all right? " she asked. " I was afraid something was wrong with him. And he is so beautiful. Or is it a mare? "

" No," he said. " It is a horse. I don't care for a mare, for riding."

" Why ? "

" She has so many whims of her own, and wants so much attention paid to her. And then ten to one you can't trust her. I prefer a horse to ride."

She saw the rugs spread on the straw.

" Who is going to sleep here ? " she asked.

" I."

" Why—but—"

He cut short her expostulations.

" Oh, but do let me bring you sheets. Do let me make you a proper bed ! " she cried.

But he only laughed at her.

" What's a *proper* bed ? " he said. " Is this an improper one, then ? "

" It's not a comfortable one," she said with dignity.

" It is for me. I wasn't going to ask you to sleep on it, too, was I now? "

She went out and stood looking at the Southern Cross.

" Weren't you coming indoors again? " she asked.

" Don't you think it's nicer out here? Feels a bit tight in there. I say, Mary, I don't think I shall ever come and live on this place."

" Why not? "

" I don't like it."

" Why not? "

" It feels a bit heavy—and a bit tight to me."

" What shall you do then? "

" Oh, I don't know. I'll decide when I'm back at the camp. But I say, wouldn't *you* like this place? I'll give it you if you would. You're next of kin *really*. If you'll have it, I'll give it you."

Mary was silent for some time.

" And what do you think you'll do if you don't live here? " she asked. " Will you stay always on the gold fields? "

" Oh, dear no! I shall probably go up to the Never-Never, and raise cattle. Where there aren't so many people, and photo-albums, and good Old Georges and Aunt Matildas and all that."

" You'll be *yourself*, wherever you are."

" Thank God for that, but it's not quite true. I find I'm less myself down here, with all you people."

Again she was silent for a time.

" Why? " she asked.

" Oh, that's how it makes me feel, that's all."

" Are you more yourself on the gold fields? " she asked rather contemptuously.

" Oh, yes."

" When you are getting money, you mean? "

" No. But I've got so that Aunt Matilda-ism and Old George-ism don't agree with me. They make me feel sarcastic! They make me feel out of sorts all over."

" And I suppose you mean Mary-ism too," she said acidly.

" Yes, a certain sort of Mary-ism does it to me as well. But there's a Mary without the ism that I said I'd come back for. Would you like this place? "

" Why? "

" To cultivate your Mary-ism. Or would you like to come to the North-West? "

" But why do you trouble about me? "

" I've come back for you. I said I'd come back for you. I am here."

There was a moment of tense silence.

" You have married Monica now," said Mary, in a low voice.

" Of course I have. But the leopard doesn't change his spots when he goes into a cave with a she-leopard. I said I'd come back for you as well, and I've come."

A dead silence.

" But what about Monica? " Mary asked, with a little curl of irony.

" Monica? " he said. " Yes, she's my wife, I tell you. But she's not my only wife. Why should she be? She will lose nothing."

" Did she say so? Did you tell her? " Mary asked insidiously.

Slowly an anger suffused thick in his chest, and then seemed to break in a kind of explosion. And the curious tension of his desire for Mary snapped with the explosion of his anger.

" No," he said. " I didn't tell her. I had to ask *you* first. Monica is thick with her babies now. She won't care where I am. That's how women are. They are more *creatures* than men are. They're not separated out of the earth. They're like black ore. The metal's in them, but it's still part of the earth. They're all part of the matrix, women are, with their children clinging to them."

" And men are pure gold? " said Mary, sarcastically.

" Yes, in streaks. Men are the pure metal, in streaks. Women never are. For my part, I don't want them to be. They *are* the mother-rock. They *are* the matrix. Leave them at that. That's why I want more than one wife."

" But why? " she asked.

He realised that, in his clumsy fashion, he had taken the wrong tack. The one thing he should never have done, he had begun to do : explain and argue. Truly, Mary put up a permanent mental resistance. But he should have attacked elsewhere. He should have made love to her. Yet, since she had so much mental resistance, he had to make his position clear. Now he realised he was angry and tangled.

" Shall we go in? " he said abruptly.

And she returned with him in silence back to the house. Mr George was in the parlour, looking over some papers. Jack and Mary went in to him.

" I have been thinking, sir," said Jack, " that I shall never come and live on this place. I want to go up to the North-West, and raise cattle. That'll suit me better than wheat and dairy. So I offer this place to Mary. She can do as she likes with it. Really, I feel the property is naturally hers."

Now old George had secretly cherished this thought for many years, and it had riled him a little when Jack calmly stepped into the inheritance.

" Oh, you can't be giving away a property like this," he said.

" Why not? I have all the money I want. I give the place to Mary. I'd much rather give it to her than sell it. But if she won't have it, I'll ask you to sell it for me."

" Why ! Why ! " said old George fussily, stirring quite delighted in his chair, and looking from one to the other of the young people, unable to understand their faces. Mary looked sulky and unhappy, Jack looked sarcastic.

" I won't take it, anyhow," exclaimed Mary.

" Eh ? Why not, if the young millionaire wants to give it you ? If he wants to throw it away—— "said the old man ironically.

" I won't ! I won't take it ! " she repeated abruptly.

" Why—what's amiss ? "

" Nothing ! I won't take it."

" Got a proud stomach from your aristocratic ancestors, have you ? " said old George. " Well, you needn't have, the place is your father's son's place, you needn't be altogether so squeamish."

" I wouldn't take it if I was starving," she asserted.

" You're in no danger of starving, so don't talk," said the old man testily. " It's a nice little place, I tell you. I should enjoy coming out here and spending a few months of the year myself. Should like nothing better."

" But I won't take it," said Mary.

Jack went grinning off to his stable. He was angry, but it was the kind of anger that made him feel sarcastic.

Damn her ! She was in love with him. She had a passion for him. What did she want? Did she want him to make love to her, and run away with her, and abandon Monica and Jane? And the babies? No doubt she would have listened close enough to this proposition. But he was never going to put it to her. He had married Monica, and he would stick to her. She was his first and chief wife, and whatever happened, she should remain it. He detested and despised divorce : a shifty business. But it was nonsense to pretend that Monica was the beginning and end of his marriage with woman. Woman was the matrix, the red earth, and he wanted his roots in this earth. More than one root, to keep him steady and complete. Mary instinctively belonged to him. Then why not completely?

Why not? And why not make a marriage with her, too? The legal marriage with Monica, his own marriage with Mary. It was a natural thing. The old heroes, the old fathers of red earth, like Abraham in the Bible, like David even, they took the wives they needed for their own completeness, without this nasty chop-and-change business of divorce. Then why should he not do the same?

He would have all the world against him. But what would it matter, if he were away in the Never-Never, where the world just faded out? Monica could have the chief house. But Mary should have another house, with garden and animals if she wanted them. And she should have her own children : his children. Why should she be only Auntie to Monica's children? Mary, with her black, glistening eyes and her short, dark, secret body, she was asking for children. She was asking him for his children, really. He knew it, and secretly she knew it; and Aunt Matilda, and even Old George knew it, somewhere in themselves. And Old George was funny. He wouldn't really have minded an affair between Jack and Mary, provided it had been kept dark. He would even have helped them to it, so long as they would let nothing be known.

But Jack was too wilful and headstrong, and too proud, for an intrigue. An intrigue meant a certain cringing before society, and this he would never do. If he took Mary, it was because he felt she instinctively belonged to him. Because, in spite of the show she kept up, her womb was asking for him. And he wanted her for himself. He wanted to have her and to answer her. And he would be judged by nobody.

He rose quickly, returning to the house. Mary and the old man were in the kitchen, getting their candles to go to bed.

" Mary," said Jack, " come out and listen to the night-bird."

She started slightly, glanced at him, then at Mr George.

" Go with him a minute, if you want to," said the old man.

Rather unwillingly she went out of the door with Jack. They crossed the yard in silence, towards the stable. She hesitated outside, in the thin moonlight.

" Come and sleep in the stable with me," he said, his heart beating thick, and his voice strange and low.

" Oh, Jack ! " she cried, with a funny little lament; " you're married to Monica ! I can't ! You're Monica's ! "

" Am I ? " he said. " Monica's mine, if you like, but why am I all her's ? She's certainly not all mine. She belongs chiefly to her babies just now. Why shouldn't she ? She's their red earth. But I'm not going to shut my eyes. Neither am I going to play the mild Saint Joseph. I don't feel that way. At the present moment I'm not Monica's any more than she is mine. So what's the good of your telling me ? I shall love her again, when she is free. Everything in season, even wives. Now I love you again, after having never thought of it for a long while. But it was always slumbering inside me, just as Monica is asleep inside me this minute. The sun goes, and the moon comes. A man isn't made up of only one thread. What's the good of keeping your virginity ! It's really mine. Come and sleep with me in the stable, and then afterwards come and live in the North-West, in one of my houses, and have your children there, and animals or whatever you want."

" Oh, God ! " cried Mary. " You must really be mad. You don't love me, you can't, you must love Monica. Oh, God ! why do you torture me ? "

" I don't torture you. Come and sleep in the stable with me. I love you, too."

" But you love Monica."

" I shall love Monica again, another time. Now, I love you. I don't change. But sometimes it's one, then the other. Why not ? "

" It can't be ! It can't be ! " cried Mary.

" Why not ? Come into the stable with me, with me and the horses."

" Oh, don't torture me ! I hate my animal nature. You want to make a slave of me," she cried blindly.

This struck him silent. Hate her animal nature? What did she mean? Did she mean the passion she had for him? And make a slave of her? How?

" How make a slave of you? " he asked. " What are you now? You are a sad thing as you are. I don't want to leave you as you are. You are a slave now, to Aunt Matilda and all the conventions. Come and sleep with me in the stable? "

" Oh, you are cruel to me ! You are wicked ! I can't. You know I can't."

" Why can't you? You can. I am not wicked. To me it doesn't matter what the world is. You *really* want it. The middle of you *really* wants me, and nothing but me. It's only the outside of you that's afraid. There is nothing to be afraid of, now we have enough money. You will come with me to the North-West, and be my other wife, and have my children, and I shall depend on you as a man has to depend on a woman."

" How selfish you are ! You are as selfish as my father, who betrayed your mother's sister and left this skull-and-cross-bones son," she cried. " No, it's dreadful, it's horrible. In this horrible place, too, proposing such a thing to me. It shows you have no feelings."

" I don't care about feelings. They're what people have because they feel they ought to have them. But I know my own real feeling. I don't care about your feelings."

" I know you don't," she said. " Good-night ! " She turned abruptly and hurried away in the moonlight, escaping to the house.

Jack watched the empty night for some minutes. Then he turned away into the stable.

" That's that ! " he said, seeing his little plans come to nought.

He went into the stable and sat down on his bed, near the horses. How good it was to be with the horses ! How good animals were, with no " feelings " and no ideas. They just straight felt what they felt, without lies and complications.

Well, so be it ! He was surprised. He had not expected

Mary to funk the issue, since the issue was clear. What else was the right thing to do? Why, nothing else!

It seemed to him so obvious. Mary obviously wanted him, even more, perhaps, than he wanted her. Because she was only a part thing, by herself. All women were only parts of some whole, when they were by themselves : let them be as clever as they might. They were creatures of earth, and fragments, all of them. All women were only fragments; fragments of matrix at that.

No, he was not wrong, he was right. If the others didn't agree, they didn't, that was all. He still was right. He still hated the nauseous one-couple-in-one-cottage domesticity. He hated domesticity altogether. He loathed the thought of being shut up with one woman and a bunch of kids in a house. Several women, several houses, several bunches of kids : it would then be like a perpetual travelling, a camp, not a home. He hated homes. He wanted a camp.

He wanted to pitch his camp in the wilderness : with the faithful Tom, and Lennie, and his own wives. Wives, not wife. And the horses, and the come-an-go, and the element of wildness. Not to be tamed. His men, men by themselves. And his women never to be tamed. And the wilderness still there. He wanted to go like Abraham under the wild sky, speaking to a fierce, wild Lord, and having angels stand in his doorway.

Why not? Even if the whole world said No! Even then, why not?

As for being ridiculous, what was more ridiculous than men wheeling perambulators and living among a mass of furniture in a tight house?

Anyhow, it was no good talking to Mary at the moment. She wasn't a piece of the matrix of red earth. She was a piece of the upholstered world. Damn the upholstered world! He would go back to the goldfields, to Tom and Lennie and Monica, back to camp, back to camp, away from the upholstery.

No, he *wasn't* a man who had finished when he had got one wife.

And that damned Mary, by the mystery of fate, was linked to him from her womb.

And damn her, she preferred to break that link, and turn into an upholstered old maid. Of all the hells!

Then let her marry Blessington and a houseful of furniture. Or else marry Old George, and gas to him while he could hear. She loved gassing. Talk, talk, talk, Jack hated a talking woman. But Mary would rather sit gassing with Old George than sleep with him, Jack, in the stable along with the horses. Of all the surprising hells!

At least Tom wasn't like that. And Monica wasn't. But Monica was wrapped up in her babies, she seemed to swim in a sea of babies, and Jack had to let her be. And she, too, had a hankering after furniture. He knew she'd be after it, if he didn't prevent her.

Well, it was no good preventing people, even from stuffed plush furniture and knick-knacks. But he'd keep the brake on. He would do that.

CHAP : XXV. TROT, TROT, BACK AGAIN

BUT as he rode back to Perth, with Mary rather stiff and silent, and Mr George absorbed in his own thoughts; and as they greeted people on the road, and passed by settlements, and as they saw far off the pale blue sea with a speck of a steamer smoking, and the dim fume of Perth down at sea-level : he thought to himself : " I had better be careful. I had better be wary. The world is cold and cautious, it has cold blood, like ants and centipedes. They, all the men in the world, they hardly want one wife, let alone two. And they would take any excuse to destroy me. They would like to destroy me, because I am not cold and like an ant, as they are. Mary would like me to be killed. Look at her face. She would feel a real deep satisfaction if my horse threw me against those stones and smashed my skull in. She would feel vindicated. And Old George would think it served me right. And practically everybody would be glad. Not Tom and Len. But practically everybody else. Even Monica, though she is my wife. Even she feels a judgment ought to descend upon me. Because I'm not what she wants me to be. Because I'm not as she thinks I ought to be. And because she can't get beyond me. Because something inside her knows she can't get past me. Therefore, in one corner of her she hates me, like a scorpion lurking. If I'm unaware, and put my hand unthinking in that corner, she'll sting me and hope to kill me. How curious it is ! And since I have found the gold it is more emphatic than before. As if they grudged me something. As if they grudged me my very being. Because I'm not one of them, and just like they are, they would like me destroyed. It has always been so ever since I was born. My aunts, my own father. And my mother didn't want me destroyed as they secretly did, but even my mother would not have tried to prevent them from destroying me. Even when they like me, as Old George does, they grudge their own liking, they take it back whenever they can. He defended me over Easu because he thought I was defending Monica, and going the good way of the world. Now he scents that I am going my own way, he feels as if I were a sort of snake that should be put out of existence. That's how Mary feels, too : and Mary loves me, if loving counts for anything. Tom and Len don't wish me destroyed. But if they saw the world destroying me they'd acquiesce. Their fondness for me is only passive, not active. I believe, if I ransacked earth and heaven, there's nobody would fight for me as I am, not a soul, except that little Jane of Easu's. The others would fight like cats and dogs for me *as they want me to be.* But for me as I am, they think I ought to be destroyed.

And I, I am a fool, talking to them, giving myself away to them, as to Mary. Why, Mary ought to go down on her knees before the honour, if I want to take her. Instead of which she puffs herself up, and spits venom in my face like a cobra.

Very well, very well. Soon I can go out of her sight again, for I loathe the sight of her. I can ride down Hay Street without yielding a hair's breadth to any man or woman on earth. And I can ride out of Perth without leaving a vestige of myself behind, for them to work mischief on.

God, but it's a queer thing, to know that they all want to destroy me as I am, even out here in this far-off colony. I thought it was only my aunts, and my father because of his social position. But it is everybody. Even, passively, my mother, and Tom and Len. Because, inside my soul I don't conform : can't conform. They would all like to kill the non-conforming me. Which is me myself.

And at the same time they all love me exceedingly the moment they think I am in line with them. The moment they think I am in line with them, they're awfully fond of me. Monica, Mary, Old George, even Aunt Matilda, they're almost all of them in love with me then, and they'd give me anything. If I asked Mary to sleep with me, as a sin, as something I shouldn't, but I went down on my knees and begged her, because I couldn't help myself, she'd give in to me like anything. And Monica, if I was willing to be forgiven, would forgive me with unction.

But since I refuse the sin business, and I never go down on my knees, and since I say that my way is better than theirs, and that I should have my two wives, and both of them know that it is an honour for them to be taken by me, an honour for them to be put into my house and acknowledged there, they would like to kill me. It is I who must grovel, I who must submit to judgment. If I would but submit to their judgment, I could do all the wicked things I like, and they would only love me better. But since I will never submit to them, they would like to destroy me off the face of the earth, like a rattle-snake.

They shall not do it. But I must be wary. I must not put out my hand to ask them for anything, or they will strike my hand like vipers out of a hole. I must take great care to ask them for nothing, and to take nothing from them. Absolutely I must have nothing from them, not so much as to let them carry the cup of tea for me, unpaid. I must be very careful. I should not have let that brown snake of a Mary see I wanted her. As for Monica, I married her, so that makes them all allow me certain rights, as far as she is concerned. But she has her rights, too, and the moment she thinks I trespass on them, she will unsheath her fangs.

As for me, I refuse their social rights, they can keep them. If they will give me no rights, to the man I am, to me as I am, they shall give me nothing.

God, what am I going to do? I feel like a man whom the snake-worshipping savages have thrown into one of their snake pits. All snakes, and if I touch a single one of them, it will bite me. Man or woman, wife or friend, every one of them is ready for me since I am rich. Daniel in the den of lions was a comfortable man in comparison. These are all silent, damp, creeping snakes, like that yellow-faced Mary there, and that little whip-snake of a Monica, whom I have loved. " Now they bite me where I most have sinned," says old Don Rodrigo, when the snakes of the Inferno bite his genitals. So they shall not bite me. God in heaven, no, so they shall not bite me. Snakes they are, and the world is a snake pit into which one is thrown. But still they shall not bite me. As sure as God is God, they shall not bite me. But I will crush their heads rather.

Why did I want that Mary? How unspeakably repulsive she is to me now! Why did I ever want Monica so badly? God, I shall never want her again. They shall not bite my genitals as they bit Don Rodrigo, or Don Juan. My name is John, but I am no Don. God forbid that I should take a title from them.

And the soft, good Tom and Lennie, they shall live their lives, but not with my life.

Am I not a fool! Am I not a pure crystal of a fool! I thought they would love me for what I am, for the man I am, and they only love me for the me as they want me to be. They only love me because they get themselves glorified out of me.

I thought at least they would give me a certain reverence, because I am myself and because I am different, in the name of the Lord. But they have all got their fangs full and surcharged with insult, to vent it on me the moment I stretch out my hand.

I thought they would know the Lord was with me, and a certain new thing with me on the face of the earth. But if they know the Lord is with me, it is only so that they can intensify and concentrate their poison, to drive Him out again. And if they guess a new thing in me, on the face of the earth, it only makes them churn their bile and secrete their malice into a poison that would corrode the face of the Lord.

Lord! Lord! That I should ever have wanted them, or even wanted to touch them! That ever I should have wanted to come near them, or to let them come near me. Lord, as the only boon, the only blessedness, leave me intact, leave me utterly isolate and out of the reach of all men.

That I should have wanted! That I should have wanted Monica so badly! Well, I got her, and she saves her fangs in silent readiness for me, for the me as I am, not the me that is hers. That I should have wanted this Mary, whom I now despise. That I should have thought of a new little world of my own!

What a fool! To think of Abraham, and the great men in the early days. To think that I could take up land in the North, a big wild stretch of land, and build my house and raise my cattle and live as Abraham lived, at the beginning of time, but myself at another, late beginning. With my wives and the children of my wives, and Tom and Lennie, with their families, my right hand and my left hand, and absolutely fearless. And the men I would have work for me, because they were fearless and hated the world. Each one having his share of the cattle, and the horses, at the end of the year. Men ready to fight for me and with me, no matter against what. A little world of my own, in the North-West. And my children growing up like a new race on the face of the earth, with a new creed of courage and sensual pride, and the black wonder of the halls of death ahead, and the call to be lords of death, on earth. With my Lord, as dark as death and splendid with lustrous doom, a sort of spontaneous royalty, for the God of my little world. The spontaneous royalty of the other Overlord, giving me earth-royalty, like Abraham or Saul, that can't be quenched and that moves on to perfection in death. One's last and perfect lordliness in the halls of death, when slaves have sunk as carrion, and only the serene in pride are left to judge, the unborn.

A little world of my own! As if I could make it with the people that are on earth to-day! No, no, I can do nothing but stand alone. And, then, when I die, I shall not drop like carrion on the earth's earth. I shall be a lord of death, and sway the destinies of the life to come.

CHAP : XXVI. THE RIDER ON THE RED HORSE

JACK was glad to get away from Perth, to ride out and leave no vestige of his soul behind, for them to work mischief on. He saddled his horse before dawn, and still before sun was up, he was trotting along beside the river. He loved the world, the early morning, the sense of newness. It was natural to him to like the world, the trees, the sky, the animals, and even, in a casual way, people. It was his nature to like the casual people he came across. And, casually, they all liked him. It was only when he approached nearer, into intimacy, that he had a revulsion.

In the casual way of life he was good-humoured, and could get on with almost everybody. He took them all at their best, and they responded. For, on the whole, people are glad to be taken at their best, on trust.

But when he went further, the thing broke down. Casually, he could get on with anybody. Intimately, he could get on with nobody. In intimate life he was quiet and unyielding, often oppressive. In the casual way he was most yielding and agreeable. Therefore it was his friends who suffered most from him.

He knew this. He knew that Monica and Lennie suffered from his aloofness and a certain arrogance, in intimate life. So friendly with everybody, he was. And at the centre not really friendly even with his wife and his dearest friends. Withheld, unyielding, exacting even in his silence, he kept them in a sort of suspense.

As he rode his bright bay stallion on the soft road, he became aware of this. Perhaps his horse was the only creature with which he had the right relation. He did not love it, but he harmonised with it. As if, between them, they made a sort of centaur. It was not love. It was a sort of understanding in power and mastery and crude life. A harmony even more than an understanding. As if he himself were the breast and arms and head of the ruddy, powerful horse, and it, the flanks and hoofs. Like a centaur. It had a real joy in riding away with him to the bush again. He knew by the uneven, springy dancing. And he had perhaps a greater joy. The animal knew it in the curious pressure of his knees, and the soft rhythm of the bit. Between them, they moved in a sort of triumph.

The red stallion was always glad when Jack rode alone. It did not like company, particularly human company. When Jack rode alone his horse had a curious bubbling, exultant movement. When he rode in company it went in a more suppressed way. And when he stopped to talk to people, in his affable, rather loving manner, the horse became irritable, chafing to go on. He had long ago realised that the bay could not bear it when he reined in and stayed chatting. His voice, in its amiable flow, seemed to irritate the animal. And it did not like Lennie. Lucy, the old mare, loved Lennie. Most horses liked him. But Jack's stallion got a bit wicked, irritable with him.

And when Jack had made a fool of himself, as with Mary, and felt tangled, he always craved to get on his horse Adam, to be put right. He would feel the warm flow of life from the horse mount up him and wash away in its flood the human entanglements in his nerves. And sometimes he would feel guilty towards his horse Adam, as if he had betrayed the natural passion of the horse, giving way to the human travesty.

Now, in the morning before sunrise, with the red horse bubbling with exultance between his knees, his soul turned with a sudden jerk of realisation away from his fellow-men. He really didn't want his fellow-men. He didn't want that amiable casual association with them, which took up so large a part of his life. It was a habit and a bluff on his part. Also it was part of his nature. A certain real amiability in him, and a natural kindly disposition towards his fellow-men combatted inside him with a repudiation of the whole trend of modern human life, the emotional, spiritual, ethical, and intellectual trend. Deep inside himself, he fought like a wild-cat against the whole thing. And yet, because of a naturally amiably-disposed, even benevolent nature in himself, he took any casual individual into his warmth, and was bosom friends for the moment. Until, inevitably, after a short time the individual betrayed himself a unit of the universal human trend, and then Jack recoiled in anger and revulsion again.

This was a sort of dilemma. Monica, and Tom, and

Lennie, who knew him intimately, knew the absoluteness of his repudiation of mankind and mankind's direction in general. They knew it to their cost, having suffered from it. Therefore the anomaly of his casual intimacies and his casual bosom-friendships was considerably puzzling and annoying to them. He seemed to them false to himself, false to the other thing he was trying to put across. Above all, it seemed false to them, his real, old friends, towards whom he was so silently exacting and overbearing.

This morning, after his fiasco with Mary, he vaguely realised himself. He vaguely realised that he had to make a change. The casual intimacies were really a self-betrayal. But they made his life easy. It was the easiest way for him to encounter people. To suppress for the time being his deepest self, his thoughts, his feelings, his vital repudiation of the way of human life now, and to play at being really pleasant and ordinary. He liked to think that most people, casually and superficially, were nice. He hated having to withdraw.

But now, after the fiasco with Mary, he realised again his necessity to withdraw. To pass people by. They were all going in the opposite direction to his own. Then he was wrong to rein up and pretend a bosom-friendship for half an hour. As he did so, he was only being borne downstream, in the old, deadly direction, against himself.

Even his horse knew it : even old Adam. He pressed the animal's sides with his legs, and made a silent pact with him : not to make this compromise of amiability and casual friendship, not forever to be reining up and allowing himself to be carried backwards in the weary flood of the old human direction. To forfeit the casual amiabilities, and go his way in silence. To have the courage to turn his face right away from mankind. His soul and his spirit had already turned away. Now he must turn away his face, and see them all no more.

" I never want to see their faces any more," he said aloud to himself. And his horse between his thighs danced and began to canter, as the sun came sparkling up over the horizon. Jack looked into the sun, and knew that he must turn his own face aside for ever from the people of his world, not look at them or communicate with them again, not any more. Cover his own face with shadow, and let the world pass on its way, unseen and unseeing.

And he must know as he knew his horse, not face to face, never any more face to face, but communicating as he did with his stallion Adam, from a pressure of the thighs and knees. The arrows of the Archer, who is also a centaur.

Vision is no good. It is no good seeing any more. And words are no good. It is useless to talk. We must communicate with the arrows of sightless, wordless knowledge, as Jack communicated with his horse, by a pressure of the thighs and knees.

The sun had risen gold above the far-off ridge of the bush. Jack drew up at an inn by the side of the road, to eat breakfast. He left his horse at the hitching-post near the door, and went into the bar parlour. There was a smell of mutton chops frying, and he was hungry.

As he sat eating he heard his horse neighing fiercely. He pricked his ears. Again Adam's powerful neigh, and far off a high answering call of a mare. He went out quickly to the door of the inn. Adam stood by the post, his feet apart, his ears erect, his head high up, looking with flashing eyes back down the road. How beautiful he was ! in the newly-risen sun shining bright almost as fire, every fibre of him on the alert, tall and overweening. And down the road, a grey horse, cloud colour, running eagerly forwards, its rider, a young lady, flushing scarlet and trying to hold up her mare. It was no good. The mare's shrill, wild neigh came answering the stallion's, and the lady rider was powerless to hold her creature back. Strong, like bells in his deep chest, came the stallion's call once more. And, lifting her head as she ran on swift, light feet, the mare sang back.

The girl was Hilda Blessington. Jack took his horse and quickly ran him, rearing and flaming, round to the stable. There he shut him up, though his feet were thudding madly on the wooden floor, and his powerful neighing shook the place with a sound like fire.

The grey mare came running straight to the stable, carrying its helpless, scarlet-flushing rider. Jack lifted the girl down, and held the mare. There was a terrific thudding from the stable.

" I'll put her in the paddock, shall I ? " said Jack.

"I think you'd better," she said.

He looked uneasily at the stable, whence came a sound of something going smash. The shut-up stallion sounded like an enclosed thunder-storm.

"Shall I put them both in the paddock?" said Jack. "It seems the simplest thing to do."

"Yes," she murmured in confusion. "Perhaps you'd better."

She was rather frightened. The duet of neighing was terrific, like the bells of some wild cathedral going at full clash. The landlord of the inn came running up. Jack was just slipping the mare's saddle off.

"Steady! Steady!" he said. Then to the landlord:

"Take her to the paddock and turn her loose. I'm going to turn the horse loose with her."

The landlord dragged the frantic grey animal away, while she screamed and reared and pranced.

Jack ran to the stable door, calling to his horse. He opened carefully. The first thing he saw was the blazing eyes of the stallion. The horse had broken the halter, and had his nose and his wild eyes at the door, prepared to charge. Jack called to him again, and managed to get in front of him and close the door behind him. The animal was listening to two things at once, thinking two things at once. He was quivering in every fibre, in a state almost of madness. Yet he stood quite still while Jack slipped off the loosened saddle.

Then again he began to jump. Already he had smashed in one side of the stall, and had a bleeding fetlock. Jack got hold of the broken halter, and opened the door. The horse, like a great ruddy thunderbolt, sprang out of the stable, jerking Jack with him. The man, with a flying jump, got on the bright, brilliant bare back of the stallion, and clung there as the creature, swerving on powerful haunches past the terrified Hilda, ran with a terrific, splendid neighing towards the paddock, moving rhythmic and handsome.

There was the grey mare at the gate, inside, neighing back, and the landlord keeping guard. The men had to be very quick, the one to open the gate, the other to slip down.

Jack left the broken halter-rope dangling from his horse's

head—it was broken quite short—and went back into the yard.

" What a commotion ! " he said, laughingly, to the flushed, deeply embarrassed girl. " But you won't mind if your grey mare gets a foal to my horse ? "

" Oh, no," she said. " I shall like it."

" Why not ! " said he. " They'll be all right. There's the landlord and another fellow there with them. Will you come in ? Have you had breakfast ? Come and eat something."

She went with him into the bar parlour, where he sat down again to eat his half-cold mutton chops. She was silent and embarrassed, but not afraid. The colour still was high in her young, delicate cheeks, but her odd, bright, round, dark-grey eyes were fearless above her fear. She had really a great dread of everything, especially of the social world in which she had been brought up. But her dread had made her fearless. There was something slightly uncanny about her, her quick, rabbit-like alertness and her quick, open defiance, like some unyielding animal. She was more like a hare than a rabbit : like a she-hare that will fight all the cats that are after her young. And she had a great capacity for remaining silent and remote, like a quaint rabbit unmoving in a corner.

" Were you riding this way by accident ? " he asked her.

" No," she said quickly. " I hoped I might see you. Mary said you were leaving early in the morning."

" Why did you want to see me ? " he asked, amused.

" I don't know. But I did."

" Well, it was a bit of a hubbub," he laughed.

She glanced at him sharply, warily, on the defensive, and then laughed as well, with a funny little chuckle.

" Why did you leave so suddenly ? " she asked.

" No, it wasn't sudden. I'd had enough."

" Enough of what ? "

" Everything."

" Even of Mary ? "

" Chiefly of Mary."

She eyed him again sharply, wonderingly, searchingly, then again gave her odd little chuckle of a laugh.

" Why ' chiefly of Mary ' ? " she asked. " I think she's so nice. She'd make me such a good step-mother."

" Do you want one ? " he asked.

" Yes, I do rather. Then my father would want to get rid of me. I should be in the way."

" And do you want to be got rid of ? "

" Yes, I do, rather."

" What for ? "

" I want to go right away."

" Back to England ? "

" No. Not that. Never there again. Right away from Perth. Into the unoccupied country. Into the North-West."

" What for ? "

" To get away."

" What from ? "

" Everything. Just everything."

" But what would you find when you'd got away ? "

" I don't know. I want to try. I want to try."

She had such an odd, definite decisiveness and self-confidence, he was very much amused. She seemed the queerest, oddest, most isolated bird he had ever come across. Exceedingly well-bred, with all the charm of pure breeding. By nature, timorous like a hare. But now, in her queer state of rebellion, like a hare that is perfectly fearless, and will go its own way in determined singleness.

" You must come and see Monica and me when we move to the North-West. Would you like to ? "

" Very much. When will that be ? "

" Soon. Before the year is out. Shall I tell Monica you're coming ? She'd be glad of another woman."

" Are you sure you want me ? "

" Quite."

" Are you sure everybody will want me ? I shan't be in the way ? Tell me quite frankly."

" I'm sure everybody will want you. And you can't be in the way, you are much too wary."

" I only seem it."

" Do come, though."

" I should love to."

" Well, do. When could you come ? "

" Any time. To-morrow if you wish. I am quite independent. I have a certain amount of money, from my mother. Not much, but enough for all I want. And I am of age. I am quite free. And, I think, if I went, father would marry Mary. I wish he would."

" Why ? "

" Then I should be free."

" But free what for ? "

" Anything. Free to breathe. Free to live. Free not to marry. I know they want to get me married. They've got their minds fixed on it. And I'm afraid they'll force me to do it, and I don't want it."

" Marry who ? "

" Oh, nobody in particular. Just somebody, don't you know."

" And don't you want to marry ? " asked Jack, amused.

" No. No, I don't. Not any of the people I meet. No ! Not that sort of man. No. Never ! "

He burst into a laugh, and she, glancing in surprise at his amusement, suddenly chuckled.

" Don't you like men ? " he asked, still laughing.

" No. I don't. I dislike them very much."

Her quick, cool, alert manner of statement amused him more than anything.

" Not any men at all ? "

" No. Not yet. And I dislike the idea of marriage. I just hate it. I don't think I'd mind men so much, if it weren't for marriage in the background. I can't do with marriage."

" Might you like men without marriage ? " he asked, laughing.

" I don't know," she said, with her odd precision. " So far it's all just impossible. I can't stand it. All that sort of thing is impossible to me. No, I don't care for men at all."

" What sort of thing is just impossible ? " he asked.

" Men ! Particularly a man. Impossible ! "

Jack roared with laughter at her. She seemed rather to like being laughed at. And her odd, cool, precise intensity tickled him to death.

" You want to be virgin in the virgin bush ? " he asked.

She glanced at him quickly.

" Something like that," she said, with her little chuckle. " I think later on, not now, not now "—she shook her head—" I might like to be a man's second or third wife :

if the other two were living. I would never be the first.
Never. You remember you talked about it? "

She looked at him with her round, bright, odd eyes, like
an elf or some creature of the border-land, and as he roared
with laughter, she smiled quickly and with an odd, mischievous response.

" What you said the other night, when Aunt Matilda was
so angry, made me think of it. She hates you," she
added.

" Who, Aunt Matilda? Good job."

" Yes, very good job ! Don't you think she's *terrible?* "

" I do," said Jack.

" I'm glad you do. I can't stand her. I like Mr George.
But I don't care for it when he seems to like *me*."

Jack roared with laughter again, and again, from some
odd corner of herself, she smiled.

" Why do you laugh? " she said. But the infection of
laughter made her give a little chuckle.

" It's all such a real joke," he said.

" It is," she answered. " Rather a bad joke."

Slowly he formed a dim idea of her precise life, with a
rather tyrannous father who was fond of her in the wrong
way, and brothers who had bullied her and jeered at her
for her odd ways and appearance, and her slight deafness.
The governess who had mis-educated her, the loneliness of
the life in London, the aristocratic but rather vindictive
society in England, which had persecuted her in a small
way, because she was one of the odd border-line people
who don't, and *can't*, really belong. She kept an odd,
bright, amusing spark of revenge twinkling in her all the
time. She felt that with Jack she could kindle her spark
of revenge into a natural sun. And without any compunc-
tion she came to tell him.

He was tremendously amused. She was a new thing to
him. She was one who knew the world, and society, better
than he did, and her hatred of it was purer, more twinkling,
more relentless in a quiet way. Her way was absolutely
relentless, and absolutely quiet. She had gone further
along that line than himself. And her fearlessness was of
a queer, uncanny quality, hardly human. She was a real
border-line being.

" All right," he said, making a pact with her. " By

Christmas we'll ask you to come and see us in the North-West."

" By Christmas ! It's a settled thing ? " she said, holding up her forefinger with an odd, warning, alert gesture.

" It's a settled thing," he replied.

" Splendid ! " she answered. " I believe you'll keep your word."

" You'll see I shall."

She rose. The horses, quieted down, were caught and saddled and brought round. She glanced from her blue-grey mare to his red stallion, and gave her odd, squirrel-like chuckle.

" What a *contretemps*," she said. " It's like the sun mating with the moon." She gave him a quick, bright, odd glance : some of the coolness of a fairy.

" Is it ! " he exclaimed, as he lifted her into the saddle. She was slim and light, with an odd, remote reserve.

He mounted his horse.

" We go different ways for the moment," she said.

" Till Christmas," he answered. " Then the moon will come to the sun, eh ? Bring the mare with you. She'll probably be in foal."

" I certainly will. Good-bye, till Christmas. Don't forget. I shall expect you to keep your word."

" I will keep my word," he said. " Good-bye, till Christmas."

He rode away, laughing and chuckling to himself. If Mary had been a fiasco, this was a real joke. A real, unexpected joke.

His horse travelled with quick, strong, rhythmic movement, inland, away from the sea. At the last ridge he turned and saw the pale blue ocean full of light. Then he rode over the crest and down the silent grey bush, in which he had once been lost.

A NOTE ON THE TEXT

THE PRESENT TEXT is an offset facsimile of the first printing of *The Boy in the Bush* (London: Martin Secker, 1924). No editorial alterations of any kind have been made in this copy-text. An American edition was published from a new setting of type later in the year (New York: Thomas Seltzer, 1924).*

There is material for a definitive edition of the novel: Columbia University has the setting-copy typescript, and the University of Texas has what seems to be an earlier typescript.

M. J. B.

* See Warren Roberts, *A Bibliography of D. H. Lawrence* (London: Rupert Hart-Davis, 1963). The extent of the authors' revisions—if any—of later editions is unknown.